UNDER A SPELL?

Create one irresistible hero, add one irrepressible heroine.
Stir in loads of sex appeal, a dash of emotion and a pinch of witchery.
Mix with adventure and excitement and a touch of danger.
Fold in passionate encounters and sparkling dialogue.
Pour in yearnings and romance, hugs and kisses.
Flavor to taste.

Repeat three times!

Satisfies everyone and created especially for you!

HEATHER GRAHAM POZZESSERE

A master storyteller with over ten million copies of her books in print around the world, Heather Graham Pozzessere describes her life as "busy, wild and fun." Surprisingly, with all her success, Heather's first career choice was not writing but acting on the Shakespearean stage. Happily for her fans, fate intervened and now she is a *New York Times* bestselling author. Married to her high school sweetheart, this mother of five spends her days picking up the kids from school, attending Little League games and taking care of two cats. Although Heather and her family enjoy traveling, southern Florida—where she loves the sun and water—is home.

KATHLEEN KORBEL

A multiaward-winning author—including a *Romantic Times* Magazine award for Best New Category Author of 1987, the 1990 Romance Writers of America's RITA Award for Best Romantic Suspense, and the 1990, 1992 and 1995 RITA awards for Best Long Category Romance—Kathleen Korbel lives in St. Louis with her husband and two children. She devotes her time to enjoying her family, writing, avoiding anyone who tries to explain the intricacies of the computer and searching for the fabled housecleaning fairies. She also publishes medical thrillers as Eileen Dreyer.

ANNETTE BROADRICK

Since 1984, when her first book was published, Annette Broadrick has shared her views of life and love with readers all over the world. In addition to being nominated by *Romantic Times* Magazine as one of the Best New Authors of that year, she has also won the *Romantic Times* Reviewers' Choice Award for Best in its Series for *Heat of the Night, Mystery Lover* and *Irresistible;* the *Romantic Times* WISH award for her heroes in *Strange Enchantment, Marriage Texas Style!* and *Impromptu Bride;* and the *Romantic Times* Lifetime Achievement Awards for Series Romance and Series Romantic Fantasy.

Heather Graham Pozzessere
Kathleen Korbel
Annette Broadrick

Destined for Love

Silhouette Books

Published by Silhouette Books

America's Publisher of Contemporary Romance

 SILHOUETTE BOOKS

 RECYCLED PAPER

ISBN 0-373-20152-4

by Request

DESTINED FOR LOVE

Copyright © 1998 by Harlequin Books S.A.

The publisher acknowledges the copyright holders of the individual works as follows:

HATFIELD AND McCOY
Copyright © 1992 by Heather Graham Pozzessere

LIGHTNING STRIKES
Copyright © 1990 by Eileen Dreyer

MYSTERY LOVER
Copyright © 1987 by Annette Broadrick

Printed in U.S.A.

CONTENTS

Dear Reader,

Hi! Welcome to a piece of nostalgia that is special for me. It takes place in an area where I've gone very often with my family, a place with a character that is unique and almost tangible in the crisp, cool air. The landscape here is beautiful, jagged cliffs, mountains, rushing water, cloudy blue skies, and at night, a mystique where it seems anything can happen.

I'm a Pisces, which is, I believe, rather a curse— except that, of course, I'm skeptical about astrology. However, Pisceans are always allowed to have two opinions—in the nature of those fishes going in two different directions—and so I believe in it, as well. Just as I'm open to belief in many areas of human mystery, such as ESP, the power of the human mind, and, of course, the power of the human heart.

Also, there's nothing like a good family feud.

Some believe the mountains to be haunted. Some believe them to carry a strange power, given by the earth, the sky, the rivers. Dusk often brings curious fogs, where we're not always sure of what we see and what we don't. Whether touched by spirits or not, there is a unique beauty to be found here. My gifted heroine is well aware that strange magic and powers can exist. My skeptical hero is taught a lesson about belief in the extraordinary, the magic of the soul—and, naturally, of love, the incredible power of love.

I hope you enjoy!

Heather Graham Pozzessere

HATFIELD AND McCOY

Heather Graham Pozzessere

Prologue

The dream came to her again that night, and she smiled in her sleep. It was a sweet dream, and she welcomed it as she would a lover.

Ah, but it was a dream that brought her a lover and warmth and soft, sensual pleasure.

She never saw his face. She was always looking out the window, looking at the rich grasses and beautiful blues and greens of summer...or perhaps it was spring. There was always a light breeze. The kind of breeze that just lightly lifted her hair.

And then she would know that he was in the room.

She would know...

Because of a subtle, masculine scent. She would know because she would feel him there.

And the warmth and tenderness would fill her. She knew him, knew the man, and knew things about him that made her love him. She didn't need to see his face. Didn't need to know the color of his eyes, or the color of his hair.

She knew all the hues within his heart and soul and

mind, and those colors were all beautiful and part of the warmth that touched her.

He could move so silently...

He would be coming across the room to her, and she would know it, and she would smile. She would know that he was coming closer, because she could always feel him near. Feel the security, the supreme sense of well-being, that came to her when she was with him.

Her lover...

Tonight...

He stood behind her and swept the fall of her hair from her neck, and she felt the wet, hot caress of his lips against her nape.

The pleasure was startling. So startling that a certain embarrassment touched her in her sleep, nearly ending the dream.

But her sleep was deep, and her enchantment was even deeper.

He held back her hair, and his kiss skimmed over her shoulder. She wore something that hugged her body. Something dark. He lifted the strap from her shoulder. Even the feel of the fabric leaving her skin was erotic.

By his touch, by his command, the garment fell from her shoulders. Bit by bit, the clothing was peeled from her body. And bit by bit it fell away to the ground, in a pool of darkness at her feet.

His arms encircled her. She could feel the strength of his naked chest as he pulled her against him. He still wore jeans. She could feel the roughness of the fabric against the tender skin of her bare flanks. Even that touch was sensual.

So vividly sensual. Even in a dream.

And she knew that she dreamed...

His whisper touched her ear. She could not hear the words, but a lazy smile came to her lips. Then she was turning against him.

She didn't see his face.

She felt his kiss.

Felt the hungry pressure of his lips, forming over her own, firmly, demandingly, causing them to part for the exotic presence of his tongue.

He'd kissed her before…

Never quite like this.

And when his lips left her mouth, they touched her throat. Touched the length of it. The soft, slow, sensual stroke of his tongue just brushing her flesh. With ripples of silken, liquid fire. She could see his hands, broad, so darkly tanned, on the paleness of her skin. His fingers were long, handsomely tapered, calloused, but with neatly clipped nails. Masculine hands. Hands that touched with an exciting expertise. Fingers that stroked with confidence and pleasure.

She allowed her head to fall back, her eyes to close. The sensations to surround her.

The breeze…it was so cool against her naked body. So soft. So unerringly sensual. Perhaps because her body was so hot. Growing fevered. But the air…it touched her where his kiss left off, and both fire and ice seemed to come to her and dance through her.

She spun in his arms. It was no longer daytime. Shadows were falling, and the breeze was growing cooler.

And his kiss went lower.

And where his lips touched her, she burned.

And where his lips had lingered earlier, the cool air stroked her with a sensuality all its own.

She dreamed, she tried to tell herself.

It was not real.

But within her dream lover's arms, his kiss lowered. And lowered until he teased the base of her spine. His hand caressed her naked buttocks and hips, and she was turning in his arms.

Her hand rested on his head, her breath quickened and

caught, and quickened again. She cried out, amazed at the tempest that rose within her, startled by the sheer sensual pleasure that ripped through her.

She cried out again and again, and then discovered that she was sinking, sinking into his arms...

Night had come. The moon remained in the sky, but she could not see clearly.

She still did not see his face. She could touch and feel, but she could not see his face.

Not that she was thinking. Not even in the dream could she reason or think, for she was with him, touching him, knowing the living warmth and fire of him. Feeling the ripple of muscle in his chest. Feeling his hands. Feeling the pulse of his body. Feeling...him.

It was vivid. So vivid.

She could feel him entering her...

She began to fight the dream. It was too vivid. It was decadent...

Even in the privacy of sleep, it was embarrassing.

And still, she knew what went on. She knew the moment in the dream when the stars burst and the sky seemed to turn a glorious gold, and then to blacken again.

She knew the absolute amazement she felt at the force of the love they shared. She knew the shattering pounding of her heart, the desperate scramble to breathe again, the sheen of perspiration that bathed them both like a lover's dew....

For it was sweet, all so very sweet. He would envelop her in his arms. She would lie upon his shoulder and feel that incredible security and the simple pleasure of being together. She would reach out and hold him and she knew that she would see his face...

But the tenderness did not come, nor did the overwhelming feeling of well-being.

A different feeling had been coming on...coming on for long, long moments.

Then it seized her. Seized her firmly. Darkness. A startling, terrifying darkness. A presence. Near them.

And she cried out.

What is it?

She heard his whisper. She tried to talk. She was choking, and she was so frightened. Her jaw was locked. Constricted. She fought so hard.

He's here! He can see us!

No…

Oh, my God! He's trying to watch us.

No, he cannot watch us.

But the feeling wouldn't leave her. She closed her eyes, tightly. Still, there suddenly seemed to be a light. A blinding light.

She saw a man's shoulder. Fleetingly, in that light. A bronzed shoulder. There was a short but jagged scar on it.

The light faded. She couldn't see anything.

She was disoriented. Confused. Frightened.

Had she seen her lover's shoulder…?

Or had it been his? The man who watched. The one who so terrified her…

Julie…

Her lover whispered to her. He tried to reassure her. He was confident in his own strength. He didn't believe. He didn't understand.

It was so frightening. Did the scar belong to a man who would hold her against all danger?

Or did it belong to a cold-blooded killer?

Julie! Julie, please…

I'm afraid, she told him. She didn't say it out loud. And he denied any sixth sense.

But this time, he had heard her.

I'm with you.

She strained. Strained against the darkness. If only she could see his face, it would be all right. If she could just see her lover's face…

But there was too much darkness. She couldn't see.

And the terror was beginning to suffocate her. She couldn't breathe.

The darkness was coming closer and closer.

She awoke with a start and realized she was screaming. "Oh!"

With a gasp, she turned on her bedside lamp. She was still shaking. She was drenched with perspiration.

She looked around the room. Nothing had changed. She was home, safe on her mountain.

"What a dream!" she murmured.

She rose, still hot and flushed, and walked into the kitchen for a long drink of water, then returned to bed. She smiled sheepishly. "I wonder if that was a defense mechanism against this dream lover of mine," she rationalized aloud. "Oh, but a shrink would have a heyday with me!"

She grinned and laid her head down. The fear was gone. Completely gone. It was incredibly easy to close her eyes and sleep again.

No more dreams taunted her. When she awoke in the morning, she had forgotten just how frightened she had been. She speculated about the dream man as she showered, grinning, wondering if she would ever meet the man. If she would stand in the breeze, and feel his caress…

She groaned aloud. Patty would blame her life-style, she was certain. Too secluded.

And so, so often, when she dreamed…

She flushed.

Maybe she would meet him.

For just a moment, she felt a tinge of fear. As if the darkness was coming over her again.

But then it was gone. She gave herself a firm mental shake.

And she started to wonder again. About him.

She showered, dressed and made herself a cup of tea

and an English muffin. She speculated once again about her mystery lover as she curled up on the huge chair on the porch that overlooked both mountain and valley. She felt wonderfully at ease.

And it was then that the phone began to ring.

Chapter 1

They were destined to come together and to clash.

But that first time Julie saw the man—for all her intuitive powers—she had no idea that she would ever see him again.

Nor did she want to!

She was in a hurry. Admittedly, she was very much in a hurry. But when she rounded the corner in her little Mazda, she was certain that she had the right of way. She hadn't even seen the Lincoln that came around from the opposite side at exactly the same time.

And so they rammed, head first, right into one another.

Luckily, they were both going five miles an hour, and both cars had huge, brand-new bumpers.

They collided and bounced.

Shaken, Julie realized that they had been really lucky. They had struck one another just as if they had been playing bumper cars. There was no damage to her car, and she was certain that there was no damage to the heavier Lincoln.

She could drive away. Thank God. She couldn't afford the time to exchange insurance information or wait around to make a police report.

The other car started to back away. She sighed with relief. She revved her car and backed away from the Lincoln. Then she paused politely.

But the other driver was pausing, too.

They both paused.

And paused.

Julie squinted, trying to see the driver. It was a man, she discerned. And he was letting her go first.

He gave a short bump to his horn.

She started at the sound, then jerked forward.

He eased forward, too.

Once again, they slammed together.

They were playing bumper cars. Julie smiled.

She started to wave at the driver in the Lincoln. But watching him, she felt her smile begin to freeze.

He wasn't smiling. Nor was he going to drive away this time.

He was getting out of his car and coming her way.

He was wearing black jeans, a black leather jacket and dark sunglasses. He was somewhere between thirty and forty—big, tall, broad-shouldered, but lean and graceful in his movements.

And he reached her window quickly. Damned quickly.

"Are you hurt?" he demanded.

"No," she said quickly. "No, I'm not hurt."

"Are you sure? Absolutely sure?"

Her smile came to life again. He seemed concerned, honestly concerned. And he had such a deep, rich, masculine voice. She didn't just hear his voice; she felt it. With all of her body. It left a pleasant, shivery warmth inside her.

He had a nice, clean-shaven jawline—a strong one. And a nice mouth. Full, broad. Warm and sensual.

He might have been the man in her dreams, she thought. Before the darkness had descended. The darkness that even now threatened an uneasy feeling.

"I'm not hurt at all," she assured him quickly.

And then his tone changed. Boy, did it change.

"What the hell did you think you were doing!" he grated out. Now his voice was full of authority and command.

It instantly struck a chord within her.

"Me! What the hell did you think you were doing?"

"You little pea brain, I had the clear cut right-of-way. I even tried to let you go first. Given the fact that you're driving with your head in the clouds, your talent for accidents makes sense."

Pea brain? No, this was not the man in her dream. Definitely not!

"Excuse me, sir," she purred sweetly, her lashes lowering over her eyes. Fight fire with oil, that's what she'd always heard. "But you did not have any right-of-way, and I'm afraid that you do seem to be in a black-leathered mental wasteland. There's no reason—"

"I was clearly—"

"You most certainly were not—" Julie interrupted. But she didn't faze him. And she didn't have a chance to explain to him that the right-of-way had been entirely hers.

"Not the one required to yield." He finished his sentence, then looked at her, the slightest curve touching his lip. "Black-leathered mental wasteland?" he repeated, astounded that she should say such a thing.

"I am not a pea brain," she said with incredible dignity.

He might have almost smiled then, but he didn't. That jaw of his squared right away.

"Never mind!" He waved a hand dismissively in the air. "I don't have the time for a petty argument. Be glad." He waged a warning finger at her. "You'd get points on your license for a moving violation."

Of all the incredible effrontery. She stared at him for a moment, then she wanted to scream. No, she wanted to jump out of the car and wag a finger at him—all the way back to that big Lincoln of his. What she really wanted was to give him a sound slap on his arrogant cheekbone. She gritted her teeth. Foolish. She couldn't see his eyes, she couldn't really see his face. She could see that he stood well over six feet tall. The better part of valor warned her to stay seated. And to smile.

"I'm quite sure you would receive points on your license, sir, for this violation. Fortunately for you, I'm in far too much of a hurry to squander time on the petty pursuit of proving a point. Now, if you'll excuse me…"

She didn't wait for a reply. She backed smoothly, then gunned the gas pedal as she hadn't done since she'd been a sophomore in high school, just learning to drive.

And then she couldn't help but smile with pure, sweet satisfaction.

Hmm. Spiteful, Julie, she warned herself. But she just couldn't help the feeling of victory and pleasure. He'd been so rude. So arrogant. He'd barely managed to keep his mouth shut about the fact that she was a woman driver.

It would have been one of his next lines, she was certain.

Still, she chided herself, you almost ran over his toes.

"Almost. But I didn't," she said aloud. "Well, he did have to step back rather quickly. But that's what he gets for being such an orangutan."

She maneuvered her small car around another curve and then saw the police station not far before her. Her smile faded. She remembered why she had been in such a hurry.

Time was so very important.

She pulled in and parked her car. She had barely opened the front door to the station, walked in and started to close the door before it was nearly ripped out of her hands. She let go of the door and stepped back.

A gasp of amazement escaped her.

It was the man. The tall blond man in the black leather who had been driving the big Lincoln.

Lord! He'd come after her, she thought in a moment of panic. She almost jumped back. He'd come after her to do her some harm for nearly running over his toes.

She was in a police station, for God's sake! she reminded herself. She couldn't possibly be in any danger here.

"Where's Petty?" he demanded of the two officers on duty, one man and one young woman.

Petty was the chief. Chief Pettigrew. Only people who knew him well called him Petty.

The man was quick to take in the office. All of the office. And his gaze, beneath the dark glasses, came down hard upon Julie.

He pulled off the sunglasses and glared at her. He wasn't smiling. There wasn't the faintest trace of amusement about him. One brow shot up, then his face creased into a deep frown. He turned to the two officers at the front desk. "Where's Petty?" he said again.

The male officer jumped to his feet. "Right this way, sir. He's expecting you. If you'll follow me—"

But the man shot Julie another hard look. One that seemed to sizzle and burn her from head to toe. Then he burst into the chief's office—with the officer following behind. A door slammed in his wake.

Staring after him, Julie lifted her chin. She took a few steps forward and sat in the plain brown chair before the desk of the remaining officer, Patty Barnes.

"Oh, no!" Julie breathed. Her abilities had certainly been failing her so far this morning. She was only now coming to see the absolutely obvious, and it was not good at all. "Oh, no..."

"What?" Patty whispered.

"Please tell me that that man isn't..."

Patty stared at her.

"Patty, he can't be!"

"But he is," Patty said.

"He's the G-man?"

"That's him," Patty replied. "The G-man."

Julie didn't get a chance to speak again. Sound suddenly seemed to burst upon them.

"What?"

Hearing the single word explode in the FBI agent's decidedly masculine voice, Julie winced.

Apparently, he wasn't very happy, either. He'd already heard about her, she realized. And he must have put two and two together and realized that she was the woman with whom he would be working.

"What?" Again he said the word. It wasn't a question. She was tempted to leap up and go striding into the chief's office.

Curiously, she was able to grant that he was an attractive man, despite his awful arrogance.

It had only been seconds that she had really seen him with those dark glasses removed. And in that little bit of time before he had crossed into the inner offices, his eyes had touched upon her.

They went well with his jaw.

They were steel-gray eyes. Eyes as hard and rigid as the structure beams for a skyscraper, eyes that were truly gray, without a hint of blue. He had sandy blond close-cropped hair, a bronzed face with rugged, well-defined features, and curiously dark lashes and brows for the blondness of his hair.

All in all, the combinations and contrasts created a very interesting face. And the face went well with the tall, taut, well-muscled body that could move with such startling ease and grace for its size. She'd barely heard his footsteps, but then she'd really only been aware of his eyes, those steel-gray eyes with their dark, probing ability.

Suddenly his voice exploded again. "I don't believe

this! You want me to work with a witch of some sort? Me? Of all people. A voodoo priestess? That—that child out there!''

Smile tiger, smile! she ordered herself. And she did so, grinning to Patty. ''I really don't think he's pleased,'' Julie murmured.

Thirty-year-old Patty had a pleasantly pretty freckled face and light red hair that was swept up in a ponytail. She arched a brow at Julie's words.

''No, I don't think so, either,'' she murmured.

Julie gritted her teeth. She'd come across the attitude often enough, and it barely disturbed her anymore. She'd controlled her temper, and she'd made herself credible by being entirely calm and dignified. It had been a long time since anyone had managed to make her feel quite so angry.

''Arrogant bastard,'' she said softly to Patty.

''Oh, he's really not that bad,'' Patty said quickly.

It was Julie's turn to arch a brow.

''Well, all right,'' Patty responded. ''He is a toughie. I really had no idea who the bureau was sending, but, yes, he is going to be tough. But the man is good, Julie. And he can be a real heartthrob when he wants. He sometimes has a smile that could melt rock, I swear it. And he's good, Julie, so good. Thorough. So he growls a bit. When he isn't growling—''

''He's probably trying to bite,'' Julie interrupted.

Patty laughed. ''Okay, so he's hardheaded and—''

''Ruthless?'' Julie suggested.

''Well, there's sort of a deep, dark mystery about the man, too. He's originally from this area, but apparently he spent about ten years out in California. Something happened out there. I don't know what it was. No one does. He doesn't talk about himself.''

''No,'' Julie said. ''He doesn't talk at all. He just barks.''

''But still,'' Patty said with a sigh, ''there's something

about him…I admit, my ticker has gone pitter-patter often enough over Robert—''

"No! It's absolutely out of the question!'' Good old heartthrob Robert was spewing again.

A quieter voice of reason must have spoken in the inner offices against the man's tirade, but that voice of reason was apparently getting nowhere. The man's argument was rising again, and Patty's cheeks grew red as she stared at Julie. The man must know that he was being heard very clearly—by everyone.

"It's not out of the question!'' Julie said firmly, her unsolicited reply in the outer office just as quiet as the man's statement in the inner office had been forceful.

"Not out of the question at all,'' Julie continued, flashing a smile at Patty. "I was asked in. I'm staying. Even if it upsets Mr. Robert—'' She broke off, looking at Patty with a frown. "What's his name?''

Patty opened her mouth to speak, then quickly paused. A long, "Oh!'' escaped her.

Julie stared at her blankly. "His name is Robert Oh?''

"Oh! No, I mean, no, of course not,'' Patty said quickly. "It's just that…''

"Well, what?'' Julie tapped her long nails against the leather of her handbag.

Patty suddenly smiled, then laughed. "His name is McCoy. Robert McCoy.''

"Oh!'' Julie said. And then her mouth curled into a smile, and she was laughing, too. "Well, maybe that just figures. Mr. Robert McCoy…'' Her voice trailed away, then she added, "If he's looking for a feud, Patty, he's going to get one. I'm needed on this case, I know it, I feel it. And I'm here to stay.''

The deep, thundering burst of a bald expletive came from the inner office. The hostility and anger behind it were enough to make Patty feel as if her red hair were standing on end at the base of her neck.

But Julie Hatfield was undaunted. Small, delicate, with a fine, beautiful bone structure and the sweet face of an angel, she sat straight on her chair. She was almost regal with her sun-blond hair caught back from her face and swept into an elegant French braid. She appeared not to have heard Robert McCoy at all.

But then Julie's eyes touched Patty's. Hazel eyes, they had the ability to glisten like gold. And they were glistening now.

Patty smiled. Perhaps Mr. Robert McCoy did need to watch out this time around.

Miss Hatfield was ready to do battle.

Inside the chief's office, Robert McCoy was prepared to go to war.

He stared hard from Chief Pettigrew to his sergeant, Timothy Riker, still unable to believe what he had just heard.

Timothy Riker, obviously dazed that he was between the chief and McCoy, looked up as a dark red flush stained his features. Robert was sorry to see Riker so uncomfortable—he was a good man, young and dedicated, but he should have known that what was going on would touch off Robert's temper.

It was all entirely unacceptable.

Timothy cleared his throat. He was loyal to the death, trying to help out Petty.

"Lieutenant McCoy—" Riker broke off. Steel-gray eyes were fixed mercilessly on him. Thankfully, the chief broke in.

"Robert, these orders aren't from me, and they aren't from any of the local police stations involved. They came direct from your own office. Now, I do admit that we've worked with—"

"This quack!" Robert McCoy said flatly.

"She's not a quack, honest, sir!" Riker piped. Then he was flushing again.

Curious, Robert decided. It was obvious that Riker was fond of the woman, whoever she was. This Julie something. Ah, but that, my young man, Robert thought, is because of your very youth! A pretty face, a soft word...

He fought to control his temper. If time wasn't entirely of the essence, he might even have been amused, intrigued.

No, he couldn't be amused. Or intrigued. He'd met others like this woman before.

He inhaled. Exhaled. That was the past. A closed door. He was going to be coolly amused. And more.

Determined, even, to unmask this so-called psychic.

And a child's life was involved.

He was good, a damned good investigative agent, and he knew it. His work was his life. He could find clues few other men would seek, and during the instances when he had been in direct contact with a kidnapper, he had been somewhat startled to realize that many of his long-ago psychology classes had paid off—he was capable of setting up a communication that could save a life.

Maybe it wasn't the psychology classes. Maybe it had just been life itself.

Life was often a wicked, wicked teacher.

None of that really mattered now. There were numerous local police stations involved in this region where the states of Virginia, West Virginia and Maryland came together in a grand cataclysm of nature. But he was the federal agent, and the man put in charge. Not that he was so much of a loner—he could work well with others. He had to. So many experts were needed, men who could comb woods, technicians who could magically read minute drops of blood and come up with incredible information. He needed others. Men and women who had some sense and could work with logic.

Not some kind of a mystic quack!

Chief Pettigrew, a man with bright blue eyes, graying hair, a salt and pepper beard and the look of a department-store Santa, sighed softly and tried once again. "Robert, give the girl a chance, eh? She's been a tremendous help in other cases."

Robert McCoy was startled when his fist landed against the desk. "Time, Petty," he said. "Time! There's a little girl missing, Petty, an eight-year-old child. We just don't have time to bring in a soothsayer!"

Time had been important to him once before.

Pettigrew stood, then sank back in his chair. Robert McCoy wasn't a stranger called in to take charge of one of his cases. Robert was the son of one of Pettigrew's oldest and dearest friends.

He wasn't going to be intimidated by the son of a friend, he assured himself.

It was just that, well, McCoy was an intimidating man. Maybe he even had the right to be so furious about this call. And despite this dark display of temper, he was a damned good man, too, Petty knew, from past experience. McCoy was passionate about his work. And he was smart, smart as a whip. He'd studied criminal law in school and he had proven time and time again his ability to analyze the mind of a criminal. He could be a hard man, almost ruthless in the pursuit of his objectives.

Especially since California. No matter how hard a man he appeared to be. No matter how silent. He had changed. And he was capable of being ruthless.

But that was exactly why he had been called in on this case. A child's life was at stake.

Of course, it was exactly why Julie Hatfield had been called in on the case, too.

"Robert!" Pettigrew leaned toward his towering blond friend. "We have nothing on this case. Nothing at all. We know that the girl disappeared from her own street, and that's all we've got. That and the suspicion—" He broke off. They all knew what the suspicion was. There had been a similar case in a neighboring county not six months ago. A young woman had been abducted from her home. A ransom letter had come, and a ransom had been delivered. But the woman had not been returned.

Julie Hatfield had been called in on that case. And she had found the young woman, barely in time, buried, but alive, in an old refrigerator upon the mountaintop.

Six months before that, there had been another similar case. The young woman taken during that abduction had never been found.

The kidnapper, assuming it was one and the same man—or woman—had struck again and was moving between state lines. And that was why Robert had been called in.

"Robert," Pettigrew said wearily. "We need Julie on this one. She can help. You just don't know her."

McCoy ran his fingers through his hair and sank into an office chair beside Timothy Riker. Why was he so furious? Because working with this girl could take time? Yes, of course. He was also bone weary. He'd just returned from a sting in Florida, and he'd thought he'd have some time off. It was moving into late spring. The fish were jumping. His own little mountaintop was beckoning to him, and for the first time in a long time, he wanted some time off.

And he was scared, too. He was always scared, though he never let it show. Dear Lord, it was always scary to hold someone's life in your hands. And now, it was a child's life, and more. The lives of her parents, her family, her friends. If she was lost forever, they would be, too. No one ever forgot the loss of a loved one. Ever.

Ever.

And he was mad, of course, that anyone could claim the things that the charlatan in the front office was pretending she could do.

It could lead to nothing but false hope.

Maybe worse.

No one but God could see into the hearts and minds of other men. No one could see the pathetic remnants of a case gone bad except for those poor investigators sent out to retrieve the body.

"It came down to us straight from the top, Robert. They say that we must use her on this one," Pettigrew said very softly.

Robert McCoy rubbed his temple with his thumb and forefinger.

"How many hours now since the little girl was taken?"

"Three," Timothy Riker informed him quickly. "And we've had men and women out scouring the neighboring woods since the call came in."

"Three hours," Robert mused. He glanced quickly at the chief. "And there's no possibility that she just ran off with friends? That she saw something interesting—"

"No, none at all. Tracy Nicholson is a very conscientious little girl. She never strayed at all. She would have never worried her mother so."

This had to be murder for old Petty, Robert thought, and he was sorry again for his outburst of temper. This was a small town, and Petty was friends with little Tracy's parents, and with Tracy herself.

"Signs of a struggle?" Robert said. He had to ask.

Riker nodded. "Scuffs in the dirt right off the road. She was definitely taken, sir."

"We've had men combing the woods since."

Good and bad. If the little girl was near, she'd be found. And if not, well, valuable clues might have been trampled into oblivion.

Riker cleared his throat again. "The child's parents are waiting at their home."

Good Lord, he was wasting time here, McCoy realized unhappily. Damn.

Swallow that temper, he warned himself, and swallow

the past. It had all been so long ago now. So long. Still, it was hard.

Hard when he knew his psychic was the soft and delicate blonde in the outer office. That dear, sweet young woman with the angelic face...

And whiplash tongue.

And wretched driving skills, to boot.

"McCoy, I swear to you," Petty said, "the orders did come straight from the top—"

"Yes, yes, fine. Riker is right. Let's get moving. Take me out to meet Miss What's-her-name."

Petty, who had started to lead the way out of his office, paused suddenly and swung back. And despite the circumstances, he was grinning.

"It's Hatfield."

"Pardon?" McCoy said.

"Her name." Petty's rheumy blue gaze surveyed him with a certain amusement. "Darned if I didn't just realize it all myself. Hatfield. Her name is Julie Hatfield. Hell, McCoy, this isn't your feud. The Hatfields and McCoys have been at it for decades, eh?"

Hatfield. Her name was Hatfield.

Hell, after everything else today, it just figured.

He crunched his jaw into the most affable grin he could manage. Only his eyes were steam.

"Excuse me, Petty."

He brushed past the old chief, letting the glass-paned door slam behind him as he strode quickly through the outer office.

She saw him coming. She stood quickly.

She was something. Petite, blond...cute. No, actually, she was beautiful. Her features were so fine, so perfectly chiseled. She was elegant. Even in jeans and a light knit sweater. And sneakers. There was still something elegant about her.

And those eyes of hers. Almost golden. With such a wicked, wicked gleam.

Two could play...And two could feud.

She was smiling. A smile plastered into place, of course. His own grin could have been rubber.

"Well, well, so we meet again," he said softly.

Don't you dare think that you've won anything! he warned in silence, offering her his hand. She accepted it. His fingers curled over hers.

"Yes, so we meet again," she told him politely.

And somehow, he sensed her silent reply.

I did win the first battle, McCoy!

His fingers tightened around hers. They were both still smiling.

And old Petty was beaming away, thinking that his team was together at last.

Subtly, McCoy pulled her a shade closer. His words were light. In jest. "So it's to be Hatfield versus McCoy, eh?" he murmured.

Her lashes, luxurious, long and honey dark, swept her cheeks. And her gaze was regal and sweet when her eyes met his again. All innocence.

"Oh, no, sir. It's to be Hatfield *and* McCoy, I believe."

Hatfield and McCoy...

His grin was suddenly real.

It just wasn't meant to be.

Chapter 2

They left the station together, and as soon as they were outside, he headed toward his car. She quickly stated that she didn't mind driving, but the force of his stride had her at the passenger door to his car before she could even complete the words. There was an incredibly firm touch to his hands as he—courteously?—helped her into the car, and an unshakable firmness to his quick, curt words. "I'll drive."

If he wanted an obedient silence from her, he wasn't going to get it. He might think she was a quack, but she'd come up against the attitude before. He might be as aggressive as a tiger when he chose, but she knew how to fight back.

Politely.

"Do you know where the house is?" she asked.

"I have the address, yes, thank you."

"But do you know where the house is? The streets around here curve."

He glanced her way with his teeth nearly bared. "I know where I'm going!"

She simply wasn't going to be intimidated.

This was a matter of life and death. They had to get along. And he had to learn that he had to listen to her.

She leaned back. "Go straight down the road here, then make a left. It should be the third or fourth house in."

He glanced her way again. There was a steel sizzle to his eyes. It was electric. She nearly jumped from the power of that gaze.

But she didn't. She'd never let him know that he managed to nonplus her.

Maybe his eyes shot silver bullets, but he didn't ignore her directions. He turned the black Lincoln just as she had directed.

There was no mistaking the house. As soon as they came around the corner, Julie saw the kidnapped little girl's parents waiting. There were other people around them. Family, friends, perhaps. The Nicholsons, she thought quickly, remembering everything she had been told. Martin and Louisa. And their little girl's name was Tracy. She would be eight next week.

The lawn, the neighborhood looked so normal, so peaceful. It was spring, and Louisa Nicholson had planted all kinds of flowers along the walkway. The house was freshly painted a bright white with green trim around the windows and doors. It was a moderately affluent neighborhood, a working neighborhood, a place where *Sesame Street* and Disney movies would play for the children, where hope blossomed for the best of lives, where the American dream could be played out.

But not today.

Robert McCoy pulled his Lincoln to the side of the road. The engine was still revving down when Julie opened her door and hurried out. She smiled reassuringly as she walked up the steps to the cement pathway leading to the broad porch and the house. She knew the girl's mother instantly—a small woman with dark curly hair and large brown eyes that kept filling with tears. She stood beside a lean man with thinning gray-black hair. "Mr. Nicholson?" She shook his hand, then turned quickly to his wife. "Mrs. Nicholson? I'm Julie Hatfield. Petty sent me from his office, and a Mr. McCoy, FBI, is right behind me. You mustn't worry, really. I don't know what Petty told you about me, but I am very good, and I'm certain that at this moment, Tracy is fine. Just fine."

Something in her words must have reached Mrs. Nicholson because some of the cloud seemed to disappear from her eyes. She smiled at Julie, then looked over Julie's shoulder. McCoy was coming toward them.

"Mrs. Nicholson, I'm—" he began.

"Yes, yes, you're the FBI man," Louisa Nicholson said. "Julie, please come in. My husband and I will help you in any way we can. Oh, Mr.—did you say McCoy, Miss Hatfield?"

They were going to go through a lot of this, Julie thought.

She smiled. "Yes, he's a McCoy. Isn't it just disgraceful?"

"Miss Hatfield—" McCoy began, that deep voice filled with all kinds of authority.

It didn't matter. Louisa Nicholson actually laughed, and her tall, balding husband at her side almost grinned.

"We're just so very worried," Martin Nicholson said.

"Naturally," Julie said softly. "Shall we go in?"

The Nicholsons excused themselves to the anxious friends and neighbors who had gathered around. Julie saw a few friends from church and waved, then hurriedly followed the Nicholsons into the parlor. Julie glanced around quickly. It was a warm house. A house, she thought, where a lot of love lived. There was a beautiful china cabinet to one side of the entry, filled with various collections of crystal and figurines. The two hutches that filled out the parlor were mahogany, rich and beautifully polished. But the sofa and chairs in the center of the room were overstuffed and very comfortable. A little girl could crawl all over them without worrying about being yelled at. She could curl into her father's lap there, rest her head against her mother's shoulder.

Robert McCoy had begun an intense round of questioning. Julie could tell that the Nicholsons had already been through it all; their answers were becoming mechanical.

The Nicholsons knew that Tracy hadn't run away. She was a good girl, she loved them both, she was an only child, and they were a very close family. She had been right out front, and then suddenly she had been gone. All the wonderful people out in the yard had searched the house, the lawn and the streets beyond, and they had even organized block searches. The police had come by, and now Mr. McCoy and Julie Hatfield were here.

Julie was surprised to find herself distracted momentarily as she watched McCoy. He had the ability to be kind, to be gentle. He spoke to the Nicholsons with a depth and understanding that startled Julie.

She had thought him all business, cut and dried. But there was a heart pumping in that broad chest.

He was a very handsome man. Those steel-gray eyes were direct and powerful in a handsome face that was strongly, ruggedly sculpted.

He probably chews nails for dinner, Julie thought.

He didn't really look like a G-man, not in that black leather jacket of his. G-men were supposed to wear three-piece suits.

Maybe he did wear suits on occasion. He would be just as tall in a suit. His shoulders would be every bit as broad. Maybe he'd be even more intimidating.

He wasn't intimidating. Yes, he was. But he did have a heart in that rock-hard chest, she had determined. Either that, or he was just so professional that he could make his voice sound as if he were caring.

Something suddenly flashed briefly through her mind.

He cared too much. That was it. He cared too much. He took every case right to his heart...

Julie turned toward the window and started. They were still talking behind her. Suddenly, she could see what had happened. She could see it all.

There was Tracy Nicholson. She was a tall girl for seven, maybe four feet three inches. And she didn't look a thing like her parents. She had bright red hair and a cute spattering of freckles across her nose. She was wearing nearly brand new blue jeans and a white blouse with a Peter Pan collar and a pretty navy sweater. She had been rolling a ball down the steps. The ball had rolled out into the street. It was then that the car...

The car. She couldn't quite see the car. All Julie knew was that it was some kind of a sedan, and not a compact car. And it seemed to be a darkish color. It drew near the curb.

The driver was calling to Tracy.

Julie inhaled and exhaled slowly. She could feel her heart thundering, just as Tracy had felt her little heart pound ferociously.

Tracy had been taught by her parents never to get into a car with a stranger. She had been taught to be polite, but careful.

And now there was this someone...

Julie tried to see into the mist surrounding the car and driver. She couldn't. She just couldn't.

Not even when the driver swore because Tracy would come no closer. Swore, and leaped quickly out of the seat, rushing for Tracy.

· Tracy tried to scream, tried to run. She could do neither. Julie could feel the little girl's terror. Her feet had felt like cement. She couldn't budge them. And her scream...her

scream had caught in her throat. And just when it might
have burst out, something was clamped tightly over her
mouth. Something with an awful, strong odor. Tracy tried
to fight then. She tried very hard, and her shoes dug into
the dirt. But that stuff on the cloth made it harder and
harder to move. She couldn't even think anymore. It was
something awful. Something that stole the light...

It was gone. A flash of blackness appeared before Julie's
eyes, and she knew. The little girl had lost consciousness
then.

"...white shirt, and jeans," Louisa Nicholson was saying. "And her high-top sneakers."

"And her navy blue sweater," Julie said softly.

"What?" Louisa said.

Julie turned around. "She was wearing her navy
sweater," she said.

Martin Nicholson gasped softly. "That's right, Louisa,
she was. She told me she was going to get her sweater
while I was fixing the pipe out back. She ran in and put
it on. I'd clear forgotten until now. We gave the other
officers the wrong description of her clothing—"

"It doesn't matter," Julie said quickly. "What matters
now is that we get her back." She glanced at Robert. He
was watching her carefully, his eyes narrowed. But he
didn't try to shut her up. He was unimpressed with her
knowledge about the sweater, certainly, but he didn't seem
to mind her presence so much anymore.

"There were originally scuff marks in the dirt on the
shoulder of the road?" McCoy asked quietly. He didn't
say it reproachfully, and he didn't let on that valuable clues
might have been gained had the dirt and grass and the
shoulder not been so trampled. It was a foolish waste, but
it wouldn't do any good to tell the Nicholsons now.

Louisa nodded and sniffed, then suddenly the tears she
had been trying to hold back came streaming down her

cheeks. "She fought him. My baby fought him. He must have hurt her, oh, how he must have hurt her—"

"No, no, Louisa!" Julie said quickly. She sat beside Louisa on the plush old comfortable couch, taking the woman into her arms. "No, please, trust me, believe in me. Yes, Tracy was frightened, and she did fight. She's a wonderfully tough little girl, and the two of you have taught her to be so resourceful. But he hasn't hurt her. He's going to ask for a ransom. He wants money, not to hurt anyone. You wait and see. It's all going to come out all right."

"The phone line has been tapped?" McCoy said.

Martin Nicholson nodded. "The police did that right away. Petty told us there would be a man listening in every time our phone rings and that if a ransom demand came, they'd try to trace the line immediately."

"That's good. That's real good," McCoy said. "Well, I think we'd better get started on what we have."

"Officer Smith is still out searching the woods around the house with some volunteers," Martin Nicholson said.

"Fine," McCoy said. "Have you got a picture of Tracy for me?" he asked.

Louisa leaped to her feet and hurried out of the room. She returned quickly with an eight-by-ten photograph in a bronze frame, handing it to McCoy.

"May I keep this for now?" he asked.

"Of course."

"Stand by your phone," McCoy said, shaking Louisa's hand, then her husband's. "We'll do everything in our power."

He started out. Julie lingered, shaking Martin's hand, too, and impulsively giving Louisa a hug. "We'll find her," she promised. Hope sprang into Louisa Nicholson's big brown eyes. Hope, and belief. Julie could have kicked herself. She'd had no right to make such a promise. Things could go wrong. Things did go wrong. Petty was con-

vinced that the kidnapper was the same one who had taken
the two young women. And one of them had been okay...

And one was still missing.

She'd had no right! No right to give that woman so
much hope for her child. A beautiful little child with red
hair and hazel eyes and those few adorable little freckles
over her nose.

"Miss Hatfield!"

It was McCoy. He was at the door, waiting for her.

She offered Louisa a rueful smile. "Now I know why
the feud began!" she whispered softly. She was rewarded
with another half smile before she and McCoy left.

McCoy waited until they started down the walk before
muttering darkly, "I wish to hell the ground hadn't been
trampled to mush! We could have learned if she really was
grabbed—"

"She was. Right here," Julie said.

He stopped dead still, his hands on his hips, his head at
an angle, his silver eyes seeming to blaze out his ridicule.

"Oh, really?"

"Yes," Julie said flatly. She walked to the spot where
Julie had been. "She was playing with her ball. A small
ball, with little stars on it, kind of like a circus motif. Then
it rolled out into the street and she came out. She looked
both ways. She's really a very good little girl. It's a loving
household. Of course, you don't have to be a psychic to
have ascertained that."

McCoy shrugged and put on his sunglasses. "You'd be
surprised," he said softly. "I've seen some awful things
in some homes that looked like paradise on the outside."

Julie shook her head. "This is a good home, and Tracy
loves it."

"If you say so."

Julie indicated the picture he was holding. "Look at her
face!"

"All children have trusting faces," he said.

"That's not true, and you know it."

He was studying Tracy Nicholson's face. Julie leaned over his shoulder and looked at the smiling girl in the photograph. "Her hair is longer now," Julie said. "Oh, and she's had her braces off since this was taken."

"Has she?" McCoy opened the car door and gently tossed the picture inside. "Let's go."

"Wait, please."

"For what?"

"Just give me a minute, please? I want to show you what happened."

"Oh, come on—"

"Two minutes, Mr. McCoy."

He didn't dispute her again. He leaned against his car, watching her.

Julie started to follow Tracy's steps. "She caught her ball here. Then she saw the car come toward her and stop. The driver asked her to come closer. I think he said that he wanted directions. But Tracy was too smart. She wouldn't go to him. So he jumped out of the car and raced to her. He had something with him. A cloth. With some kind of dope on it. I don't know what. He came down this street with the intention of taking someone. He probably even watched Tracy before." She hesitated, then walked a bit. "This is where he took her from. He clamped the cloth over her mouth. And she fought until she lost consciousness."

She watched McCoy inhale and exhale. "Get in the car, Miss Hatfield. You can sit here and play charades. I have work to do."

"You are an arrogant buffoon! I only want to help you, and I can. And Petty says—"

"Yes, yes, Petty says. Okay, so Petty wants you in on this. And your friends inside want you in on this—"

"I've never met the Nicholsons before, McCoy, so they aren't my 'friends inside.'"

She couldn't see his eyes behind the sunglasses, but she could sense them narrowing. Speculatively. Maybe he was just beginning to believe...

"Get in the car, Miss Hatfield."

"Then—"

He stopped, glaring at her. "What kind of car, Miss Hatfield?"

"I don't know! I can't quite—"

"And is it a man driving? What does he look like? Is he alone? Is he tall, is he short?"

"I can't quite—"

"You're right. You can't. You can't give me a damn thing except that a little girl was kidnapped. Well, we all have that one figured out, Miss Hatfield."

"I've just told you—"

"Nothing! You haven't seen a thing."

"I've seen a lot! But no, I can't see everything, I'm not God! I've given you a good picture—"

"You've made some pretty good guesses. Now, let's go. I need to make phone calls. Set up a more organized search. I want to get out in the field myself. I—"

He broke off as the front door to the Nicholsons' house burst open, and Martin Nicholson was hurrying toward them.

"It came! A ransom call came. It wasn't long enough— they couldn't trace it. You've got to come in quickly. Petty is on the phone for you now."

McCoy could move faster than lightning. He was already on the phone with Petty by the time she came inside. Sunglasses pushed back on his head, he watched her as he grunted to Petty. Then finally he hung up the phone.

"The kidnapper has called. He wants a hundred thousand by tonight, small, unmarked bills, et cetera."

Julie nodded, feeling a tightening in her stomach. They had all suspected that this might be the same criminal.

Now they knew.

"You two seem to know something!" Louisa Nicholson said, fear rising in her voice.

McCoy exhaled softly. He shook his head. "Not really. Petty played the recording for me. Our man—or woman—is disguising his voice. But…"

"But what?" Julie said.

"Don't you know?" he taunted.

She stared at him, gritting her teeth. McCoy, to his credit, changed his tone quickly. Neither wanted the Nicholsons to realize that he didn't have faith in Julie.

"Our kidnapper seems to have eyes in the back of his head."

"He knows that the police are in on it already?" Julie asked softly.

"Oh, yes, he knows." McCoy watched her curiously. "He asked specifically for me to be the one to deliver the money."

"Where?" Julie asked.

He shrugged. "There's a phone booth by a gas station near the highway. I'll get the first call there."

Martin Nicholson stepped forward. "You will do it, Mr. McCoy, won't you?" he asked anxiously. "I'll get the money, I'll get it within an hour. There won't be any problem. I'll put the house up for what I don't have. The banks here will help out. They'll get the money for me by tonight. I don't want to take any chances."

"Mr. Nicholson—" McCoy began.

"It doesn't matter. The money doesn't matter at all. The house, none of it matters. Not without Tracy," he said.

Julie felt his pain so intensely, she could scarcely breathe.

"Mr. Nicholson," McCoy said quietly. "Of course, I'll take the money. Please, don't worry. The FBI likes to arrest kidnappers, too, especially the kind that travel over state lines. We don't like them to go on kidnapping other people. But please, I swear to you, we have a policy, and

I have a personal commitment here, too. I swear that I'll not endanger your daughter's life in any way. Do you trust me?"

After a moment, Martin Nicholson nodded.

"Especially with Miss Hatfield along," Louisa Nicholson said.

McCoy looked at her, startled. "I should go alone. This might be dangerous—"

"Oh, Miss Hatfield!" Louisa's eyes were starting to fill with tears again. "You have to go along, please!"

"It isn't FBI policy—" McCoy began.

"On this case, it is," Julie reminded him pleasantly. Damn him, he still didn't quite seem to understand. The kidnapper could run them on a wild-goose chase. He could take the money, and fail to return Tracy Nicholson.

Maybe McCoy did understand. Maybe he just didn't believe she could do anything about it.

"I've got to get down to the bank right away," Mr. Nicholson said. "And get things in motion for the money."

There was a knock at the door. Tense, pale, Martin Nicholson threw open his front door. He seemed relieved. There were two uniformed officers there, a pretty young woman and a slender young man. "Is Lieutenant McCoy here?" the young man inquired.

McCoy nodded. "I'm here."

"I'm Jenkins, and this is Officer Daniels. She's going to stay with Mrs. Nicholson. I'll escort Mr. Nicholson to his bank and back here."

"Fine," McCoy said. "Mr. Nicholson, Mrs. Nicholson, I'll be back at seven. That will give us an hour before I'm supposed to be at the phone booth with the money. Miss Hatfield, if you're with me..." He waited, arching a brow at her.

Julie smiled reassuringly at the Nicholsons, then hurried along behind McCoy.

He had very long legs. He strode ahead of her to the car and got in. She thought he was going to gun the motor and escape without her.

But that wasn't his intention. She had nearly reached the car when he pushed open the passenger door from inside. "Get in, will you?"

She crawled into the car quickly. She was barely seated before they were pulling out onto the road.

"McCoy," she said, "I *am* coming with you tonight."

He didn't answer her.

"McCoy?"

"Damn it! Don't you know that these things can be dangerous? I've got to confer with Petty. We've got to be very careful. There's going to be backup on this, but it's damned hard when you're sent from phone booth to phone booth—and when this guy seems to have eyes in the back of his head. If you're with me, you could be putting your own life in jeopardy."

"How charming! I didn't realize that you were so concerned for my health and welfare."

His dark glasses were on but she could feel the heat of the glance he cast her way.

"Miss Hatfield—"

"The name seems to be giving you problems. Perhaps if you called me Julie—"

"Perhaps I would like it very much if I didn't have to speak to you at all!" he exploded.

"But you do have to speak to me! Damn you, don't you understand? I might be able to find Tracy. And that is the most important thing."

He was quiet for a long moment, then he sighed. "I do realize that Tracy is our priority. What do you think I am, Miss Hatfield, a block of ice?"

"Well—"

"Never mind, don't answer that. It's just that maybe I don't believe you can do Tracy any good."

"But what if I can?"

"I don't believe in—"

"You don't believe! But what if I *can* help Tracy? What if it's even a one out of a hundred shot? What if I could even make a lucky guess?" She had grown very passionate in her argument. She was almost touching him, she realized.

And then she felt a set of hot, electric fingers dancing a pattern down the length of her spine.

Julie moistened her lips. The passion remained in her voice. She had to convince him. "Give me the chance. Give Tracy the chance!"

"All right, all right, you're with me!" he exploded.

She settled back in her seat, strangely worn, as if she had just completed some great feat of manual labor.

"Where are we going now?" she asked.

"Back to see Petty first. I have to set up whatever cover I dare with him. There are the usual warnings. If I'm seen being followed, he'll kill the girl. We have to be very careful."

"Then where are we going?"

He cast her a quick look. "Dinner, Miss Hatfield. It's been a long day, and it's going to be a longer night. I haven't had a chance to eat. Any objections?"

Julie shook her head. "No," she said pleasantly. "No, none at all."

"If you really have any abilities, close your eyes and picture me the best steak in the area."

She sniffed and sat back. "I thought you knew where you were going around here."

"I do. But it's been awhile…well?"

"That's easy," Julie said softly. And she named her favorite steak house. "But how on earth you can eat—"

"Hunger. It does it every time," he told her. "Of course, I can leave you off—"

"And not come back for me," Julie said sweetly. "No, no, I think I can manage one meal with a McCoy."

But that same curious warmth that had traveled her spine seemed to have spread.

Was she going to share much more than one meal with this man?

For a moment, she saw darkness and shadows. And the silhouette of a man, a lover, walking slowly, surely toward her through those shadows...

The moon rose. She saw a scar etched across the man's shoulder.

And she felt the danger...

She shivered fiercely. All pictures faded away.

"Miss Hatfield?"

His voice was deep, sensual.

"I'm fine, Mr. McCoy. I was just wondering..."

"What?"

"Do you have a scar on your shoulder?"

He was very still. She wondered at first if he had heard her.

"Well, Miss Hatfield, if you ever see my shoulder bare, you'll get to find out, won't you?" he said, turning his attention to the road.

And she was left to wonder.

Chapter 3

McCoy was, Julie decided later, the ultimate professional. She watched him speak with the officers who would be assigned to wait patiently at various points in the region. There was a tremendous network of communication going on, for in a period of less than ten minutes, it was possible to go from West Virginia to Maryland to Virginia to West Virginia, and back through all three again.

And they were surrounded by countryside where a man could easily get lost among the foliage. Forests carpeted the mountainsides. In the darkness, movement could be tricky business. In certain areas, rock was sheer, with precipices that led nowhere—except straight down to more rock.

McCoy made it clear to the force working that night that they were in a difficult—perhaps in a no-win—situation. The girl's life was most important, and they must do nothing to jeopardize little Tracy.

Sitting in the back while McCoy spoke to Petty, who would be manning phones and radio, and the six officers who would be assigned the task of trying very hard to be in the right place at the right time, Julie was startled by McCoy's knowledge of the region.

"How does he know this place so well?" she whispered to Pettigrew.

He grinned. "He grew up here, just the same as you did. Except he comes from a Maryland mountain and you come from a West Virginia mountain."

Julie frowned. Putting all the mountains together, they still hailed from a small region.

"Why haven't I ever seen him before?"

He took so long to answer, she wondered if Petty heard her. "Well, he's been gone for a long time, that's why."

"Then—"

"Any more, Miss Hatfield, and you'll have to look into that crystal ball of yours."

Julie sighed. He just didn't want to tell her any more about McCoy. Well, that was all right. All she had to do was get through the night with the man. Then she'd never have to see him again.

No. She would see him again. She knew it.

It was a quarter to six when they finished at the station and headed to the restaurant.

"Since you're from this area, why didn't you pick your own restaurant?" she asked him in the car.

"Because restaurants change constantly," he told her. "And it's been a long time since I've been home. Is this it?" He pointed to the sign advertising the best steaks anywhere in the state.

"Yes."

"Is the advertising true?"

"I doubt it, but the food is good."

He smiled, pulled off the street and parked. To Julie's surprise, he walked to the passenger side and opened the door for her.

The beast came with manners on occasion, she thought.

Julie greeted the hostess who seated them, then smiled to the cute, young brunette, Holly, who waited on them.

The restaurant was brightly lit for a dinner place, with booths surrounding the walls, and tables covered with snow-white linen cloths. Julie was glad to be sitting across the table from McCoy at a well-lit booth rather than in a more romantic, candle-brimming room.

She needed distance with McCoy.

Holly, it seemed, didn't.

Even after McCoy ordered his steak and Julie ordered her salad, the young woman hovered until Julie formally introduced her to McCoy. Julie felt annoyed at the way Holly looked at McCoy, as if she had walked in with Mel Gibson or his equivalent.

"Are you staying in the area, Mr. McCoy?" Holly asked.

"Maybe, I'm not sure yet."

"Well, we certainly hope that you do. Don't we, Julie?"

"Oh, sure, yes, of course," Julie said blithely. McCoy cracked a crooked smile, which probably caused Holly's heart to flutter. Finally, another couple came into the restaurant, and Julie and McCoy were left to sip their coffee in peace.

"A salad, huh?" McCoy said, pressing his fingertips to his temple. "Let me see. A vegetarian?"

"No," she said, trying to keep an edge out of her voice. "Just a very nervous person who is too worried about a little girl to dream of digesting a steak."

McCoy's hands moved idly over the heavy white coffee mug before him. They were large hands, with very long fingers. Well-kept hands. The fingertips were calloused, but the nails were neat and clean and bluntly clipped. To Julie's distress, she found herself imagining those hands against her skin. Covering her fingers. Moving softly against her arm.

She looked quickly into his eyes as he said, "I'm worried, too."

Julie would have responded, but Holly was back. She set a nice-size Caesar salad in front of Julie and a sizzling steak platter in front of McCoy.

Then the young woman proceeded to fuss. Did he want steak sauce? Sour cream for his potato?

"Butter for his beans?" Julie suggested pleasantly.

"Pardon?" Holly said, wide-eyed and innocent. "Oh." She blushed. "Oh, I know! More coffee."

She brought the pot. She filled McCoy's cup and forgot all about Julie's.

"Holly!"

"Oh, sorry," she said as she filled Julie's cup.

McCoy studied Julie when Holly left. "So the little blond angel has claws," he said softly.

"That's right," Julie agreed pleasantly. "And best you remember it."

"Should I?"

She arched a brow.

"Well, are we going to be together again for any reason in the future?"

"I don't know," Julie said evenly. "Are we?"

"You're the psychic."

"But you don't believe in me."

"All right. Let me ask you this. Is Tracy going to be all right?"

Julie looked at him across the table. "I don't know."

"Then…"

"I told you before. I'm not God. I can't see everything."

"Then what good is any of it?" he demanded, his tone suddenly so harsh that her fingers curled tightly around her cup. Instinct warned her that she should jump up and run.

"Sometimes, Mr. McCoy," she said quietly, meeting his hot silver gaze, "sometimes my ability can do an awful lot of good. Sometimes I can see people, I can see them exactly as they were...or are. Not every time, but sometimes. I don't know why I have this gift. When I am able to do something, I don't question it. I'm thankful for whatever the ability is. That's it. There's no more to it. I try. I try with all my heart. And on occasion, I have been able to save a life. And to me, Mr. McCoy, just one life is worth it all!''

She expected some burst of emotion from him in return. She didn't get it. He stared at her for what seemed the longest time, then he set his fork and knife into his steak again. His eyes were on his meal. ''Just one life,'' he murmured.

''Pardon?''

''Nothing. Aren't you going to eat your salad?''

''For your information, Mr. McCoy—'' Julie began, leaning close to him across the table.

''For my information what?'' he snapped. His eyes blazed into hers. Little silver arrows seemed to pierce her flesh, to sweep inside her, raking through her with heat and fury. She didn't think she'd ever felt a look so physically before—ever.

Nor had she expected the anger that filled her, or that other emotion.

Attraction. Stark, sharp, physical attraction. So strong that it sizzled and whiplashed, and seemed to create electricity in the air between them.

She sat back. His gaze, too, was quickly masked, but Julie knew, suddenly and fiercely, that he had felt it.

''I...'' She began. What? Her mind was a blank. She didn't even like him, she reminded herself dismally. And it didn't matter. They were out to catch a kidnapper. Possibly a murderer.

Tracy. They were out to save Tracy.

''What?'' he demanded, exasperated.

''It's getting late,'' she said.

He glanced at his watch. It wasn't really so late, but he didn't dispute her.

"I'll get the check from your friend."

"I think she's *your* friend," Julie told him sweetly.

"Claws out, Miss Hatfield?"

"Hey, what do you want? I'm with a McCoy."

Two hours later they sat on the steps of a long walkway that led to an abandoned antebellum home outside the city limits of Harpers Ferry and Bolivar, but still on West Virginian soil.

Something felt right about being with him. Maybe it was his size. He was tall, with such impressive shoulders.

No...it didn't have anything to do with his size. He simply had that air of confidence about him.

Aggression, she warned herself. Bald aggression.

And no matter how strongly attracted she was, he was the last man she wanted to find herself involved with. She did not like being laughed at. Or doubted.

It was a beautiful spring night. Even in the shadows and darkness, shades of spring seemed to cover the land. The forests rose like deep, rich green sentinels, the sky was cast in cobalt and black, and the silver-white glow of the moon touched down on it all. Even where they were right now, with the night hiding the chipping paint of the old home, and the moonlight giving a past glory to the tall white columns on its porch, even the house looked beautiful.

But despite the warm spring air, Julie shivered. He was out there. With Tracy.

She closed her eyes. The phone should be ringing soon.

She gasped suddenly. Tracy.

She could see the little girl. And see what Tracy was seeing...

Darkness. Tracy was crying. It was hard to breathe. And

hard to move, because she was boxed in. The smell around her was a rich one. Dirt.

"Oh, God!" she breathed.

"What, what?" McCoy demanded. His arm was around her shoulders. Tightly. Supportingly. Maybe he didn't believe—

Maybe he just felt the loneliness and the fear of the night.

She had to draw in a very deep breath. "He—he's got her buried," she said.

And just then, the phone rang.

McCoy leaped up, leaving the briefcase containing the money Martin Nicholson had obtained by Julie's feet. "Where?" he snapped into the receiver. McCoy was wired, so that the others would know where they were going next. He repeated the instructions given to him by the kidnapper.

When he hung up, Julie was already on her feet. "He hasn't left her enough air!" she said anxiously. "Where does he want us to go now?"

"Maryland side of the border," he said briefly. "Let's go."

Both of them were deadly silent as they moved on to the next phone booth. They barely reached it before the phone started ringing.

This time, McCoy came back to Julie looking perplexed. "He knows that I'm wired. And he knows exactly how many other cars are out."

"We have to do whatever he says!" Julie whispered softly. "She's running out of air. Tracy is running out of air."

He hesitated, gritting his teeth. Then he spoke loudly. "Petty, I'm getting rid of the wiring. He's on to us. And Julie says I don't dare take any more time."

Somewhere, Julie knew, Petty was cursing away. He didn't like the idea of putting her or Robert McCoy at risk.

But he liked the idea of what could happen to Tracy Nicholson even less.

"Come on," McCoy told Julie.

"Where now?"

"Virginia," he said curtly.

They drove to another phone booth, both hoping that the task force might still be around them. "How the hell does he know so damned much?" McCoy exploded. Then he mused softly. "Unless he's bluffing. Maybe he doesn't know. Maybe he's just guessing, and making darned good guesses."

"He's not bluffing about Tracy," Julie said.

They came to the next phone booth. The kidnapper had planned well. The phone booth was off the beaten track, away from any convenience stores or gas stations.

No one could have easily followed them to it.

And once again, just as McCoy stopped the car, it was ringing.

When he hung up that time, he came back to the car for the briefcase. "I'm walking it up the mountain," he told her.

"I'm coming with you."

"You're staying here—"

"Oh, no, I'm not! Don't you ever watch movies? The man always thinks he's being the hero by walking off alone into the night. And while he's gone, the monster comes back and gets the woman. I am not staying here alone."

He smiled. It was that same crooked smile that had so captivated Holly.

"You think there are monsters in these here hills, Miss Hatfield?"

"Yes, and more than just McCoys!" she answered sweetly. "Please! We're almost out of time."

He didn't argue with her any longer, but keeping up with him proved to be a trial for Julie.

She was mountain born and bred, and she could scamper up heights and over rocks with a fair amount of agility and ease.

But he had such long, long legs.

And it was apparent that he was mountain born and bred, too. He climbed without his breathing even deepening, and he seemed to have the agility of a mountain goat. He only turned back once or twice, however, reaching to drag Julie along with him.

Then they came to a plateau with a sparse clearing. "This is it," McCoy said.

"It's what?"

"It's where I'm supposed to leave the case."

Julie nodded. McCoy set the case down.

"Now what?" Julie asked.

He swore softly. "Now we go back to the phone."

"No!" Julie exclaimed suddenly.

"No? What do you mean, no?"

She shook her head fervently. "Tracy isn't here. She's—" Julie paused. "She's near the river. She can't hear the water rushing now because he's buried her. She couldn't even hear it once he had dragged her up. But she could see it. She could see it from the rock. And he thought it was funny. Really funny when he buried her. He kept laughing. He was careful, he didn't talk. But he laughed. There was something funny about it. Something really funny. He was so proud of himself. For being so bold. And he has no intention of letting her out."

"Where is she?" McCoy demanded harshly. He dropped the briefcase at his feet and grabbed Julie's shoulders. Roughly, he swung her around, studying her intensely. "Damn you, where is she? And if you're wrong, Julie Hatfield, I'll wring you out and hang you up to dry myself!"

"I'm not wrong!" she gasped. "I'm not wrong!" Julie shook her head. "She's not here, not here, not here…"

She paused, feeling the sensations as they began to steal over her. Tracy...

Tracy, where are you?

It came to her, slowly, then more quickly. Then frantically.

Can't breathe, can't breathe, can't breathe...

What happened, where are you?

Can't breathe, can't breathe, Mommy, where are you, please, I'm so scared...

Tracy...

And then Julie was with Tracy. She was with her as it had happened.

He was there. The kidnapper. And she was Tracy.

She was over his shoulder. He was panting, and they were climbing. Higher and higher. There were people around. No one could see Tracy, though. She was packed up like painting equipment. Lots of people sketched or painted here. They stopped, they milled around. They chatted, they saw things. Saw the rock, saw the water. Saw...

Tracy couldn't see, though. There was canvas over her head. She was still so dopey. She knew she needed to cry out. She couldn't. She felt him climbing. She'd been here before. It was so obvious.

And it was getting dark. Nearly dark. The people were gone, there were no lights. It was perfect. Such a perfect place to bury someone. And he had planned it all out. The hole was there, the box was there...

"Damnation!" McCoy shouted suddenly.

Julie's eyes flew open. She had been talking out loud, she realized. Describing what she had seen—and what she hadn't seen.

"What?" she cried.

"Come on, hurry up, I know the place you're talking about."

He had the briefcase in his left hand, her fingers in his

right. With her in tow, he began to plunge down the mountainside, running, balancing, running harder.

She stumbled. He paused to pick her up. He halfway carried her all the way to the car.

Then he was on his radio, calling Petty. Demanding that he get the cars to the cemetery, telling him to get people up there right away.

It took them at least ten minutes to drive into town and park the car among all the official cars already there.

Then there was the climb up the pathway to the old cemetery.

When they reached it, Petty already had search lights going. He saw them across the broken and angled tombstones as they arrived. "Robert, are you sure?"

McCoy said something. Julie stopped in her tracks. Yes, yes, this was it!

Tracy, where are you?

Can't...breathe. Mommy, want Mommy, can't...

She could hear it. Julie could hear the awful, ragged, desperate sound as Tracy Nicholson struggled for the last of her air.

Julie spun around. She could hear it...

"There, over there!" she cried.

McCoy was ahead of her. "There's dirt plowed up here!" he shouted. There was a man nearby with a shovel. Without a word McCoy snatched it up and began to dig. Julie was quickly by his side. "Hurry, oh, hurry."

Mommy, Mommy, Mommy...can't breathe...

"Please, dear God, hurry!" Julie cried frantically. A pick lay nearby. Men were running toward them, but she was so desperate. She grabbed the pick and slammed into the ground.

Someone else was there. She looked up. It was one of Petty's regular men. Joe Silver. He smiled at her. "Julie, I'm stronger. Hand it over."

She did.

Joe swung the pick while McCoy shoveled.

"Easy!" she cried suddenly to Joe. The shovel struck something hard. She was afraid that the pick might crash through wood and enter into delicate flesh.

"It's some kind of a coffin, I think," McCoy said.

"It's a cemetery! There's probably hundreds of coffins up here!" Petty roared.

But not like this coffin, Julie knew. Her chest hurt. She couldn't speak because she couldn't breathe.

Tracy Nicholson was in that coffin, in the square box deep down in the hole. This time, the kidnapper had employed a truly bizarre sense of the macabre. Had his victim died, there would be no need to move her. Had she never been found, hundreds of years from now she might have been dug up just like any other corpse in the graveyard.

"Julie—" Petty began.

"Hurry!" She felt as if her chest were caving in on her. She gasped, deeply, desperately, drawing in air. "It's Tracy. She only has minutes left. He never intended to return her. Never."

Maybe Robert McCoy didn't believe in her, but he answered the desperation in her voice. He was down in the hole, having discarded the thought of attempting to drag up the box. Heedless of the dirt, he slammed the spade against the latch on the side of the coffinlike wooden box. There was an awful, wrenching sound. His hands on the rim, he tore at it. Julie heard the groaning of wood, then the lid gave at last to the power in his arms. There was a splintering sound, and the lid popped open.

And there was Tracy Nicholson.

She was just as Julie had seen her, dressed in her jeans and her pretty white shirt and her navy sweater. Her red hair was all tangled and askew.

Her freckled face was pale. Her eyes were closed. Her lips were silent.

"Dear God—" McCoy breathed.

She couldn't be dead, Julie thought. No, she just couldn't be dead. She would know; she would feel the loss.

McCoy had the silent girl in his arms and quickly stretched out on the ground. His fingers closed her nostrils as his lips descended over the girl's mouth, forcing air into her lungs.

Once, twice, three times...

Suddenly the little girl gasped, choked, coughed and choked again. Her little chest rose and fell on its own. "Oh, thank God!" Julie shrieked. McCoy moved aside. Tracy's eyes were opening. She looked right at Julie.

"Thanks," she mouthed softly.

Her eyes closed again, but she was still breathing. Evenly.

A cheer went up in the cemetery. Almost loud enough to wake the dead, Julie thought. And that was almost what they had done. A few more minutes, and there wouldn't have been a prayer for Tracy. Julie was shaking. She had seen. Yes, she had seen Tracy. But she hadn't seen the cemetery. She would have never made it on her own.

McCoy...

He had known what she was saying. He hadn't believed, but he had taken a chance.

He was looking at her now. She was on her knees in the middle of all the dirt that he had dug up. She was covered in it.

So was he.

"Make way for the medics!" someone called.

"Her parents are here, down on the street," someone else said.

"Here's the doctor!"

"And her folks!"

The Nicholsons didn't notice either McCoy or Julie as they rushed for Tracy. "My baby!" Louisa shrieked. Tracy's eyes opened at the sound of her mother's voice. She didn't seem to have any strength, but she could talk.

"Mommy! I called you. I called you and called you."

"And I'm here, my dearest, I'm here, I'm here."

Tracy was quickly wrapped in her mother's arms. Martin Nicholson supported his wife as she stood with their child. The two of them turned away, stunned with the wonder of their daughter's return.

People were following behind them, Petty and Joe Silver and some of the other officers. The hole in the earth still lay gaping open. There would be investigative work on it. Fingerprints would be taken, the area would be searched for the minute clues.

But for the moment, it was just a hole. This time, the grave had been cheated.

They were nearly alone. And McCoy was still staring at Julie. Then suddenly his arms were on her and he was lifting her, nearly throwing her into the air.

"Damn it, we did it! We made this one, we made it!"

And as he dropped her, she came sliding down against his chest. She felt the tight, hot ripple of muscle in his arms, in his torso. She felt the silver fever of his eyes, blazing into hers.

Then she felt the rough, searing enthusiasm of his kiss as his lips suddenly and passionately covered hers.

Lightning seemed to strike. Julie might have heard thunder crashing across the heavens.

Heat, startling, sweet, astounding, swept in her and throughout her.

He started to raise his lips, started to pull away.

But he did not...

His mouth settled more firmly on hers, and his arms wound around her. A searing pressure forced her lips to part for his. The amazing fever held her still in his grip, responding almost savagely to his touch, tasting his mouth, savoring the feel...

Oh, no! This just couldn't be right. She wanted to go on and on.

She barely knew him.

No, she had met him in a dream.

Demon or lover?

She didn't know. All she did know was that the electricity was nearly more than she could bear, that she had never felt like this about any man, anywhere, be it real or in a dream. And it was wrong. He didn't even believe in her...

But she didn't pull away. He was the one to do so, his arms still around her, his eyes a silver fire as they stared into hers.

"Now this—is madness!" he said hoarsely.

Julie pulled furiously away from him. They were alone with an open grave site and dozens of broken-down tombstones. Voices were growing faint in the distance.

"Yes, it is. You don't even like me, do you?" Julie accused him.

"I never said that—"

"Well, it is certainly extreme madness," Julie insisted. "The moon is out, that's my only excuse. Really. A handshake would have sufficed!" Confused, flushed, dismayed, she turned, nearly stumbling over one of the old tombstones. He caught her arm. She wrenched it free. "Good night, Mr. McCoy." Determined not to trip again, Julie kept walking. She heard his soft laughter behind her.

"Miss Hatfield?"

"What?"

"Am I going to see you again?"

"No!"

Again, his laughter touched her. She spun in a new fury. "All right, McCoy, what is it now?"

"All right, Miss Hatfield. You're the psychic. But you're wrong. I will see you again. I'm very certain of it."

And smiling like a self-satisfied cat, he shoved his hands into the pockets of his black leather jacket and sauntered confidently past her.

Chapter 4

McCoy was right.

Julie did see him again, and much sooner than—but certainly not where—she had expected.

Just five days later she saw him in church, sitting just a few rows ahead of her. He was with a tall, slim woman with dark sandy hair and two children. An uneasiness spread throughout her. She hadn't thought that he could be married.

No, she couldn't be his wife. Not even someone with McCoy's inborn arrogance could have kissed her the way he did if he had a wife.

Still...

When the woman turned enough so that Julie could see her face, she saw that the woman was beautiful. She had bright blue eyes and fine, stunning features. At her side was a little girl, maybe a year or two older than Tracy Nicholson. She had soft, pale blond hair that waved down her back. She must have sensed Julie watching her, because she turned and her eyes met Julie's. She smiled. It was a wonderful smile.

Then the boy turned, too. He was about twelve. His eyes weren't blue. They were that steel gray color, just like McCoy's.

So he did have a wife and family...

No, he couldn't have. She was certain she would have known.

Maybe not. Inner sight could be blind at the strangest times.

The woman, realizing that the two children were staring at someone or something behind them, turned, too. Of course, she caught Julie staring right at her.

She smiled.

Well, it was time.

McCoy turned, too.

He wasn't in his black jacket, but neither had he really dressed for church. No one really dressed up in the spring and early summer; they didn't want the many tourists in the area to feel awkward for dressing casually. Julie was casual herself in a short denim skirt and short-sleeved tailored white blouse. A little bit of warmth went a long way. She was wearing sandals and no stockings.

McCoy wore black trousers and a turquoise knit shirt. The buttons were open at his neck. She didn't meet his eyes. She was staring at the tiny space of chest covered with coarse, sandy whorls of hair that was just visible at the opening of his shirt. He was tanned, so the skin beneath the springy feel of hair would be bronze. And tight. He was very well muscled. A powerful man. She had noted that when he had ripped the coffin open, and she had felt it the several times that he had touched her.

Her eyes met his. She was suddenly convinced that Robert McCoy had a few powers of his own. He'd been reading her mind. And of course, her mind had been on his body.

Right in the middle of the last amen!

He smiled. Smiled just as he had the night they had found Tracy. Smiled like a man who knew something. As if he held something over her.

She nodded briefly, then tore her eyes from his and looked straight ahead.

But by then, the service was ending. And when she slipped from her pew and started out, she stiffened. She didn't need to turn to realize that he was right behind her.

As soon as they stepped from the church and into the daylight, she felt his hand on her arm, stopping her. "Why, Miss Hatfield! Good morning. Were you in there praying for divine guidance?"

She spun, smiling sweetly. "On the contrary, Mr. Mc-Coy. No one wants to see things that others don't."

He arched a doubting brow, then turned quickly as the woman he had been with emerged from the church. "Julie Hatfield, this is my sister, Brenda Maitland. Of course, underneath she's really a McCoy. Being as you're a Hatfield, I feel obliged to remind you of such a thing."

"Oh, Miss Hatfield!" Brenda Maitland extended a hand to her and offered her a broad smile. "How nice to meet you. And how very wonderful that the two of you found that little girl." She shivered, looking up the cliff toward the old cemetery. The church was on the pathway that led to the burial ground. The view from the church was stunning. There was the street, which was part of the National Park Service now, handsome with its ages-old buildings. And there were the rivers, the Shenandoah meeting the Potomac, beautiful blue with little whitecaps as water rushed over rapids. Then there were the mountains stretching onward, the spring greenery of Maryland Heights.

To reach the church from the valley below was easy enough. Some of the original settlers had carved steps right out of the rock. The climb became more difficult once there were no more steps, but the mountain residents were accustomed to climbs. It was the tourists who panted as they walked the trek to Jefferson rock and onward to the cemetery.

But all in all, it was a long climb to reach that cemetery.

"We're so close to where it all happened. Imagine! Someone managed to bring that box up there, dig a big hole, then drag that poor little girl up, and no one even noticed all of it going on!"

It was extraordinary, Julie thought. Especially when they were already into the spring tourist season.

"But it turned out well, at least," Julie said.

"Are you really a witch?"

Julie started at the softly spoken question that seemed to come from nowhere. She looked down. The little girl with her mother's blue eyes and the beautiful cascade of blond hair was standing right before her.

"A witch?" Julie repeated.

"Well, Uncle Robert said that—"

"Tammy!" Brenda said, distraught.

"Did I say witch?" McCoy asked, his hands on his niece's shoulders, his eyes sizzling as they touched Julie's with no apology whatsoever.

Fine. Julie looked from McCoy to his niece. "I don't cook with toads or snake's eyes or anything like that, if that's what you mean. I'm sorry."

"But you are a witch in a way, right?" Tammy insisted.

"Well, I think your uncle is convinced that I am," Julie said sweetly.

"Let me finish the introductions," McCoy interrupted. Still no apology, but he was suddenly determined not to let it go any further. "This impudent little piece of baggage is Tammy Maitland. And my nephew here is Taylor Maitland. We were on our way to Sunday brunch. Care to join us?"

"Oh, no, I—" Julie began.

"Oh, please!" Tammy insisted.

"I really—"

"Please? I promise, I won't ask you anything more about being a witch!"

Julie gazed at the little girl. *What if I told you that your uncle really doesn't like me? That I spent the majority of a night with him and he still didn't believe in a single thing I told him?*

"Please, do come," Brenda insisted. "Of course, I suppose that you have been hounded. Robert was saying that you were lucky you're not an official, and that you could crawl away to that house of yours up in the mountain. The station was just plagued with phone calls from newspapers and the television stations. Fending off the media is worse than coping with the criminals at times, so my brother tells me. We really won't plague you. Yes, we will, but just a little."

Julie had to laugh. She was surprised then to catch McCoy's silver gaze upon her. And she was startled by the softness of his voice when he bid her a simple, "Come?"

Julie shrugged. "I suppose. Artemis will miss my speedy return."

"Who's Artemis?" Taylor asked.

Julie widened her eyes. "Artemis? He's my cat. My black cat," she added, smiling as she looked at McCoy. "My familiar, I believe."

He groaned. "Shall we go?"

They went. Julie didn't need to speak with McCoy as they walked to their cars because Brenda Maitland managed to keep Julie at her side. "You'll have to forgive my brother. His feelings on this subject are wickedly single-minded. Of course, it is natural, I suppose." She seemed grave. "After everything that happened."

Julie's curiosity was instantly piqued. "What happened?" she asked.

But her question came too late. Brenda didn't hear it. She had stopped to look back. "Where's Taylor now?"

"Up here with me," McCoy called. They had reached the church's small parking lot. "Miss Hatfield, will you ride with us?"

"I have my own car," Julie said.

"I'll get you back to it."

She hesitated. He hadn't gotten her back to her car the last time she had seen him. Of course, that hadn't really been his fault. She'd been so mad that she'd stayed with Petty until he'd been able to drive her to her car.

"But I—"

"Come on!" He walked to her. His body blocked her from the others. "You're dangerous on the road, you know."

"I am not."

"You should have seen me coming."

"You should have seen *me* coming."

"No, Miss Psychic. You should have *seen* me coming!"

"Oh, no, I'm not going through this—"

"Yes, you are. Come on." He raised his voice. "She's driving with us."

"Great!" Brenda called, climbing into the back of her brother's Lincoln along with the children.

"I never said—"

"What's the matter, don't you like kids?"

"I like kids just fine. I have problems with adults at times!"

"I won't spill a thing or throw a single pea, I promise," McCoy vowed gravely.

He was shoving her again. Or dragging her. One or the other. She was nearly in the passenger seat and she hadn't agreed in the least.

But she couldn't disagree, because McCoy was quickly in the driver's seat, and they were already moving. And while they drove, Julie discovered that she hadn't seen Brenda before because McCoy's sister usually attended a little church two towns over.

"Why were you in today?" Julie asked.

"Oh, Robert convinced me. Quite honestly? I wanted to meet you. And Robert said that you'd be there today."

Julie cast McCoy a quick glance. Petty knew she came to church here almost every Sunday. He could have told McCoy.

But had he?

Julie wondered again at Brenda's comments about her brother—that it was natural for him to feel the way he did about psychics. Why?

The question plagued her, but she couldn't ask it now. Yet as she studied McCoy, she felt a trembling steal over her fingers again. Was he the man in her dream? Her cheeks felt hot as she remembered the dream. It had been so real. She could almost feel the man's body. They had been so close, so intimate. She barely knew McCoy.

His eyes touched hers suddenly. Silver. Sharp. Like blades, they seemed to pierce right through her.

He knew, she thought in a sudden panic. He knew what was going on in her mind!

He couldn't. She tore her eyes from his. He looked at the road. He was smiling.

He hated psychics, he wanted to deny them all. But the way he had just looked at her...

A hot sizzle streaked along her spine. He could deny it, but Julie was absolutely convinced that Robert McCoy had certain powers of his own.

And oh, the things that he could read in her mind!

"Have you always lived here, Miss Hatfield?" Taylor asked.

"Always," she said softly.

"A Hatfield from the hills!" Brenda said, laughing softly.

"Well, it seems to me that these hills are brimming with McCoys," Julie returned good-naturedly.

"Yes, I suppose it's true. We have lots of cousins

around us. Of course you're the first Hatfield I've ever met," Brenda said. "Do you think there really was a feud at one time?"

"Think?" McCoy snorted. "I could almost guarantee it—seeing as how we've met a Hatfield now."

"Whoa!" Brenda protested. "Julie, ignore him!"

"Oh, don't worry about it," Julie said. "I have it on the highest authority that there was a feud—and that the Hatfields won. So there."

Brenda laughed softly. Julie felt a silver gaze on her, and she quickly looked down.

Her fingers were trembling again. She could feel the man's warmth as if it touched her.

What is he doing to me? she wondered.

They were barely friends. They were more likely enemies.

She had never wanted anyone more. She felt the tension building in the car between them. Bit by bit. The air didn't seem to touch her. The heat was building. Explosively.

Brenda was talking. About something. Julie couldn't hear her. She suddenly wanted to be alone with McCoy. She wanted to shout at him. She wanted to tell him to leave her alone, to get out of her life.

And if he didn't...

Well, then, he needed to hold her.

No. He needed to make love to her.

The car pulled off the road. They had reached the restaurant in Charlestown.

Julie nearly catapulted from the car. Taylor was emerging behind her, pointing out a place where his Little League team had played the year before, and thankfully, a feeling of normalcy settled over her once again.

She didn't know about McCoy. He had already walked into the restaurant.

Once they were all inside and seated and Julie had a cup of steaming black coffee in front of her, she felt better.

The brunch buffet featured all sorts of magnificent things to eat, and when Julie returned with her plate, she was surprised to see that McCoy's choice of foods might have been a copy of her own. They had both piled their plates high with peel-and-eat shrimp and marinated artichokes and sweet-and-sour pickles.

"I'm going back for an omelet and red meat later," McCoy assured her, pulling back her chair. And at that moment, she had to smile.

The meal progressed. Brenda Maitland's children were charming and very well behaved. There was a closeness to their family group that she found herself enjoying.

Maybe the Hatfields had won the feud, but it hadn't done much for her. She was an only child, and her mom had passed away over ten years ago, her dad a year ago last spring. She did have aunts and uncles and cousins, but they had slowly moved toward the big city, Washington, D.C. She saw them as often as she could.

But then, McCoy lived in Washington, she remembered. And he would probably be going back there. Soon.

"Tell us more about Tracy Nicholson," Brenda said suddenly. "She really wasn't much help to the police after she was found, was she?"

Julie shrugged and glanced at Robert. "Your brother knows more about that than I do. I wasn't there when they questioned her. Tracy had been taken to the hospital immediately, and they questioned her there. I wasn't needed anymore, and there were plenty of people who were."

"She didn't see anything," Robert said. "Nothing at all. She couldn't even tell us what kind of car it was."

"I know," Julie murmured.

"You know?" McCoy said.

Julie gritted her teeth to hang on to her temper. "When we were at the house, when I was coming down the steps, I saw the ball go into the road. Then I saw the car. But it was—it was in a mist."

"How convenient," McCoy said dryly.

Brenda elbowed her brother. "Did you see the man, Julie? *Was* it a man?"

Julie shook her head. "Yes, I think so. I mean, I think it's a man. But no, I didn't see him. He must have been..." She paused, her voice breaking off. She had a sensation of...

"A stocking!" she exclaimed suddenly.

"What?" McCoy demanded.

"That was it!" She stared at him. "He scared Tracy right from the start because his face was so strange. He had a stocking pulled over his face. He wanted to make sure that she didn't see him!"

"But she would have run right away," Brenda protested.

"No, no," Julie said excitedly. "She was already in the road, remember? She was smart, but she was scared. And he realized just how smart she was quickly, so he jumped out of the car to take her."

"But what a dangerous thing to do!" Brenda exclaimed. "For the kidnapper, I mean. Anyone could have seen him. And he wouldn't have looked normal in the least. How recklessly brazen—"

"Brazen and smart, and laughing at the pack of us all the while," McCoy muttered. "Brenda, somehow this guy walked to the cemetery, dug a hole, planted a box and then a little girl. I have no problem seeing him as brazen or reckless."

"Well, Julie has just explained to you why Tracy Nicholson can't help you."

"Why can't she tell me about the car?" he demanded. He stared straight at Julie.

"Tracy doesn't know cars," Julie said softly. "And there—there was mist around it."

McCoy sat back. His gaze was an open challenge.

"What mist? There was no fog that day. Nothing. Unless a little cloud descended right around the kidnapper's car."

"No, of course not—"

"Then why can't you tell me about the car?"

Julie sighed. "I can only tell you what Tracy saw. My connection always seems to be with the victim."

"That's convenient, too," McCoy commented dryly.

"Excuse him for being so rude," Brenda said with a long sigh. "He can be such a pest."

"I've noticed."

"Maybe he knows that," Taylor said suddenly.

They all started. The children had been so quiet that Julie had forgotten Taylor and Tammy had been listening. Now they stared at the handsome boy with McCoy's steel-gray eyes.

"What was that, Taylor?" Brenda said to her son.

"I'm talking about the kidnapper. He must know something about the people around here, right? He wanted Uncle Robert to carry the case. And maybe he knew something about Julie." He stared at his uncle. "He meant to kill the little girl he kidnapped, right? He meant to kill her all along. So why cover his face to Tracy? Unless he knew that Julie was going to be called in, and that she might be seeing him through the little girl's eyes?"

They were all dead silent for the longest time, staring at Taylor in amazement.

His words had made so much sense.

"Well, I'll be darned," McCoy said softly. "That's great reasoning, Taylor."

Taylor flushed, pleased. McCoy tousled his hair. "Of course, it's possible, too, that the kidnapper knew that he was running the risk that Tracy might be found before she did run out of air."

"Maybe," Julie murmured. Then she suddenly gazed at Brenda, feeling guilty. "And maybe we shouldn't be talking about this all in front of your children—"

"Are you kidding?" Brenda demanded. "I want them to know what happened, *and* what almost happened. That way, they'll watch out for one another, and they'll be doubly careful. It's not the same world we grew up in, Julie. Children have to be aware of the maniacs out there. They have to be. For their own safety."

"We're very careful, Mom. Aren't we, Taylor?" Tammy demanded.

Taylor nodded. "I'm right about the kidnapper, though. I know it. He's not afraid of his victims seeing him. He's afraid of Julie seeing him."

A chill streaked along Julie's spine. Was Taylor right?

McCoy groaned. "Not another psychic, please. This is all getting unbearable."

"You know your uncle doesn't believe in psychics," Brenda reminded her son gently.

"You don't believe in Julie?" Tammy asked.

"Not a whit," McCoy replied pleasantly. "Where is the waitress? We could use more coffee."

"And we could use more milk," Tammy agreed. "But if you don't believe in Julie, why did you make her come to breakfast?"

Brenda gasped. Julie felt a grin tugging at her lips, then she felt McCoy's eyes on her again.

"Well, she is attractive, isn't she?"

"Beautiful," Taylor agreed, and then blushed. Julie felt her cheeks growing red. McCoy could be so light and personable one minute, and then come down like lead the next. She could almost like the man, and then...

"The most beautiful charlatan I've ever come across," he said smoothly.

"Maybe I can entice the waitress to serve the coffee over his head," Brenda murmured. "Robert—"

Julie had had enough. She was suddenly heedless of Brenda and heedless of the children. She leaned closer to

McCoy. "If I'm such a charlatan, how did we find that little girl?" she demanded.

"Luck, maybe," he replied, his gaze hard. "Perhaps you even noticed him going through town. Maybe you saw someone with a spade heading for the cemetery."

"I don't even live in town!"

"Maybe a friend mentioned it."

"But I didn't know it was a cemetery. You're the one who found the cemetery, McCoy!"

"Look, I'm not trying to say that you lie on purpose—Hatfield. But perhaps you build on some sort of suggestion in your mind—"

"I was with that child, and you know it!"

"Well, her parents think so, and that's enough, isn't it? Petty is fooled." He looked quickly at Brenda. "Joe Silver and I were the ones digging away, covered in dirt, and the Nicholsons just wanted to thank Julie. It's a great life, right?"

"Don't you believe in anything?" Julie exclaimed.

"Oops, here's the waitress!" Brenda said cheerfully. "I think they both need a bath in cold water, but we'll take a little more coffee, please. And milk for the kids. And the check, if you don't mind," Brenda said.

She kept talking cheerfully, determined to keep up a monologue so Julie and McCoy would both shut up. And they did.

But through the rest of the meal, Julie could feel his eyes on her. And more.

She could feel the heat rising again. It was anger. Really. He was so arrogant, so damned sure of himself.

Was it really anger?

She had become tense. The brush of his napkin over her fingers nearly made her jump a mile. He glanced her way. She stared furiously at him. *Don't you dare call me a charlatan!* she silently yelled at him.

But you are, you have to be...

She gritted her teeth. She was not reading his mind—she didn't read minds. And she wasn't a witch. Still, she could scarcely sit in the restaurant a minute longer. She had to do something.

Touch him.

Her heart was pounding too quickly; she had difficulty breathing. And it seemed that a sizzle of fire danced up and down her spine.

Just when she didn't think she could take another minute, McCoy stood. "I'll just pay up front."

"I'll leave the tip," Julie said, leaping up. McCoy might have argued with her. Then she realized that he was in as big a hurry as she was.

But if Brenda was aware of their distress, she gave no sign. When they reached the car she nimbly climbed into the backseat saying, "Robert, drop the kids and me off first, will you? As long as you don't mind, Julie."

No! Julie wanted to shriek.

She kept her jaw locked. McCoy grunted some kind of an agreement.

As he started the car, he slid his dark glasses on against the bright glare of the spring day. Julie sat silently in her seat, noting the way the wind tousled his hair. She looked straight ahead. She wanted to strangle the man. She had also been tempted to reach out and run her fingers over the rugged line of his cheek.

He pulled off the highway to follow a small, winding pathway up to an old farmhouse. He stopped in front of it. "Well, this is home," Brenda said, getting out with the children. She paused to stand by Julie's window and shake her hand. "Can you come in?"

"Oh, thank you. But I think I'd best get home myself," Julie said.

Brenda nodded. "Well, we won't be strangers now. We live close by each other. And I'll even admit defeat in the feud for the McCoys, if we can all be friends now!"

Julie laughed. "I really haven't the faintest idea who won," she said. "And it was wonderful to meet you."

The kids told her goodbye and ran around to kiss their uncle goodbye. Then Julie and McCoy were back on the road. Neither of them spoke.

When they neared the lot where her car was parked, Julie spoke at last. Politely. "Thank you for brunch. Your sister is lovely."

"Thank you," he said curtly. He came to a stop. He was going to get out to open her door, but Julie moved too quickly.

"I'm fine, thank you. Goodbye, McCoy."

"Miss Hatfield—"

"Don't you mean, 'Miss Charlatan,' McCoy?" she asked, her door half open.

"You've known my opinion—"

"Well, then, I'll tell you mine. You, sir, are an ass!"

With that, she slammed his car door shut and hurried to her own vehicle. She smiled grimly—she could hear the thunder of his retort following her.

She ignored it, revved up and quickly swung from the parking lot.

Several minutes later, her smile faded.

He was following her.

Just how mad had she made him? she wondered. And despite herself, she felt a jumping in her heart.

She was almost home. And he was following her still. Right to her house.

Well, she'd wanted to have a fight with him. A real, live fight.

She wanted to vent some frustration. To hit him good.

She just didn't want him to hit back.

And that annoying sizzle of heat was back, racing up and down her spine...

She pulled off the highway, and up the long patch that

led to her house. She parked in the big expanse of her front yard, slamming out of the driver's seat to await him.

He braked to a halt right behind her and got out.

"What!" Julie shrieked. "You have to follow me to hand out more abuse! You are an ass, a complete fool, as hardheaded as rock. And you had no right to follow me just to argue that point. You—"

"I followed you, Miss Hatfield, because you left your purse in my car!" he bellowed in return.

"Oh. Oh!"

For a moment Julie just stood there, a column of fury and tension. She strode quickly to where he leaned against his car door, holding her small white leather clutch bag. "Thank you!" she snapped, taking the bag and hurrying to her front door.

He was right behind her. She opened the door, and he followed her in.

"And I'm an ass, am I? You tell me, Miss Hatfield, what happens when this voodoo doesn't work? When you have people believing in you and following your every lead. Only you're leading them down the wrong damned path?"

"I don't go down the wrong path!"

"Well, just what happens if you do?" he demanded heatedly.

He was backing her down the hallway, past the stairs to the rear wall.

Then she was against the wall, and his hands were on her shoulders. His body was nearly touching hers; she could feel his fingers so acutely through the thin fabric of her blouse.

"I don't owe you any answers, McCoy!" she flared. "You're in my house—and I don't remember inviting you in!"

He stopped, suddenly seeming to realize that he'd barged in.

"I'm leaving!"

"Good! Fine!"

"And I won't be back, Miss Hatfield. We've done what we were supposed to do. It's over. I don't have to see you again."

"And I don't have to see you again. I don't have to listen to you, I don't have to talk to you!" Julie said.

"That's right," he agreed savagely. He was still touching her, though. His hands were still on her shoulders.

He dropped them. Julie gritted her teeth.

He turned, striding to the front door, which he opened and slammed shut behind him.

Julie winced at the sound. She leaned against the wall, closing her eyes. If only her heart would stop beating so stridently. If the pulse that throbbed against her temple would slow down.

If only the sudden...

Emptiness, yes, emptiness...

Would go away.

There was a thundering on her door. She started, then yanked it open.

He was back. McCoy was back. Tall, imposing, towering there in her doorway.

"What—what else did I leave in your car?" she demanded.

"Nothing," he said briefly.

"Then?"

He could be a bully when he wanted. He stepped inside, closing the door behind him.

Julie backed up just a bit, watching him.

He pulled off his sunglasses, and in his eyes she saw a tumult that matched her own. She swallowed, and her eyes lowered to his throat, and she saw the same pulse beating there.

"Then?" She repeated softly. "What..."

He groaned. "Then—then this!" he stated flatly. Suddenly he was reaching out, and she was drawn irrevocably into his arms. His mouth was on hers, wet, hot, open. Demanding. Parting her lips. And all the heat and electricity that had played between them suddenly met and seemed to explode there in the hallway like soaring red fireworks. The fever scorched along her back and settled into her.

And the kiss went on and on...

The kind of kiss that could never, never stop at the lips.

Chapter 5

His kiss was the most wonderful thing Julie had imagined, sweet water on dry earth, magic and mystery, and a slow, burning lesson in the ways of sensuality. His lips touched her lips, but the fire they created touched her skin, swirled to her belly and found root in some central place of her being. Every shift, every movement, each touch, each stroke…all were so natural and fluid, and all touched her anew. She felt the roughness of his fingertips against the bare flesh on her arms, her cheeks. His lips, his tongue…he kissed her and kissed her. Tasting, demanding. Savagely and tenderly at the same time. The feel of his body against hers was overwhelming. The driving tension, the engulfing heat, the steel power seemed to enwrap and encompass her. Then his lips rose briefly, and his eyes touched hers. She didn't know exactly what he sought, but he seemed to have found it. Once again, his lips found hers. His teeth gently caught her lower lip, and the searing warmth streaked through her once again. Her knees were weak, and a fierce trembling had begun within her.

His tongue bathed her lower lip, then he kissed her cheek, her forehead, her lips again. His movement was slow...

And so anxious. So leashed. As if he hungered greatly, but dined slowly to savor each morsel of a meal.

Julie gasped softly, clinging to his neck. He brushed aside her hair and kissed her throat. His tongue teased her flesh; his teeth barely brushed it. His lips moved again, just beneath her ear. Then lower, against her shoulder.

The buttons of her blouse were slipping open. As if they had life of their own, as if they approved of the assault on her senses, as if they gave blessing to it. He found the flaring throb of her pulse and left his kiss there. And then his head moved lower, and she vaguely thought that he had wonderful, thick rich sandy hair, then the thoughts were stolen from her mind, for his kiss was pressed against the rise of her breast, searing hot and more arousing than she could bear. She moaned softly, and her fingers knotted into his hair.

"Julie..."

"Yes..."

She didn't know if the whisper of her name was a question or not. She knew only that he had touched her in some way from the first moment she had seen him. And they had both known that coming to this point was inevitable.

He was the man...the man in her dream. The man who had brought heaven to her, here on this earth. The man who...

A chill swept through her. Danger. There had been so much danger in the dream. Ecstasy followed by fear.

But she wasn't afraid.

Perhaps he felt her tensing. Perhaps not. His arms were more securely around her. His kiss was more tantalizing. No fear...

Either that, or the desire was simply greater. So great that she could not care. Her blouse had fallen open all the way. He moved deftly, swiftly, knowing what he wanted. His fingers brushed against her back, freeing her breasts from the restraints of her white lace bra. His lips kissed the rise of flesh, then his mouth took her in, his tongue brushing her nipple fiercely, his hands...caressing.

A long, low moan escaped her. All thoughts of fear evaporated. She had never felt more sheltered.

Or more aroused.

His lips covered hers once again, then his head rose suddenly and she felt the silver fever of his eyes tense on hers. She was in his arms, half naked now, parts of her clothing barely dangling from her shoulders.

"You do live alone, I hope?" he said.

She smiled, a slow, warm smile that curled across the fullness of her lip. She nodded.

Then she was swept urgently into his arms. Her arms curled around his neck.

"Where?" he demanded huskily.

"Upstairs."

Julie closed her eyes and leaned against him, secure in his hold. McCoy took the stairs two at a time.

There were five doors on the second floor, all standing ajar.

Perhaps he did have a touch of some form of power within his own doubting heart, for he chose the second door, the one that led to her bedroom. It was a beautiful room, with age-old mahogany furniture and a bed with a tall canopy and a plush, deep red, patterned comforter that matched the valances above the lighter drapes. Julie was glad she had made her bed that morning.

And then she knew it would not have mattered in the least because McCoy managed to one-handedly strip off the comforter and top sheet before placing her within that cocoon of covers. He came with her, not just a graceful lover, but an urgent one, his lips finding hers again before her head touched the pillow. Graceful, able, nearly frantic.

His kiss broke as he found her shoes and dropped them heedlessly to the floor, his eyes on hers. Julie simply watched him for a moment, then she roused herself, shimmying from the remnants of her top garments and reaching out for him. Her fingers seemed so small and delicate against his chest as she worked at the two buttons on the turquoise knit shirt. Perhaps she didn't move them quickly enough. A strangled sound seemed to escape him, and he wrenched the shirt over his shoulders. For a moment they paused on their knees, watching one another, and then he pulled her into his arms, and the feel of her naked breasts against his hair-roughened chest was exquisite.

His hands covered her as he pressed her to the bed again, then he found the zipper at the rear of her skirt, and the rasp as it went down seemed to fill Julie with an ever greater longing. He slipped the skirt from her hips and she was left in a wisp of white lace bikini underwear, and for the first time, something gave him pause.

He stared at her as seconds ticked by. Then he touched her lip, and delicately drew a line from her mouth along her throat, between her breasts, down past her navel and straight to the throbbing center of all her heat and desire. She moistened her lips, amazed that such a delicate touch could create such a sensation. She could lie there no longer, her body on fire. She started to rise, but he pressed her back, his lips covering hers, then tracing that same pattern he had already drawn down the length of her body with his finger.

Julie twisted violently as the sweet sensation tore wildly through her. A flick of his finger had broken the thin band on the panties, and the wisp of lace was tossed away with no apology. And once again, she found the heat and desire within her rising to an unbearable point, half agony and half ecstasy, the longing and the pleasure so acute.

Then he was with her. His own clothing was shed and strewn, and the magnificent warmth of his body covered all of her. She entwined her arms around his neck and touched his lower lip gently with the tip of her finger. She stroked his shoulders, her fingers trailing down his back. He groaned, and she brought her delicate, sweeping touch around, teasing his midriff, his hip. Lower. Closing her fingers around him...

Some harsh sound emitted from him and it was over, this brief, sweet time of play and exploration.

It could be no other way.

Julie wrapped her arms and legs around him, welcoming him as he thrust into her, gasping, shivering, trembling, as she accepted the whole of him. He paused. He moved so slowly. Drawing out the touch, the wonder...

The longing.

She cried out, rising against him, but then he moved slowly no longer. A whirlwind swept around them. Magical, wonderful. She was aware of the cool feel of the air around them, because her flesh was on fire. She was soaring upward, but she keenly felt the softness of the comforter brushing against her flesh. She rose to some distant plain with him...

But she was so aware of his body. His thighs, so rough against her own, muscled, huge, taut. His belly, flat, damp, teasing her with every brush, every stroke and movement. His fingers, his hands...now at the side of her head, for anything held back was unleashed, and a sweet rhythm was rushing by faster and faster. Wonder filled her again and again, rising. Going even higher. She met his eyes, then she cried out, startled, almost frightened by the volatility of the sweet climax that seized hold of her. She closed her eyes against his, suddenly, ridiculously shy. She wound her arms around his neck, turning her face to the side and holding tight to him. Then she felt a great quaking within his shoulders, a stiffening like rock, and then a slow relaxation. Hot mercury seemed to fill her body.

He held deadly taut for what seemed like forever, then he slowly eased himself down beside her.

Neither of them spoke. He held her easily within his arms, and still the seconds ticked by. Hot, damp flesh cooled in the spring mountain air.

Then he gently ran his fingers over her shoulder. "I told you that I'd see you again," he reminded her.

Julie smiled. He had banished any discomfort she might have felt over her more than abandoned behavior.

"Yes, you did. You must be psychic."

It was the wrong thing to say. She felt the tension snake into his body, and it wasn't a sexual tension. He didn't exactly toss her away from him, but she felt him withdraw. Confused, hurt, she determined to draw away herself. Blindly she groped for something to cover herself with so that she could walk to the shower. There wasn't anything there. Her discarded clothing had gone flying and he was halfway lying on the comforter.

She didn't need anything. That would be like closing the barn door after the cow had run away, she reminded herself dryly. She just needed to leap up proudly and stride for the shower.

A long, tightly muscled arm fell over her. She couldn't hide forever. She met his eyes, a steady gray now, hard on hers.

"Julie," he said huskily, "I don't suppose I ever told you this. I really think you're the most beautiful woman I've ever met."

She was going to melt. She had to take great care. She sometimes felt as if she was dealing with Dr. Jeykll and Mr. Hyde. "That isn't necessary now, McCoy, is it? We've been where you wanted to go."

His brow flew up incredibly and he was suddenly sitting, staring her down.

She wasn't going to be intimidated. It was time to make

that proud march into the shower. She stood up. "Yes, excuse me—"

He stood and blocked her path. He didn't seem at all alarmed at his own nudity.

It alarmed Julie.

She had more time to look at him now. And she certainly had a more complete picture.

Her knees were weak all over again. She really did like everything about him. Even his arrogance. He was standing there with his hands on his hips, the breadth of his shoulders very straight, and the whole of him seeming to tick and pulse with tension once again. Bronze, taut and big. She felt her palms going damp and her eyes drawn just where they shouldn't be.

He smiled suddenly. "Yeah. I got what I wanted. Like you weren't ready to jump my bones, Miss Hatfield."

"If you will just excuse me—" she said again, trying to stride imperiously by him.

It wasn't easy. He caught her by the shoulders and swung her around. And she struggled and started to shout out a real protest but she never found her voice. He was kissing her again. That same kind of kiss that seemed to bathe all her insides, that had gotten them here to begin with.

She pulled away from him determinedly. "I'm taking a shower, McCoy."

She moved quickly, before he could stop her again, her mind in a whirl. What was it with him? There were moments when they seemed so close.

Moments when it seemed as if he was a lover she might have waited a lifetime to meet.

And then...

Then something leaped up between them. A wall, a barrier, as cold, as hard as stone.

She was still a charlatan. Sweet and simple.

That thought gave her the strength to slip by him to her bathroom.

Once the bathroom had been a bedroom. Julie had always wanted a huge bathroom. One with double sinks and a separate shower and tub, and she'd been determined that the tub would be huge and deep and have a nice hot whirlpool in it. Once she had saved enough of the money she received from the sale of her short stories, she had invested it immediately in her bathroom. It was a wonderful place.

But she didn't give it the least heed as she marched in, slammed the door and slipped into the glass-enclosed shower. She jerked the water on. It came out freezing cold. So cold that she gave a little scream, then stood beneath it anyway. Maybe it was exactly what she needed.

Suddenly the glass door opened. McCoy was right behind her.

"What the hell happened?"

She stared at him blankly, water dripping over her eyes.

"You screamed."

"Oh! The water. It was cold."

"That's all?" he demanded incredulously.

"Well, I didn't mean to scream. It was just cold."

McCoy was wet now, too, with the water spraying over his naked body.

"Move over, Hatfield," he said softly.

"I will not—" she began, but he was already inside the shower stall and closing the door behind him. He stepped behind Julie, then reached over her shoulder to adjust the temperature. The water became much warmer quickly.

She felt his hands, slick with soap, on her back. "Julie, I meant what I said."

"What?"

She knew what he had said. She just wanted to hear it again.

"That you're beautiful," he said softly. "Really beautiful. So small...so delicate..." His soapy fingers accentuated his words, sensually moving against her shoulders and spine, curving and finding the pattern of muscles and bones. "So damned...perfect." The whisper came against the lobe of her ear. And as he whispered, his hands moved around, slipping and rubbing over her breasts and belly, and below.

"McCoy," she protested, turning in his arms. Her eyes widened as she seemed to fit right against the renewed arousal of his body.

Then she found herself pressed against the wall of the shower stall with the water hot and rushing over them. She kissed his soaking chest, tasting the salt of the man and the heat of the water.

And as it rained down around them, he made love to her once again.

The water turned cold. They were still entwined, still breathing heavily and still leaning against the wall. McCoy swore beneath his breath.

"What kind of a hot water tank do you keep?" he demanded.

"Well, we have been in here a very long time," Julie reminded him.

He shut off the water and pushed open the door, snaking a towel quickly off the rack to wrap her in before finding one for himself. She watched him curiously as his eyes met hers again at last.

"Do you or do you not like me, McCoy?" she asked frankly.

A handsome smile curved his lips. "Obviously, I like you, Miss Hatfield."

"Then why do you suddenly get so mad at me all the time?"

"Because I don't want to hear about this ridiculous psychic business!"

"Ridiculous?" Julie said. He didn't answer. His jaw

was set in that line again. The barrier was up. Hot and cold.

She swung around and walked to her room. She ignored him as she dug into her drawers for clothing, choosing jeans and a T-shirt. He watched her as she dressed, seeming to be in no hurry to do so himself. Then he suddenly strode across the room and gripped her shoulders.

"Julie, damn it, we both knew we were coming to this. You are beautiful. I have never wanted anyone more. And it's more than wanting…it's your eyes. It's your voice. It's the way that you care about people. Hell, yes, I like you. I just don't want to hear about the voodoo bit when we're together!"

She pulled back, staring at him. "You say that you care about me, McCoy. But don't you see? It's part of what I am! I can't take it on and off like a coat!"

"What do you mean, it's part of what you are?" he demanded. His voice was rough and angry. "That's it, that's your whole function, your life?"

"You're a G-man, right?"

"That's a job, Julie. It's what I do for a living."

She sighed softly. "And you do it day and night."

"I don't—"

"But you do. It's not just a job to you, it's more. If you're needed at night, you're there. I wouldn't ask you to change."

"It's not the same at all! Unless you're trying to tell me that you do this for a living—"

"No!" Julie said. "I would never charge anyone to help them. I've never taken a penny and I wouldn't. There's no way to put a price on human life."

His jaw was still at that angle that meant trouble.

"No tea leaves during the week, no crystal balls?"

She gritted her teeth, spun around and hurried down the stairs, leaving him behind.

From the main hallway she walked through the formal

dining room to the kitchen. She was muttering beneath her breath as she filled the teakettle.

"Tea leaves, my foot!"

She slammed the kettle on the stove. When she turned around he was behind her again, barefoot and bare-chested.

And he didn't have a single problem making himself completely at home in her kitchen. He opened her refrigerator.

"I'm making tea," she said.

"Thanks, I'll have a beer." He found one, flipped the pop top and grimaced at her. "You're driving me to drink. What have you got to eat?"

"We just came from brunch."

He looked at his watch. "That was five hours ago."

"You're kidding!" Julie gasped, glancing at her watch. He wasn't kidding. And she was suddenly starving.

"Haven't you got anything in here that isn't green?"

"I do not have molded food in my refrigerator!"

"No, but the only thing you do have seems to be lettuce."

"Well, it isn't," Julie said indignantly. She came to the refrigerator and pushed him aside.

Maybe tea wasn't the right idea at exactly this moment after all. She had a chilled bottle of white Zinfandel, which she set on the counter with a bang, then she opened the freezer. He had simply been looking in the wrong place. She had lots of food. Chicken, lamb, pork, beef. She even had a turkey. Microwave defrostable? She had to stick with the beef.

"Is stir-fry too avant-garde for you?"

"I do stretch to a bit more than meat and potatoes," he said. "Especially if you're cooking."

"We could call for a pizza with the works."

He grimaced. "Not on your life. Cook, woman."

She arched a warning brow. "You'd best be careful. You're coming very close to having a greasy pizza."

For some reason, she didn't mind the idea of cooking for him, although she should have minded. She tossed the package of sirloin strips into the microwave and dived into the green stuff in her refrigerator, some of which wasn't green at all. She had red bell peppers as well as green, and mushroom caps and onions.

"Should I pour you a glass of wine?" he asked her.

"Please."

She began chopping vegetables while he opened the wine bottle. She noted that he knew right where to go for the corkscrew, but she didn't comment on it because he didn't seem to realize it himself. And since she had already started chopping the vegetables, she didn't want to get into another of their arguments where he could either stalk out—or she could become determined to throw him out.

If she was capable of carrying out such a deed.

"So what do you do?" he asked her.

"What?"

"For a living. You said you aren't paid for being a—"

"Charlatan?" she asked sweetly. She pulled out the wok, then dug out her peanut oil and teriyaki and oyster sauces. "Well, I was left some money."

"Nice," he commented.

"No, not really. I'd much rather have my parents back."

"Sorry," he said softly. "I didn't mean it in that way. But does that mean that you're independently wealthy?"

She shook her head. "I write short stories."

"Really?" He poured her glass of wine, handed it to her and propped himself up on the counter with his beer to watch her. "What kind of short stories?"

"Charlatan short stories."

"Now really, the question was civil."

"By your standards, I imagine it was."

"Testy, testy."

"We charlatans get that way."

"Are you going to finish slicing that onion or do you need help? I'm hungry. Let's get going!"

She stared at him, amazed, then saw the silver glitter in his eyes and knew he was doing his best to get beneath her skin. "I think I'd rather do the chopping. And you're the guest. And not really invited. Therefore, you can just wait until I'm done."

"Just remember, I have to report to work in the morning."

Julie sipped her wine and looked at him. A sharp tremor seized her. Was he leaving the area already? She was startled by the sharpness of the pain that seized her. They were scarcely friends.

They were lovers.

And with her whole heart, she didn't want him to go.

"Here? Are you still working out of the station—or do you have to be back in Washington, or wherever it is that you usually do work?"

"No, I'm still working here," he said softly, the humor gone from his eyes as he studied the beer bottle. "Tracy Nicholson came out of it okay, and that was the most important thing. But we didn't catch our man."

"You think he'll strike again?"

"Yes."

Julie stared at her wok. There was a very frightening criminal out there. A kidnapper, a murderer.

And all she could think for the moment was that she was absurdly pleased McCoy wouldn't be leaving the area.

"Do you want—" she started to ask, then broke off. No, he wouldn't want her help.

"Do I want what?"

"Wine with dinner, or would you like another beer?"

"I'll have a glass of wine with you, if you don't mind making some coffee after."

Julie laughed softly.

"Coffee is funny?"

"Well, you found the beer yourself, managed to inveigle dinner—"

"And sex. Don't forget the sex."

Julie flushed. She hadn't forgotten it.

She never would.

"At any rate, I just can't imagine you asking for the coffee so politely. Not when you tend to see what you want and merely take it."

"Do I do that?"

"Yes."

"Did I do that with you?"

"Yes."

He grinned slowly in return. "Good. That means I can probably do it again."

"McCoy, damn you—"

"Your meat is sizzling," he told her. He leaped from the counter, still grinning. "Shall we eat?"

"I'm not so sure," Julie murmured. But he was already reaching for the plates he could see through the glass cabinet doors.

"I think we need to eat really quickly."

"Why?"

"Because we just might have another argument coming on. And your stir-fry smells delicious. And I'm starving. And I don't want you to throw me out of the house before I get a chance to wolf it all down."

Despite herself, Julie was smiling again.

How was it possible to want to hang a man one minute and find herself laughing the next?

Well, that was McCoy. He was complex and hard. Sometimes distant, and sometimes as weary as if he had already lived out a whole lifetime.

And then there were times like this. When his chest muscles gleamed like copper and his dark blond hair was still damp and falling disobediently over his forehead and one eye. When some of the silver edge had left his eyes, and he seemed so young, so handsome...

And so damned sexy...

"Yes! We need to eat. Quickly!" Julie said. She was not letting her mind wander in that direction again.

She scooped the concoction from the wok onto two plates.

"Where shall we eat?" McCoy asked.

"The dining room?"

"Too mundane."

"The kitchen?"

"Too tight. Ah," he said softly. "The bedroom?"

Julie shook her head warily. "Too intimate."

"Well, that was the idea."

"You have to work tomorrow," Julie reminded him. "Remember, you've got to get going. We'll eat in the parlor."

It would be safe, Julie thought.

But it wasn't.

McCoy just wasn't a safe man.

They dined slowly. They talked politely. Mostly about Brenda and her children. Julie learned that his brother-in-law was a serviceman based in D.C. but on loan to a base in California at the moment. Their conversation remained pleasant, easy, casual.

"I have to go," McCoy said softly. "Go—or stay," he added.

"Oh, no," Julie said. "Not tonight. You're not staying tonight. We hardly know one another."

"I thought we were getting acquainted rather well."

"No. You have to go," she said. But his eyes were on her lips. He watched her speak with fascination. He reached out and touched her lip gently with his fingertip.

"I'm going."

But he didn't leave. He pulled her into his arms again.

His lips came down on hers. Tasting them, brushing them. Slowly, slowly savoring them.

Julie broke away, looking into his eyes. "You have to...to..."

Damn, but she liked his mouth. It was full and generous. And sensual. And when it met hers...as it was doing again...she felt such a startling arousal and sweet birth of emotion.

"I have to what?" he whispered softly. The warmth of his breath touched her ear. Seared her throat. Entered into her.

They hadn't had an argument for well over an hour, she realized.

She met his eyes, secure in the warmth of his arms, and she smiled. Slowly. Wickedly.

"You have to stay, McCoy. That's what you have to do."

He laughed softly.

And kissed her again.

Chapter 6

Julie hadn't expected to find herself at the police station the next morning, but by ten o'clock, that was exactly where she was.

And the man with whom she had shared a warm and passionate night was staring at her as if she was a distasteful stranger. A thunderous frown knotted his forehead, and his lips were drawn tight and thin.

It hadn't been Julie's idea to come. She had considered herself done with the case for now. She could help with the victim—not with the criminal.

But Petty had wanted her called in.

McCoy had left her house very early, just about with the crack of dawn. He'd gone home, showered, shaved and changed, and this morning, he looked just like a G-man.

He was wearing a three-piece suit.

And like black leather and casual knit shirts—and nothing at all—he wore it very well. The suit accentuated the tightly-muscled leanness of his physique and the breadth of his shoulders. His hair this morning was firmly brushed back from his forehead—the better to see the scowl, my dear, she thought—and he was all business.

Well, she wasn't particularly pleased about the turn of events herself. She had been so tired when he had left. Deliciously sleepy, worn and warm. She had barely roused herself when she'd heard him whisper that he was leaving and felt his kiss on her forehead. And when she had fallen asleep again, it had been a deep, comfortable sleep.

Then her doorbell had seemed to shrill with the force of a million banshees, and she had shot up, disoriented. The doorbell had continued that awful screeching as she promised herself that she was either going to get a new one or rip the entire thing out while she hopped around, quickly trying to drag on a pair of jeans so that she could answer the summons and make the noise stop.

Joe Silver and Patty had been on her porch. "Petty wants to see you, Julie. He said that we're not to let you escape. We're to sit right here until you're ready to go to the station."

"You're kidding," Julie told her.

"No. I'll make the coffee. Have you any of that mocha blend to grind? I love it. It tastes better at your house than any other place in the world."

"Thanks, yes, grind away," Julie called after her, looking at Joe Silver. He was a nice-looking man, mid-thirties, medium height and build, dark brown eyes, with a great smile. Julie had wondered for a long time if there wasn't something going on between him and Patty.

Patty always denied it.

"What does Petty want?" Julie asked Joe.

"He wants you to talk to a police artist from Charlestown, a man who's supposed to be one of West Virginia's finest."

"A police artist?"

"Yes. To give him a description."

"But a description of what? I didn't see anything!"

Joe shrugged. "Well, I told Petty that. He's just grasping at straws, but you know Petty when he gets something set in his mind."

"Yes, I know Petty."

"Coffee's on. Get ready, Julie," Patty said. "We're not allowed to let you dawdle."

"Does our G-man know I'm coming?" she asked, trying to keep her tone light.

"Yes, he knows," Joe told her. He was watching her closely. So was Patty. Had they both guessed that there was something going on between her and McCoy?

"And?"

"And what?" Patty demanded.

"He can't be pleased."

"Oh, he isn't," Patty assured her cheerfully, waving a dismissive hand in the air. "But it is Petty's station. And even our real McCoy respects that. Um, wake up and smell the coffee. Isn't that a great aroma?" she asked Joe. "I'll get you some. Julie Hatfield, you go get ready!"

So she'd gotten dressed, choosing a light knit business suit with a soft white lace-trimmed blouse beneath, and stockings, fully aware that she'd need to be composed around her doubting McCoy.

She hadn't quite expected the look she was getting from him now. He hadn't addressed her since she'd come into the station.

Now he was half leaning and half sitting on Petty's broad desk, his arms crossed, one long leg firmly on the floor, the other dangling. The police artist was sitting next to Julie, and Petty was in front of her, straddling an office chair and resting his chin on the high arched back of it as he watched Julie. Joe and Patty had been dismissed after bringing her in. Timothy Riker, the chief's right-hand man, was there, too.

If McCoy wasn't speaking to Julie at the moment, then Julie made sure she didn't have anything to say to him.

She addressed Petty and the artist. "I didn't really see the man, Petty. If I'd had any kind of a picture, I would have told you. You know that."

"Yes, Miss Hatfield, but anything would be helpful at this point. Any impression at all. All I want you to do is close your eyes and think—and give me anything at all that comes into your mind."

Julie leaned forward, closing her eyes. At first she couldn't think at all.

McCoy had been staring at her with daggers in his eyes, and that made concentration hard. Even when she wasn't looking at him, she could feel the heat of his gaze.

Pity they didn't need a description of McCoy. She could have told them inch by inch exactly what he looked like, his face, his legs, his chest, his...

Shoulders...

No, she couldn't see the kidnapper's face. But she could see his shoulder.

Fear ripped through her, suddenly, vividly.

Then the visions rushed in upon her. She was with Tracy again. Tracy as she stood in the road, Tracy as the man jumped from the car to sweep her up.

Tracy, struggling...

She couldn't see the man's face. Couldn't see it at all because a stocking was pulled over it, distorting his features. But as Tracy fought with him, she pulled at his shirt. A long-sleeved tailored shirt. But he wasn't wearing a tie, and several buttons were undone.

Tracy ripped another one off. And the shirt slid off his shoulder. And there it was.

A scar. About three inches, jagged. Maybe it had come from a fall or a knife wound. At one time, the tear had been deep. And it had left behind that scar...

The same scar that Julie had seen in her dream. That dream she had nearly forgotten this morning, that dream in which her lover came to her...

She was trembling, yet she was achingly aware that she had been afraid the scar had belonged to her dream lover. And now she knew.

No, they were not one and the same.

And then the realization struck her. They were coming closer and closer to the time when the terror would not come to her through another.

The terror would be for her...

"Julie! Julie! Are you all right?"

Her eyes flew open. Petty was on his knees before her, grasping her hands. They were cold and clammy. Timothy was standing right behind the chief, his eyes wide with alarm.

Even McCoy had jumped off his doubting perch on the desk. Julie stared at him and felt the remnants of her fear send chills dancing down her spine. *I can't see you again, ever,* she thought wildly.

But could that help her? Had what she had seen in that dream already been set into motion?

And were the feelings she had for McCoy stronger than fear...

Stronger than destiny.

"Julie?" Petty said anxiously.

"I—I'm all right. I'm sorry," she said. She looked at the artist. She shook her head. "Honestly, I can't help you. Tracy didn't see his face. All I can tell you is that he was wearing a stocking over his face, that he's probably about five feet ten inches, dark-haired—and that he has a scar, like a jagged knife scar, on his left shoulder."

She heard a soft explosion of sound.

McCoy. The sound was one that ridiculed her. Angrily.

He suddenly strode across the room, leaving the office. The door snapped sharply behind him.

"You're sure of this?" Petty asked her.

Julie nodded. "Petty, I've never been more sure."

Petty nodded and shrugged to the police artist. "That's

about all we're going to get. Medium height, medium build, darkish hair.''

"And that scar," Timothy said.

"Yeah, the scar," Petty said. "Too bad it isn't on our fellow's face. It might be kind of hard walking around trying to get the populace to bare their shoulders."

Julie grimaced. "I'm sorry."

"You've given us plenty, Julie. Thanks," Petty told her.

She nodded and started out. "Tracy is doing fine, right?" she asked Petty.

"Tracy is doing wonderfully," Petty told her. "No problems at all. It's great to be young, huh?"

"Probably. I don't remember."

"Ah, you're just a babe yourself, Julie Hatfield. Wait till you reach my age, then you'll know!"

She smiled and turned to leave.

McCoy was sitting on the corner of Patty's desk in the outer office. He was glaring at her, a deep frown imbedded in his forehead. Patty had moved to Timothy Riker's desk and had her nose stuck in her typing. Joe Silver was trying to look every bit as busy, going through the files.

Everyone was aware that there was a storm brewing here, and everyone seemed determined to avoid it.

Well, there wasn't even going to be a raindrop, Julie decided. She smiled pleasantly, gave an easy wave to Patty and Joe and walked out of the building.

That was when she remembered she had been driven in by Patty and Joe.

Well, hell! She had made it out so smoothly. She didn't feel like ruining her fine exit by going back.

She gritted her teeth as she stood there. Then the door opened behind her and she knew it was him. "Come on," he said curtly. "I'll get you home."

It would be rather futile to argue. It was a long walk.

But still, even as she crawled into the Lincoln and he

sat down beside her, she felt as if she were next to dynamite about to explode.

"All right, McCoy, just what is your problem?" she demanded.

"Nothing. Nothing! I have no problems, Miss Hatfield. It's just that we have a psychic here, but funny, she can't give us a description of a man—"

"He was wearing a stocking!"

"He's of medium height and medium build and probably dark haired. Well, let's see. That probably describes half the men in the immediate area. Hell, it describes half of the men in our law-enforcement agencies!"

"It lets out Petty," Julie remarked coolly.

"That's right, it does. And thank God, my hair is fairly light, so maybe it lets me out, too. Except maybe not. After all, you did ask me if I had a scar on my shoulder."

Julie stiffened, remembering the occasion. Yes, she had asked him! Because she had seen the scar. She had seen it in the dream, and he had been in the dream. And she had been left to wonder...

But she knew now that he was the man in her dream. The lover in her dream.

But he was not the man who brought the awful, shattering sense of danger...

"You did ask me about a scar, Julie!"

"Yes."

"Yet it seemed in the office just now as if you were seeing that scar on the kidnapper for the first time."

Damn, he was still so angry! Well, maybe it did look as if she was a charlatan.

"I just saw the scar through Tracy's eyes in the office," she said. He was never going to understand. He didn't believe in her to begin with.

"Where did you see it before?"

"In a—dream."

"A nightmare, huh? And I was in it, right? Before or after we met?"

There was a tight note of sarcasm edging his voice.

Julie sat back, gritting her teeth. "If you recall, McCoy, you didn't answer me about whether you did or didn't have a scar."

"That's right, I didn't, did I? Is that why we made love? Were you checking out my shoulder?"

"Oh, McCoy, you are really something, do you know that? A true prize!" Julie exclaimed furiously. "Stop the car. I'd rather walk."

He wouldn't stop the car. She knew that.

But he did stop it. He pulled abruptly off the road onto the narrow shoulder and turned to her with a sudden, startling passion. "Did you check out my shoulder? Did you check it out really well? Did you think long and hard about what you were doing?"

Had she thought long and hard? No, she hadn't thought for a single second.

But she knew his shoulders bore no scars. She knew simply because she had been so fascinated by his body, by every minute stretch of bronze flesh.

"McCoy, obviously, neither one of us gave it long, hard thought, or else last night would have never happened! And it's probably best if we pretend that it never did happen. And if you don't mind—"

She started to reach for the door. If he really meant to let her out on the side of the road, then she'd just get out on the side of the road.

"What do you think you're doing?" he demanded.

"I'm getting out."

"Here?"

"Well, you stopped."

He exploded with an oath. The Lincoln suddenly roared to life.

He didn't speak again until they were in front of her

house. Then he leaned over and opened the passenger door for her. "Julie, you go ahead and get as mad at me as you want to, but don't you suppose that you'd better start thinking?"

"What are you talking about now?"

"You don't ever just get out on the side of the mountain and start walking. And you don't leave your doors open, and you take care when you're alone."

Her heart suddenly slammed against her chest. "Why?"

Was he worried? Did he think that just maybe his nephew had been right? That the kidnapper knew about her, that he had worn the stocking over his face because he knew that Julie might be called in on the case?

"Because every woman in this area is at risk right now, Julie. You can't behave foolishly."

She remembered the force of her dream. Yes, she had been in danger. But the danger had involved him.

She just needed not to see him again. That was all. And she would be all right. Since he was so angry, so disgusted, that should be easy.

"I'll be careful," she told him, slipping out of his car.

The Lincoln remained parked in front of her house until she let herself in and locked the door.

"He's angry. He won't come back," she whispered.

But he would come back.

She could refuse to see him.

But already, an ache was growing in her heart. She didn't want him out of her life. She wanted him back, now. She wanted to sleep beside him again through the night. She wanted to go on discovering more about him. She wanted to go on...

Falling in love with him. A little bit more every day. Needing him as badly as she wanted him.

"Destiny is not preset!" she announced aloud. He wasn't the man she wanted or needed in her life. Once before, she had fallen in love with a doubting Thomas.

With tragic consequences. From every single direction, it was better to stop this now.

Three days later, when Julie had convinced herself that he wasn't going to return to her life, McCoy appeared on her front doorstep.

It was early, barely eight in the morning. No dream or inner sense had warned her that he might appear.

She had finally begun to work last night on a story for a mystery magazine and she had stayed up very late.

When the doorbell rang she barely managed to find an old terry robe and wrap it around her long johns and stumble down the stairs.

And stupidly, she threw the door open without glancing through the peephole, without even pausing to wonder who it might be.

"What in God's name do you think you're doing?"

That was McCoy's greeting.

He was freshly showered and shaved, and she could smell the faint and pleasant aroma of his after-shave. His hair was slicked back, still damp from the shower. But he wasn't wearing his three-piece suit today. He was very casual, wearing cutoff denims and an old football jersey and sneakers that had a few holes in the toes.

Julie stepped back, rubbing her forehead. "Answering my door."

"What did I tell you the last time I saw you?"

"McCoy—"

"Julie, damn it—"

"I saw you through the peephole—"

"You're lying!"

"How the hell would you know?" she demanded. But he did know. Was it because of the expression on her face, or was it maybe true that McCoy did have a hint of second sight of his own?

"Okay, I forgot. I was working last night—"

"No good, Julie."

"Okay! I'll be more careful in the future, I promise. What do you want, McCoy, or did you come over just to torture me?"

"No." He hesitated a minute, then sighed. "I was at a standstill. Getting nowhere. I thought some time off might help. I came to take you out."

She arched her brows, a smile curving her lip as she stared at him from head to toe, indicating his outfit. "Out? Where?"

"Tubing."

"Tubing?" Then she looked past him to his car. Three heavy black tire tubes were strapped on top of the elegant Lincoln.

"Are you game?" he asked her.

"Well, you know, McCoy, I might be working. Or I might have had other plans for the day—"

"Oh, you did not. You told Patty you might go to a movie with her tomorrow night, and if you worked till the wee hours last night, I don't think that you're going to slam right back into it this morning."

"As a matter of fact—"

"Yes?"

She had been going to work. She had proofed her story last night—all she needed was a clean copy. "Can you give me thirty minutes?"

"I can give you a couple of hours. The sun will be stronger by then."

"All right. Can we run by the post office?"

"Anywhere you want."

"All right. You're on then. Make yourself at home. I'll hurry."

Julie suspected that he might follow her up the stairs and into the shower, but he didn't.

She was alarmingly disappointed. She dressed quickly in a bathing suit, T-shirt and shorts and managed to find a pair of sneakers just as full of holes as the pair he was wearing.

When she hurried downstairs, the coffee was ready, and he had toasted several English muffins.

"Thanks," Julie told him, biting into one and pouring herself a cup of coffee. He was on the back porch, at the round wooden table, sipping coffee, reading the paper and looking over the hills and valleys. He looked up, nodded and smiled, and looked back to his paper. "Go ahead. Go to work. You don't need to worry about entertaining me."

She didn't worry about him. She took her coffee and muffin into the office behind the parlor on the left side of the house and sat down. She concentrated on making her changes, then sighed with satisfaction as she sat back, delighted with the way that things had fallen into completion. After she turned on her printer, she wandered into the kitchen for a second cup of coffee.

McCoy was still on the porch, still looking over the mountains. Julie felt a soft warmth steal over her.

There were so many things against them. One of them being the way he felt about her second sight—or whatever he wanted to call it.

But there was something nice between them that she hadn't realized until then. They were both mountain lovers. They loved this region. They loved the foliage and the greenery, and the hills and the curves. They loved the way the sun rose here, and the way it set. They loved the quiet, and the serenity.

She hadn't made a sound. He turned suddenly, and Julie knew he had been aware she was there.

"How's it going?" he asked her.

"Fine. I'm just about done."

"Whenever. Let me know."

Julie went into her house and sipped the rest of her coffee while the printer finished throwing out her pages.

He did know how to make himself at home here. He'd

been into the various bags of coffee beans she kept in the freezer, studying and selecting his choices.

She had a tendency to add heavily on the various flavors, like cinnamon or nut, while McCoy, she was learning, liked a stronger basic blend of coffee with just a hint of flavor.

Opposite ends of a pole, she reminded herself.

But then, opposites did attract.

Julie let out a sigh of exasperation with herself, collected her long line of paper from the printer and began to tear at the perforations, creating a neat little stack of manuscript. She dug out an envelope, quickly addressed it and hurried from her office.

She certainly hadn't had any bad dreams about tubing down the river. And the weather was beautiful; the day ahead looked bright.

"All set?" he asked her when she appeared in the kitchen.

"All set. Where are we starting from?" she asked him, as they left the house together.

"Maryland side," he said, frowning at her as he slipped on his sunglasses.

"What now?" Julie asked.

"The door. You didn't lock the door."

Julie exhaled slowly and hurried back to lock her front door. "Well, it's your fault, you know. You're so willing to jump down my throat all the time, I must be thinking inwardly that I need to give you a good reason to do so."

"Right."

Julie walked by him to the car. She smiled when she saw the ice chest wedged into the one tube. "What are we bringing with us?"

"A fine, vintage Bordeaux, how's that sound?"

"Elegant."

"Well, I'm afraid that it goes with unelegant cold fried chicken, potato salad, slaw and chips."

Julie grinned. "It will do."

The conversation was easy and light enough while he drove to their point of debarkation. It was public ground, not a spot owned by any of the rafting companies. While McCoy brought the tubes down, Julie watched him. She grabbed the first one as he tossed it her way.

"Hey, McCoy!"

"What?"

"Tubing down with the current is going to be great. How are we getting back to the car?"

He walked up to her and tweaked her cheek. Since she was balancing two tubes, she had no power to stop him. "Oh, ye of little faith!" he said. "I have a friend who has a little coffee spot almost right on the water some miles down from here. By then we'll have something warm like chocolate or coffee and tea, and then he or one of his kids will drive us to the car. How does that sound?"

"Great. Let's get started," Julie said. She stripped off her T-shirt and shorts then flushed as she realized McCoy was staring at her. She had worn what she thought was a fairly demure bathing suit. It was one piece and black, but the French cut rode high on her thighs, and the back was very low, falling an inch beyond her waist.

He wolf whistled. She wasn't sure whether to thank him or slap him.

She threw her shirt at him. "You've seen me in less."

"Yes, but I'm afraid to bring you in front of others in that getup. They might want to see you in less, too."

"McCoy—"

"Don't worry, Miss Hatfield. We McCoys are the proprietarial type. No one would dare come near, I promise. Want to throw the shorts over?"

She did so, then she decided that she had to hand it to McCoy—he really was prepared. He had a waterproof sack for them to stuff their shirts and her shorts into, and then a place to set the sack on a wire shelf in the cooler. He had a thin rope to connect the cooler tube with his own tube, and while Julie touched the water—letting out a yelp as its spring freshness touched her skin—McCoy was managing as only a man who had grown up playing with tubes on rivers could do. He was all set and ready while she was still wincing.

"I thought you grew up here!" he called to her. "Come on, get a move on!"

"Well, the water just wasn't quite this cold when I was younger," Julie assured him. She settled into her tube despite the cold washing over her. "And I did grow up here. And I've tubed this very water eighteen trillion times."

"Eighteen trillion?" McCoy said, grinning broadly.

She smiled, glad that she had come with him, wondering how she had managed to get through the days when he hadn't appeared.

Don't, don't, don't fall in love, she warned herself. But she was too late. It was already happening.

She was comfortable in her tube at last, accustomed to the water. A surge came rushing by her, lifting her along. Her feet trailed over the muddy and rocky bottom, but her hole-filled sneakers protected her feet. White caps lifted her over a smooth rapid in the way, bringing her tube crashing against McCoy's.

"Hey!"

"Oh, buck up!" Julie retorted. "There's calmer water ahead."

His arm snaked out, and his hand caught her wrist. For a moment their tubes twirled in a wide circle through the water, then they reached a patch of calm past the rocks, in the high water. He smiled and leaned back but didn't release her. Julie closed her eyes and felt the sun on her face.

She was quiet for a moment, then she asked him, "Why did you come back today?"

He didn't move. He was stretched comfortably, basking in the sun. "I wanted to see you."

"But nothing has changed about me," she reminded him quietly. "I'm still a charlatan."

She saw his jaw harden. "If only we didn't have to talk about it all the time—"

"But trying to pretend—"

"Julie, it's a beautiful day. Do we have to go through this?"

She gritted her teeth and closed her eyes. A sudden flash of sight came to her, and she smiled. "All right, McCoy. In a matter of minutes, we're going to pass by a large rock in the middle of the river. And there's going to be a big black snake sitting on it, sunning itself."

"Oh, yeah?"

"Yeah!"

Julie was right. They came upon the snake just a few minutes later.

"Don't you see?" she pleaded. "I do know things sometimes. Not always, but sometimes."

McCoy was silent.

"Well? What do you think now?" Julie persisted.

"I think you bribed the snake," he said very seriously.

"Oh, come on!"

"All right, Julie. Maybe you were out here a few weeks ago. Maybe you knew the rock was there. Maybe you didn't know that you knew the rock was there, the memory was just sitting there, somewhere in the back of your mind. And if there had been a snake on it before, why couldn't there be a snake there again?"

Julie groaned and leaned back again. The swirling waters brought them crashing together. Her leg brushed his.

"McCoy?" she asked softly.

"What?"

"If I asked you not to do something—if I were really passionate about it—would you listen to me?"

"Julie—"

"McCoy, please, this is important to me. If I sensed that you could be hurt...really hurt...would you listen?"

"Julie, you know how I—"

"Even if it was just to humor me?"

"Let's stop over there, on the rocks, and pull up the cooler."

"McCoy!" Julie snapped. But it didn't matter. He wasn't listening. The water was hip deep, and he'd slipped from his tube. He dragged the tube with the cooler along with him to where some high, flat rocks were rising out of the water.

Julie slipped from her tube, too, and followed him. By the time she dragged her tube beside his, he had opened the cooler and pulled out the bags of food.

"Have a seat, Miss Hatfield. Lunch is served."

Julie sighed and sat in the sun. It was high in the sky now, bright and warming. There was a soft breeze moving through the trees that lined the river bank. The water was so many colors, blue and green and aqua and white where it dashed over the rocks. The scenery was incredibly beautiful.

McCoy passed her a plastic picnic plate with chicken and little containers of potato salad and cole slaw. He sat beside her, munching a drumstick.

Julie glanced at him and felt a fierce pang in her heart as she studied him. She cared about him so much. From the hot steel in his gray and silver eyes to the tight cords and muscles of every inch of his body. Someone like this came by only once in a lifetime.

And still...

"Is lunch all right?"

"It's amazing. Especially for a single man."

"Single men are extremely inventive and imaginative," he informed her. He suddenly passed her the wine bottle. "My sister made the lunch," he admitted.

Julie laughed softly. "We're supposed to drink this great wine out of the bottle?"

"I packed the wine. Can't you tell? I forgot the glasses."

She smiled again, laughed and swallowed a sip of wine before turning to her chicken. She was amazed at the appetites they had built up, and they ate in a companionable silence, waving at times as other tubers and rafters passed by their spot on the rocks.

When the food was gone, McCoy stuffed their plates and garbage into the cooler, but he didn't seem to be in any hurry to leave. They stretched out on the rocks, feeling the sun. Julie closed her eyes. Then she realized that he was leaning on an elbow beside her, staring at her.

She gazed into his eyes.

"That suit should be illegal," he told her. His finger traced a pattern softly over her hip.

"McCoy—"

"You should be illegal. Damn it, Julie, you're just the very last thing I needed now in my life. If only you weren't so damned beautiful…"

He leaned over and kissed her gently. Julie swallowed as his lips parted from hers. His kiss had promised more. So much more.

And she wanted it all.

But the pain was suddenly with her. "Answer me, McCoy," she said.

"About what?" He hedged again.

She touched his cheek. "If I was really certain that you were in danger, would you listen to me? Please, Robert, it's important."

"Well, I'll be damned. You do know my first name."

"McCoy!"

He laughed softly, then his expression became very serious. He traced the fullness of her lip with his thumb.

"All right, Julie. Yes. If you were really afraid. If only to humor you."

She smiled, content.

He leaned close to her. "It's getting kind of cool now, isn't it?"

"Maybe. Just a little."

"I know how to get warmed up."

"Do you?"

He nodded gravely. "Come home with me, Miss Hatfield. I'll show you how."

She smiled and nodded. "Yes. I'll come home with you. And you can show me how."

Chapter 7

"**W**here is your home?" Julie asked, after McCoy's friend Jim Preston had taken them from the coffee shop, where she and McCoy had hot chocolate, to McCoy's car. She'd been somewhat surprised to discover that Jim's coffee shop was in the central Harpers Ferry area, one of the quaint and rustic eateries that catered to tourists.

She knew Jim Preston herself, if only casually. Like her and McCoy, Preston was a native of the area. He was a handsome man of medium height and build with dark sandy hair and dimples when he smiled.

Julie liked Jim and his two teenage children, and she was impressed with the warmth he and McCoy seemed to share. They were very old friends.

"I wonder why you and I never met before," Julie mused out loud, not realizing that she hadn't waited for an answer to her first question.

McCoy grinned, casting her a quick glance. "Well, Madam Curiosity, I imagine that the answers are the same to both questions. My mountain is on the Maryland side of the region.''

She arched a brow. They had dropped his sister off near Charlestown on Sunday, and that was West Virginia, near the sight where Old John Brown had been hanged.

"My sister's home is new, remember. I still have the old family home in the hills, Miss Hatfield.''

"Oh,'' she said, smiling. And then she waited, intrigued.

"Actually, I hadn't opened it up in years,'' he said softly. ''My sister and Jim had painters in and got the place cleaned up when they heard that I was coming in from Washington. I hadn't thought I wanted to go back. But I've loved it since I've been here.''

"Are your folks—gone?'' Julie asked.

He smiled. ''Gone to St. Petersburg. I bought this house from them when they moved. They didn't want to keep it, but they didn't want to let it out of the family, and at one time…'' His voice drifted for a moment.

"At one time?'' Julie persisted.

He shrugged. ''It's a big place. Too big for them to keep up anymore. They've had it with ice and snow, and the only thing they say they really miss are the kids. That's not really true, though. They come back every year. Can't keep old mountaineers away from the mountains once it really turns to spring and summer.''

"That's nice,'' Julie murmured. He hadn't said what he had been about to say.

He closed off frequently, she realized. There was something there that he didn't talk about. Or something that he didn't trust her enough to talk about yet.

She made a mental note to call his sister and see if they couldn't meet for lunch one afternoon. She had the feeling that McCoy's sister might be willing to tell her lots of things she wanted to know.

He turned up one of the old dirt mountain trails and the Lincoln began to climb in earnest. They moved through a deep forest area that was richly and heavily treed, and then the clearing with the house on it seemed to burst out in front of them.

It was stunning. Made of a rich dark wood that had been kept to natural shades, the house was as old or older than Julie's own family home, built big and broad, with wide, embracing porches. Four gables adorned the upstairs windows, while the back porch, enclosed by glass, seemed to jut over the mountain peak and look down on the beauty of the valley.

"Wow!" Julie said softly. She looked at McCoy. "This is some family home."

He shrugged. "My great-grandfather was a senator from the region, a man with a great dynasty in mind. Life is fickle, though. He had only one son, and that one son had only one son, my dad."

"Poor man," Julie said.

"He was probably the one who started the feud with the Hatfields," McCoy said lightly. "I hear that he was a very cantankerous old man. Maybe he started a feud with my great-grandmother, too. That would explain things."

"Was there really a feud, do you think?"

"Well, we seem proof of that, don't you think?"

"Maybe," Julie said, but she was still smiling.

"I love the house, though. I always have. It was a great place to grow up. Come on in."

Julie's smile deepened and she hurried out of the car and ran up the steps to the house. McCoy opened the front door, and they entered a great room with naked oak beams. It was full of overstuffed furniture and bookshelves, a warm, delightful and inviting room.

"This is the best," McCoy advised her, lifting a hand to indicate that she should pass through an arched opening to the back of the house.

Here was the porch that extended over the back. At one end of it was a massive fireplace that stretched from wall to wall. Before it was a large, thick fur rug, and just beyond the rug, close to where a blaze would flame, was a setting of furniture, an older wicker sofa and matching chairs and occasional tables. A comforter had been tossed over the back of the sofa.

At the other end was a very modern entertainment center. There was a table and chairs set out, and Julie quickly imagined that this was where McCoy came mornings.

Then she glanced at the thick fur rug and the comforter again, and she smiled. This was his favorite room. It was where he came to sleep. It wasn't because of the fireplace, it was because of the view of the sloping, forested fall to the valley deep below. A bubbling stream could be seen rushing down the mountain. The trees and bushes waved softly in the spring breeze, so deeply green, alive in shades of forest and kelly and the lightest of limes.

Julie inhaled softly and walked across the room to better see the view. McCoy stepped past her and slid open one of the windows. The soft, cool mountain breeze swept in around her. It touched her cheeks. It gently ruffled her hair.

"Like it?"

"I love it."

"Want something? Coffee, wine, water, anything? How about an Irish coffee? I think I have a can of whipped spray stuff in the fridge, I had the kids up here last night."

Julie smiled, feeling him beside her, but still stared at the view. "Irish coffee with whipped spray stuff sounds great."

"Don't make fun of my culinary talents," he warned her sternly.

"I wouldn't dream of it. You make wonderful coffee," she assured him as he left for the kitchen.

His view was even more spectacular than her own. She certainly didn't want to tell a McCoy that his mountain was better than hers, but it was an awfully pretty mountain.

Night was coming now. Here, up high and almost in the

clouds, it came very evidently, and with an even greater array of color. She could still see the sun in the western sky, a brilliant orange, emitting streaks of that same shade across the sky. In places, the orange was tempered by a softer yellow, and down by the trees there seemed to be a darkening frame of shadows in shades of violet and purple.

He came gently into the room. She didn't so much hear him come as she sensed him. But she knew that he was with her.

She still looked out the window, looking at the extravagant colors, the sheer richness of spring. She felt the breeze. It moved through her hair, caressing her throat and her neck, touching her cheeks as gently as the soft movement of invisible fingers.

He was with her. She still hadn't heard his movement. She just knew. And she knew the scent of him. Subtle, masculine.

A slow, burning warmth began to fill her. Just because he was near.

Because he would touch her.

She knew the touch, and she knew the tenderness. She knew him, knew the man and knew things about him that made her love him. She didn't need to see him to know the contours of his face, the deep sandy shade of his hair, the compelling steel and silver of his eyes. She didn't need to see him to know the generous fullness of his mouth, the sensuality.

She knew all the hues within his heart and soul and mind, and those colors were all beautiful, and part of the warmth that touched her.

He could move so silently...

He would be coming across the room to her.

Yes, now.

A smile curved her lip.

He was coming closer and closer. Moving with long strides but silent grace. She felt him, and felt cocooned in the special warmth that he brought, felt a supreme sense of well-being come over her.

He was going to make love to her. Now. Prove that he knew exactly how to warm her.

He stood behind her and swept the fall of her hair from her neck, and she felt the wet, hot caress of his lips against her nape.

The pleasure was startling. So startling. Hot tremors swept instantly along her spine. Danced there. Her knees grew weak as swift-flowing desire came cascading into the depths of her being.

He held her hair, and his kiss skimmed over her shoulder. As he kissed her, he lifted the shoulder of her T-shirt. The soft knit slid from her shoulders. It fell to the floor in a pool of lilac. The feel as it left her flesh was so sensual. Soft, warm, exquisite, leaving her skin bared to his kiss.

The straps of her suit fell from her shoulders. The dampness of it peeled from her body, leaving more skin bared. Sensitive. Waiting.

She felt his hands on the snap of her shorts. She heard the long rasp of the zipper. The flutter of fabric as they fell. Then the coolness of her still-wet suit slid against her, landing discarded at her feet.

His arms encircled her. She could feel the strength of his naked chest as he pulled her against him. He still wore his cutoffs.

She could feel the roughness of the fabric against her tender skin. Even that touch was sensual.

His whisper touched her ear. The words, each breath of air, brought aching new sensation. "You are...exquisite. You do things to me that I hadn't imagined could be done..."

A smile curved her lips. She turned in the circle of his arms.

She stared up into his eyes and felt the driving passion in their silver depths.

And then he kissed her.

And she felt an explosion deep within her. She felt the hungry pressure of his lips, forming over her own, firmly, demandingly, causing them to part for the exotic presence of his tongue.

He'd kissed her before...

Never quite like this.

And when his lips left her mouth, they touched her throat. Touched the length of it. The soft, slow, sensual stroke of his tongue just brushing her flesh. With ripples of silken, liquid fire. She could see his hands, broad, so darkly tanned, upon the paleness of her skin. His fingers were long, handsomely tapered, callused, but with neatly clipped nails. Masculine hands. Hands that touched with an exciting expertise. Fingers that stroked with confidence and pleasure.

She allowed her head to fall back, her eyes to close. The sensations to surround her.

The breeze...it was so cool against her naked body. So soft. So unerringly sensual. Perhaps because her body was so hot. Growing fevered. But the air...it touched her where his kiss left off, and both fire and ice seemed to come to her and dance through her.

She spun in his arms. It was no longer daytime. Shadows were falling, and the breeze was growing cooler.

And his kiss went lower.

And where his lips touched her, she burned.

And where his lips had lingered earlier, the cool air stroked her with a sensuality all its own.

And still his kiss lowered. And lowered until he teased the base of her spine. And his hand caressed her naked buttocks and hips, and she was turning in his arms.

Her hand rested on his head, her breath quickened, and caught, and quickened again. She cried out, amazed at the tempest that rose within her, startled by the sheer sensual pleasure that ripped through her.

She cried out again, and again, and then discovered that she was sinking, sinking into his arms…

Night had come. The moon remained in the sky, but she could not see clearly.

Darkness was falling over the mountains. She reached out and touched his face, stroked the contours of his cheek. She pressed her lips against his, then against his forehead, then against each cheek. She groaned softly, kissing his throat, just teasing it with the barest brush of her teeth.

It was incredible to touch him. She was in his arms, and she was barely aware that they moved. Then they were sinking once again, down, deep, deep down into the fur before the fireplace.

She touched him then, again and again. Touched him, knowing the living warmth and fire of him. Feeling the ripple of muscle in his chest. Feeling his hands. Feeling the pulse of his body. Feeling…him.

It was so good to be with him. Life, feeling, sensation, all were so wonderfully vivid.

In the shadows he rose above her for a moment. Once again, she found that even sound could be scintillating as the quick rasp of his zipper tore against the silence of the darkened night.

She stretched out her arms, and he came down with her. He came down silently, gracefully. He braced himself over her, and then she cried out softly, wanting him so badly.

And finally having him.

She could feel him entering her…

The fur touched her back. She felt the softness, and the roughness. Her hands splayed over his chest, and she felt the rigor of his muscle, the exciting, slick feel of his bronze chest. In the near darkness, she could see his eyes, nearly a pure silver now, all sizzle and passion.

She could feel…

Movement. Slow, sure, then subtle, the pace quickening. Each stroke, faster, the rhythm growing. The wonder inside of her growing as his body touched hers, and touched it…inside and out.

She watched his eyes. Watched his tension, and watched his smile.

His lips touched down on hers. Took them hungrily, passionately, while his body filled hers.

She closed her eyes, but even in the darkness it seemed that stars suddenly burst in the middle of the heavens, like the births of a thousand suns. She quivered like a bow strung too tight, and then she catapulted into a sweet recess where wonder and magic all seemed to crash down upon her.

His arms were suddenly laced around her, tight. Great shudders racked the whole of his body, and the length of him came against her tautly. Then his arms eased, and he whispered something erotic in her ear and fell by her side. He lay there a second before sweeping her into his arms, his kiss brushing her forehead.

Silently, she curled against him. She wasn't going home. Not tonight. They both knew it. She let her fingers play over the crisp hairs on his chest. A wonderful warmth came slowly sweeping over her again. It was so damned good to lie with him. There was such a sense of comfort and security here.

"Hey," he said softly.

"Hmm?"

"You're falling asleep."

"Am I? I'm just so comfortable."

"What about the coffee?"

"Um," she murmured. She didn't want any coffee. She didn't want to move. She didn't even want McCoy talking.

She felt too relaxed, too happy. And so wonderfully drowsy.

She didn't want to feud.

Neither did McCoy, it seemed. He wasn't moving.

"Will we burn the house down if we don't go for the coffee?" she whispered.

"No. It has an automatic turnoff."

"Good," Julie breathed softly. She closed her eyes. It had been a long day. Tubing…and now.

She must have drifted off to sleep, because she was quickly dreaming.

And it was so strange, for in her dream, she saw all that had just been. She saw herself coming into McCoy's house. She saw the glassed-in porch and the blue-green beauty of the mountains beyond.

She saw him open the window, and saw herself lift her face to the breeze.

And then she realized that the reality that had just passed had been her dream before. She had known that McCoy was her dream lover…

And now the lovemaking in the dream had come to pass…

Darkness seemed suddenly to descend, and with it a sense of absolute and acute terror.

Yes, the time had come.

He was out there.

The kidnapper. The murderer.

He was staring at the house. Staring, as if he could see her. As if he watched her, with McCoy.

As if he knew…

Julie awoke abruptly, a scream tearing from her lips.

He could be out there. Anywhere. Close. He could be lurking in the darkness. He could be any one of the shadows.

"Julie!"

She didn't hear McCoy call her name. She screamed again, shaking furiously, blinded by the darkness, by her fear.

"Julie!" He called her name again, pulling her into his arms, shaking her.

She didn't recognize him, McCoy thought at first. She stared straight at him, but she didn't see him. He shook her again, gently, then more fiercely. "Julie—"

"He's out there!" she cried.

"Julie, you were dreaming."

"No, no!" She fought his hold, trying to pull away from him. "You don't understand. He's out there! He's watching us, he knows us!"

"Julie, it's all right—"

"You don't believe me!" she cried frantically.

What was he supposed to believe? McCoy wondered. Her eyes were frantic. Wide, gleaming, beautiful—but frantic. He couldn't doubt the fear within them. Nor the quivering that tore at her body.

"Julie, Julie, it's all right. I'm with you." He pulled her into his arms. She was still trembling. No, shaking. Hard. He rocked with her.

A sharp unease snaked its way up his spine. She believed. No matter what, he knew that she believed. And try as he might to deny her, the creeping feeling sinking into his system seemed to say that what she told him was true.

She did know things. Julie Hatfield knew things. She had seen the black snake...

No, God! I do not believe in psychics! I believed once, I was willing to hope and pray and believe, and look what happened! I will not believe. I will never believe again.

But I love her, he thought.

And once I said I would never love again...

"He's there!" she cried more softly, her face buried against him. "The man with the scar on his shoulder."

McCoy was suddenly convinced that they were being watched.

She moaned softly. He sifted his fingers through the beautiful, tousled silkiness of her hair. It was like spun gold in the night.

"Julie, I'm with you. I won't let anything happen to you," he promised her.

She was silent. He kissed her forehead, then he rose. She started as he released her, swallowing hard, afraid for him to leave her in the darkness.

"It's all right!" he promised.

His cutoffs had dried and he slipped them on, then found the light switch. Bright light dazzled throughout the porch.

"The light!" Julie cried.

"Julie, no one can see in this room—not unless they are hovering outside in a helicopter. Look, sweetheart, you can see for yourself."

She had pulled the comforter to her chest. Wide-eyed, incredibly feminine and vulnerable with her pool of pale hair a fascinating mane around her, she turned as he directed her. And she knew that he was right. The porch did jut out to the edge of the mountain. It was a totally private retreat.

No one could see in.

But still...

"McCoy," she said softly, moistening her lips with her tongue, "he was out there. He was close. Watching. I know that he was watching the house."

He didn't say anything, but looked at his toes for a moment.

"How about that Irish coffee now? It's decaf, so we won't be up the rest of the night because of it. And we're not driving anywhere for awhile, so I can pile it high with Irish whiskey."

She almost smiled. "And add that whipped stuff, too."

He walked across the room to a closet and found her one of his terry robes. He tossed it to her. "The fit might be a bit large, but it will do in a pinch."

She slipped it on. The fit was huge, but she seemed warm and happier.

In the kitchen, they heated the coffee. Julie poured the coffee into cups, and McCoy added the whiskey.

As he had promised, he was generous. He was certain, though, that she was going to need help going back to sleep.

But even as they worked in the kitchen, he could see that she was beginning to relax again. He suggested raisin toast, and she agreed, glad to be doing something.

· Their food all prepared, he suggested they take it to the porch. She tensed for a moment, then nodded and followed him as he carried the coffee and toast on a tray to the porch.

"Maybe there's a good movie on cable," he said, setting down the food tray and reaching for the remote control.

He sat cross-legged beside her before turning on the TV and cable box and flicking through the channels.

"You're going awfully fast!" she said with a laugh. "How are you going to know if you find something you want to see?"

"Oh, I always know what I want right away," he told her.

She smiled. He didn't try to pretend anymore. He took her into his arms.

"Are you okay now?"

She nodded. Then she hesitated. "He's gone."

"What?"

Her lower lip trembled just a little. "He's gone now. He was here, but he's gone now."

The feeling of unease went snaking through McCoy again.

Damned if he didn't believe her...

No. She couldn't really know things like that.

But Julie did.

Where others had failed...

He didn't want to think about it. He picked up his coffee

cup with the whipped cream piled high. He touched it to hers. "Julie, I'm here. I'm with you."

"I know," she said. She leaned against him. He hadn't found a movie he wanted to see, so they watched an *I Love Lucy* rerun, an exceptionally funny one.

When they had finished the coffee and the toast, she crawled sweetly into his arms, and he made love to her again.

Afterward, he held her, smoothing her hair while she slept. No dreams marred her sleep again.

But hell, the night was shot for him.

With a sigh, he sat up and watched her. After awhile, he lay down and simply held her.

It was a long night.

In the morning, he drove her to her house before reporting in to the office.

He sat at Patty's desk, his head held morosely between his hands.

He had no leads. No damned leads at all.

"McCoy!"

He looked up. Patty gave him a friendly freckle-faced smile from over by Joe Silver's desk. She held Joe's phone receiver in her hands.

"Yeah?"

"A call for you."

"Who is it?"

"I don't know."

McCoy pushed the blinking button on the phone and picked up the receiver.

"McCoy here."

"Is that you, McCoy?"

The voice was a raspy one. Faint, almost like a whisper. It sent chills up his spine, just like nails against a blackboard.

"I just said my name." He was careful to be irritable and slow.

"She's a real looker, McCoy."

"Who are you, and what are you talking about?"

"You took her home with you last night, McCoy. And she stayed. All night."

The chills turned brutally icy. They stole his breath while fear and fury streaked through him.

"Who the hell are you—"

"Oh, no. I can't tell you that."

McCoy motioned wildly to Patty to get a trace going on the call. "Well, what can you tell me at the moment?"

Soft, husky, rasping laughter came his way. His fingers tightened around the receiver.

"You're not going to trace me, McCoy. We'll talk later."

"Wait! When? I don't know who—"

"Ah, but I know who you are. You kept my money, McCoy. Yes, I know you well. And I know her."

"What the hell—"

The phone clicked dead.

He stared across the room at Patty. She shook her head sadly.

Not enough time for a trace.

She had known! Julie had known!

Someone had been watching them on that mountaintop!

Chapter 8

It was strange, but by the morning, Julie didn't find herself plagued at all by the fear that had come to her in the night.

She knew she had lived out her dream, and she and McCoy had made it through the night.

McCoy wasn't part of the danger—he was her only protection from the danger, she was certain of it. The danger came from the kidnapper, the man with the scar on his shoulder, the man who had taken Tracy Nicholson and the other two young women.

And maybe the man had been somewhere near them last night. He was certainly still in the vicinity. That was why she was so certain that she was being watched.

McCoy had been wonderful last night. He hadn't ridiculed her. But then, she had been so terrified, and he had known it.

By morning, though, he had been very quiet. Pensive. She couldn't tell if he had decided she was neurotic or that there might be something to her perceptions. He was too hard-nosed to give her a clue. And he had let her off with the usual stern warnings. Don't open the doors. Be careful. Be really careful. Use the peephole, and the latches.

After he had brought her home, she convinced herself that she was going to tackle her office—clean out all the paperwork and pay her bills before someone came after her—and then vacuum, dust, rearrange, the whole nine yards. She wanted to call Brenda Maitland; she was certain that Brenda wouldn't mind telling her all sorts of things about McCoy that Julie wanted to know.

Julie didn't want to call Brenda too early just in case she slept late, but then, halfway through what she liked to think of creative money management—making sure that she paid the bills that politely reminded her that she was late—she realized that Brenda Maitland couldn't possibly sleep late, she had two children to get off to school.

She pored through the phone books, looking for Brenda Maitland. She couldn't find the name, so she called information, only to discover that Brenda's number was unlisted. She almost called the station to see if McCoy was there and ask him for his sister's phone number, but then, she didn't want him to know that she meant to give Brenda the third degree on him.

Perplexed, Julie sat on the porch, looking out over her own mountain, wishing she had the power to foretell the future at will, and wondering if she and McCoy would ever manage to really get along.

Then she jumped up. Maybe she didn't know Brenda's number, but she did know where Brenda lived.

Within thirty minutes she was standing in front of Brenda's old farmhouse, perplexed once again. No one answered when she rang the bell. Right when she was about to give up and go away, a car pulled off the road and into the driveway. It was an old silver BMW, beautifully maintained.

"Miss Hatfield! What a delight!" Brenda said, stepping out of the car.

Julie smiled. Brenda already looked as if she had mischief on her mind.

She would spill all the beans, Julie knew.

"I wanted to call you, but your number wasn't listed."

Brenda smiled, wrinkling her nose as she walked to the porch and shook Julie's hand. "Actually, my number is listed. One of them, at least. I'm a realtor, but I always worked under my maiden name and the business is under McCoy, too. The private line, under Maitland, is unlisted to avoid the eighteen million salespeople I seemed to attract. Anyway, I'm pleased to no end that you decided to come on out. Want lunch? Should we eat here, or would you like to go out? I have to pick up the kids at three in town—"

"Then how about that new salad place in Charlestown?" Julie suggested. "I've been dying to try it."

"Perfect!" Brenda said, laughing. "I was about to suggest it myself. Robert mentioned that you liked green things."

"Did he?"

Brenda smiled. "Shall I drive? Or do we need both cars? Like I said, I have to pick up the kids, and if we should run late, I just don't want to inconvenience you."

"I don't mind seeing the kids again at all," Julie assured her. "If you don't mind driving—"

"Not in the least."

They were on the road within minutes. Brenda had to be one of the easiest people to get to know. She was quick to smile, and she had a great sparkle in her eyes. Julie was barely in the car before Brenda began telling her about it. "I had always told my dad that I wanted a BMW when I graduated from college. I knew that I wasn't getting it, of course, because my folks just didn't have that kind of money. Robert was already in college—he's a year and a half older than I am—and they had my tuition coming up, too. We were both working through school to help, but you know colleges. Anyway, Robert was coming in from Washington to have dinner with the family for the occasion, and to my absolute amazement, he came driving up in this very car! It was already ten years old at the time, and one of his well-off college friends had fender-bendered it and he had another friend who knew exactly how to put it back together again. I was so excited. I told him I would never want another car as long as I lived. I'm still driving it." She hesitated for a minute. "Well," she added softly, "my husband was the college friend who knew exactly how to put the car back together again, so there's the real sentimentality, but no matter how crazy my brother makes me, I love him with all my heart." She glanced quickly at Julie. "I just thought you should know that."

Julie smiled slowly. "Brenda, the last thing that I'd ever want to do is hurt your brother."

"Right. I knew that. But I wanted to give you fair warning just in case…oh, never mind. Now, of course, you want to know just what his problem is with you, right?"

Julie inhaled quickly, then laughed. "Well, yes, in a nutshell, that's it."

"He doesn't believe in psychics," Brenda said softly.

"Yes, he's made that very clear. I can't even mention anything about it, or he's down my throat."

"He doesn't mean to be," Brenda said. She smoothed a strand of hair, biting softly on her lower lip. "There's the restaurant. Let's wait till we get inside, shall we?"

"Yes, fine," Julie said. But it wasn't fine. Her curiosity was driving her crazy, but what Brenda had to tell her seemed to be something very important.

The restaurant was pretty and bright, with broad picture windows and lots of ferns. They were led to a table by one of the big windows. The hostess chatted until the waitress brought the menus.

Then the waitress chatted, pointing out the different specialties, making suggestions. Julie kept smiling politely, wishing with all her heart that the waitress would go away.

"What do you think? Cajun chicken salad and gumbo sounds intriguing."

"It sounds just great," Julie said. Anything sounded great, just so long as the waitress would disappear.

"I don't know. I'm still wavering between that and the Hawaiian Caesar," Brenda murmured. "Or then there's the taco salad—that looks great, too."

"Oh, the taco is super!" the waitress said.

"Let's make it tacos, then," Julie said enthusiastically.

To her relief, Julie saw that she had won Brenda over. They both ordered iced tea, too, and then the young woman left them. Julie leaned forward, waiting expectantly.

"Okay, Brenda, please! Explain to me your brother's big problem with psychics!"

"Well, you see, he was married," Brenda began.

"Married!" Julie murmured.

"She was beautiful, really sweet. Serena was a Californian. He met her at George Washington University. They were really perfect for one another."

Julie shook her head. "Brenda, what would your brother's marital status have to do with psychics? Oh! Did they have problems because of an astrology reading or something?"

"Oh, no!" Brenda exclaimed. Then she fell silent, smiling. Their iced tea had arrived.

The waitress left them once again.

"Oh, Julie, if only it were something that simple!"

"Then…"

"You really do care a lot about him, don't you?" Brenda asked her.

"I—yes," Julie admitted flatly.

"Umm. And you're sleeping with him, huh?"

"Brenda, I—"

"Never mind, don't answer that. It's none of my business, and it was an awful question." But she smiled. "Especially when I know the answer."

"Brenda!" Julie moaned. "Will you please tell me what happened with the psychic?"

"I am sorry. Well, it had to do with his work," she began, then she broke off abruptly, frowning. "I don't believe it!" she said, looking over Julie's shoulder through the glass window and out to the parking lot.

"What?" Julie demanded. She swung around. To her amazement, she saw McCoy's big Lincoln parked next to his sister's BMW.

And McCoy was coming through the door.

He stopped as the hostess addressed him, but Julie saw him pointing toward her and Brenda. She couldn't begin to read his thoughts because it was anoth- er black-leather-jacket-and-dark-sunglasses day. He seemed casual enough, clad in jeans, his hands in his pockets. But Julie sensed a tension about him that hadn't been there before.

Certainly not last night. When she had been so unreasonably frightened, he had been like a rock. He hadn't ridiculed her, but she had been certain that he hadn't put any credence in her belief that they were being watched.

What was he doing here? she wondered. Was he looking for her, or for Brenda?

And why had he shown up just when she had discovered that he'd had a wife, and that something had happened to her?

Something that had had to do with a psychic.

"Robert!" Brenda said, her voice echoing the amazement Julie was feeling that he could have stumbled upon them.

Had he sensed that she planned to talk to his sister, trying to delve into his life?

Perhaps. His tension seemed like anger when he reached the table and sat beside Julie. He scarcely gave her a chance to move over. With him next to her, she felt his tension more keenly.

"Things slow down at the station?" Brenda asked, trying for a smile. Maybe she was feeling a bit guilty, too. As if he might have known that she was waiting to spill the beans about him.

"No, things were not slow at the station," he replied, scowling. "I was looking for Julie."

"Why?" Julie asked, surprised.

"Because I've got something for you."

"Really?" Julie said. He had something for her. He had that look that he had worn when they had first collided. It was not a look she expected to see on the face of a man who wanted to give her a present. "What is it?"

"It's in the car," he began.

"How did you find us?" Brenda demanded.

Intuition, Julie thought suddenly. Simple intuition. He denies it, but he has a certain power all his own.

"Easy. She wasn't home—I couldn't find you at home or at your office. And I know that women love to gossip."

Brenda wrinkled her nose at him. "Julie is going to think you're incredibly rude."

"Julie knows he's incredibly rude," Julie said.

She felt the sharpness of his silver gaze, right through the darkness of his glasses. "You should keep that in mind, Miss Hatfield," he murmured.

She didn't have a chance to wonder what he meant, for the waitress was back with their salads. McCoy looked at the giant shells piled high with lettuce and ground beef, olives, salsa and sour cream.

"What is it?"

"Something green," Brenda said. "I don't think you'd care for it. They do have hamburgers."

McCoy shook his head and waved over the waitress. "I'm not hungry—but I'll have a cup of coffee," he told the young woman.

"How did you find us?" Brenda persisted.

McCoy sighed. "I figured you might be together."

"Almost as if you had second sight," Julie murmured innocently.

He made a not very delicate snorting sound. "Once I knew you were together, it was easy. I just needed to think of a place where the food was all green. And I knew this place was here, near Brenda's, and new. It has nothing to do with second sight. It has everything to do with logical thinking," he said. His tone was almost fierce.

Julie stared at him, startled by his tone, wondering what had happened to cause the change in him since he had left her that morning.

"Well, you're a great lunch companion," Brenda said, attacking her salad. "If I'd had any idea you were going to be so charming, I would have called and invited you."

He drummed his fingers on the table, eyeing his sister. "Why? Am I disturbing you?"

Yes! Julie wanted to shout. She had just been on the verge of finding something out. And now...

"Why did you have to hunt us down?" Brenda demanded.

"I told you—I have something for Julie."

"Well, couldn't it wait?" Brenda demanded, exasperated.

He shook his head. "No, Brenda, it couldn't wait. It's not even going to make it through that salad if you don't hurry up!"

The waitress brought McCoy his coffee.

"I'm chewing, I'm chewing," Brenda said.

McCoy looked into Julie's bowl. "That's red meat in there," he warned her.

"I do eat red meat, McCoy," she reminded him.

It didn't matter. Since he had arrived, Julie had lost her appetite. Her nerves felt all twisted into knots. He was angry, he was tense. She didn't think that his anger should

have been directed toward her, but somehow she was receiving the brunt of it.

And he had something for her...

Brenda's mind was moving in the same direction. "Isn't
it wonderful to receive gifts from nice, handsome, charming men?" she commented sweetly.

"Eat, Brenda," McCoy said.

"I know!" Brenda exclaimed. "It's a diamond!"

They both glared at her. Brenda chuckled softly. "Well,
is it intimate? Should I slink out and leave in my own
car?"

"Brenda, you should finish your lunch," McCoy said
flatly.

Julie could see the steam issuing from his coffee, but he
managed to gulp it down anyway. He noticed that Julie
was finished with her lunch, and he turned his attention to
Brenda.

"Aren't you done yet?"

"Well, yes, I suppose, if you want me to be!" Brenda
exclaimed.

"You know, McCoy, this better be good," Julie warned
him, her eyes narrowing at his impatience with his sister.

"It just can't wait in the car any longer," McCoy said.
"Come on."

"Gee, let's remember not to invite him to lunch anymore, shall we?" Julie said to Brenda.

"Never," Brenda agreed solemnly.

"Would you just—"

"We have to pay the check!" Julie said. "They frown
on people who eat and leave without paying. They might
even call in the police!"

Brenda said she'd leave a tip, and Julie pushed past
McCoy, catching their waitress by the cash register. When
she turned, McCoy was waiting at the door. He was holding it open for her.

Julie watched him as she walked out the door, wonder-

ing how someone could seem so furious with her and be
so determined to give her a gift.

"Will you please hurry?" he demanded.

"I'm here now!" she exclaimed. "But what can make
you so impatient I can't begin to—"

She broke off because she suddenly saw why he hadn't
wanted to stay in the restaurant.

His gift, waiting in the Lincoln, was panting.

Just as she came outside, the creature stuck its huge head
out of the window.

She'd never seen such a large head on a dog, nor had
she ever seen a dog quite like this one. For a moment she
wondered if it was beautiful—or the ugliest dog she had
ever come across.

It was certainly the biggest.

"You're giving her a monster?" Brenda demanded incredulously.

"He's not a monster," McCoy said indignantly. "He's
half shepherd and half Rottweiler."

Julie stared blankly at McCoy. Of all the things she
might have expected, it was certainly not a dog big enough
to eat her out of house and home.

She searched her mind frantically. Had she ever given
him the slightest reason to think that she had wanted a
dog? No...she was certain that she hadn't. And if someone
had asked her to please think about what kind of dog she'd
like, she'd have probably said that her favorite might be a
beagle or a Scottie, or something fairly small—and cute.

This dog could never, never be described as cute.

"You'll get to like him," McCoy assured her. He
walked to his car and opened the back door. The creature
hopped out. His head came nearly to McCoy's hip.

"He's bigger than Julie is," Brenda stated. Brenda
seemed convinced that her brother had lost his mind. "Actually, Robert, it might have been a bit premature, but per-

sonally, I think that the diamond would have been a better idea.''

McCoy ignored her. ''His name is Rusty,'' he told Julie.

''Rusty. Nice name,'' Julie murmured. She stared at Rusty. He cocked his head at her, as if he knew he was being judged. A massive, shepherdlike tail began to wag, and Rusty gave a little whine.

He had great eyes, Julie decided at last. Big, brown, mournful eyes. He looked at her as if he knew that she was supposed to be his master, as if he knew it was necessary for her to like him.

''Rusty, Julie,'' McCoy said. The dog trotted forward a few steps to Julie. He pressed a cold nose against her hand.

''Hi, Rusty,'' Julie said.

''Robert, this is a restaurant parking lot,'' Brenda reminded him. ''We're going to scare away all the clientele with that monster.''

''He's not a monster.''

''He's ugly as hell!''

''He was the best in his class,'' McCoy retorted.

Julie stared at him again, her eyes narrowing. ''Maybe we should head back to Brenda's,'' she murmured.

''Rusty's not getting in my car!'' Brenda said with a laugh.

''No, he's not, he's getting in mine,'' McCoy told her. ''And don't you ever beg me for a fine dog like Rusty, little sister, because after this, you'll never get one from me!''

''Thank God!'' Brenda said, laughing. ''Julie, you go ahead with that new creature of yours. Or both those creatures of yours. I'm going for my kids. I'll meet you at my house.'' Brenda waved and started for her car.

''Come on, Rusty, let's go,'' McCoy told the dog.

As obediently as if he understood every inflection of every word, Rusty turned and hopped into the backseat.

Julie walked around to sit next to McCoy in the front passenger seat.

As they headed out of the parking lot, she exploded with a, "But why?"

He hesitated, as if he didn't want to answer her. Then he smiled. "Didn't you always want a big old dog?"

"No, not really," she admitted, but she had to smile. He was trying. She'd give him that.

"How about a thank-you gift?" he said huskily.

"Flowers would have done fine," she said.

He was silent for just a second. "Julie, the kidnapper called me today."

"What?" she gasped, turning to him. Despite his dark glasses, she could see the gravity in his features. She bit her lower lip.

The kidnapper had called him. Was that the danger she had seen in the dream that had become reality now?

"What—what did he say? How did you know it was him?"

McCoy shrugged. She wondered if he was hedging. "He didn't say too much of anything. I knew it was him because I'll never forget his voice. Julie, he knows me. He knows what is going on around me. I'll just feel better if you're not alone."

She looked at her hands. They were shaking. She clenched them, determined that he wouldn't see she had suddenly felt a terrible sweep of fear come rushing over her.

"McCoy, I keep a gun. It's a little ladies' Colt. Petty taught me how to use it. I'm actually pretty good at a firing range."

He turned to her, a wry smile twisting his lips. "Is poor Rusty really that ugly? I thought he was a great-looking dog. I spent hours with the trainer before making my final choice. He was on special request for a cop in the D.C. area, but I convinced the guy I needed him more. He's perfectly housebroken. And he'll obey every command you give him.''

"A dog is better than a gun?" Julie said.

"A dog senses things when you're asleep. Can a gun do that?"

Julie laughed softly. "I guess not." She was suddenly touched. McCoy had taken a lot of effort to get the dog for her. He had probably done some heavy-duty bargaining. And a dog like Rusty had probably been a very expensive investment, too.

Maybe more than a diamond—a small diamond, anyway.

She turned to look at Rusty. His face was a perfect cross between Rottweiller and shepherd, with shepherdesque markings. Those huge brown eyes looked at her soulfully. He wagged his massive tail, and barked once.

"He's...he's great," Julie said.

She saw McCoy smile, and was convinced that he thought she was merely humoring him. It didn't seem to matter.

Just so long as she kept the dog.

Julie sat back as he drove. "It's very strange, you know."

"What's so strange?"

"Well, you don't seem to have any problems thinking that a dog can have a sixth sense."

She watched as his fingers tightened around the wheel. "I never said that a dog had a sixth sense. A dog has an excellent sense of smell and very acute hearing. And this fellow should scare away almost anyone."

Julie couldn't argue with that.

They pulled into Brenda's driveway well ahead of Brenda. McCoy said that she needed to get to know Rusty. And although Rusty might be one of the most obedient dogs in the world, McCoy seemed determined to teach her how to give instructions. So out in front of Brenda's farmhouse they worked with Rusty. Julie told him to come, to heel, to lie down and to play dead. She told him to bark, and she told him to be quiet.

"Is that it?" Julie asked McCoy.

"Not quite," McCoy said grimly.

"Well?"

"You can tell him to attack," McCoy said very softly. "Just remember that if you do, he'll take hold of the person by the throat and throw the full force of his weight upon him."

"Will he…"

"No, he won't rip the throat out, he'll just stay there, forever if need be, until he's told to get off. I watched him working with the dummy. If a fool tried to fight him, the fool could be pretty well ripped up."

Julie turned away uneasily.

McCoy spun her around. "Julie, this man has tried to kill three times. We can only assume that he succeeded once, since only one young woman has never been found. He tried to kill a child, Julie."

She nodded. "Yes, I know."

Brenda's car pulled up the drive. She had barely braked it to a halt before Taylor and Tammy leaped out and ran to McCoy. "Uncle Robert, Mom's been telling us about the dog for Julie!" Taylor called out. Then he saw the dog. "Oh, wow, he's great!"

"He's not as ugly as all sin, Mom," Tammy cried, puzzled as she studied poor Rusty.

"Well, maybe he's only as ugly as half of all sin!" Brenda called out cheerfully. Then she became somber as she stepped out of the car. "Robert, Rusty won't hurt the kids, will he?"

"Definitely not," McCoy said. And it was a good thing, of course, because the kids were already on the ground with Rusty, shrieking with laughter as they rolled over and over with the giant canine. Brenda, coming up to stand between McCoy and Julie, gave her grudging approval at last.

"Well, he is quite a creature, isn't he?" she said. "Julie, before you leave, I thought of a few things my brother didn't. I have some bowls and a twenty-five-pound bag of dog chow in my trunk. That'll last you until at least tomorrow."

Julie smiled. "Thanks."

"And since my brother decided not to let anyone enjoy lunch, I picked up some burgers to barbecue."

"Brenda, I have to go back to the station," McCoy began.

"Oh, you have another hour, I'm sure."

"They're turkey burgers, Uncle Robert," Tammy said. McCoy groaned. "I don't think I have an hour—"

"You weren't supposed to tell him!" Brenda moaned.

"Honest, Uncle Robert," Taylor advised him, one man to another. "You really can't tell the difference. They're pretty good. I eat them."

"Oh, well. If my nephew eats them, they can't be all bad. But really, Brenda, I've got to go back to work. Hurry it up, will you?"

"Yes, sir!"

"I'll give you a hand," Julie said.

"No, no. You get to know your creature. There really isn't anything to do. The barbecue is all set, I have those quick-burning coals. And I have store-bought tossed salad, macaroni salad and chips. It will only take a few minutes."

She smiled merrily and went off, Tammy following behind her like a very mature little helper.

"He really is a great dog, Uncle Robert," Taylor said.

"Yeah? You think so?" McCoy said, ruffling his nephew's hair.

"You can come see him anytime you want," Julie said. "And if your mom is real busy, I can bring him here sometimes."

McCoy knelt by Taylor and threw a stick. Rusty began to bark and bellow, then chased after it. "Guess what, Taylor."

"What?"

"Rusty has a brother. But don't tell your mom yet. I want her to suffer."

"Uncle Robert, I'll be the one suffering!" Taylor said.

McCoy laughed. "Well, we'll see. I'm going to have to break this to her gently." He glared at Julie. "Don't you say anything to her, either."

"Not a word!" Julie said.

Brenda poked her head out the door. "Come on in. Taylor, you can give that monster some water and a bowl of dog food. Julie, Robert, you can wash up and grab the plates—it's paper and plastic tonight, all right?"

"Sounds great!" Julie said.

"Taylor, get the hose out in back for his water, huh?"

"Yes, ma'am." Taylor went off as he was told. McCoy and Brenda watched as Julie knelt and patted Rusty on the head. He rewarded her with a lick of the tongue that seemed to encompass her entire face. "Yuck!" She laughed. "Brenda, I think I need a bath!" she wailed.

"Oh, quit being such a fuss!" McCoy said flatly.

She stood indignantly. "Well, excuse me. You just remember that if he decides to sleep in bed with me. My room is small," she warned McCoy softly.

"What was that?" Brenda asked. She had heard. That soft blue glitter of mischief was in her eyes.

Julie flushed and McCoy laughed. "Do you ladies have to tell each other everything?" he whispered.

She let out a sigh of exasperation and spun around, heading for the house. "He deserves turkey burgers nightly!" she told Brenda.

Actually, the turkey burgers were very good, and piled high with lettuce and tomatoes and pickles, they resembled their beef cousins to a T. McCoy commented to his sister that they were delicious.

They ate at the picnic table in the backyard. The children sat for at least ten minutes, dutifully eating one burger each, making their mother happy by quickly consuming salad, then jumped up to play with the dog.

Rusty hadn't stayed around the table. Julie hadn't had the heart to send him away when he had come sniffing, but McCoy had ordered him to go sit, and that was exactly what the dog had done.

But when the kids rose to go play with him, McCoy let them each take half a turkey burger to give to Rusty. The kids, delighted, fed him.

And Rusty, delighted, lapped up the turkey burger.

Then the three of them raced around the big lawn. The kids shrieked with gales of laughter. Rusty barked now and then, his furry tail flying.

"I think I'm going to feel guilty taking him home," Julie said.

"Oh, no, no, no!" Brenda laughed. "The housing market hasn't been that good lately. I sprung for the puppy chow today. Now it's in your lap."

McCoy took a long swig of soda. "Every boy should have a dog," he said. "And that Taylor, he's a good kid."

"Didn't you say that you had to go back to work, Robert?" Brenda asked him.

He laughed. "Yeah, I do. Come on, Julie. I'll follow you home."

She looked up, startled.

"Julie doesn't have to go to work, you do."

"I'm going to follow her home," McCoy said simply. He stood and kissed his sister on top of the head. "Thanks for dinner. It was great. Julie, come on."

"Has he always had this illusion that he's a drill sergeant?" Julie asked Brenda. She wasn't going, she decided.

"It only comes out at times," Brenda promised her.

"Julie!" He turned to look across the yard where the kids were playing with Rusty. "Hey, Rusty, come!"

Rusty barked and came bounding toward him. "See? Look how good Rusty is—no complaints," McCoy told Julie.

"That's right, McCoy. Something you should bear in mind. Rusty is obedient, and I am not," Julie said with feigned patience. "Rusty is a dog, and I am a woman."

McCoy laughed. "All right. Come here, woman. Let's go. Please!"

All right. It was the "please" that did it. She'd go. She didn't know why he was so determined to follow her home, but he was.

She thanked Brenda for dinner and was pleasantly touched when both kids—manly Taylor included—offered her a kiss on the cheek goodbye. Then she was packed into her car, and McCoy was behind her with Rusty in his backseat, his big head sticking out the window.

"You should be the one to keep that dog, McCoy!" she said softly beneath her breath.

She pulled up to her own mountain. McCoy came behind her just as she was dragging Brenda's gift of the twenty-five pounds of dog food out of the car. "I'll get it," McCoy told her. He carried the food into her kitchen, Rusty following behind him, his tail wagging.

"There are rules here," Julie warned the dog. "The kitchen is yours, the porch is yours. Upstairs is a no-no. I will not have fleas where I sleep."

"Are you insinuating that I would buy you a dog with fleas?" McCoy inquired. "Or are you just trying to keep him out of my half of the bed?"

She had to laugh at the inquiry. Then she realized that his eyes were on fire, that a slow grin was sensually curling his lip. He took a step toward her.

"McCoy, you said you have to go back to work," she reminded him.

"I do," he told her. But he was closer. And she was suddenly in his arms. And his kiss had the same sizzling appeal it had always had.

Yes, he had to go back to work. But apparently, he had a little time. Before she knew it, they were upstairs. And their clothing seemed to be melting away.

And the world disappeared as he made love to her.

Yet, as he lay beside her later, his chest glistening in the moonlight that flickered into her room, he seemed more distant than ever before. He rose, walked to the window, then came back to her.

"I have to go."

"Are you coming back tonight?" she asked.

He hesitated. "No. I'll be busy."

She gritted her teeth. He wasn't going to be busy. And he wasn't coming back tomorrow, or the day after. She knew it. What she didn't know was why.

"Fine."

"Julie—"

"Never mind! Just go."

"Damn you, Julie, if you just understood—"

"Well, I don't, because you never want to tell me anything. And you're making me neurotic. One minute you can't leave my side, and the next minute you're climbing out of bed to tell me that you don't want to see me again."

"I didn't say that—"

"I'm a psychic, remember?" she said curtly. He wasn't coming back, she thought with panic. At least, that was what he was thinking at the moment.

And everything still seemed so intimate between them. They were both naked, slick, warm. They should have been content. They should have been curled into one another's arms.

She leaped up, wrenched her robe from the foot of her

bed and slipped into it. She tied the belt in a knot as she
continued speaking to him.

"But then, that is the problem, isn't it? You'd be perfectly happy if I'd just pretend that none of it existed. Well,
I can't!"

"Julie, damn you!"

He was sputtering. She was right. But suddenly he
jerked her into his arms.

And kissed her again.

And it was all there. All the passion, all the demand.
All the hunger.

Maybe even love...

But then he broke from her abruptly. "I have to go."

She stepped back, tears stinging her eyes as he dressed.

"Julie—"

"You said that you had to go," she said flatly.

He didn't try to argue with her. He left her in the room.
She heard his footsteps as he hurried down the hallway—
and then the door slammed.

Then she heard his bellow far beneath her. "Come lock
this door!"

"I have a monster of a dog," she muttered to herself.
"Why do I have to lock the damned door?"

But she went downstairs and did so. She leaned against
the door while she heard him gun his motor, then drive
away.

"I hate him!" she said out loud. Then she added softly,
"I think I love him. I really do."

Rusty came and stuck his cold wet nose into her hand
while he wagged his tail, waiting to be petted. Absently,
Julie obliged him.

"What makes him tick, Rusty?" she said to the dog.
"He can't seem to stay away, he buys me presents—like
you. And then..."

She paused, realizing that she still didn't really know
what Brenda had been about to tell her about her brother.

He had been married. That was all she knew.

"So what happened to his wife, Rusty? And why did it make him hate psychics?"

Rusty barked.

"I swear, I am going to find out tomorrow!" Julie vowed.

But the questions seemed to plague her relentlessly.

It was going to be a long, long night.

Chapter 9

By the next evening, Julie was frustrated. She hadn't heard from McCoy.

And she hadn't been able to reach Brenda, either. She had tried the business number through most of the day, but had managed to speak with nothing but Brenda's answering machine.

She had tried to concentrate on a new story, but had quickly given up the effort. Then she had tried to read a new mystery that she had been dying to sink her teeth into, but she couldn't concentrate on any printed matter any more completely than she could concentrate on her own.

At six she sat on her front steps, idly patting Rusty, who had worn himself out running around, and now sat contented by her side, half of his big body on one step, half of it on another.

Suddenly, Rusty sat up and started to bark.

"What is it?" Julie asked the dog. Then she saw. One of Petty's police patrol cars was winding its way up her little patch of mountain.

"Who is it, huh?" She felt herself tighten from head to toe, hoping that it was going to be McCoy. She knew, though, that he wouldn't be in the cruiser. And when the car pulled to a halt in front of her house, she quickly saw that Patty was driving and Joe Silver was at her side.

The two exited the car smiling. Then Rusty started to bark and bellow.

The smile quickly left Patty's pretty freckled face and she stopped dead still. Joe's brown gaze became somber, and he, too, stopped walking.

"It's all right!" Julie called quickly. She put a firm hand on Rusty's collar. "Rusty, these are the cops!" she remonstrated to the dog. "He's supposed to be so damned well trained!" she called out. "A burglar will come and good old Rusty will probably lead him to the silver! Rusty, they're friends. Sit!"

Rusty whined but immediately dropped at her feet. He put his nose between his paws.

"Where on earth did he come from?" Patty asked her.

"You didn't know anything about him?" Julie said.

Joe walked up, smiling again. "I didn't know anything, but I imagine that I can guess. McCoy bought him for you, right?"

Julie glanced at Joe and shrugged. "Yes, McCoy gave him to me."

"The guy doesn't believe in flowers or candy, huh?" Patty said, still studying the dog. She gazed at Julie again. "Is he hideous or beautiful? I'll be damned if I can tell."

Joe laughed. "Shepherd and Rottweiler, I think. Look at that head! What does he eat?"

"Anything and everything, so it seems," Julie said with a sigh. He was a great dog, really. He was housebroken, and he did have the biggest, most soulful brown eyes she had ever seen in that huge head of his.

But last night he hadn't liked being kept downstairs

while Julie slept. He'd found one of her old slippers and chewed it into pulp.

"What's his name?" Joe asked.

"Rusty."

"Hello, Rusty," Patty said.

Rusty growled.

"Never mind, Rusty."

"There's nothing wrong, is there?" Julie asked, looking from one to the other. "Did Petty send for me for some reason or another? You know, he can just call. He doesn't need to send you two out all of the time."

"Petty didn't send us at all," Patty told her.

"McCoy asked us to come out."

"McCoy!" Julie said, startled. But then it all made sense. He wasn't coming around himself. He was going to do his best to distance himself from her.

He was worried about her, though. So he'd given her a dog, and now he was sending out his troops.

Patty shrugged. "I told him that I'd call you, but he wanted us to come out and take a look around. Who knows, maybe he wants *someone* to see that police cruisers can be at your house very quickly."

"Maybe," Julie murmured. She gritted her teeth, wondering why it hurt so badly that McCoy suddenly seemed so determined to shake her off. She should be furious. He was absolutely incredible. He came on like a cyclone. He seemed to be following her wherever she went, and he had appeared at the lunch table when she had least wanted him to do so.

And then her house…

The sweet tension had been there. The electric need. And he had seemed to want her so damned badly…

But as soon as that tempest had ended, he had withdrawn. Completely.

"Well," she said brightly, determined not to let anyone see that she could be affected by Robert McCoy in any way, shape, or form. "What are you two up to now?" She gazed at her watch. "It's past six. Want to come in for a while?"

"I'm not so sure that we can," Joe said, laughing. He pointed at Rusty, who had lodged his bulk in front of Julie's door.

"Rusty!" Julie moaned. "Give me a second. I'll put him in the basement."

Rusty whined and cast all his weight on his haunches, but Julie was determined. She dragged the huge dog through the front door, the entryway, and into the kitchen. She panted as she held him by the collar and opened the basement door. "I'm sorry, Rusty, but you just can't be nasty to my friends like that!"

When she turned around, Joe and Patty had followed her into the kitchen. Patty was in the refrigerator. "What have you got that's cold?"

"Are you off duty?" Julie asked.

"Yep. You were our last official project. You're fine. At least, she looks fine to me," Patty said.

"Looks great to me," Joe agreed. "Have you got any cold beer in there?"

Julie stepped around Patty and found a can of beer and tossed it over to Joe. "White Zinfandel, white Zinfandel," Patty murmured.

"Boy, she's even specific," Julie moaned to Joe.

"Hey, Patty, beggars are not supposed to be choosers," Joe reprimanded her.

"But I know she's got it in here somewhere—beyond all the green stuff," Patty teased.

"Move!" Julie commanded. She found the wine and poured a glass for Patty, then sat on one of the bar stools at the kitchen counter. "How are things going?" she asked.

Joe shrugged. "There was a break-in at Mike Geary's souvenir store," he said.

She shook her head. "I'm talking about the kidnapping. Or kidnappings. Any news?"

Joe shook his head. "Not that I know of."

"Something happened yesterday."

"What?" Julie demanded.

"Yeah, what?" Joe echoed.

Patty stared at him incredulously. "You didn't hear? Oh, I can't believe I forgot to tell you. I was alone in the office with McCoy when somebody called and asked to speak with him. I didn't think anything of it at first. Then all of a sudden McCoy is waving at me madly, indicating that I should get a trace going on the call. I tried, but I'd barely gotten things started before the caller hung up."

"The kidnapper?" Julie said.

"I imagine. Or else somebody claiming to be the kidnapper."

"What did he say?" Julie asked.

"I didn't get a chance to hear—"

"Well, what did McCoy say?"

"McCoy didn't say anything, not to me. He was closeted with Petty this morning for awhile, so I guess the two of them really hashed it out. Whatever he said, though, it disturbed the hell out of McCoy."

Julie stared at Joe. He shrugged helplessly. "This is the first that I'm hearing about it, too."

"Well, they must be trying to keep a really low profile," Julie mused. "But—how could he be sure it was the kidnapper?"

"I think," Patty told her, pulling up a bar stool, "that McCoy had no doubt. Don't forget, Julie, McCoy listened to the kidnapper's voice time and time again on the night you two went from phone booth to phone booth trying to find Tracy Nicholson."

"I had forgotten," Julie said thoughtfully. She shrugged. "I don't know. Maybe he's just trying to make sure that he doesn't say anything to the two of you, or to

Timothy, or even Petty—anyone who might say something to me. He's probably afraid that I hear things and then imagine that they're part of my abilities.''

"Oh, don't take it that way!" Patty said.

"And why not?"

Patty paused, blinked, then shrugged. "He must think a great deal of you."

"He must," Joe agreed cheerfully. He leaned on the counter, cupping his chin in his hand. "Hey, kid, that's an expensive dog he bought for you!"

"Yeah, boy," Patty agreed. "I didn't even know that you were actually dating."

"I don't think that we are actually dating," Julie said. She didn't want to discuss it any longer. She leaped off her seat. "So, Patty, are we going to see a movie, or what? I'm sorry, Joe, do you want to join us?"

"No, thanks," he said. "I've got plans."

"I think he has a very hot date, but he doesn't want to tell me about it," Patty moaned.

"Yeah. Every law-enforcement official in the next three states will be talking about my love life if I tell Patty anything," Joe said flatly.

"Oh, come now!" Patty protested.

"Timothy Riker went out with a Las Vegas showgirl last year and I swear, they knew about it in Maine," Joe told Julie. "Ladies, with that, I am leaving. Have a nice night." He paused a moment. "Hey, Julie, will you see that my partner here makes it home?"

"Of course," Julie assured him. He waved again. Patty made a face at him, and he was gone.

"What do you want to see?" Patty asked Julie. "Have you got a newspaper around here?"

Julie indicated the newspaper at the end of the counter. Patty started looking through it. "I wanted to go home and take a shower," she murmured. "But if we want to eat first—do we want to eat first?"

"Yes," Julie said. "And I want to eat somewhere with lots of alfalfa sprouts."

"Alfalfa sprouts?" Patty said.

"Never mind," Julie murmured. "How about seafood?"

"Whatever," Patty said, poring over the movie section. "Comedy? History? Drama, suspense, murder—no, no murder. How about the new thing they've been advertising—"

"Comedy?" Julie asked.

"Yeah."

"Perfect," Julie agreed. She wanted to see something she could just sit through. Her concentration probably wouldn't be the best. She glanced at her watch. "Hey, we'd probably best be getting a move on here. Although, if you want to shower here, there's probably time. You can find something of mine to wear, and we can still make dinner in plenty of time if we go to that seafood place right by the theater."

"Well, it sounds like a hunk of heaven," Patty said dryly. "All I'd need is a good-looking guy to go with it."

"They're not all that they're cracked up to be," Julie said.

"I'd like the chance to find out," Patty said with a laugh. Then her eyes twinkled with merriment as she studied Julie. "I just can't wait to get all the dirt on McCoy. Is the feud over? What do you mean, you're not dating? Just flat out sleeping together? What's he like in bed? Is he just great?"

"Patty, you are asking very personal questions," Julie moaned.

"Hey. They're the best kind. Come on. Tell all."

"Patty, you've got about five minutes to shower."

"Hell, I'll give up the shower for the information."

"Well you're not getting any information, so go get ready."

"Well, all right. But as good-looking as McCoy is, I think you need to think about this one seriously. After all, if he bought you this giant dog after just a few dates, or sessions, or whatever you're having, imagine what he'd get you for a first anniversary present? An African elephant would not be out of the question."

"Would you please go get ready!" Julie commanded. Patty laughed and went upstairs.

Julie started to lock up the house, then remembered Rusty in the basement. She opened the door, calling to him. Absently she patted him on the head and straightened the kitchen. She heard Patty ask if she could wear a certain pair of jeans and Julie called back that she could wear anything that she wanted.

Then Patty came running down the stairs, and Julie went up to brush her teeth and her hair. She grabbed a jacket and her shoulder bag and hurried down the stairs.

Patty had stepped outside and was sitting on the porch, as Julie had been when Patty and Joe had arrived. Rusty had decided to like her. He was slumped on the porch, his nose in Patty's lap. "Sorry, Rusty, we've got to go," Julie said. "I've got to put you inside."

"He seems to like the outside. Maybe you should just leave him on the porch."

"But he's supposed to protect the house. I think he needs to do that from inside."

"Maybe," Patty agreed.

Julie shooed the dog in the house, and the two of them left. She winced, hearing him bark mournfully as they drove away.

"So what is the story with McCoy?" Patty persisted, watching Julie as she drove.

"I don't think there is a story right now, and I really don't want to talk about it," Julie told her.

"Oh, come on——"

"No. I'm serious. Patty, you believe in me, even if he

doesn't, right? Well, I knew when he left last night that he didn't mean to come back, that he intends to stay away. For some reason. I don't know why. And he hates psychics to begin with. For—'' She broke off, ready to kick herself. She still hadn't gotten hold of Brenda.

"For?" Patty persisted.

"Nothing. I really don't know, and I really don't want to talk about it, all right?"

Patty sighed. "But—"

"Whatever was is over. All right?"

"Fine! I won't push the future! But you can tell me about the past, okay? Is he just the greatest thing since the invention of chewing gum?"

Julie groaned out loud. "Patty!"

"Okay, okay."

And Julie was certain that Patty did try, but try or not, all she did was ask questions about McCoy all through dinner.

And even during the movie, despite the fact that Patty was entertained at last, Julie couldn't get her mind off McCoy. The whole thing was so crazy.

It must have been a good movie, because everyone else in the audience kept laughing hysterically. Patty was laughing so hard that she punched Julie on occasion.

Damn McCoy. She couldn't even enjoy a movie anymore!

She stood up suddenly, determined to leave the theater and find a phone.

"Julie!" Patty said. "I've got more popcorn here—"

"I'm not going for popcorn," she whispered.

"Ladies, please?" the fat man behind them intoned.

Julie apologized, quickly slipped from her row and hurried from the movie. In the lobby, she found a phone, and dialed Brenda's number.

She had no difficulty. She had called McCoy's sister so many times now that she knew the number by heart.

"Oh, Brenda, come on, please!" she murmured. She was delighted when the phone was answered.

"Hello?"

"Brenda, it's Julie!"

"Julie! Hi, I've been trying to get you back—"

"I know. I'm not home. I'm at the movies."

"Oh. What are you seeing?"

Julie told her.

"Oh, I've been dying to see that! Is it as good as they say?"

"I guess so. The whole audience is laughing."

"Oh, my lord, but I never finished telling you the end of the story about Robert! Oh, Julie, I forgot, or I would have made sure to reach you today."

"Can you tell me now?"

"Yes, of course. Julie, he's really not as bad a bear as maybe he seems at times. And he's worried about you. And all right, he has a real problem with psychics. Julie, his wife was murdered."

"What!" Julie gasped. She must have been very loud. She was standing in the lobby, but the theater manager frowned at her. "Sorry," she mouthed.

"Yes, she was killed. And under very similar circumstances to those right now. They lived in California. Mc-Coy was already working on the case when Serena was taken from a shopping mall. It was entirely coincidence. This man locked his victims in freezers. And McCoy was desperate so he listened to the psychic they had brought him, and, well, she directed him into the heart of L.A. when Serena was out in the suburbs."

"Oh, God!" Julie breathed.

"I'm sorry. It's awful, but I thought you should know. Maybe you would understand him a little bit better."

"I'm not sure if it matters or not."

"I know that it matters. I've seen him date since then,

and I've met some of the women. I haven't seen him care since then. And he does care now. Very much.''

"Very much—but maybe not enough. I don't know," Julie said. "But whatever, Brenda, thank you. Thank you very much.''

"Of course. Well, you can't possibly enjoy that movie now. Go try, though.''

She thanked Brenda again and hung up, feeling numb. She stood in the lobby, leaning against the wall. Okay, so she understood him now. Or at least she understood an awful lot.

She stared blankly at her fingers. All right, so this was hard for him. But it was hard for her, too. She should have run from him the moment she met him. He had been hurt.

Maybe she'd never had to deal with anything quite so horrible, but she'd had her own losses.

She hadn't cared. Her feelings for McCoy had just been too strong.

The movie was letting out. She stood by the phone until Patty came by.

"You are a rotten date, Miss Hatfield! Has anyone ever told you that before?''

"I'm sure they've thought it on occasion," Julie said.

"Well? Did you make your call?''

"Um—it was busy," Julie said. She wasn't ready to talk about the information she had received—not with anyone. She felt too numb.

"Come on—let me get you home," she told Patty. And she feigned a cheerful interest in the movie as they left.

It was late and dark in the mountains by the time she had driven Patty to her home, an old house almost on top of the park area, then driven to her own mountain. She was surprised at how nervous she felt approaching her house. She hadn't thought about the night, or the darkness, or anything but McCoy.

And now...

It was just that the place seemed so dark.

She parked the car and stepped out, staring at the house. Why hadn't she left on more lights?

And why wasn't the dog barking?

Julie bit her lip. Her breath seemed to catch in her throat. She wasn't alone...

She swallowed the sudden certainty, then tried to decide if someone was outside, near her, watching her.

Or if someone had gotten into the house.

"Rusty!" she called softly.

There was no answer. Only the soft whisper of wind through the trees.

It was suddenly cold, very cold. Was there danger outside?

Julie raced for the house, then paused on the porch. Had she locked the door? She remembered ushering Rusty into the house, but had she locked the door?

Oh, God! She didn't know in which direction she should be running.

All she knew was that she was not alone on her mountain that night.

"Rusty!" she called softly again. She looked down. Her keys were in her hand. Should she open the door or run to her car and drive away as fast as she could?

Could she reach her car?

Suddenly, her front door swung open.

And someone was there. Someone tall and unearthly dark in the night. Someone towering and staring at her and—

A scream tore from her throat, and she turned to run. Too late. A hand shot out and fingers curled around her upper arm like a vise. Another scream ripped from her lips, and she turned, swinging, only to be caught in a set of powerful arms.

"Damnation, Julie, what the hell is the matter with you?"

McCoy. It was McCoy! She gasped, stepping back. Her eyes were adjusting to the darkness. "McCoy!"

"Yes, damn it, it's me."

Relief flooded through her.

"You all right now?"

"Yes, I'm all right now." He released her. She slammed her purse against his arm with all the power she could muster.

"What the hell—"

"You scared me to death!" she gasped.

"I scared you! I came out here and you had left the place wide open!"

"I left it with my attack dog waiting right in the entryway!"

"But you still need to lock your doors!"

"Well, who the hell knew you would just step right into my house?"

"Fool woman, I was trying to make sure that you weren't in trouble somewhere in it!"

"Well, I'm not. I'm just fine, thank you. With no thanks to you. And what are you doing here, anyway? You said that you—you said that you weren't coming back!" Her voice had broken. She was dismayed by the emotion she had betrayed with her words.

Then she felt his eyes on her in the darkness. "No, Julie. You said that I wasn't coming back." He sighed. "And I didn't come back. Not last night. And I didn't mean to come back. Not tonight."

"Then why are you here?"

"I don't know," he said very softly. "Yes, I do. I'm back because I want to go away. With you."

She gasped, stared at him, then brushed past him in a fury. "Oh, no, no, no, no! I will be neurotic by the time you finish with me, McCoy. First you can't seem to live without me, and then you don't want to be anywhere near me. Then you say that you're not coming back—"

"Wait a minute!" The door slammed behind them. Rusty barked at last, wagging his tail.

McCoy caught Julie's shoulders and spun her around to see him. "I will remind you, Miss Hatfield, you were the one who decided that I was not coming back!"

"But I was reading your mind!"

"I do not believe in mind reading!"

"That's right! You don't believe in anything. You don't believe in me, and I don't even know if you really believe in the possibilities of love anymore! I'm trying to understand, and I do understand, and I'm so sorry—"

"So sorry about what?" he exploded suddenly, wrenching her close to him. "What are you talking about?"

"I'm talking about your wife!"

Suddenly, he thrust her away. His eyes narrowed. "Who told you about Serena?"

"Your sister."

"Did she tell you that a wonder woman, the marvel of the state of California, sent me on a wild-goose chase while Serena lay in that freezer, suffocating to death?"

"Yes, she told me."

He exploded with an oath and stared at the ceiling, as tense as a man could be, his hands braced at his hips. "Then have some mercy, Julie! Understand that I don't want to hear anything about what you think you're seeing in any visions!"

"And understand why you want me one day, and not the next, too? I'm sorry, McCoy. I can't. I gave you faith, I gave you everything. I need some of it back."

"Julie, damn you. After what happened, what the hell do you want out of me?"

"I want you to believe in me!"

"Damn you, I don't believe—"

"I know you don't! You don't believe in anything! Maybe you can't believe in anything. And that's why I don't want you back!"

"What are you talking about?" He stepped back and hit the light switch. Julie blinked against the sudden harsh glare. She bit her lower lip.

"Nothing," she said wearily. But she had gone too far, and she knew it. He was going to hound her until she said something to him.

"Julie—"

"All right!" she flared, staring at him. She took a step toward him. "All right, McCoy, so you don't believe in psychics. I do understand. But you don't want anything to do with that part of me. Well, I don't want any part of the disbelieving part of you. Because I really couldn't stand it. A time could come when I'd know you were in danger, serious danger, and you wouldn't listen to me—"

"Wait. Wait right there, Hatfield!" he warned her suddenly. She had advanced on him. Foolish. He was bigger. And now his hands were on her shoulders, and his eyes were silver as they glared hotly into hers. "We went through this once. You asked me if I'd listen to you if you warned me about danger. Even if it was only to humor you."

"Yes," she said.

"And I said that I would."

"You just said that to shut me up!" Julie told him angrily. "So you go right ahead, McCoy! You just keep shutting me out and walking away, because that's the way I want it! I can't take any more."

She was amazed at the emotion that had suddenly risen within her. Her words were hot, impassioned and furious. And there were tears stinging her eyes. She didn't want to see him any more. She spun blindly and headed for the stairs.

"Julie!"

She ignored him and raced to her bedroom. She slammed the door behind her. It didn't deter him in the least. A second later he was behind her, catching her on her bed, flipping her over to meet his eyes when she would have kept her back to him.

"Stop. I know all about Michael Grainger."

Julie gasped, amazed that he knew. Then she wasn't so amazed. There were any number of people whom he might have asked about her.

"Well, if you know—"

"He was killed two days before your wedding, Petty told me. And he was killed because he rode his motorcycle when you warned him not to."

"Yes! Yes!" Julie shouted at him. "And you'd be just like him, telling me that I was wrong all the time. No, you're not just like him. You're worse. You've been hurt once. You won't take any chances. There are no hard and fast guarantees in this life. Not in love, and not for life itself. And, oh, God, McCoy, I really am so sorry. So very sorry. But I do have something. It isn't there all the time. It isn't mechanical. It didn't come with a warranty. It is a gift, and I have to use it when I can. But in my own life, McCoy, I have to have someone willing to believe!"

"Julie…" He started to kiss her forehead.

"No!" she cried out brokenly.

He braced himself against her. Tension knotted throughout him like wire.

Then he gently pulled her into his arms.

"McCoy—"

"Will you listen to me?" he asked softly. "Julie, maybe you could have stopped him from riding the motorcycle. Maybe he would have been killed anyway."

"And maybe he wouldn't have been!" It had been a long time ago. Over five years. But then, she'd known Michael a long time, too. They'd gone to school together. They'd gone to proms together. And they'd grown up feeling the same deep attachment.

The wedding had been planned. Her dress had been

bought. The church had been arrayed with half of the flowers.

Then she'd had that awful feeling. The surety of danger. And she'd called him in town and told him not to come out to the house, to wait. And he'd laughed and he'd told her that no one was as good on a bike as he was, and that she was having pre-wedding jitters. He teased that she just wanted to get out of the ceremony.

And he'd hung up on her, telling her he'd see her in just a few minutes.

She'd never seen him alive again.

"Julie..." McCoy whispered softly. He wiped away a tear that had formed at the corner of her eye.

"McCoy."

"Julie, it's wrong to live in constant fear."

"I don't live in fear! And it's insane not to listen to an inner warning—"

"Julie," he interrupted her. Moonlight streamed in through the windows. It lit up the silver of his eyes and fell upon her as he spoke. "Julie, I think that I love you. I can't promise to believe."

"Then—"

"But I can promise to try," he said softly. He cradled her gently against him. "We can both try. And if we can believe in love again, maybe both of us can believe in life again."

Julie looked at him. She felt the brush of his thumb against the dampness of her cheek.

His lips touched hers.

They would try...

And for the moment, it seemed to be enough.

Chapter 10

McCoy looked from the handsome buildings of the Smithsonian Museum that surrounded him on the green of the mall to Julie, stretched out on the grass by his side. Something tugged at his heart, and he realized, almost miraculously, that yes, he really did love her. It was hard not to do so.

She lay flat on the grass at the moment, her blond hair spilled over her, her eyes closed and her face to the sun, the slightest curl of a smile on her lips. He knew why. The sun felt good. The air felt good. Spring air. Not too hot and not too cool.

She loved it. She loved the air, she loved the sun, she loved the white and pink beauty of the cherry blossoms that were bursting in Washington, D.C., today. She had thought his suggestion that they drive into the capital strange, but he had convinced her that a few days away from everything might be a very good idea.

It was another thing that he loved about her. She was so vibrant, so very alive. And she was always willing to

listen, to do things, to see another point of view. Against
the grass, she was beautiful. Small, delicate, feminine, her
facial features so fine. She was wearing a white tailored
dress that was perfect for spring, and as she lay on the
grass, he suddenly and fiercely wanted to preserve the moment forever. The skirt of the dress had billowed over her.
Its soft color lay against the natural earth, the hem just
above her knees, her legs bare beneath it. They were
bronze against the whiteness of her dress. The outfit
shouted of spring. There was a narrow gold belt around
her waist, and she wore slim white sandals on her feet.
She looked so lovely that he wanted to encompass her in
his arms and draw strength from the serenity in her features.

He hadn't wanted to care so deeply for her—he certainly
hadn't wanted to fall in love. He hadn't thought that he
could ever really love any woman again, not after Serena.

And certainly not Julie McCoy. Not a woman with any
kind of psychic abilities. Not when the hurt was sometimes
so deep that he would shudder walking down the road
when the memories came upon him too strongly.

But somehow, she had managed to dull some of the
memories. She wasn't Serena. Maybe there were things
about them that were similar. The easy ability to smile.
The independence.

The love of life.

The relaxed feeling that had come to him at last while
they had prowled through the Museum of Natural History
abruptly left him.

He should have stuck like glue with his initial determination to stay far away from Julie Hatfield. He had lost
Serena.

And now Julie was threatened.

Her eyes opened and she stared at him thoughtfully.
"What's the matter?"

He groaned softly. "Nothing is the matter. Are you determined to try mind reading now, too?"

Julie sat up. "If I could read your mind, McCoy, I wouldn't be asking. You've just suddenly grown so silent. I don't need any special powers to know that something is bothering you."

He hadn't told her yet what the kidnapper had said to him. She knew that the man had called—Patty had told her about the call.

But he didn't want her to know that he was especially worried about her. She thought he had tried to stay away because of her psychic abilities. It wasn't the time to tell her that he had stayed away because he had been afraid.

The kidnapper had watched them together at his house. Rusty had seemed like the best idea in the world then. Then McCoy determined he would stay as close as possible himself, as well. Between him and Rusty, they had to be able to keep her safe.

Coming into Washington for the weekend had seemed like the best idea yet. There'd been no difficulty with Rusty because McCoy had a town house here. They'd have to be back for Monday morning, but it wasn't more than an hour and a half away, even if the traffic was a little rough.

We are going to enjoy this weekend, he assured himself. They already had. They had both been in the museums on the mall dozens of times. They both still loved them.

"McCoy—"

"There's nothing wrong. I'm just hungry, that's all."

"Want another lemonade?" she asked.

They had just shared one. He shook his head. "No, I want food, real food."

She laughed softly. "Man's food, right? Nothing green, something thick and heavy and really bloody and red, huh?"

"It doesn't have to be really bloody and red—although that doesn't sound bad. And I wouldn't mind eating something green along with it, as long as it's supposed to be green, rather than mold or the like. You got any ideas?''

''Yeah, there's the Associate's Court in the museum. They'll probably have red things and green things. We can run through the Exhibit on Man that we missed after lunch, then we'll have time to move on over to the Museum of the American People, and you can buy me some kind of big slushy float or sundae in the ice-cream parlor. How does that sound?''

''Slushy. Sounds great. Then what?''

''Then we have to head back to your town house. We've left Rusty alone, remember?''

''He's a big dog, he can wait awhile,'' McCoy said. Then he reflected on the matter. ''Actually, though, I don't mind the idea of heading back.''

''No?''

''Well, this is supposed to be a lover's retreat, a decadent sort of a weekend.''

''Really?'' Her eyes were soft. Shimmering. Such a hypnotic color. Green and brown mingling to gold. Just the look in them stirred him, sending wild messages to his mind—and groin.

''Yes, and you're making me feel very decadent. Don't look at me like that. Not unless you want to forget all about the ice-cream.''

She laughed softly, and that sound, too, did exciting things to his system. She was so remarkably natural. If he lived to be a hundred, he could never stop wanting her.

If only…

He hesitated, disturbed to discover that he was not at all relaxed anymore. He felt like a caged tiger.

No, he felt as if he had just missed something.

Something was wrong. Or would be wrong.

''McCoy—''

He stood up, drawing her to her feet. ''Come on. The evolution of man awaits us—and so does some good, artery-clogging red meat. And then ice-cream. And then dec-adence. In that order. But only if you quit looking at me like that."

"Culture, McCoy," Julie reminded him.

"They all started with decadence," he assured her. "Every single culture out there!"

With his arm at her waist, he led her around a softball game that had just begun and across the green to the stone steps of the museum.

While they ate, he relaxed again. Julie quizzed him about living in the city. "It's all right," he told her. Then he mused. "No, it's more than all right. D.C. is fascinating. There's always something going on, good or bad. The air here has a crackle to it, a tension. Almost like New York. But it isn't as big as New York. New York doesn't have the cherry blossoms in spring."

"It's different from California," Julie noted.

He felt the tension winding around his neck again. "It's very different from California," he said aloofly.

She wasn't to be deterred. "You were married a long time."

"Long enough."

"No children?"

"Have you seen any?"

She might have been offended. If she was, she didn't show it. "McCoy, you might well have children that you've never mentioned. Nearly grown, living with a rel-ative of your wife."

"No, I don't have any children."

"Did you want any?"

He shook his head irritably, staring at her. "Am I under an investigation here?"

She shrugged. "Maybe. In a way. You should have chil-dren. You like children. I've seen you with your nephew and your niece. You're very good with them."

"Thank you. If I ever need a recommendation, I'll let you know."

She picked up her glass of iced tea and sat back, studying him. Then she spoke very softly, but he sensed the seriousness of her words. "I was under the impression that we were going somewhere with this relationship. I was asking you about things that are rather important to me. Are you sure you wanted me on this trip with you in the first place?" she asked him.

He sighed. "Yes, I want you with me."

"Why? Just because it's hard to have a decadent weekend alone?"

He laughed. "No, I'm sorry, I don't know why I'm so tense. Yes, I like children. I never gave it that much thought. We were young—we both thought we had lots of time. Good enough?"

"It will do for the moment."

"Good. What about you?"

"What about me?"

"Children, Miss Hatfield."

"No, I don't have any. I was never married, McCoy."

"Marriage is not a necessity."

"For me, it is," she said.

"Marry me, Hatfield, and your kids will be McCoys."

"Oh!" she said worriedly.

"I kind of like that," he told her smugly.

"Is that a proposal then?"

He smiled. "Maybe." He leaned forward. "What do you think, Miss Hatfield? Is this spring fever? Opposites attracting? What would your answer be?"

She was smiling. She opened her mouth to reply, but then she fell silent. He watched as a curious darkness seemed to slide over her eyes.

"Julie—?"

"I think that…yes," she murmured. She was distracted, though. Curiously breathless.

"What is it?"

"I think that I..." She paused, shaking her head. "There's something there. Between us."

"Oh, damn it!" he swore. He spoke so loudly that the elderly lady at the table next to theirs looked at him with a condemning frown.

"McCoy!" Julie murmured.

"Julie, I don't want to hear any more of the mumbo-jumbo stuff, please."

"Then what the hell is the matter with you?" she demanded in a heated whisper.

"I don't know what you're talking about!"

"You do! Something is bothering you, really bothering you, and you won't admit it to me."

"Can we forget it for the moment, please? Can we just have one day of peace?"

She looked as if she wanted to argue, but she didn't. She lifted a hand and waved it in the air. "Fine."

He leaned forward. "I like kids, Julie. I'd like to have them with you. Maybe two, a boy and a girl, like my nephew and niece. Or two boys, or two girls—since you don't get to pick them. Is that good enough?"

"Yes, thank you," Julie told him primly. Then she rose, still angry, but a smile curling the corner of her lip. "If you've had enough artery-clogging red meat, let's head on to that exhibit."

"Wait! There's something green left on your plate."

"Where?"

"Oh, no, I'm sorry! It's simply part of the pattern there. Come on, let's go."

Julie nudged him in the ribs with her elbow and they left the dining court behind.

She still felt that he was uncomfortable. She didn't think it was because he was with her, and she didn't think it had anything to do with his initial anger when she had said that something still lay between them.

No...

This was him. He'd been just a little bit distant all day long.

She didn't want to press it, though. At this point, if he wasn't answering her, he wasn't answering her. And on the whole, it had been a wonderful day. It was fun being together. Fun waking together, fun showering together, fun jockeying for a position in front of the one bathroom mirror in the town house, he trying to shave, she grappling with her makeup.

Like playing house...

She did want to marry him, Julie realized. Very much. She wanted to live with him and wake up with him every morning of her life.

She wondered if his thoughts on the subject were as intense as her own. They were walking through the exhibit on the evolution of man and she was giving half her attention to a case that showed skull surgery.

McCoy suddenly caught her arm, and pulled her across the room to another case. The nine months of development of the human fetus were shown in the case, with small exhibits of minute but perfectly formed little bones.

"Look. There's little Hatfield-McCoy at ten weeks," McCoy said. His arms came curling around her waist and he rested his chin on her head. "What do you think?"

"I think it's remarkable," Julie said, studying the tiny skeletons.

"And miraculous," McCoy agreed softly. "Can you believe it? The very idea of just how one goes about creating those little guys has caused all kinds of reactions in my, er, mind. Let's move on to the ice-cream part of the afternoon."

Julie laughed. "We've barely finished lunch."

"Hey, I promised ice-cream, we're having ice-cream. And it's a good walk over. We'll be ready for dessert by the time we get there."

They were ready for it because each became distracted by one exhibit or another. They just made it to the ice-cream shop before it was ready to close. Julie decided on a shake; McCoy ordered a monster sundae, but he did manage to convince her to share in the whipped cream. Then he managed to make a curiously sensual event out of the eating of their ice-cream, even in such a public place. When they left, Julie was laughing and more than ready to return to the decadence part of their weekend.

They drove to the town house and were barely inside the front door before McCoy turned to her, sweeping her into his arms, kissing her fiercely. Julie shrieked with surprise, then pleasure, then fell silent as the aggressive pressure of his lips brought a sweet pounding to her heart and mind and senses. Her hands caressed his cheeks, holding him to her. She delicately traced a finger over the pulse at his throat. His lips raised from hers, and his whisper, insinuative, suggestive, entirely sexy, touched her earlobe. All sorts of delicious sensations came to life within her.

"Damn!" McCoy swore suddenly. His expletive was followed by a loud woof, and as he swung around, Julie began to laugh.

There was Rusty, sitting patiently by McCoy's feet, one paw gently reaching out to scratch at McCoy's beige trousers.

"You're supposed to be man's best friend!" McCoy reminded the dog. "Why the interruptions?"

"Because he's been locked up for hours now," Julie said serenely. She hopped out of McCoy's arms and found Rusty's leash on the entryway sideboard. "Your turn. You give him a little walk."

"Why me?"

"Because I'll make it worth your while," Julie promised cheerfully.

"I'll only be a few minutes," McCoy warned. She smiled and nodded and ushered him out the front door with

Rusty. As soon as he was gone she quickly snapped the
door shut and raced into the kitchen. She found a bottle
of wine cooling on the lowest shelf of the refrigerator, and
the cheese and sandwich meat she had packed in the cooler
for their trip. Digging through his cabinets, she found a
tray and an ice bucket and arranged everything to bring
into the bedroom.

The town house was nice. She had liked it from the
minute she had seen it. It had an easy flow, with a short
hallway leading in from the street, a handsome parlor to
the left with a formal dining room behind it, a kitchen
straight ahead and two bedrooms to the left. It was laid
out well, and the neutral carpeting and tile and drapes were
all attractive. It was lacking something, though. As Julie
raced through the hallway to the bedroom with her sup-
plies, she realized just what it was.

McCoy had never really made it a home. He had come
here after he had lost his wife. Serena had never been here.
McCoy had slept here, he had changed his clothing here.
He had never made it a home.

Maybe she could make it one.

But that was for the future. Today, she wanted nothing
more than to ease the tension that seemed to plague him.

He was always angry with her for the second sight.

But today...

She could have sworn that he sensed something. Something that was very wrong. Something that he couldn't
quite see or define, but that bothered him nevertheless.

"I'm going to make sure that your mind is on me when
you come back in here!" Julie promised. With that she
kicked off her sandals, stripped off her dress and dived
onto the bed.

Beyond a doubt, Julie Hatfield had a way with her, Mc-
Coy decided. When he returned to the house, he released
Rusty from his leash and called to Julie.

"Come this way, McCoy, over them thar hills!" she called back.

He grinned and followed the voice to his bedroom.

His bed had never looked so good.

She was stark naked, stretched out on his sheets on her stomach. She leaned on her elbows, waiting for him, a wineglass held easily, invitingly in her hands. His own glass was on the dresser, and a tray of cheese was at the foot of the bed, embellished with grapes and bite-size pieces of apples and wedges of orange. They were all displayed beautifully.

Not quite as beautifully as Julie.

He walked to her and slipped the wineglass from her hand, then sipped from it. His eyes met hers. "How the hell did our families ever have a feud?" he wondered aloud.

She smiled, coming up on her knees, deftly undoing the buttons of his light, short-sleeved, pin-striped shirt. She nuzzled her face against his chest as she did so, her nose and cheeks so soft against the coarseness of the hair there.

"Oh, I can see where a McCoy might be an argumentative type," she said flatly.

"Oh, yeah?" He set the wineglass down and threaded his fingers gently through her hair, lifting her face to his. He kissed her. Deliberated. Kissed her again. Then spoke softly. "I think I know what the feud must have been over."

Her eyes were nearly closed. "What's that?"

"A McCoy must have ravaged a Hatfield daughter. What do you think?"

"I think that maybe the daughter changed sides afterward," she said innocently, laughter in her eyes. "Then again..."

"Yes?"

"Maybe the Hatfield daughter ravaged the McCoy." With her words, she slipped the cotton shirt from his shoulders. She pressed her lips against his shoulder blades. She teased the flesh with the soft trail of her tongue, then moved her face against his chest again.

Slowly, with a sensuous, circular motion, she moved downward against him. Her fingers moved just beneath the delicate caress of her lips.

She found the buckle to his belt and deftly undid it. His zipper gave to her touch, and she heard the soft groan that left his lips and felt the wild shudder that ripped his body. His hands landed gently on her naked shoulders, but for a moment he let her have her way.

She peeled the trousers and briefs from his hips. She nuzzled him, stroked him, teased him in every manner. Then she felt a second groan, almost a growl, stirring within him, growing within him, suddenly erupting from him, and she was lifted up, crushed into his arms, held against him. Her breasts were pressed against the rugged hardness of his chest, and at the juncture of her thighs, she felt an explosive heat of desire.

In seconds she was aggressively lifted up, only to find herself falling back, McCoy with her. The bed seemed to encompass them. Then quickly, fiercely, he was one with her, and sharp rays of fire seemed to shoot out from the searing center of her to radiate through her limbs and beyond. Her arms wound around him, and she felt the slickness of their bodies touch again and again. She'd never felt him quite so tense, quite so explosive. Muscles knotted and eased beneath her fingertips; drumbeats seemed to throb throughout her, rising to a blinding pitch.

Then the world seemed to explode into tiny fragments of light and dark. She gasped and trembled with the rocking force of magic that touched her.

His arms came more tightly around her. He eased to her side, enveloping her.

And for the first time that day, he seemed to be really at ease, entirely relaxed.

Julie smiled, trailing her fingers over his arm. She leaned her head back. He stroked her hair lightly.

"Was it worth your while?" she teased.

"Entirely," he replied in muffled tones. McCoy closed his eyes. He did feel great. Not only sated, but at peace. And tired. He wanted to hold her now, just hold her, and sleep. Perhaps she felt the same. She didn't speak again. He heard her breathing slow, heard it soften.

"I'll walk the dog whenever you want," he promised lightly.

"Um," she murmured.

Seconds later, he was convinced that she was asleep. He closed his eyes. All the little things that sometimes troubled him were gone. He didn't hear creaks in the flooring or feel a cramping in his leg muscles. He didn't feel anything but good. And relaxed.

"I love you, Julie," he whispered. She didn't hear him. She was already sleeping soundly.

Soon he had drifted off himself.

When the phone began to ring, it sounded like an air-raid siren to him. He bolted up, fumbling for the receiver.

"Hello?"

Beside him, Julie, too, was stirring. She had been deeply, deeply asleep. Her blond hair was a wild, beautiful cascade all around her. Her catlike eyes were unfocused, barely opened. He wanted to reach out and touch her, reassure her. To cradle her against him.

"McCoy, it's Petty," McCoy heard. Then he realized that he was listening to something in the background.

Someone was sobbing...

And it came back, the feeling that had plagued him. It was dread. It slammed against him with the force of a brick wall, and he could barely catch his breath.

"What is it, what's happened?"

"McCoy, you need to get back here right away. He's struck again."

"The kidnapper?"

"Yes." There was a hesitation again. McCoy could still hear the sobbing.

"Petty, damn it, tell me, what has happened? Who—"

"He's taken your niece, Tammy Maitland. Brenda is here with me. She's in pretty bad shape. And the kidnapper says that you'd better get back fast if any of us ever wants to see Tammy again."

Chapter 11

Julie sat on her front porch, alone, and still stunned by what had happened.

And stunned by McCoy's behavior.

She had been nothing short of horrified, her heart as torn as his, when she had learned that Tammy had been kidnapped. She knew the value of time, and she could have been ready to travel with him in a matter of minutes.

Except that he didn't want her with him.

"I'm going now," he had told her, sitting on the side of the bed, pulling on his shoes. "I have friends who can get me back quickly with the chopper. You can bring the Lincoln for me. Drive to your house. When it's over, I'll find you there."

"When it's over? But, McCoy, I can help—"

"No!"

She had never heard the word snapped out more emphatically in her whole life.

"McCoy, I know that bad things have happened to you

in the past, but damn it, I can help you. This is your niece!
My God, you should be using every possible means—"

"Julie, no, and I mean no! I don't want you in on this!
If you get in my way this time, I'll have you arrested."

She'd never been more stunned, and despite the fact that
she knew he was emotionally involved and in pain, she
struck back, in pain herself. Now she didn't remember all
she had called him and told him. He had pushed her away
from him and left.

He had taken the dog, and not her.

Julie hadn't wasted any time. McCoy could feel any way
he wanted to feel, but if there was anything she could do
to help Brenda and Tammy, she was going to do it.

Tears stung her eyes. They'd been so close. It seemed
that so many arguments had slid into the past, lost to the
incredible warmth and attraction between them.

Lost to love.

But the love hadn't really been there, not deep enough.
Not deep enough to sustain them in the face of this crisis.
Not when Tammy…

She hadn't driven by the station—she had come straight
home. Then she had called in and spoken briefly with Timothy Riker, who had whispered to her that the kidnapper
was supposed to be calling in a few hours.

He had waited for McCoy. He would negotiate with
McCoy only.

Tammy was out there somewhere. Brenda was hysterical. And McCoy wouldn't let Julie near.

Julie closed her eyes. She had always managed to help
through the victim. She knew Tammy Maitland. And
Tammy wasn't stupid or foolish—she would never have
just gone off with the kidnapper. Unless it was someone
she trusted. Or unless she was taken completely off guard.

This was her expertise, she told herself. Even if you
can't be there, think. *See* Tammy…

She concentrated very hard. In a minute, she began to

see a blurred vision of Brenda Maitland's old farmhouse. She saw the front lawn and the porch. There was another blur, and she saw the back. The barbecue was there, and the big picnic table where they had eaten that night.

And there was Tammy. Yes...she saw Tammy.

The little girl was sitting at the table. Her light hair was drawn back with a blue ribbon. Her blue eyes were focused on a pile of sticks before her. Popsicle sticks. She was busy building something with the pile of sticks and some glue.

A cloud passed overhead. Tammy shivered. She was wearing blue jeans with little bows at the ankles, pink socks, white sneakers, a pink T-shirt and a big crimson pullover sweater. With the cloud passing, the breeze picked up.

Julie could feel it. Feel the breeze. It was cool against her cheeks, but pleasant. It was a soft breeze. A spring breeze.

Taylor came striding out of the woods behind the house. "Could have sworn someone was back there," he said, shaking his head. "Sure wish we had a dog. I heard something."

"You heard a skunk. Or a raccoon," Tammy told her brother. She bit her lower lip, dedicated to the task before her. Taylor snorted and walked toward the house. "Where's Mom?"

"Inside somewhere. Bring me a drink, Taylor, will you?"

"Tammy—"

"Please?"

"Yeah, all right, give me a minute."

Taylor was gone. The cloud overhead moved on. Tammy glued another piece to her Popsicle house.

Then she felt a queer sensation and turned around. The woods were still quiet. She frowned. She quickly forgot the interruption and turned her attention to her project.

She felt it again. An eerie sensation, shooting up her spine. She heard a rustling. She tried to turn to discover what it was.

Too late. She tried to scream as the sudden darkness descended upon her, but something hard and tight was over her mouth. And something harsh and rough had been thrown over her head, like burlap. There was a smell to it, too.

She didn't see anything or anyone. She felt the material, abrasive against her skin. And all her senses seemed to fade away. There was that awful, sickly scent. And the hand outside the burlap, pressing down against her mouth.

Julie suddenly cried out and leaned over. She could feel Tammy's terror, the very last thoughts traveling through her mind. Taylor. Taylor would come. He was bringing her a drink. Mommy would come, Mommy would see that she was missing.

He was going to hurt her. He was going to try to, he was going to try to…

And then nothing.

"Oh, Lord!" Julie whispered. She sat straight up in her chair on the porch.

Tammy, I can touch you, where are you? she wondered desperately.

No answer. Nothing. Nothing at all to help her.

Dear God, was she dead?

No, no, she would feel it. Julie would feel it.

Wake up, Tammy. Please wake up! She prayed silently.

And that was when Brenda Maitland's BMW pulled into her driveway.

Petty had given McCoy his office the moment McCoy made it back. He had been certain that McCoy needed the time to be alone with his sister, and McCoy was grateful.

He had never seen Brenda in such bad shape. His own fear was so rife that it was almost impossible to hold a rein on his panic. He had to. He was the G-man. And he was Tammy's uncle.

But he couldn't begin to deal with the situation until he had dealt with Brenda. And he couldn't even talk rationally with Brenda until he had managed to get her to calm down. She had been sobbing for hours, from what he understood. She had refused any kind of a sedative.

Men had begun combing the grounds as soon as they had discovered that the little girl was missing. It hadn't helped.

Then the call had come. The kidnapper was playing cat and mouse with McCoy. Tammy had been especially selected.

Not Julie, McCoy thought. Because the kidnapper hadn't been able to get to Julie. He was using Tammy to hurt McCoy instead.

McCoy knew Julie must hate him now. But he didn't dare bring her in on it. The kidnapper could make his try for Julie then, and McCoy might well lose them both. No, this time, he had to find Tammy. He had to best the kidnapper; he had to catch him.

It took him ten minutes with Brenda to calm her down enough to utter one comprehensible word. Then he managed at last to get her to agree to a sedative, and Dr. Willoughby, her local physician, managed to give her a shot. ''She'll be all right—it will just take the edge off her. She'll be able to help you more,'' Willoughby told McCoy.

And in a matter of minutes, it had worked. Her eyes swollen and red, Brenda described the day to her brother. Tammy, determined to play outside with her Popsicle sticks. Taylor in the woods. Brenda had come into the kitchen when Taylor had been pouring apple juice into a plastic cup to take outside for his sister.

But Tammy hadn't been there. Tammy had been gone.

"He's got her, McCoy." Tears welled in Brenda's eyes again. "He's got my baby."

"I'll get her back, Brenda. I'll get her back."

"How?"

"He's calling me, Brenda. He wants me. I'll let him have me. We'll get Tammy back."

She stared at him, her eyes glazed. "I want Julie, Robert. I want Julie here. I want her to help."

He stiffened.

"You blame her for what happened before, Robert! You can't do that! She can help me. Please, Robert, she can help me!" Brenda was starting to sob again.

It was then that the phone rang. He gave a quick motion to Patty to see that a trace was started, then he picked up the receiver.

"You know the phone booth, McCoy, and you know the price. I want my money this time. Be there. Seven o'clock tonight."

The line went dead. There was no possibility of a trace.

He swore and slammed the line down. Brenda stared at him hopefully. "It's going to be all right. He wants to meet me. I'll get her back."

But Brenda wasn't falling for it. "I want Julie," she said stubbornly. "You can't hate her—"

"Brenda!" he exclaimed, coming to his knees before his sister. "I don't hate Julie. I don't know—I don't know what powers I believe in, but I promise you, I would try anything in the world for Tammy. It's just that—Brenda, don't you see, we're risking Julie if we bring her in on this. He's called before. He watches Julie."

Brenda didn't care. She knew that her brother liked Julie, really liked her.

But Tammy was at stake. And Brenda was nearly hysterical.

"Robert, Julie will be with you. And Rusty. Nothing will happen to her."

He sighed, looking at his feet.

"Robert, he would have killed that other little girl if it hadn't been for Julie." She paused. "Julie, and you. She had the perceptions, you had the logic. Robert, this is my daughter!" Her voice was rising hysterically.

He knew when he was beaten. "All right. Let's go out and see Julie. I'm sure she's home by now."

"Get Rusty," Brenda said vaguely.

McCoy frowned. He had sent the dog with Timothy Riker to go over every inch of his sister's property. But Brenda wanted the dog.

"Patty, radio Riker about the dog," he said. "He can meet me at Julie's with Rusty. Chief, I'll be back once I've set Brenda up with Julie."

"We'll get the stakeout cars arranged," Petty said wearily.

He had a right to be weary, McCoy thought. It was happening all over again.

Just the same way.

They had saved Tracy Nicholson.

Now they had to save his niece.

But this time, they had to catch the man.

The car had barely come to a halt in front of Julie's place before Brenda leaped out of the passenger's seat. Julie stood, waiting tensely. She saw that McCoy had been driving. Brenda raced toward Julie. McCoy got out more slowly, staring at her. Julie tried not to meet his eyes. It wasn't difficult because Brenda reached her. She needed to be embraced.

"Julie, please. You have to find Tammy."

Julie held Brenda, looking over her shoulder toward McCoy. He was silent, standing there by the car. There was no welcome light in his eyes. He still didn't want her involved.

There was nothing about him to suggest that they had been very close just hours ago.

She squared her shoulders. What happened between them didn't matter anymore. He had said that he would try. He didn't intend to try.

That didn't matter. Tammy mattered.

"We'll find her, Brenda," she said softly, assuringly.

Brenda drew away, staring at Julie, the hope in her tear-stained eyes heart-wrenching. "Julie, she's alive, isn't she? Please, you'd know, wouldn't you, if she weren't. Please, Julie, oh, please—"

"She's alive, Brenda," Julie said. "But she's—" She hesitated. She didn't want to tell Brenda that her daughter had been drugged into unconsciousness. "She's sleeping right now. I know that she's all right, but I'm not quite sure where she is."

Julie expected to hear a sound, some snort of derision, from McCoy. But he didn't say a word. He was dead silent, watching them both.

"Should we go to my house?" Brenda suggested. "Maybe—"

"I don't think that will really help," Julie said. "She was taken through the woods at the back of your place, I'm pretty sure. But she didn't see where she went, so I can't be much of a help there." She stared at McCoy.

"I have to be at the phone booth at the same time tonight," he said tonelessly.

"You'll let me come?"

He shrugged.

"Yes, yes!" Brenda cried. "He'll let you come."

"So what do we do now?" Julie asked.

"We wait," McCoy said flatly. "Brenda, go on in with Julie. I'll have to go into town and see about getting the money. Oh, Timothy Riker will be by with Rusty. I want him with us tonight, too."

"Oh! The money—" Brenda began worriedly.

"I'll take care of it," McCoy said. Julie felt his eyes on her again. "If you'll take care of my sister?" There was just the slightest suggestion of a plea to his voice. Julie nodded. Of course, she would take care of his sister.

McCoy left. Julie led Brenda into the kitchen. She quickly surmised that Brenda had been given some kind of a sedative, so she made her a herbal tea, a warm drink that wouldn't affect the drugs. Then she tried to talk, reassuring her. They sat in the parlor. She managed to get Brenda to lie back on the sofa. Julie wondered if it might not have been better to have Taylor here, too, but Brenda told her that she had taken him to a friend's house because she hadn't wanted him to see her in this kind of a panic.

"But he must be worried sick, too. I shouldn't have left him," Brenda said.

Then to Julie's amazement, Brenda yawned. A few moments later, Brenda's red-rimmed eyes closed. She had dozed off.

Julie was greatly relieved. She tiptoed from Brenda's side and went to sit on the porch again. Sometimes it was best to be alone.

She closed her eyes. She concentrated.

Suddenly, a jolt tore through her. A wild jolt of fear.

Tammy. Tammy was awake now. And she was in darkness.

The panic washed over her like great waves of the ocean. It was a darkness unlike any darkness she had ever seen before. It was horrible. She was trapped in it. It was an enveloping, engulfing, awful darkness.

She raised her arms, trying to fight against it. Her arms hit something hard with a thunk. Oh, it was close, so close. She tried to shift her position. It was all around her. She could barely move.

She'd heard about the other little girl. She'd heard about Tracy.

She was buried alive…

Julie cried out, hearing Tammy's scream echo and echo in her mind.

Oh, Tammy, I'm with you. I'm with you. You're not alone. It seems so very dark, but I'm with you there, I promise. Tammy, I'll be with you.

So dark, so dark, so dark.

I'll be there, Tammy.

I'm scared, I'm so scared. It's so horrible. I can't move. I can hardly breathe.

Tammy, calm down. You have to calm down. You have to lie very still. I'll find you. Oh, Tammy. Your mother loves you so much, so be strong and brave, and we'll find you. Don't panic. I'm here. Close your eyes. Try to rest. Try to dream sweet dreams and don't let yourself be so scared...

"Julie?"

She started, rising up from the ball she had bent herself into, to look into Timothy Riker's young, worried face.

"Timothy!" she gasped.

"Are you all right? I didn't mean to startle you. I've got the dog. McCoy wanted the dog."

"Oh!" Julie exclaimed. Then she laughed nervously. How could she have missed the arrival of Rusty? He was straining at his leash to reach her, panting as if he had just run a mile.

Riker let him go. He bounded toward her, licking her face in one long lash and trying to land his bulk on her lap. "Some well-trained creature you are!" she told Rusty. She smiled at Timothy. "Thanks for bringing him."

"Well, McCoy's right—he could prove to be a big help. We gave him one of the little girl's sweaters and he just about went wild. He barked all over the property, but he lost the scent after the woods in back."

"That's because she was driven away," Julie said.

"Oh," Timothy muttered, a little uneasily. "Well, I'm going to get back now. Petty needs to set us all up for tonight. I imagine McCoy will be back for you right after. Patty is going to stay with Mrs. Maitland.''

"That's good," Julie said.

Timothy smiled and waved goodbye and walked to the patrol car. Julie closed her eyes again. She waited. Rusty was licking her hands. She tried to concentrate. Tried to reach Tammy.

She found her. She was still breathing hard. Her little heart was beating wildly. But she was trying. She was saying her prayers. Saying them over and over again.

She was using too much air...

Tammy, don't be afraid. Please don't be afraid. Help me. Try to help me. Did you wake up at all before? What happened? What happened after the yard?

The car. I think I remember a car.

How far did you go? Up a mountain? Down into a valley? Did you see anything? Did you see his face?

There was darkness for a moment. Only darkness. Tammy hadn't seen anything. But she had come in and out of consciousness on the drive.

The drive. I knew the drive. I've done it, exactly the same. You know how you can just feel the way that you're going? I've done it before. I've done it before. So many times. We came someplace that I know really well...

"Julie."

She heard her name. The other voice faded away. She looked up.

McCoy was back. One foot was on the bottom step. He was leaning his elbow on his knee, trying to get her attention. Rusty was barking wildly.

She stared at McCoy, disoriented for a moment. Then she gasped.

"McCoy, I know where she is."

"For the love of God, Julie—"

Julie leaped up, heedless of his heartache and his anger. "Damn you, McCoy, you promised to at least try!"

"We're talking about my niece's life!" he ground out in bitter agony.

"And I can save it!" Julie shouted. "I know where she is!"

He looked at his watch. "Julie, we're just an hour away from the first call at the booth—"

"I can find her in twenty minutes, McCoy!" Julie pleaded. "Give me that. Just give me that."

"Robert! Do what she says. Please!" another voice suddenly begged from behind them. Brenda was up. She was standing in the doorway. Tears streamed down her cheeks silently. She appealed mutely to her brother as they all waited.

"Julie, if we miss this call—"

"Please, believe in me! It won't matter if we miss the call. All we need is Rusty. Please!"

McCoy looked at his sister, then he sighed. "All right, get in the car. Hurry."

Julie raced for the BMW, calling Rusty along with her. Brenda followed.

"Brenda," McCoy began. "Brenda, you shouldn't—"

"We haven't time, Robert. Please!"

Julie knew that listening to her at that moment was against everything he had ever been trained to do. But for once, he didn't argue. He slid into the driver's seat and revved the motor. He gazed at Julie, in the backseat with Rusty, through the rearview mirror. "Where are we going?"

"Your place," she said huskily.

"What?" He seemed so amazed that he might refuse to do what she had asked. "Did Tammy see the kidnapper?" he asked her.

She shook her head. "He came up on her from behind. But he came through the woods and through the yard. He threw something over her head, something scratchy, like burlap. And he had it soaked in—" She hesitated, remembering that Brenda was in the car, turning paler with every word. "He drugged her. He didn't want her fighting or afraid."

Brenda drew in a breath that turned into a ragged sob.

"She's all right, Brenda. I know it. She's just frightened, and trying very hard to be brave. It's all right. We'll reach her."

She met McCoy's eyes in the rearview mirror again.

If they didn't find Tammy all right, he would personally take *her* apart. Piece by piece.

"What makes you think she's at my place?" he demanded.

"Because she knew the drive."

"What do you mean?" he barked.

"She knew the drive. Even drifting in and out of consciousness, she knew the drive. All the curves and turns and climbs were familiar. Something she had done many times. Going from her house to yours. Maybe she even had a peek at something familiar there. I don't exactly know how I know, McCoy, but I do. She's at your house."

She didn't need to argue any longer. They were climbing McCoy's driveway.

He pulled the car to a halt in front of his house. Before the motor had died, Julie threw open the door, letting Rusty bound from the car. She jumped out after him. "Okay, Rusty, you've been working at it all day. Find Tammy now. Find Tammy."

Rusty barked, as if he had understood every single word perfectly. Then he started to run.

He ran in a wide circle.

"Oh, dear Lord..." Brenda wailed.

Then Rusty barked again, and leaped in the air, and started to run.

McCoy was right behind him. Fast. Like a streak.

Julie followed the best she could, with Brenda right behind her. She gritted her teeth. Tammy, Tammy, we're coming. We're close, we're so close. Just hang on.

Can't! Can't breathe. It's so stuffy. Julie, help me, help me. Oh, Mommy, I want my mommy, I want my mommy, so scared, so scared...

Tammy, don't fight. Lie still. Breathe slowly, really slowly...

Julie's heart was in her throat. The kidnapper hadn't left Tammy any air. He'd meant her to be dead before Julie and McCoy reached the first phone booth.

"McCoy, hurry!" she called out.

She heard Rusty barking and carrying on something awful. Julie burst into the clearing before her.

Rusty was standing on a mound of uprooted grass and weeds and dirt.

McCoy was beside him, digging through the dirt with his hands.

Julie fell beside him and did the same. A second later, Brenda was with them. They worked furiously.

Then, at last, beneath them, they saw the wood. "Get out of the way," McCoy commanded them both. They jumped away. He found the edge of the wood and began to wrench at it with his bare hands.

Julie had heard that desperation gave men strength.

Now, it did. She heard the boards groan, then snap, broken by his hands. The dirt they had dug up fell into the coffin.

"Tammy!" Brenda screamed. "Oh, Tammy, Tammy, my baby, please, baby, speak to me, oh, Tammy..."

Now it was Brenda who thrust aside her brother. She reached into the coffin, pulling her dirt-laden daughter into her arms. "Tammy, oh, please, oh, please, God—"

Tammy's eyes opened. She stared at her mother. She started to cough and choke, and then she started to cry. She reached out, her arms winding around her mother's neck. "Mommy! Oh, Mommy!"

"Oh, thank God!" Brenda gasped, and then, there in the mound of dirt, she started to cry. "Thank God, thank God, thank God."

"No," McCoy said softly. Julie realized that he was staring at her across the open coffin that had been relieved of his niece's body. "Thank Julie."

Chapter 12

The kettle whistled and Julie roused herself, then hurried into the kitchen to take it from the stove.

She was alone again, but that didn't really matter. Tammy was fine. She'd be going home soon, Julie was certain. She hadn't seemed to have had a scratch on her, but they had taken Tammy to the hospital for observation. They'd probably keep her overnight, and Brenda could sleep in one of the chairs by the bed. Patty had gone to pick up Taylor and take him to the hospital, too.

All was well. McCoy would be with her soon.

She made herself a cup of tea, absently patting Rusty on the head as she did so. McCoy had never explained his feelings to her.

It had been Brenda who had given her the glimpse of the insight. "He's not against you, Julie. Not anymore. He's afraid for you, don't you see?"

At that exact moment she hadn't. But since McCoy had promised to be with her as soon as possible, she did understand. Especially since she had seen the very proud and determined man say, "Thank Julie."

He hadn't wanted to leave her then, but there had been so much confusion. The ambulance arriving, and all the police cars coming. Then Patty had gone off to get Taylor, and everyone had to be called off the search.

Then there was the nagging thought that the kidnapper had not been apprehended.

And the even more frightening thought that he had never, never intended for Tammy to be found. But for tonight, all was well. There might be a long climb ahead. Julie didn't mind the idea of climbing anymore.

He believed in her, she was certain. More importantly, he loved her. He loved her enough to believe in her.

"Hey, Rusty, what is it? Is McCoy back already?" she asked the barking dog. Julie walked to the entryway, taking care to look out the peephole. She didn't want to ruin an emotional homecoming with him yelling about the fact that she hadn't looked through the peephole.

She saw the police car parked on her lawn and breathed out a little sigh of relief. Then someone moved outside and she saw that Joe Silver, still in his uniform, was waiting patiently on the porch.

She started to open the door. If Joe was out there, McCoy had probably sent him for her. He'd probably been delayed and wanted her to come to him.

Rusty kept barking, slamming his weight against the door with such a vehemence that Julie couldn't open it. "Rusty, get down!" she commanded. She caught hold of his collar and managed to open the door. "Hi, Joe. I'm sorry. Rusty, Joe is a good guy. I swear, when a robber comes, Rusty will wind up leading him right to the family jewels. Well, not that I have any family jewels, but you know what I mean."

Joe laughed, stepping in. "Hey, Rusty, you and I are going to get to be friends eventually. Yeah, boy."

Rusty didn't believe him. "I'll just put him in the basement again," Julie said with a sigh. "Come on in," she
called over her shoulder. He followed her to the kitchen
as she dragged the dog along. "Did McCoy send you?"
she asked, shooing Rusty down the stairway at last. He
was a heavy dog. She was somewhat distracted when Joe
answered her.

"Well, yes, in a way he did."

She closed the basement door and turned to smile at
him. "Well, am I supposed to be somewhere? Has he been
held up? Have there been any leads? Oh, I forgot! Did he
go to the phone booth, did anyone go to the phone booth?"

Joe shook his head, his brown hair slipping just a little
over his eye. "I don't think there's anything new. I wasn't
on call tonight."

"Oh," Julie said. Rusty was still carrying on in the
basement. "What am I going to do with that dog? He can't
seem to tell the good guys from the bad!"

The phone starting ringing then, just to add to the confusion. Julie reached for it. "Hello."

"Julie." It was McCoy.

She covered the receiver with her hand. "It's McCoy
now," she told Joe. She turned to the phone. "McCoy?"

A shiver went along her spine. The phone was dead.

She turned. Joe had jerked the phone wire from the wall.
Her mouth fell slowly open with astonishment.

And then she felt like a fool. A complete fool.

He was of medium height and medium build. His hair
was darkish.

Rusty hadn't been confused in the least. Rusty had
barked the night Patty and Joe had come over, but when
she and Patty had been getting ready to go out, Rusty had
been with Patty on the steps, calm, content, his nose on
Patty's lap.

"Oh, God," she breathed. "You?"

He nodded. "And you know what, Julie, you are remarkable. I wanted to test McCoy. They always said that he was the best. But I never could get to him. Not with you in the picture. So, Julie, now it's your turn."

Her turn.

He could never quite get to McCoy—because of her.

She couldn't breathe, her heart was racing so horribly. It was all so obvious now. Joe. Right there in the office with them all, watching everything they did, knowing ahead of time what they were going to do.

And no one would ever think that a patrol car racing through the night held evil. No one would have searched his car for clues.

Then there was Patty. Julie had always thought that they made a cute couple, but Patty never wanted an involvement. Even Patty had sensed that there was something not quite right about him. She had worked with him day after day, and she had known...something.

How long had he been among them? Two years? Three years? Long enough to watch, to learn.

And Julie, with all her great powers, had never seen. Rusty had known instantly. While she...

She had to get away from him, that much was simple. If she could stall, McCoy would come.

He took a step toward her. "Come along easily, Julie. I don't want to hurt you."

She started to laugh, and the sound rose. "You just want to kill me, not hurt me."

"You can come peacefully," he told her.

"You know that you are really sick. You can probably be helped if—"

"Now, Julie, I don't want to be psychoanalyzed." He sprang for her suddenly. Her hot tea was sitting on the counter. She threw it in his face.

It was still hot enough to cause him to pause and shriek. She didn't think it would cause him any permanent damage, but maybe it gave her a chance to move.

She sprang for the door, desperate to get Rusty out. Hell! She had even locked up the dog for the man.

But she fell short of the door because he threw himself against her before she could quite reach it. She fell with a ferocious force, his weight on top of hers. She gasped for breath, swinging and fighting. She managed to gouge his cheek nicely with her nails, and then she started for a second because she saw the lethal fury in his brown eyes.

The eyes of a murderer, unveiled.

"He'll get you!" she shrieked. "He'll get you this time. And he'll kill you. He'll kill you for what you did to his niece. And for what you're doing to me. Don't you see, you will get caught in the end. And if it is McCoy—"

She broke off because Joe Silver was laughing. "If McCoy catches me, he'll take me in. He's a G-man. He'll have to. And who knows? I could plead insanity. You just said that I was crazy. I may get off."

"And you may not."

"Then maybe that will be for the best," he said.

It was the scariest thing Julie had heard yet. He knew he was sick.

He wanted McCoy to catch him.

"Joe, please. You don't want to do this to me," she said desperately, trying a new tactic. "Look, the tea burned your face. You're getting a blister on your cheek. Let me get something for it."

"No good, Julie," he said. His weight was holding her to the floor, his knee in her stomach now, his fingers wound around her wrists, holding them to the floor.

Nearby, Rusty barked and howled. Julie prayed that he might be heard.

Her mountain was quite remote.

He started to shift his weight, trying to grasp both her wrists with one hand. Julie took advantage of the moment, struggling fiercely once again. She tore at his shirt and ripped it from his shoulder.

She paused, gasping.

It was there. The scar that she had seen in her dream. It was just as she had envisioned it, there, cut into his flesh, near his collarbone.

"Yes, I heard that you described the scar," he said distantly. "But I hadn't been out with anyone without a shirt. Not in a long time. And no one was looking at me suspiciously anyway. You're the only one who saw."

Fear swamped her. The awful, dark terror of her dream. The fear that had haunted her ever since. The danger had come. The danger McCoy had tried to keep her from by keeping away from her himself.

You didn't bring the danger, my love. It was there, facing both of us. But, please, come now. Come quickly. Keep me from it...

She lashed out, trying to kick him. She almost dislodged him from her, but he fell hard against her again. Before she could move, he caught her in the jaw with the back of his hand.

She tasted blood. Her head spun. She fought it because she knew she might die.

But Joe was shifting, reaching into his pocket. A handkerchief was stuffed over her face. There was an awful, sickly sweetness to the smell.

He was drugging her. She couldn't be drugged. She had to pretend that she was docile. She couldn't breathe in too much of the drug.

But it was powerful. Despite the strength of her will, a blackness descended over her.

The fight was over.

McCoy drove swiftly into Julie's yard, one of the patrol cars directly behind him.

It hadn't been necessary for him to lose contact with her to know that something was horribly wrong.

And while he had been sitting at the hospital with Brenda, the logic of it all had been building in his mind.

The man had to be someone close. Someone who knew him.

He wasn't that close with anyone here anymore. He'd been away too long. He still had friends, yes, but not anyone who knew his every move.

But the kidnapper knew about him and Julie. And he knew about Brenda, and Tammy, and Taylor. He knew just about every damn thing McCoy did.

A psychic, like Julie?

No, because Julie didn't know everything. What she had was a startling gift.

A gift...that gave life. They would have never reached Tammy without her. He knew that now, beyond the shadow of a doubt.

And it didn't matter. Julie had swept away all of the past for him. She had never questioned the attraction.

She had never questioned him. She had given him her faith from the beginning. She had given him her love.

And thoughts of her were distracting him now. He sighed.

Who...

It had to be someone he knew.

Someone who could ride around easily. Someone with an airtight alibi. Someone who heard his words.

Someone involved with the investigation.

He sat up on the bench, stunned that he hadn't seen it before.

Yes, someone at the station.

Who?

Eliminate the impossibilities...

He rose restlessly and walked to the nurse. "How's my niece doing?"

"Fine, Lieutenant McCoy, just fine. She's sleeping a

very natural sleep, and her mother is right by her side. Shall I get her for you?''

''No, no, I'm sure she's fine. If she asks for me, just tell her that I had to go out for a while. I have some things to do, and then I'll be at Julie's.''

The nurse nodded, promising to deliver the message.

McCoy left the hospital quickly, feeling as if there were some sort of urgency on him now. He drove to the station. It was open. There was no one in the front office.

There was someone in the chief's office. McCoy looked in. Pettigrew was there, his head clutched between his hands. He looked at McCoy. ''There's got to be something we're missing.''

McCoy nodded. ''I'll be in the outer office.''

He sat down at Joe Silver's desk.

Eliminate...

And so he did. Petty—of course not. Patty—no, she was always with him when the kidnapper called. Timothy Riker? No, not Timothy. McCoy squinted, trying to remember. Had Timothy ever been there...

It wasn't right. Timothy just wasn't right.

Damn, I don't work on intuition alone! he told himself. But it wasn't Timothy. And if it wasn't...

Joe Silver. He hadn't been on duty the night they had gone to try to find Tracy Nicholson. But suddenly he had been there. He had been there, at the graveyard, helping him to dig up the little girl.

Then there was Julie's description. A man of medium build, of medium height. Brown hair, probably.

A man with a scar on his left shoulder.

McCoy jerked the desk drawer open. Paper clips, file reports, pencils, pens. He jerked open a bottom drawer. More papers. McCoy rifled through them.

Then he found it. It must have been taken a couple of years ago. There was Joe Silver with a tube in his hand.

He was standing near the spot where McCoy and Julie had gone tubing.

He wasn't wearing a shirt, and there, on his left shoulder, was either an imperfection in the film—or a long, jagged scar.

McCoy stood abruptly. He needed proof. But more than that, he needed to know that Julie was safe. He shouldn't have come here without her.

He stuck his head into Petty's office. "Petty."

"Yes."

"You sent someone to the phone booth, right?"

"Of course. I sent Joe. But the phone never rang. Our fellow knew the little girl had been found."

McCoy felt panic growing inside him. "He knew. Right." Then he exploded. "Petty, damn it, it is Silver!"

"What?" To Petty, it was inconceivable.

McCoy didn't have to the time to explain. "I've got to get hold of Julie. I've got to reach her. I'll radio to Timothy for some backup."

He picked up the phone on Silver's desk.

He heard the sound as the phone began to ring at Julie's house. Julie answered. Relief flooded him. Then she turned away from the phone. "It's McCoy now," he heard her say.

And then the line went dead.

He'd never driven so fast in all his life. The patrol car could scarcely keep up with him.

It was too late anyway. When he burst into the house, he knew that she was gone. The phone line was ripped out of the wall. Julie's teacup was on the floor, shattered. Tea soaked the tile on the kitchen floor.

She had fought. Julie had fought. He hadn't taken her by surprise. She had seen the face of her assailant.

She knew...

But she hadn't known soon enough. If she had, Rusty

would never be in the basement, barking in a frenzy. No, she had put the dog in the basement because she had assumed that the man was her friend.

He released Rusty. The dog came rushing out, barking, jumping, swirling his massive body around in circles. McCoy knelt by him, trying to calm him down.

It was hard. He didn't feel very calm himself.

Steady, steady. The word echoed in his head. It had worked out before...

But Julie had been there to help him before. Julie had seen. And now he was alone. She was depending on him, and him alone.

He groaned. "Okay, Rusty, we've got to think. We've got to think."

Patty and Timothy Riker burst into the house behind him. "We've got an all-points bulletin out on Joe," Patty said quickly. "He's driving around in a station car."

McCoy shook his head. "Not any more, he won't be."

"But where will he be able to get to?" Patty said, trying to reassure him.

It didn't matter to McCoy where Joe Silver could get to—what mattered was Julie.

How much time had he given her?

"Damn, just think of it. You work with a guy every day of your life, and wham!" Timothy said. He cleared his throat. "Where do we begin, lieutenant? What do you want done? Should we start combing these woods?"

McCoy didn't have a chance to answer. Julie's phone began to ring. McCoy automatically began to answer it in the kitchen, then remembered that the cord had been ripped out. He shoved past Timothy, anxious to pick up the parlor extension.

"Hello?"

He knew instantly from the slow breathing that it was Joe Silver.

"Hello, McCoy."

He fought frantically for control. "All right, Silver. We know it's you. I want Julie back. I want her back right now. We can deal with this—"

"When did you know it was me?"

"Not too long ago," McCoy said. He strained hard to listen to the background noise coming over the receiver. He heard a sound that he recognized.

Water. Running water.

He tried to keep talking. "It had to be someone who knew what I was doing all the time. Someone in the station. I thought it was you. Then I saw the picture. I saw your scar."

"And Julie knew about the scar. She discovered it just as you were thinking of it, I imagine."

A wave of fury and fear rose in McCoy. "What did you do to her?"

"What did I do to her? Why, I buried her, of course."

"What do you want? The money—"

"No, it isn't the money."

"Then—"

"You haven't much time to find her. Then you have to find me."

The line went dead. McCoy sat, numbed, staring at the receiver. He gritted his teeth, fighting for reason. There were things that had to be set into motion. They had to start combing the woods. He had to act.

"Riker!" he barked. Timothy was standing before him in seconds, waiting. McCoy told him to get in some emergency help, to get patrol cars on all the main roads in all three states. He wanted more men out—they could be borrowed from any city in the region. Hell, they could borrow them from Texas, it didn't matter, just so long as they got them out. He wanted the area by Brenda's place covered, the area by his own house, and by Julie's. He wanted someone up to the cemetery quickly.

But would any of it do any good? And where did he go himself?

Water. He had heard water. His only clue was water.

Rusty barked. McCoy looked at the dog. "You can find her, can't you? If I can just get you to the right place to start looking!"

It was dark. Dark beyond any darkness she had ever imagined. Darker than any darkness she had touched through others.

And when the drug wore off, the panic was greater and more horrible than anything she had ever dreamed.

A scream rose in her throat, and madness seemed to race through her. She tried to slam against the coffin, she tried to fight the weight of the earth that had been planted over her. She knew what had happened. Exactly what had happened. She had come in and out of consciousness. She had seen, without the ability to do anything. Her eyes had opened, but her limbs had been weighted down. She hadn't been able to move.

He had brought her through the trees, near the water. Briefly, as he carried her, she had been able to look through the trees to the very spot where she had warned McCoy that he would see the black snake—and where the snake had been.

Then she had seen the ground dug up through the trees. She had seen the coarse, makeshift wooden coffin—waiting for her. She had seen the hole in the ground.

McCoy!

She had cried out to him in her mind.

He could not hear her.

Thump, thud, thump. She had heard the dirt falling, falling on the coffin. Then blackness had descended, she had lost consciousness again.

And now...

Now the darkness.

Don't cry out, don't move too much. Breathe slowly, breathe shallowly, preserve your air.

But what good would it do? How would he ever find her? There was so much land to cover, and so little time. And Joe might have buried her anywhere.

McCoy! She thought again. Tears were welling in her eyes. He had finally come to believe in her. And he loved her. Oh, yes, she knew that he loved her. He'd even listen to her. It had all been there, beautiful and glorious. Little things wouldn't have mattered because the love had been so strong. She wouldn't have minded her children being McCoys at all.

Except that now she would never have any children. She would never see the silver sizzle in his eyes again. Feel his hands on her shoulders.

Never argue with him again. Never feud.

Never make up, never make love.

"McCoy!" she whispered the name. She couldn't do it. She couldn't waste her breath. But her mind raced on. Desperately, she reached out with it. McCoy, McCoy, I love you. I love you so very much. Please, you can't let it be the end. You have to find me.

You have to believe...

In the unbelievable.

Think of me. Remember me. Remember the laughter, remember the longing. Remember the picnic on the rocks, and wanting to be home. Remember that you told me I had probably paid the snake to appear.

I love you, McCoy. Touch me.

Water.

He was halfway out of the house, determined that he'd lead Rusty around Julie's house before trying the forest near his own house when he remembered the sound of the water.

McCoy...

He started. It was almost as if he had heard her whisper his name. God, his mind was playing tricks on him.

Julie! I love you. I can't make it without you. Not this time. Julie…

Think! He commanded himself.

The picture! The picture of Joe Silver at the water, his shoulder bared, the scar visible.

Rusty was running around wildly. Julie hadn't been buried anywhere on her own property.

The picture. Down by the water. Down near the place where they had gone in with their tubes.

His heart was sinking. There was so much ground to cover.

He blinked. He could almost hear her laughter. See her in that sexy black bathing suit that day, her hazel-gold eyes narrowed as she challenged him. There'd be a snake on a rock.

And he'd been amazed. Yes, she knew things.

I love you, McCoy.

He could have sworn that he heard the words. Perhaps he did. Perhaps they echoed in his heart.

"Let's get going," he told Patty and Timothy. "I want to try a place by the water." He told Timothy exactly where. Timothy rolled his eyes, as if assuming that McCoy had lost his mind. "Shouldn't we try his old haunts first, sir? Perhaps the cemetery—"

"No. I know where I'm going. I heard water. I heard the sound of water. And there's a phone booth not twenty feet from the river there. I heard water," he insisted.

But it was more than the sound of the water. Instinct was guiding him.

Instinct, or Julie.

And his love for her.

It didn't matter. They were there at last. "Here!" he shouted to Timothy. "There's the phone booth. Stop here. Rusty, come on, boy, get ready!" He turned to Patty. "I'll take the dog. You get hold of Petty. Get more men out here. We'll have to comb the whole area. Rusty can probably find her, but if not..."

Her air was running out. It was becoming more and more difficult to breathe. She choked and coughed, and then she choked and coughed again because she couldn't take in enough oxygen. The blackness was something imprinted on her mind then.

McCoy, please...

She couldn't think anymore. She couldn't think at all. There was only darkness, and the most horrible sorrow. Just when everything had been so beautiful. She had never imagined that she could love any man the way she loved McCoy. She had never imagined that there could be a man like McCoy.

I love you, she thought. Tears welled in her eyes. Tears that didn't matter in the darkness.

Then she heard the barking.

Her eyes opened in the darkness. She strained for breath.

More and more, the darkness wrapped around her. The barking faded. She was suffocating.

"Rusty! Good boy! You've found her!" McCoy shouted.

He came tearing through the trees into the copse. Rusty was standing over a mound of freshly dug up dirt, barking and carrying on.

"Julie, hang on. Julie, hang on, hang on!" He started digging with his bare hands, shouting, hoping that Timothy could hear him. "Bring the shovel! Get help quickly. Come on!"

He had barely shouted the last words when suddenly a shot burst through the night.

Rusty let out a whimpering cry and fell atop the earth.

McCoy stared at him for a split second in astonishment,

then, out of the corner of his eyes, he sensed movement. He fell to the earth. A second shot came bursting through the night—one intended for him.

He leaped to his feet then, slamming against the man behind him. He saw the silver nose of a pistol go flying over his head as the force of his blow dislodged the weapon from his opponent's hand.

But the force of his impetus sent him flying to the ground while his opponent reeled to his feet. Again, McCoy sensed movement.

Then a shovel came slamming down on his shoulder. The blow had been meant for his head, but he had turned just in time to avoid it.

And Joe Silver was there. Still in his uniform. He was covered in dirt, but somehow, he was still the same man he had always been. And he was smiling. Smiling his usual, good-natured smile.

"Missed," he said, raising the shovel to strike again.

McCoy rolled out of the way in the nick of time. He leaped to his feet, watching Joe carefully. "You fool! You can't possibly beat me!"

Joe Silver smiled. "No, you're the big strong G-man. You can beat me. Or you can catch me. But to do either, you let your precious Julie's life slip away. Tick, tick, tick. The seconds slip by. I didn't give her any air at all. I couldn't." He smiled, then swung the shovel again. McCoy ducked just in time, then bounded up.

This time, he caught Joe in a giant bear grip that brought them both crashing down into the trees. He didn't waste a second's time. He looked into the ordinary features of the man, into the face that housed the charming smile.

The man was sick.

He didn't care. Julie was dying. He slugged Joe as hard as he could with a solid right fist. He heard a sickening sound from Silver's jaw. The eyes went glazed as Joe Silver lost consciousness.

Julie…

"Lieutenant McCoy!"

It was Timothy Riker at last with Patty on his heels. They were both carrying shovels. McCoy grabbed a shovel from Timothy and started digging again.

Patty and Timothy were on their knees. Dirt flew.

Hope flared in McCoy's heart. Joe hadn't managed to bury Julie as deeply as he had buried Tracy and Tammy. The earth wasn't packed. Within minutes his shovel slammed against the wood of one of Joe's makeshift coffins.

"Grab it up!" he commanded Timothy. Between them, they brought the coffin to the surface. With the end of the shovel, he wrenched open the lid.

She was there. His Julie. Her eyes were closed. Her face was as pale as snow. Beautiful, ethereal, surrounded by a mist of gold and platinum hair. Her hands were folded over her chest.

"Julie!" he screamed her name. Screamed it loud enough to wake the dead. Screamed it to the heavens. Not again, dear God, not again…

He reached for her. He would give her life. He would give her air from his lungs, and life from his soul. "Julie, please…"

His arms encircled her as he lifted her from the coffin to start CPR.

His lips lowered to hers.

And then…

Her eyes flew open. She inhaled on a ragged gasp and began to cough and choke. He held her up, whispering her name.

"McCoy!" she wheezed it out.

"Julie." He enfolded her against him. He held her there, rocking her with him, smoothing her hair. "It's over, Julie, you're safe." He looked at Timothy. "Get Silver. Cuff him, even if he is unconscious. Bring him to the car."

Timothy nodded. McCoy stood, staggering somewhat with her in his arms. He started walking to the car. Her golden eyes were on his. Her lips were curled into a beautiful smile. Her cheeks were becoming a beautiful blush rose once again.

Thank you, God, thank you, God.

"You were wonderful, McCoy. Just like in the fairy tales. A kiss from a knight in shining armor."

He was choking. "Julie, if I hadn't found you—"

"But you did find me. I was calling to you and calling to you. And you heard me."

"Julie, I didn't hear you."

"In your heart, McCoy. You heard me in your heart. You believed in me."

"Julie, I knew you were near water—"

"McCoy, face it. You have powers of your own."

"Julie," he groaned.

"You loved me. You believed in me. And you believed in yourself. And you found me."

"Rusty found you—" he began. His face clouded over. Julie's arms clutched more tightly around him. "Silver shot Rusty." He turned back. "Timothy, get a move on back there! I want my dog taken to a vet. Maybe there's hope for him."

"Your dog?" Julie said.

He looked at her again. "Our dog."

There were sirens shrilling in the night. An ambulance came shooting in beside the Lincoln, then a patrol car. Petty leaped out, nearly ripped Julie from McCoy's arms, then began a barrage of questions.

"Patty's bringing Silver to the car," McCoy began, but then he frowned, watching as Patty came walking up to them, shaking her head.

"What happened?"

"I—I'm not sure," she murmured. "Silver's dead."

"What?" McCoy demanded.

"No, you didn't kill him, lieutenant. He must have come to. And he raced for the water. But he didn't find a level entry. He threw himself from high ground. He struck a patch of rapids. He's dead."

Julie, held in Petty's fatherly embrace, exhaled on a long, jagged sigh. "It really is over then," she whispered softly.

"Amen," Petty said. "Young lady! Let's get you into this ambulance—"

"No, Julie is coming with me," McCoy said. "Rusty goes in the ambulance. He needs the best vet in town. I'll get Julie to the hospital— Riker, will you please go with my dog?"

"My dog," Julie said.

"Our dog," McCoy reminded her.

A second ambulance had pulled up, and another police car.

Others were there now. Others to deal with the remains of Joe Silver.

Perhaps he had been the most tortured soul, Julie thought. She was still too shaken to know. He had found his peace now, and she wasn't sure that she could help but be glad.

For her, it was over. Resting her head on McCoy's lap, she could only be grateful for life.

She told McCoy that she didn't need to go to the hospital—but he insisted. And once she was there, it was decided that she should stay a night, too. And so she was bathed and poked and tested, and dressed in a clean gown. And a bewildered Brenda came in to see her, and then returned to her daughter. Then McCoy was back, just holding her hand by her bedside.

Within an hour, the phone rang. McCoy took it, and she watched as a boyishly delighted grin appeared on his face as he listened.

He hung up.

"Rusty's going to make it. He'll be in something like a doggy cast for a long while, but he's going to make it. My dog is going to be fine."

"My dog."

"Our dog."

"But he lives with me—"

"Julie, we're going to be married. That means we live together."

She smiled. She wasn't in the mood to argue with him. "Oh." Then she sat up and threw her arms around him. "Oh, McCoy, I love you so much. I didn't mind the idea that I was going to die. I just minded the idea that I was going to die now that you were in my life. But you found me. Oh, McCoy, you had that wonderful power, and you found me."

"Julie, it was logic. I saw the picture—"

"It was instinct."

"Logic."

"Instinct."

"Julie—" McCoy began. Then he smiled slowly. And he looked into her beautiful hazel eyes. "All right, Miss Hatfield. Let's end this feud right now. It was instinct, and it was logic. And..." He kissed her lips gently. "It was love."

"Oh, yes!" she whispered agreeably. "Above all, McCoy, it was love!"

And she kissed him in return.

The feud was, indeed, over.

Epilogue

The dream had become her life.

And there was no mistaking the man in the flesh for the haunting lover who had teased her senses for so long.

She knew him, knew him so well. She knew the very handsome curves and contours of his face, knew the silver sizzle of his eyes, the curve of his lips.

And she knew when he came behind her.

Every time…

Because of a subtle, masculine scent. She would know because she would feel him there.

And the warmth would fill her, the tenderness. Yes, she knew him, knew the man, and knew things about him that made her love him.

She knew all the hues within his heart and soul and mind, and those colors were all beautiful, and part of the warmth that touched her.

Tonight…

He stood behind her, and he swept the fall of her hair

from her neck, and she felt the wet, hot caress of his lips against her nape.

He held her hair, and his kiss skimmed over her shoulder. She wore something soft and slinky. Something silk. Something that fell from her body, rippling against it, touching her hips and his thighs, then drifting down to a pool on the floor. The fabric was so cool...

And that touch of his lips against her flesh was so very, very hot...

His arms encircled her. She could feel the strength of his naked chest as he pulled her against him. He still wore jeans. She could feel the roughness of the fabric against her tender skin. Even that touch was sensual.

She felt his kiss.

Felt the hungry pressure of his lips forming over her own, firmly, demandingly, causing them to part for the exotic presence of his tongue. Teasing her lips, dancing against them...taunting them, forcing them apart to a new, abandoned pleasure.

And when his lips left her mouth, they touched her throat. Touched the length of it. The soft, slow, sensual stroke of his tongue brushing her flesh. With ripples of silken, liquid fire. She could see his hands, broad, so darkly tanned, upon the paleness of her own skin. His fingers were long, handsomely tapered, calloused, but with neatly clipped nails. Masculine hands. Hands that touched with an exciting expertise. Fingers that stroked with confidence and pleasure.

She allowed her head to fall back, her eyes to close. The sensations to surround her.

The breeze...it was so cool against her naked body. So soft. So unerringly sensual. Perhaps because her body was so hot. Growing fevered. But the air... It touched her where his kiss left off, and both fire and ice seemed to come to her, and dance through her.

She spun in his arms. It was no longer daytime. Shadows were falling, and the breeze was growing cooler.

And his kiss, the tip of his tongue, stroked a slow, searing pattern down the length of her spine. It touched her nape, and the building tempest within her suddenly seemed to engulf her.

And his kiss went lower.

And where his lips touched her, she burned.

And where his lips had lingered earlier, the cool air stroked her with a sensuality all its own.

His kiss lowered. And lowered until he teased the base of her spine. And his hand caressed her naked buttocks and hips, and she was turning in his arms.

She was touching him then. Touching him, knowing the living warmth and fire of him. Feeling the ripple of muscle in his chest. Feeling his hands. Feeling the pulse of his body. Feeling…him.

And he was with her. Her lover, her husband. A part of her. And when he touched her so, when the rhythm of his love brought her soaring so high, the night could seem to be lit with sunlight, and the air was eternally charged with magic.

As always…

When he touched her, the world spun, and split, and lightning seemed to sizzle. And then it came, the moment when the stars burst and the sky seemed to go a glorious gold, and then to blacken again.

As always…

There was the desperate scramble to breathe again, the sheen of perspiration that bathed them both like a lover's dew…

As always…

His arms came around her, warm, tender, inviting. She kissed his hand and lay still, savoring their love, and their life together.

No words came to either of them for the longest time.

It was too beautiful. It was spring. They were nearing their first wedding anniversary, and both of them were content to hold one another.

But then McCoy shifted at last. He ran his hand over the growing contour of her stomach.

"You're sure our little McCoy is okay?"

She smiled. "Quite sure."

"Are you sure you don't know what it is?"

"Yes, I do. It's a baby," Julie said solemnly.

He made a face in the darkness. "Is it a boy or a girl?"

She shook her head. "I don't know." She did know. She was convinced it was a boy. But she wasn't going to tell McCoy. He was going to have to be there with her in the delivery room and find out for himself.

"Have you thought more about names?" he asked.

"Yes. If it's a boy, we should call him Hatfield. After all, he'll have McCoy for a last name. He can be Hatfield McCoy."

"Do you really want him growing up with that name?" McCoy rolled to his stomach and stared at her very seriously, as if warning her that their child could fight his way through school because of it. "And what if the baby is a girl?"

"Well, we'll just call her Hatfield, too," Julie told him, very seriously.

"Julie—"

"Then again, I'm fond of Robert. Not a Junior. I like Bobby. When he grows up, he can be a Robert if he wants. Or a McCoy."

He smiled, and kissed her. "Mrs. McCoy, you do know how to flatter your man."

"I try," she said serenely.

"Well, we do have about two months left to decide," he said, and then he sighed. "But we've got to get going now. Brenda expects us there by eight."

"And we really have to be there on time?" Julie asked.

She didn't like being late, but it was so nice here tonight. They were living in the town house in Washington most of the time—it was necessary for McCoy's work. And Julie loved roaming the various libraries and archives to find years-old scandals and murder cases for her stories.

But both of them loved to come home. Rusty could run around the mountains. They could both breathe again, really breathe.

They could go anywhere, she thought. Anywhere in the world. This would always be home to them both.

They didn't need to say it. They knew it.

"We can't be late. Brenda is having a surprise anniversary party for us, and if I know it, I'm sure that you do. Petty will be there, and Patty, and Timothy—and from what Brenda said, I think that those two are going to have an announcement of their own."

Julie started to bound up. It wasn't easy with her stomach in the way. McCoy gave her a hand. "Patty and Timothy!" she exclaimed.

There was a teasing light in McCoy's eyes. "You didn't guess?"

"Not for a moment. How wonderful!"

"Yes, I guess so. Anyway, we've got to get going." He pulled her to her feet. "Hop in that shower, ma'am. I'll be right behind you."

He was right behind her. She smiled as the water cascaded over her. Life was really so good. They still argued. Everyone argued.

But she was never afraid anymore. She knew that he was with her, and she knew how deeply he loved her.

Both of them had put to rest the ghosts of their pasts and found something precious and rare. Not many people were so blessed. She had never imagined the danger between them, but they had met it, and the reward had been more than life, it had been this wonderful love.

"Hurry," McCoy warned her later, pulling on his

jacket. "You know, I heard that it might get a little chilly tonight. I'll throw our coats in the car, too."

Julie patted powder on her nose. "No, bring the raincoats."

"Julie, there wasn't a cloud in the sky all day long—"

She turned around, smiling sweetly. "Please?"

And McCoy, watching his beautiful imp of a wife—who now, quite admittedly, did resemble a little blond blimp—had to smile.

And shrug.

And kiss her lightly on the lips.

"All right, my love, raincoats it is."

And later that night, when the last of the guests were leaving Brenda's, huddled against the drizzling raindrops, McCoy set his hand into the pitter-patter that was falling down. And he laughed.

His life was incredible. Wonderful, incredible.

And beyond that, it even had special advantages!

* * * * *

Dear Reader,

My father set the challenge of *Lightning Strikes* when I was still a child. My father, you see, is a CPA. And he's awfully tired of the cliché that a CPA is a nerd with a pocket protector and no sense of humor. My father was a big band singer in the forties, a great dancer, and the most romantic man on the planet. When my mom had a baby (which was often), he'd send her eleven roses with a card that said, "The twelfth rose is you."

So when Alex Thorne made his first appearance in a previous book, *Perchance to Dream*, I decided to make him a CPA. And the minute he showed up in print, I knew he'd be a great romance hero. Alex may be a logical man, but he's hardly dull. And, like a certain other CPA I know, he couldn't be called a cliché. He just isn't ready to meet a woman who lives by instinct rather than logic. Which means, of course, that I had to introduce him to Sarah Delaney, commune child, psychic and design artist. Having grown up with my own parents, I not only consider it a perfect match, but one that creates amazing sparks.

Kathleen Korbel

LIGHTNING STRIKES

Kathleen Korbel

To Dad
(who loves me best)
the man who taught me
that CPAs make great heroes

Chapter 1

At first he tried not to listen. After all, it was only a three-floor elevator ride.

"Oh, no," she was saying behind him, her voice as breathy as a breeze. "Not now. I don't have time to fall in love."

Alex couldn't figure out who she was talking to. He hadn't really paid attention to the other people who'd stepped from the cool stucco-and-tile lobby of the Sunset Building into the elevator. He hadn't noticed who'd gotten off on the second floor. His attention had been on the heat he'd left out on the Phoenix streets and the job that he was headed toward.

A favor for a friend was the only thing that would get him out of Colorado during the height of the hiking season. An independent look at the finances of Sunset Designs to settle the vague unease felt by its director. Alex hadn't been looking forward to the job. He hadn't been looking forward to two weeks in the heat or another round of hotel living.

And now, even before he got started, like an ill omen, he was momentarily stuck in an elevator with a woman who was setting up to confess all her innermost yearnings within inches of his left ear. A woman who sounded uncannily like his ex-wife.

"I don't want to marry him. He's not even my type."

Alex wished the other person would answer. He wished the light would flash for the third floor. He wasn't comfortable with this kind of thing. It was the aristocratic Southern accent, the kind that had once drifted from plantation house porches, that made the admission so disturbing, so personal.

This had to be the slowest elevator in the Western hemisphere.

"Oh, my God." Her voice sounded suddenly distressed.

Alex reacted instinctively. He turned around.

She was alone. Worse, she was looking directly at him. Even worse than that, she was blond. Blond and petite and vulnerable looking, with curls in sweet disarray and eyes the size of China-blue saucers. Alex noticed all that in the same instant he realized that she was going to reach out to touch him.

"Turn down the case," she pleaded, those devastating eyes treating him like an accident victim as she took hold of his arm.

It took a minute for the words to register. Alex was too distracted by her looks—the very looks that always got him into trouble. Blond and sweet and fragile and as dumb as a brick.

"Case?" he finally echoed a bit stupidly. Who had she been talking to back there? And who was it who wasn't her type?

Eagerly she nodded, her loose flaxen curls dancing on her shoulders. "Tell your captain that you can't do it. Tell him you'll take the next murder or robbery or whatever it is you investigate. If you do this one, you'll be hurt."

"Murder?" Alex demanded, the words finally sinking in. "Lady, what are you talking about?"

Pulling her hand away from him to brush at her hair, she bobbed her head again, her expression intent. "It's a little hard to explain," she said. "I know you police don't give much credence to things like this—"

"Police?" he said, trying to pull his gaze away from her petite hands only to find it firmly snared by all that China blue. "What makes you think I'm a policeman?" Alex noticed the bracelets that jangled on her arm, the voluminous teal silk trousers and paisley blouse.

"The case you're about to work on," she said, doing her best with that sweet honeysuckle accent to impress him with the gravity of the matter. "I know that it's going to be dangerous. Please don't take it."

Alex sighed and shook his head. "I appreciate the warning. I really do. But I think you have the wrong guy. I'm a CPA. And the only danger I'm going to be in is if I don't get up to the company who hired me to check their books."

She blinked a bit owlishly. "Oh. Then it doesn't make any sense, does it?"

"No," he admitted, doing his best to step by her. "It doesn't."

Her hand shot out again. Her face folded into sincerity. "Please, believe me. I'm not making this up."

Who could? he wanted to say. Instead he smiled. "Thank you. I appreciate the concern. Now, I have to be going."

And Alex Thorne, who had been an expert at disengaging himself from some pretty intense holds, peeled her fingers from his arm and turned for the door.

Not surprisingly, Sunset Designs took up most of the Sunset Building. A small company that had been founded no more than four years ago by two college roommates, it

provided graphic designs for industries as diverse as linens
to corporate logos. Alex had slept on Sunset Design sheets
and flown on an airline with a Sunset-created logo.

In researching the company before his trip, he'd discovered it to be well managed, imaginative and aggressive in
an oddly polite way. Most of its promotion had been accomplished by word of mouth. Customers glowed about
genius, innovation and unparalleled creativity. Detractors
were still trying to come up with a good reason to complain. The company's profit margin was good. It manufac-
tured some of its products in Phoenix and others in a plant
in Virginia, and it was turning over business in the comfortable seven-figure range each year.

And, much to the chagrin of the competition, its sights
were as limitless as they were diverse. No one knew quite
what market Sunset Design would choose to tap into next.
This, in a company whose president, cofounder and inspi-
rational leader still personally approved every job appli-
cant.

"Oh, my God. You're Alex Thorne!"

Alex had just stepped through the glass door into the
Sunset Design offices. He was still trying to get over a
purple-green-and-blue color scheme that shouldn't possibly have worked as well as it did. Suddenly, a tall, bright-
eyed receptionist was standing before him, smiling with
every tooth in her head.

Instinctively Alex smiled back. "I'm here to meet Ms.
Delaney," he said, a little surprised at the openmouthed
shock on the secretary's face. He still elicited this kind of
reception on occasion in the Denver area, although most
of his recognition came at bars with big-screen televisions.

She was still shaking her brunette head, not sure whether
to hold out a hand or straighten her hair. "I can't tell you
how many Sundays I spent watching you." She glowed
with sincere delight. "God, you were the best. Not to mention being possessor of the nicest set of buns in a huddle

in either league. I could spot you from the cheap seats at the ten-yard line.''

That seemed to quell her indecision. Giving her head another shake, she held out a well-manicured hand. ''I knew Sarah was expecting a Mr. Thorne. I didn't know it was you.''

''It's nice to meet you,'' Alex greeted her, long since comfortable with letting the rest slide. It had been three years since he'd last suited up and one year since the beer-commercial offers had stopped coming in. He was just as happy that way. Giving up football had been the hardest thing he'd ever done. And, in the long run, the most intelligent. Every time he had to ride up in elevators with talkative lunatics instead of being able to take the stairs, he remembered why.

''Kim,'' she offered, belatedly letting go. ''I'm the receptionist. I'll let Randolph know you're here.''

Randolph was the executive secretary, a serious, studious young man who seemed to harbor no fond memories of Alex and Sundays, which was just as well. Alex was ready to get to work.

''Let's see if we can raise her,'' Randolph was saying as he walked on around to the double doors at the end of the hallway, his attitude resembling a librarian headed for the rare-book section. ''She's been asking about you for two days.''

Alex couldn't help but wonder how Randolph anticipated raising his president. By radio? Ouija board? Well, Ellis had said that this would be an interesting job. So far, Alex couldn't say he was disappointed.

Then Randolph opened the door onto the president of Sunset Designs, and Alex understood what the secretary— and Ellis—had meant. The woman who rose to her feet behind the cluttered cherrywood desk was the same woman who had accosted him on the elevator. The blonde with the warnings and the sky-blue eyes.

Alex felt the groan escape before he could do anything about it.

Sarah couldn't believe it. She'd just made it into her office, the nausea still chasing her from the incident on the elevator. Randolph hadn't even brought in her tea yet. And suddenly she was hit with it again.

"You," she whispered, stunned, shaken, falling.

"Sarah?" Randolph asked, stepping in to intercede.

Sarah waved him off, knowing that Randolph understood. He wouldn't cosset if she didn't need it. Slowly Sarah steadied herself, wishing the dread would recede, an evil tide slipping away to leave her with sense and sunlight.

But he was here like a reprieve. A second chance to make matters right. To prevent him from making mistakes that could cost his life. All she had to do was convince him. All she ever had to do.

She couldn't believe that she hadn't anticipated this on the elevator. Oh, well, that was how it usually went.

"Are you Mr. Thorne?" she asked with a smile, making it around her desk to meet him.

"Alex Thorne," he answered, taking her hand as if expecting to find a joy buzzer nestled inside. "Ellis told me all about Sunset Design."

He didn't tell me about you, he was thinking. Sarah could see his thoughts on his face and couldn't hide her smile. She knew people like Alex Thorne, and they didn't accommodate themselves easily to the Sarah Delaneys of the world. She was going to have to explain everything very carefully. Looking way up at him, she thought she wouldn't mind at all.

"Ellis recommended you highly," Sarah offered, and then motioned to the chairs clustered over by the window. "Why don't we sit? Would you like some coffee or tea?"

"Coffee," Alex acquiesced. "Thanks."

"Coming right up," Randolph said, and swung out the door.

Sarah led Alex past her cluttered desk, video station and overflowing drawing board to where she'd set up an oasis of quiet in the office. A small island isolated by potted plants and focused on a picture window out to the mountains, it was here she conferred with clients, here she brainstormed with staff and here, often, she napped when she forgot to go home.

Shoving a nest of magazines and a peacock-blue afghan onto a third chair, she settled herself into the purple sectional sofa and curled her feet up beneath her. She'd forgotten to put her shoes back on when Alex had entered the room. She imagined they were still somewhere under her desk with the stuffed pig.

He was so big. Alex, that is. The pig was only big enough to rest her feet on.

Sarah couldn't get over it. She was five foot five in socks and only came up to his collarbone. He had shoulders that almost shut out the sunlight and arms that could probably crumple furniture. And yet his hands hadn't been all that big. They'd been gentle and warm, a friend's hands.

He had tawny looks, with sun-bleached hair and eyes the color of toffee. His face was squared and solid and lined with laughter. It was a face Sarah instinctively liked. A face that gentled his strong, athletic body, eyes that betrayed the intelligence that had brought him here.

She saw openness and logic and a certain hesitancy for the off-kilter world he'd stepped into in her building. A mathematician's personality. A left-brain mind-set. Orderly, logical, fiercely loyal.

Sarah liked him. She thought he was probably one of the ten best-looking men she'd ever sat close to. Still she wasn't sure that was enough to provoke what had happened in the elevator. But then, she'd never had such an instant reaction before. Maybe she'd read it wrong.

No matter, she had other things that needed talking about. The dread, the overwhelming tide of emotion, refused to go away. The sensations so washed her that they swept away her balance and blotted out the sunlight on this bright desert afternoon. These were the things she needed to tell Alex Thorne, and they were the things he wouldn't believe.

"You think I'm crazy," she said baldly.

He seemed a bit disconcerted by her frank appraisal. Sinking into the easy chair with unconscious grace, he settled into comfort without slouching a millimeter. "You...surprised me, Ms. Delaney."

Sarah couldn't help but laugh. "I surprise everyone," she admitted, taking an absent swipe at her hair. "A lot of times I surprise myself." It was always a shock, that sudden drop in the pit of her stomach, the noises in her head. The borders that shifted in her vision, tilting her world into suspension. She often wondered whether, if she could anticipate them, she could settle herself, curl upon the couch and offset the physical reaction the worst ones brought.

And the one in the elevator had been one of the worst. It had been one without pictures, without smells or sounds. It had been pure emotion, raw possibility and loss.

"Sarah," she said, lifting her head.

"Pardon?"

She saw him start, as if waiting her out, warily watching for surprise moves. Sarah smiled apologetically. "Sarah," she repeated with a small wave of her hand. "My name. I hate being called Ms. Delaney. It makes me sound like an English Lit teacher—or a character in a Tennessee Williams play." Without realizing it, she reached to pull back the afghan, bunching it into her lap. "I've changed my mind."

He looked even more confused. "About your name?"

Again she laughed, a light, airy sound. "No. I'm sorry. About hiring you. I changed my mind. It was probably a rash decision. That's what Randolph says, anyway."

"That's what you've waited two days to tell me?"

The people she knew trusted her. If Sarah told Randolph not to get on the elevator because it would hit bottom, he would take the stairs. If she told Ellis that there was something wrong with the home he wanted to buy, he'd pull his offer. But this man sitting before her didn't know her. He didn't know how to trust her advice yet. And Sarah truly didn't have the ability to think along his logical pathways to convince him. So, she'd decided that firing him from a potentially dangerous situation was the way to go.

"But why would it be dangerous?" she asked herself without realizing it. She couldn't seem to pull her gaze from the path of his golden eyes, caught by the pull of anticipation and danger. Torn by the ambivalence of the dilemma.

"You're talking about this…case," he said quietly, his brows gathered—trying to understand.

"I'm talking about my company," she answered, her own gaze still lost in her question, her hands worrying at the use-softened cover. "What could be here that would be dangerous to you?"

"Is that why you don't want me around?" Alex asked. "Because there's going to be some trouble?" He couldn't seem to take his eyes from where she was twisting the knitting in her hands.

Sarah noticed peripherally. She was trying to resurrect the feeling, searching for some kind of clue that would lead her. Maybe it was merely coincidental. Couldn't Mr. Thorne simply step out in front of a drunk driver or slip down the steps at the hotel? Something that wouldn't have happened if he'd stayed in Denver, but that wouldn't necessarily have anything to do with her company.

"I...I don't know," she finally admitted, still focused inward, her head tilted as if to better hear or see. There was no message in the turbulence, though, no guideposts. Only elemental energy. "I'd just rather not risk it."

Alex Thorne didn't appear very convinced. Leaning forward a little, he rested his elbows on his thighs and folded his hands. "Why don't you tell me the financial problem and let me decide?"

Before Sarah could get a chance to formulate an answer she'd been working on for almost two weeks now, Randolph knocked and entered. Sarah saw that his eyes were on her. His forehead was creased with worry, but he didn't say anything. That would be up to her. He'd been through this often enough that he knew how to take it.

"Connie says she'll be in as soon as she's finished," he told her, skirting the potted figs and schefflera to set down the ladened tray on the table between Sarah and Alex. Briefly his eyes strayed to Sarah's guest, and she could tell he wasn't comfortable.

"Thanks, Randolph," she said with a smile. Randolph hadn't been any happier about outside interference than anyone else at the company. "The new design for Intertell is over on the board somewhere. Could you take it down to production for me, please?"

Randolph took a few moments to unearth it. It wasn't until he had come up with the sheet of paper and carried it out that either Sarah or Alex moved.

"You'll like Connie," Sarah said, reaching to dump two or three teaspoons of sugar into her steaming mug. "She's the sensible half of the partnership. I'm afraid she's not any more fond of this idea than anybody else in the place, though."

"Which idea?" Alex asked, lifting his coffee without embellishment. "Me?"

Sarah grinned. "Do you believe in intuition, Mr. Thorne?"

He was about to take a sip of coffee. Her words stalled his cup halfway to his mouth. "Do you always converse like this?"

Sarah's grin broadened as she once again waved at her hair with her free hand. "If you mean, is it impossible for me to approach a problem head-on, yes. Connie says I think in circles. Ellis says I think in no pattern known to man. It makes sense to me, but explaining the process to anybody else is a bit futile."

"I see." He finally sampled his coffee and grimaced.

Sarah grimaced right back. "Oh, I should have warned you. Randolph's coffee is lethal." She caught a smile from him on that one.

"Which is why you drink tea?"

Sarah nodded with a sheepish grin. "I hired him for his organizational abilities, not his cooking talents."

Another grimace. "Obviously." Alex considered the mug a moment, obviously weighing his health against continued contact with the contents. He kept the cup in hand, but didn't return to it soon. "Why is he so thrilled to see me?"

"That goes back to the question of intuition."

Alex's glance sharpened a little. "His, yours or mine?"

"In this case," she said, holding very still, wanting him to understand, "mine."

Sarah saw him give a little shake of his head, almost as if he'd anticipated this. "Is that what all that on the elevator was about?"

"No," she answered more quietly than she realized. "That was...different. I'm talking your garden-variety feeling that something is more or less than it seems without obvious proof."

Alex nodded, finally ventured another sip and commented without words. "I've been called out a couple of times because a businessperson saw something wrong without realizing it. Is that why I'm here now?"

Sarah tried to hold on to his gaze, to impart comprehension to the honey brown of his eyes. Leaning forward, she balanced her mug on her knee and excluded the rest of the world from her consideration. "Something's wrong with my company, Mr. Thorne. I don't know what. I couldn't find out if I tried. I just don't have that kind of brain. I see the world in shapes and compositions, not in linear progression. What I see is that somehow there's a piece missing, and I can't find it. I'm not even sure which piece it is. I need somebody else to do it for me."

Frustration took hold of Alex. He shook his head and narrowed his eyes. "And nobody else agrees with you?"

Sarah felt the frustration infect her, too. Sighing, she straightened. "Everything looks fine. We've checked ourselves. But something…smells wrong, and I don't know how to search it out. As for the rest of the company, we're kind of a tight unit here. It's almost like a family. I hired everyone myself, and we've fought pretty hard to make it where we are today. To them, you're like an outsider moving into a small town. Of course they're going to be a little resentful."

"Besides the fact that just by hiring me you're accusing one of them of something illegal."

Sarah stiffened, hating what he said. Hating the fact that she'd even thought it herself. "I don't know that. I just know that something isn't right, and we need to fix it."

For the first time, Alex Thorne smiled, and Sarah saw how very rich it could be. There was a wealth of memory in his eyes, both pain and joy, and all of it escaped into his smiles. It didn't negate his size as much as complement it, showing an unexpected depth to the man, an endearing warmth.

"But if nobody's doing anything illegal," he said softly, leaning forward again, "how can it be dangerous?"

"Dangerous?"

Startled, Sarah whipped around. She hadn't even heard

Connie come in. Closing the door behind her, Connie bore down on them, the worry in Randolph's eyes magnified tenfold in hers.

"Randolph said you'd had a premonition. Are you all right? Is that what it was about?"

Sarah was on her feet almost as quickly as Alex. First she had to defuse Connie, then deal with Alex. And then deal with herself. She never even noticed that the afghan had fallen into a bright puddle at her feet or that a magazine fluttered after it.

"Premonition?" Alex echoed, eyes on Sarah, cup held as stiff as an alms request. "You have premonitions?"

"So," Connie greeted him, smiling, hand outstretched. "You're Alex Thorne. It's a pleasure to meet you. Ellis had quite a bit to say about you. I'm Connie Mason."

Sarah envied Connie her easy business manner. Connie was the company's public image: confident, self-assured, meticulously correct. She knew two hundred business associates by name and family history and could quote closing prices in seven countries. Sarah couldn't even find those countries on a map. Come to think of it, she'd be hard pressed to know where to find a map.

Alex shook Connie's hand and returned the greeting, his attention already taken. Sarah wished Connie hadn't spilled the beans so ungracefully. The fact of her "X-ray vision," as Ellis was wont to call it, was something that needed gentle introduction. Especially to someone like Alex, a man who occupied such a solid, unyielding place in the real world.

She could almost read his mind. Premonitions. Next it would be channelers and ancient Egyptian mystics. Usually that kind of attitude didn't bother Sarah. It was the way of the world, especially here in America where everything was built on tangibles. But with Alex, it did make a difference. It had made a difference since she'd looked up and seen his broad back taking up most of the light in the elevator. Since the moment she'd known.

"Are you all right?" Connie repeated, turning worried hazel eyes on Sarah.

"I'm fine," Sarah assured her with an airy wave of her restless hand. "Randolph has dosed me with tea, and Alex is listening to why I'm letting him go."

"Premonitions?" he asked again. "Is that what this is all about? Crystal balls?"

Sarah turned a disparaging smile on him. "You don't have to sound quite so stricken about it."

"You don't know?" Connie demanded of him. "Ellis didn't tell you?"

"All Ellis said was that this would be an interesting job. And that I'd find out when I got here."

Connie laughed. Sarah did not.

"Sarah doesn't just have premonitions," Connie said, weight shifted to one leg, arms crossed in amused challenge. "She has the sight. ESP. She's as fey as a Scottish witch. Has been ever since I've known her. Whatever she says is worth listening to. Now, then, hon," she said, turning her business eyes on Sarah. "What's this about danger?"

Sarah could do no more than shrug in the glare of Connie's immense pragmatism. "I have a...feeling that Alex could be hurt it he takes on this job, that's all."

"That's enough," Connie answered, straightening.

"Doesn't the victim have anything to say about it?" Alex demanded, his attention divided between the women.

Both Sarah and Connie turned on him. He was still looking at Sarah as if she were going to disappear into a puff of blue smoke.

"Your warning has been noted," he assured her, and then lowered his coffee cup in a gesture that said they should be getting down to business. "Now, why don't you show me the books?"

Sarah's heart sank. "No," she objected. "You can't."

"I can," Alex retorted. "And I will. Ellis is an investor in this company, and he wanted me here. *I* want me here."

"I don't," Sarah insisted, feeling the weight of guilt. Torn by already wanting him to stay when she knew he shouldn't.

"She's probably right," Connie suggested. "She's been known to be annoyingly accurate in the past."

"I've survived more than the CPA boards in my life," he said quietly. "I'll keep an eye out. Besides, if it's going to be dangerous for me—" Sarah wished his expression showed that he believed it "—it's probably going to be dangerous for the next guy coming in. And I'll guarantee you that he won't be able to handle himself as well as I can."

He seemed as implacable as a mountain, solid angles and strength. In that moment, as Sarah watched him, as his golden gaze warred in silence with her blue one, she believed him. She thought that nothing could bring down this tower of a man. And, unforgivably, she wavered.

"I don't want you to be hurt," she insisted, her voice already surrendering.

He smiled, and she saw those memories again, felt the amassed strength of trials she knew nothing about. Trials that had nothing to do with size and stamina.

"I'll give you a list of referrals," he promised. "They'll tell you how invincible I am."

"Connie," Sarah said, unable to look away from Alex. "Do you want to introduce Alex around?"

Connie let go with a dry laugh. "Kim spread the word half an hour ago. But I'll make it official."

Both Sarah and Alex nodded, each still challenging the other and unsure how to back down, each still curiously caught in the other's gaze.

"Thank you, Alex," Sarah finally said.

Alex gave a shrug of deprecation. "Thank me when I find something."

Sarah couldn't help but smile. "I'm not sure I'll be grateful then."

Alex was headed out the door behind Connie when he turned one last time. "By the way," he said, a hand on the door. "That premonition thing in the elevator."

Sarah stilled. "Yes."

"Who is it you don't want to marry?"

Sarah saw Connie stop and spin, and knew that behind her Randolph did the same. Even so, she couldn't help but grin. She kept her eyes on Alex, anticipating his reaction. "You."

His reaction was everything she could have hoped for.

Chapter 2

It was enough to give Alex a headache. Not only was he
stuck in a city with the mean temperature of a well-done
slab of beef, he was trapped with a sweet ditz of a blonde
who had premonitions.

Premonitions, for heaven's sakes. He couldn't have just
gotten another blond bimbo like his ex-wife, Barbi, whose
recommendations began and ended with her wide blue
eyes and drop-dead figure. He couldn't have found himself
corralled with a legitimate airhead. He had to trip over one
who managed to squeeze hocus-pocus in between those
cute little ears of hers.

The CPA's manual never covered this one.

"Does she do this all the time?" he finally asked, not
exactly sure how to deal with Sarah's last pronounce-
ment—or the delighted grin that had accompanied it.

Connie barely broke stride as she led him down the
hallway decorated in Georgia O'Keeffe prints. "Ever since
I've known her. And we became roomies in our junior year
of high school."

Alex could do no more than shake his head. "Takes some getting used to."

Connie just laughed as he led him down the hall. "Tell me about it. Within fifteen minutes of meeting Sarah for the first time, I'd been given instructions on how to best decorate my half of the room, the names of my proposed suitors for the year and a rather uncomfortable insight into my problem with James Joyce."

"You couldn't understand James Joyce?"

"I *hated* James Joyce. I thought it was because he refused to make sense. Sarah informed me that he made perfect sense, but not to somebody who insisted on thinking logically."

Alex couldn't help a grin as he nodded. "At least that explains my 'D' in Twentieth Century Lit. I'm just having trouble understanding how she gets along in the business world."

Connie shrugged offhandedly. "She doesn't. That's what I'm for. Sarah is like the bright, creative child who has a hundred wonderful ideas every ten minutes."

Alex looked over at the handsome woman who strode through her company like most of the women executives he'd known. Brisk, intelligent, composed. An interesting contrast to the gypsy fortune-teller he'd just left. "And you?"

Connie smiled, and it lit her face with soft whimsy. "I'm the mother who makes her go in one direction at a time."

The two headed on in unspoken agreement. Alex was still trying to piece together the different angles of Sarah he'd gotten so far. "Just how accurate is she with this sight of hers?"

Connie shrugged. "Sarah says nobody scores a hundred percent, but I've turned into a percentage player. I'd rather look foolish than really stupid."

"Does she still supervise your love life?"

Connie shook her head with a wry grin. "Nope. She won't try anymore. Says we're too close. That throws it all off somehow."

"What number prospective husband am I?"

They reached another glass door at the far end of the hall, which Connie held open before answering. "Oh, that. You're the first."

Alex tried his best not to come to a complete halt in the middle of the doorway. Three people looked up inside the modern black-white-and-red office where a mainframe computer whirred and clicked, and a small herd of PCs blinked in syncopation. Connie waited with the door held open, and Alex felt as though he'd just stepped through the looking glass.

Instead of commenting on the feeling of impending doom that was blossoming in his chest as Sarah had predicted, he took a look around at the jarringly spare room that reminded him of nothing so much as Early Hamburger Joint. Found at the end of the purple-and-green hallway, it pulled a person to a standstill. Alex took a minute to look over his shoulder at the lush colors behind.

Connie was already grinning. "Meet the computer staff. They have a very warped sense of decorating."

Alex couldn't help shaking his head. "What does the billing department look like, something out of *Bleak House*?"

"It's all Sarah's fault," Connie admitted brightly. "She encourages the lunatics to take over the asylum." When Alex looked up, she shrugged. "My office looks like a House of Denmark showroom."

He ended up just shaking his head. Suddenly he couldn't wait to get back to the hotel, where all the rooms looked alike. This place was straight out of a Rorschach test.

"Thaddeus," Connie was saying as she stepped into the bright room. "Unpeel yourself and come meet the company."

For the first time since he'd stumbled into this alternate universe, Alex could say he wasn't surprised. The person who came forward was the one he'd expected—an intense-looking young man with a wild thatch of red hair and a mad twinkle in his eye. He looked as if he'd been born with pocket protector in hand. The nineties equivalent of the born accountant. Alex had run to football to survive high school. Thaddeus had obviously escaped into computers.

Thaddeus didn't look terribly enthusiastic to see Alex. Even so, he left his two gaping associates to present himself.

"Thaddeus," Connie said with subtle relish, "this is Alex Thorne. He's going to check on the books for Sarah. Alex, this is our resident genius. Thaddeus is the real brains behind Sunset Designs."

Alex held out a hand that was taken in a slightly damp shake. "All computerized?" he asked.

"Right down to some of the designs," the programmer said with an edge to his voice. His handshake wasn't much, but he had a smile like a pirate's, brash and full of himself. A genius with a special spin on the world. Alex had met a few Thaddeuses in his career and had ended up liking the majority of them.

"Sarah's terrified of him," Connie announced with delight. "She says he's possessed by the spirit of Hal from *2001*."

"In that case," Alex assured them both, "we shouldn't have any problem at all. You design your own software?"

Thaddeus nodded, the hair that was shorn just shy of his ears flying. "Some. I adapt others. Come back after the tour and I'll explain it all."

The billing department was almost a disappointment. Cherry paneling and celery carpet and white walls. Alex met two key people there, Hector Yglesias, the supervisor, and Jill Bramson, who ran accounts receivable. Jill was a slightly overweight blonde with a bad dye job who chewed pencils, and Hector was a man "on his way up." Energy and hunger radiated from him in equal amounts as he pushed his wire-rimmed glasses back up his nose and extended a dry, firm hand.

"I saw you in the Superbowl," he greeted Alex. "The year you beat Pittsburgh. How do you get to accounting from there?"

Alex shrugged. "I was in accounting first. Football paid for college."

Neither of them wanted him here. Alex couldn't miss the chill that had spread out from the computer section and followed him through the billing department to the yellow design floor. Friendly poses and a lot of reserve. A goodly sprinkling of resentment. Just as Sarah had said, the sense that he was an interloper.

At least that was something with which Alex was comfortable. He'd investigated more than one company that really didn't want him there. He'd do this one the same way and then get the hell back to Denver.

"Where would you like to start?" Connie asked.

"Lunch," Sarah answered from the doorway.

Both of them turned in surprise. There in the hallway, still in stockinged feet, stood the president and cofounder of Sunset Designs.

"It's only eleven," Connie reminded her with the sound of someone who did this regularly.

Sarah grinned. "I know. I didn't eat breakfast, and I'm finished with the proposal for Endicott. I need a reward."

"What about Bartonberry?"

A shrug. "Safely shoved into the subconscious ooze. I expect a flash anytime soon."

Connie frowned. "They've been screaming all week."

Sarah gave an expansive shrug, sending her hair bobbing about her shoulders. "Nothing I can do. Everybody in design is backed up on the new lines and I can't seem to pull an idea out of thin air. I figured a timely break might help. Do a little food association,'' she said to Alex as if he'd understand, her smile as bright.

Still plagued by the feeling that if he turned around quickly enough he'd catch sight of the White Rabbit, Alex smiled back.

Connie instinctively checked her watch. ''I have an appointment with Susan over at Dallyripple in half an hour. Sorry, hon.''

Sarah turned her attention to Alex. Caught by her bright blue eyes, he had the unsettling feeling that she'd known all along exactly what Connie's plans were. ''Alex?''

''Might as well go on.'' Connie sighed. ''She'll drive you nuts until you do.''

Alex couldn't help but think that he'd been there less than two hours, and that he had work to do. And damn it if that bright, sweet smile wasn't sapping away all his hard-won common sense. He knew better. *Ellis* had known better when he insisted Alex come down here. Alex had no business getting involved on any level with women with breathy voices and guileless eyes. But here he was passing up a chance to tell her that what he really needed to do right now was dig into her books like she'd wanted him to. Instead he acquiesced with a smile.

''Lunch is fine.''

''Great,'' she sang with impulsive delight. ''I'll get my purse.''

''Don't forget your shoes,'' Connie suggested.

Startled, Sarah looked down. ''Oh, yeah,'' she murmured with another grin. ''That'd probably be a good idea, wouldn't it?''

Alex was building up for another groan when Connie shook her head. ''Don't let her get away from you, will you? She might not find her way back.''

It didn't take a fortune-teller to know what Alex Thorne was thinking. No matter how polite he tried to be, or how tolerant, Sarah knew that he was being just that. It should have frustrated her, especially since the more she saw him the more clearly she saw the future that trembled before the two of them like an apparition on the desert.

He had choices. Everybody had choices, and it was those choices that fashioned the shape of the future. Each decision made narrowed the path taken. What Sarah saw were the possibilities that lay beyond those choices. She saw what might be instead of what would be.

At least that was the way she'd always thought of it. When she'd first encountered Alex, she'd seen both joy and grief, a beginning and an end. She'd seen the major pathways he might take. Something he would do might lead him to her. The same thing, or something else, might lead him to harm. She couldn't say what, and more importantly, she couldn't tell him what decision to make. With his resolution to stay, both possibilities shimmied into better focus. The dread crept as close as the anticipation.

"I did this on purpose," she said as Alex held the front door open for her. He smelled like soap. Sarah liked that. She liked the economy of his movements, the way he tilted his head to listen to her, as if what she said were important, even though she knew how uncomfortable he was with her. "I wanted to give us a little time to talk, away from the office."

"To begin the courtship?"

Sarah made it a point to grimace. "I don't interpret 'em. I just have 'em. I'd be as happy as you if nothing came of that one." She wasn't being entirely honest. She'd never considered falling in love before. Well, not since Billy Peterson in junior year of college, anyway. But now that it was an option, she couldn't say she minded terribly. She could do worse than Alex Thorne.

"What are our chances of escaping the inevitable?" he

asked, his voice colored with a healthy dollop of skepticism.

They'd reached the rental car he'd left on the lot. After several false starts against the hot metal, Alex unlocked the doors and opened one for Sarah. She offered him a bright smile, wondering if he heard as much history in those words as she did. She wondered what the woman had been like who had hurt him.

"I don't know," she admitted, sliding into the seat. "I've never been in this situation before."

He joined her, but waited to introduce the key to the ignition. "Oh, I have," he announced with dry humor. "My ex-wife had visions, too."

Sarah brightened. "She did?"

He scowled. "Yeah. She saw dollar signs over my head and camera lights in her future. That was her idea of Kismet."

Sarah couldn't help a knowing grin. "And you fought her off until you were too weak to struggle anymore."

She was glad to see that Alex Thorne could take a little heat. Tilting his head slightly, he offered her a particularly dry smile. "You *do* have ESP," he said, and finally turned on the ignition. "Where are we going?"

At that, Sarah blinked. "Uh, my house."

She should have anticipated this. Alex was having enough trouble getting used to her as it was. The last thing Sarah needed at this point was to betray the full extent of her limitations. If she hadn't been so distracted by the premonition, by the Bartonberry account that lay open on her desk like an unsolved homicide, by the surprising warmth of Alex's eyes and the way his hand felt wrapped around hers, she probably would have had the problem covered.

No, she wouldn't. She would have jumped to her feet just as quickly, the impulse propelling her instead of logic, like always.

Alex turned with a particularly pained expression on his

face and Sarah bluffed. "I'd rather not discuss the problems of my company in public," she said. "We can get some lunch delivered and sit out by the pool. Now, turn onto Bell, and I'll direct you from there."

"Does this have to do with the wedding-in-the-chapel part of the premonition," Alex asked dryly, "or the villain-lurking-in-the-bushes part?"

"It has to do with business," she insisted, unable to quite face those knowing eyes.

"Sarah, I don't want to insult you—"

"You're pretty gun-shy," she accused, head up, eyes challenging as she tried to deflect him. "Aren't you?"

"I'm *very* gun-shy," he admitted, refusing to be deflected. "But that doesn't have anything to do with why I don't like this idea."

Finally Sarah sighed, slumping back into the seat. "I don't know how to get to anywhere else," she admitted.

Alex blinked. "You're kidding."

Sarah shot him her first glare. "Some people have a bad sense of direction. I have no sense of direction at all. Are you happy?"

But Alex persisted. "How long have you lived in Phoenix?"

She shrugged. "Two years." He probably knew every street name in Denver and where they intersected.

"How do you shop?"

Sarah groaned. This was one area of her capabilities— or lack thereof—that had always bothered her. In the glaring light of Alex's competency, it frustrated her anew. "I walk. Now, can we please go?"

Alex wasn't finished shaking his head. "I'll pick the place," he decided. "I can usually find my way around."

"Of course you can."

That's why the gods had picked Alex for her, she thought with sudden, inexplicable frustration. He was a male Connie, all common sense and logic. It was a darn good thing he had such beautiful eyes, such a nice set of shoulders, such a surprising smile. It might offset that insurmountable pragmatism of his.

"I don't suppose you're left-handed," she tried.

"Sorry."

She sighed. "I didn't think so."

The gods weren't giving her a soul mate. They were giving her a new baby-sitter.

Alex turned the car left onto Bell, and Sarah was immediately lost.

Alex felt like one of the moon walkers. He'd just landed in a completely alien atmosphere, and he didn't know which way to step first. There were so many questions he wanted to ask Sarah. Not just about the company, but about her, about Connie, and about Ellis, who never mentioned the founder of Sunset Designs without a certain amount of awe in his voice.

Before him, Alex saw a gamine with a brain that seemed incapable of any recognized pattern of thought, a grown woman who got lost in her own neighborhood and yet convinced a gathering of very intelligent people that she could foray into the future and bring back treasures.

It wasn't that Alex didn't believe in intuition. He'd shared a pretty surprising communication with his sister over the years, a sixth sense of danger or excitement or pain that had united the two of them more than with the rest of his family. But that communication had been honed out of trouble. He and Lindsay had suffered together; they had forged their bond out of long years of love and struggle. Alex considered it a natural outcome of their special relationship.

He really didn't know how to take this capricious lightning that struck from the woman across the table. Could she really have a gift so startling? Did it have the right to exist without effort, without the years of sharing that became the currency exchanged for such an ability?

Lindsay would say yes. Lindsay, though, was a psychologist, a student of the vagaries of the mind. The unknown excited her. She lived for possibility. Alex was a craftsman, stolidly plying his trade, his brain a tool best suited to a well-defined task. He wasn't sure he could allow Sarah her magic. CPAs weren't a breed of animal that found comfort in the great unknown.

But he couldn't say he disdained her intent. He'd known her for two hours and could already feel the tendrils of her bright, winsome charm wrapping around him. He didn't really want to believe her, but he wanted her to believe in herself.

"What do you think of the company?" Sarah asked between bites of enchilada.

Alex wanted to smile at her. She had an appetite like a lumberjack. All that prophesying must tax a woman's strength. He took the time to swallow his first mouthful of *fajita* before answering. Around them, the cool white-tile restaurant was beginning to fill up. Laughter echoed from the bar, and a party of vacationers with New York accents took over the next table.

"I've only had two hours so far to look at it," Alex reminded her.

Sarah flashed him an unrepentant smile. "That's not my fault," she said. "I was going to try and talk to you last night at the hotel. I even left a message, but you didn't answer."

"I didn't get in until late," he retorted. "But if you're psychic, you should have known that."

She set her fork down, obviously well used to the challenge. "Your sister's overdue for her first baby and went into false labor. You stayed until she went home from the hospital. I know."

Alex actually paused, snagged by her trick. Then he saw the grin peek through and shook his head. "I told Ellis."

His reward was another of those quicksilver smiles. "How is she?"

"Frustrated. I'm glad I'm not her husband. Lindsay can be a real bear when she wants to."

"I'm sure when you're pregnant someday, you'll understand what she's going through," Sarah baited him.

Alex had the good grace to grin. "This is the payback. She was unmerciful when I was recovering from my last football season. Something about, I was around for the fun, the least I could do was pay the price."

"Which was what you said to her."

He liked the playful sparkle in her eyes. "Something like that."

Alex expected another comment from her on the subject, something akin to Lindsay's outrage at his very male goading. But when Sarah returned her attention to him after polishing off her rice and beans, she surprised him again.

"Why football?" she asked.

Alex lifted an eyebrow. At his size, that had never been tops on any list of questions he'd been asked. It had usually been the other way around, like Hector's question. Why accounting?

"Why not?" he countered, distracted by the way she tilted her head when she concentrated, consumed by the dreamy soft blue of her eyes.

She always looked as if her mind were absorbed by more than she was saying, as if inner voices diverted her. It should have warned him away. Instead it intrigued him. Alex was never going to get anything done on this job if he stayed around her. Already he was wondering what it would be like to kiss her.

"You're basically a left-brain person," she said. "Very logical, practical. You like computers, don't you?"

Alex tried to concentrate on the question. The slightly

distasteful frown Sarah proffered betrayed her own feelings on the subject. Alex grinned in return. "Some of my best friends are computers," he said.

That was actually an accusation Lindsay had made once when she'd tried to unravel a program he'd been teaching her. Since that had been scant months after the Barbi debacle, he'd seen no reason to disagree with her. Now, three years later, he still didn't.

Computers, no matter how stupid, how exacting, how frustrating, always gave back just what they got, no more, no less. They never let prejudices or greed or infatuation or even hormones get in their way. Not like people. You never knew what you were going to get from people—if you got anything at all.

Especially women, he thought, looking at the woman who should have reminded him so much of the late, unlamented Barbi.

Sarah nodded, as if he'd been perfectly serious. "I'd think that with your education and talents, you'd be more inclined to avoid sports. Especially something as punishing as football." Zeroing in on him with those sweet, wide eyes of hers, she frowned. "Is it really worth that kind of sacrifice?"

Alex directed his attention to his lunch when he answered. It was a question he'd often been asked, one he'd considered in a hundred different ways both before and since his retirement. Was it worth the aching knees and accumulated hospital time? The Mondays lost to whirlpools and physical therapists and the rest of his life squeezed into the spring months until football passed him by? Was it worth the years it had taken to move beyond retirement?

Alex felt Sarah's eyes on him, like warm light. Interested, concerned, empathetic when she shouldn't have known how to be. He knew he'd give her the same answer he always gave. And yet he was surprised this time at the sudden stab of loss her question incited.

For a moment those years rose in him like blood from a newly opened wound, bright and hot and life-giving even as they drained away. Impressions of friends and fans, of road trips and games and thundering crowds, of biting winter afternoons and the endless repetition of practices. And in that moment he suffered again the cost of walking away.

"It was for me," he said as he always did, bare fact always an easy shield behind which to hide. But when he lifted his eyes to her, ready to push the memories back, he was silenced by the wonder in her eyes. The pain. She understood, and he hadn't said a word.

She saw it. In a bright flash, almost like film playing at fast forward, Sarah saw the camaraderie, the exertion, the struggle...the pain. She saw the exultation of achievement echoing from an empty stadium. Sarah saw a man with the strength to fight for what he wanted and the courage to walk away.

More than a baby-sitter, she thought. Someone who has had it all and given it away with grace. Someone with a passion buried deep beneath the calluses he's formed. A harsh ache ignited in her chest for the pain that had escaped him. An awe bloomed for his determination.

"Ellis wasn't as gracious about quitting," she said.

Alex shrugged, returning his attention to his *fajita*. "Ellis didn't have as much to go back to."

Sarah nodded. Ellis, the rising mercurial black star of Penn Tech. The brightest new rookie, and the sudden has-been when his leg was broken in the first game of his third season in the pros. Ellis, who came from the ghetto, became no more than an illiterate ex-football player with no skills and fewer prospects.

"How did you meet Ellis?" Alex asked. "He never told me."

Sarah smiled, her food temporarily forgotten for the memories. "When he won his suit with Penn Tech for having graduated an illiterate college senior, he took the money and went to University of Virginia. He was a thirty-year-old freshman when Connie and I started. And he still couldn't read. He ended up sleeping in our bathtub a lot. He sneaked in there when cramming got too rough and just fell asleep. I never saw anything like it."

Alex chuckled. "Yeah, he slept in my tub a lot, too. Usually when he was really hung over. He said that it had been the coolest place back home in Bed-Stuy, and that he'd just gotten used to escaping there."

Alex leaned into his chair then, eyes assessing and controlled, the moment of betrayed pain neatly tucked away. He was again in control, buttoned down and purposeful. "And when you got out, Ellis invested in Sunset Designs," he said.

Sarah set down her own cutlery, already missing the other Alex, knowing that he wouldn't allow himself back out yet. "It's Ellis's law school money. It's also our way of having some street smarts on this team. Neither Connie nor I excel in the cutthroat school of business acumen."

It had been a standing joke among the three of them. Sarah had the insight, Connie the common sense and Ellis the passion. He'd been the one who'd pushed Sunset into reality.

Ellis had always had a need to seek, an unquenchable hunger for more that fed his rage as well as his enthusiasm. After he'd lost football, his rage had been impressive. Football, he'd said, had been his release. His catharsis. There were still times when Sarah thought he hadn't found a suitable substitute.

"What do you do with it all?" she asked.

Alex frowned. "With what?"

Sarah waved a hand. "All that…emotion. The passion of the sport. Ellis talked for hours about the incredible highs, the surges of energy, the...the lust for what he did. What do you do with that now?''

Alex shook his head a little. ''You did it again.''

Sarah lifted an eyebrow. ''You'll get used to it. How *do* you deal without that kind of release?''

His smile was dry. ''I live vicariously through others.''

''I'm not sure Ellis would agree with you.''

''I *know* he wouldn't.''

Passion, she thought, buried deep and rigorously controlled. Peeking out in the guise of consternation, betrayed in little frowns and the softening of those honey-brown eyes. Slipping through when he wasn't watching.

It was there, she realized, caught beneath layers of pragmatism, waiting to be mined, waiting to be tapped like a hive until it flowed over her like sweet, hot nectar. Until it surprised her, overwhelmed her.

Sarah couldn't help smiling with delight at the thought of well-composed Alex wild and abandoned. And all for her. The taste of honey was already sweet on her tongue.

Honey. Hives. Pollination.

Bees.

''That's it!'' she cried, suddenly scooping up her purse.

Alex looked around. ''What's it?'' he asked.

''The Bartonberry logo. A stylized bee. Why didn't I think of it? Do you have a pen?''

She was flattening out her napkin, the shape already formed in her mind. When Alex handed over a gold pen, she arced lines in the center of the paper, suddenly oblivious to Alex's bemused frown. She'd been struggling with this idea for a week, and one lunch with Alex had provided it.

''We have to get back,'' she said, her eyes on her work as she scribbled away.

''I thought you wanted to talk about the company,'' Alex objected.

Sarah flashed him a quick grin. ''Well, I guess you'll

have to come by my house after all. I have to get this down to design. We're a week behind on it as it is."

She didn't even see Alex pull out his wallet and cover the check. Sarah was involved with intersecting semicircles and complementary colors, already seeing the logo on natural-food packages all across America.

"That's it," she announced with finality as she clicked the pen closed. The napkin disappeared into her purse and would have been followed by the pen if Alex hadn't reached over and gently plucked it out of her fingers.

"From my sister," he said. "She'd kill me if I lost it."

"Sorry," Sarah apologized brightly, a feeling of well-being suffusing her. Everything would work out. Alex would find the mistake, Bartonberry would love the design, and the company would settle back into regular chaos. For the minute she didn't have to even think far enough ahead to consider marriage or disaster. "Are you ready to go?"

Alex was already on his feet. "Don't forget your shoes."

Surprised, Sarah looked down. She'd instinctively slipped them off and wound her feet together, the usual position for creation in her office. With a guilty grin, she retrieved her shoes and followed Alex.

The heat struck them the minute they walked out the door. The sun was blinding, the streets shimmering and the low buildings in the neighborhood crouching beneath the stunted trees for shade. Sarah barely noticed. She was still flushed with her inspiration.

"Thank you, Alex," she said when they got to the car.

He turned without opening the door. "For what?"

Sarah blinked up at him. "I got the idea for the logo from you. And you can't imagine how hard I've been trying to come up with something."

Alex didn't seem quite sure how to react. Giving his head another one of those little shakes, he nevertheless smiled. "You're welcome," he said. "For whatever I did."

She saw that he still didn't understand. He didn't even realize how important this moment was to her. Sarah couldn't think how to explain it any better, so she showed him. Stretching up on her toes, she wrapped her arms around his neck and kissed him.

Chapter 3

"Ellis, what did I ever do to you to deserve this?"

Alex wasn't in the least appeased when he heard Ellis's chuckle rumble over the long-distance wire.

"You tellin' me you don't appreciate my good friend Missus Wizard?" the ex-wide receiver demanded.

"I'm saying that you could have warned me before shoving me headlong into *The Twilight Zone*." That wasn't what was really bothering Alex, but he wasn't about to admit it to his gloating friend, no matter how many hundreds of miles away he was. "I bet you knew all about those premonitions she says she has."

The new round of laughter neatly answered his question. "Boy, I always said you was the marryin' kind. If you live long enough, anyway."

Alex took to rubbing his eyes. The light was soft in his suite, the furniture muted Santa Fe pastels, the only sounds he heard were those invading from the pool outside his window. Still, it all seemed too loud and irritating. And Sarah had made him promise to come over for dinner.

"Do you know the worst part?" he demanded. "After hearing all that, *I* was the one who insisted on staying. I *still* can't figure out how that happened."

Ellis made commiserating noises. "Yeah, Sarah can do that to you."

"You might have warned me that your good friend was a little different," he accused.

"Different?" Ellis demanded with too much humor. "What's so different about her?"

"Oh, that's right," Alex retorted. "I'm talking to a man who blessed his football with chicken skins. You wouldn't recognize different if it fell on you."

"Don' be makin' fun of my mama, Alex. She *gave* me those skins."

Ellis's mother was a bona fide Haitian priestess. Alex wasn't sure whether she practiced one of the religions unique to the Caribbean or had just made up one that appealed to the same sense of theatrics her son had inherited.

"I bet your mama likes Sarah."

"You kiddin'? They're soul mates."

"Well, I'm not. That entire place is just a little too Zen for my tastes. I can't wait until my partner finds out I'm down here investigating a 'premonition.' He'll have me committed."

"What'd you tell me when I had to quit football? Broaden your horizons, you said. There's more out there than pigskins and cheerleaders. Well, that's what I'm tellin' you. Do you some good."

Alex growled. "It's giving me a headache. It's bad enough working a job like this when everybody talks the same language. I have people there I'm not even sure are from the same *universe*."

"Don't hurt her. She's my friend." This time, Alex heard the concern escape into his friend's voice. Hurt her? Alex hadn't even managed to anticipate that far. He couldn't seem to drag himself past the immediacy of her, the stunning sensuality of her spontaneity.

Alex thought of the kiss they'd shared. She'd surprised him with it, impulsively wrapping herself around him as if it had been the most natural thing in the world. Kissing him with no more intention than gratitude and celebration.

Somewhere in that kiss his intentions had changed. His surprise had given way to pleasure, and pleasure had evaporated into hunger. Alex had found himself enfolding her with arms that ached. He'd curled impatient fingers into the silk of her hair and devoured the taste of her lips.

Honey. He could swear he had tasted honey on her. Her scent lingered on his clothes, a light aroma that reminded him of summer and mornings. He could still feel her vibrant body against his chest, her breasts straining and soft. And, just as he had out on that broiling parking lot where only a moment before he'd been suffering no more than the heat, Alex was struck with the harsh ache of sudden desire.

Within seconds, the room that had been so cool and quiet had become an oven, and Alex needed to move.

"The only thing I'm going to do," he grated out, knowing already that he was lying, "is check the company books and get myself back to Denver."

"Just make sure to watch your back," Ellis warned.

"Goodbye, Ellis."

"Alex? I mean it."

"So do I. I'll call when I have news." Without waiting for Ellis to reply, Alex hung up.

A swim. He needed a swim.

Jumping to his feet, Alex stripped out of his work clothes. Suit pants and tailored shirt hit the carpet and, for once, stayed there. He pulled on his swimming gear and doused himself in a cold shower until it was safe to be seen outside.

And then he stalked out to the pool and dove in.

People on deck chairs turned when they saw him coming. A few flinched from the scowl on the powerful features, and the tight set of the sleek muscles. One or two of the women took appreciative breaths and strolled over to intercept him when he surfaced.

But Alex hadn't come to socialize. He'd come to work off the sight of Sarah's eyes when she'd backed away from that kiss. The confusion, the vulnerable yearning that had softened them to the color of morning clouds. The languor of desire that widened the pupils and pulled him unforgivably close to kissing her again.

"Bartonberry," she whispered distractedly.

"Bartonberry," he'd answered, and the moment had been broken.

But it returned now, her startled face materializing beyond closed eyes, her erratic breathing sounding now to him like the slap of water as he cut through it.

Hormones. That's all it was. It was all it had been with Barbi, a raging case of infantile star ego exacerbated by the predilection for females of the blond persuasion. He'd been horny and he'd been full of himself and he'd fallen like a ton of bricks for the woman with the biggest eyes and the bounciest assets.

Alex's fingertips touched the side of the pool for the fourth time, and he flipped into a turn and headed the other way. He didn't see the heads above the water, following his progress like the sirens watching unwary sailors.

It wasn't ego this time. He'd learned that lesson the hard way, through courts and cameras and abstinence in the face of fame. But he'd been putting most of his energy into the business in the past few years—and Sarah had nailed it on the head. He liked computers. He trusted computers. Computers didn't have eyes the color of morning and lips that begged for kissing.

Computers didn't seduce you with their joy.

Alex dated nothing but businesswomen in Denver.

Savvy, ambitious, intelligent women who enjoyed the outdoors and fit comfortably into social and official occasions. He'd been looking for a while now for a wife, a partner, a companion to share his life. He'd met each woman with a kind of anticipation.

Not one of them had elicited this kind of anxiety.

Not one of them had been a blonde with big blue eyes who was everything Alex did *not* want in a wife.

Not one of them had looked at him the way Sarah had when he'd talked about football, as if she'd walked off the field on the last day right alongside him.

Lindsay would probably have something to say about this. Maybe when he got home, after Lindsay had the baby and felt better, he might sit down and talk to her. He might ask her what this weakness of his was, and how to avoid it in the future.

But right now, he had to work it off or screw up the job he'd come to do.

It took almost an hour to dissipate the ache. Alex could feel his shoulders tighten and his knees start to tremble with the exertion. A pleasant lethargy began to invade his body. Pulling himself up to the edge of the pool, he swept his hair back with both hands and vaulted out. He didn't see the gazes follow him with growing disappointment as he bent to scoop up his towel and walk back to his room.

He heard the phone ringing even before he reached the door.

"Hello?"

"Thirty-five!"

Alex frowned. "Excuse me?" Then he recognized the voice.

"It rang thirty-five times," Sarah said. "I was getting worried. Are you all right?"

"I'm fine, Sarah. I was swimming."

The silence on her end of the line was a taut one. Alex realized that she really had been worried.

"Oh," she almost whispered. "I'm...sorry...."

"Another premonition?" he asked, settling onto the bed without thinking of the wet suit.

"No," she said quickly. "Nothing new. It's just that I haven't really paid attention to it much today. What with everything..."

Alex understood perfectly. He'd been dealing with "everything" himself. "I'm fine," he repeated, wondering if he was going to have to make a habit out of that statement. "I'll be over in—" quickly he scanned the clock "—a half hour. Okay?"

She didn't answer him right away. Alex found himself leaning into the phone a little, wanting to hear her assurances.

"Sarah?"

"I'm sorry, Alex. I don't mean to hover. It's just a big responsibility...oh, well. Get changed before you ruin the bedspread."

Alex looked down, startled. "You—"

"Heard the bedsprings," she answered. "I'll see you in a few minutes."

What surprised Alex was that he wasn't really surprised. He was grinning—and he was looking forward to seeing what kind of gypsy caravan Sarah Delaney lived in.

Fruitcakes. He'd definitely developed a taste for fruitcakes. Shaking his head one last time, he got to his feet and headed for the shower.

"I told you he'd be there," Connie was saying.

"I know," Sarah sighed, settling into her favorite wing chair. Her feet—shoeless—were curled up beneath her, and she had a glass of iced tea in her hand. Outside her windows, her garden sagged from the heat. Not a leaf rustled. To the north the sky was sketched with naked mountains. The evening was stark in its golden light, the setting sun magnifying the desert colors, the harsh desert lines, wilting the greens and hardening the reds. Sarah closed her eyes against it and pressed the glass to her forehead to ease the ache.

"I don't know what to do, Connie," she said, hanging on to her friend's voice like a lifeline. "I'm not handling it right and I can't seem to…I don't know."

"You've said it yourself," Connie reminded her. "You're never a hundred percent right. Let's say you're having an off day here."

"I wish you were right," she said. "This is so hard. Premonitions feel bad enough without kissing interfering."

There was a pause as Connie digested Sarah's words. "It affected you that much?"

Sarah had to smile. Images tumbled. Sensations skittered along nerve endings. Her chest swelled with the intimate memory. Her belly tightened.

Connie needed no more than the suspicious silence for her answer. "I'm still not sure that your keeping such a close eye on him's going to save him from anything."

Sarah tested that thought and came away unconvinced. There wasn't a reason to explain her need to keep Alex close—not one she could successfully discuss with the pragmatic Connie, anyway. She just understood that, even only knowing Alex no more than a few hours, she already wouldn't forgive herself if something happened to him and she could have somehow prevented it.

She'd lied to him. Well, she'd fudged a little. She'd said there had been no new premonition. If it all happened that cleanly, she could have better explained. But the truth was, since that kiss in the parking lot, she'd felt a greater sense of urgency—and a growing impatience.

But for *what* she didn't know. It wasn't as easy as saying, "Watch out for that falling tree branch, Alex." It was more as if the air were disturbed around her, charged like just before a lightning strike. The kiss had stirred it up further. It had agitated the delicate balance until the possibilities roiled in her like acid—like an ulcer on an empty stomach.

She was anxious to keep Alex close to her, but she couldn't tell whether it was to further a destined relationship or prevent a potential disaster.

Or it could have simply been because she liked the way he kissed.

It was getting all too complicated. And it was getting in the way of the reason she'd asked Alex to come down in the first place.

"Earth to Sarah."

Snapping to attention, Sarah took tighter hold of the receiver. "I'm sorry, Connie. I'm trying to hammer this all out."

"Don't try," her friend suggested. "Logic isn't exactly your long suit. Just go with the flow, like you always do. *Which* reminds me, what provoked the Bartonberry logo? Design is in ecstasy."

"Lust."

Connie didn't so much as hesitate. "Uh-huh. Well, I have to get ready for my own date here. Maybe I can come up with a new bed sheet or something."

Sarah chuckled. "You told me yourself that Peter wasn't that kind of guy."

"Well," Connie retorted. "I figure if a CPA can inspire creativity, a computer system salesman should, too."

Sarah smiled. It was good to hear that kind of talk from Connie—from both of them. They'd put so much into Sunset that neither had had much chance for outside interests. Neither had had the time or energy. Sarah was glad they were moving past that. She wanted Connie to have a full life.

It would have been nice, though, to know this time whether Peter was the one to provide it. Sarah hadn't paid enough attention when he'd courted the company as a representative from Landyne Systems. Now that Connie had begun to see him away from business, Sarah would have to reassess. Maybe she'd have a chance when she saw Peter again.

"Have a good time," Sarah said. "I'll see you tomorrow."

"You, too, hon. Tell Alex 'hi' for me. And tell him to watch out for himself."

"He's a good man," Sarah said. "Isn't he?"

"Yeah," her friend answered. "He's a good man. I hope he's a smart man, too. See you."

Sarah sat for a long time without moving, the phone receiver still in her hand, the tinny beeping lost to her. She didn't know what to do. She knew what she *wanted* to do, but that might not have anything to do with what she *should* do. She wanted to ease into love with Alex just like sliding into the comfort of the whirlpool on her patio, steeping in it until it drove everything from her mind. But if she did that, the rest would become muddied. The clarity that enabled her to see farther than most people saw would dim, just as it had with whatever was happening with her company.

The light outside changed to mauve. The garden rustled, and somewhere a coyote anticipated the moon. Inside Sarah's house only the grandfather clock in the front hallway spoke, counting out the marching seconds with comforting familiarity. Linear progression, logical movement. A straight line. Except that Einstein didn't think time moved in a straight line. Sarah felt her life curling back in on her, bending and warping with the whims of whatever it was that held her sway. The past skidded close, and the future leaned back until it almost touched. And Sarah was caught in the middle, not knowing how to keep both of them in their places without sacrificing the insight she'd gained over the years.

How did she move in a logical progression when the next step she took could cost Alex his life? How did she act toward him so to settle the future into place? And in the end, did it matter what she did? Did she really have a choice? Or was she doomed to fall in love with Alex Thorne only to lose him?

Without thinking, Sarah lifted her forefinger to her lips, as if she could still feel the imprint of Alex's mouth there. As if she could rub the scent and taste of him onto her finger and then observe it.

It had been a long time since she'd become lost in a kiss. It had been a long time since she'd even wanted to. But out in that parking lot, where the asphalt sent the temperature soaring, her own temperature had risen, too. Her cheeks had flushed. She wouldn't have been surprised if her nose had flushed, as well. She'd stepped away from him, stunned and shaken and suddenly alive. And the only thing she could remember—except for the sweet ache that still refused to recede—was that all she'd wanted was more.

Out in the hallway, a bell chimed. Her finger still playing against her lower lip, Sarah didn't hear. She faced the fireplace, but she saw the crimson oleander that had edged the restaurant lot. She heard the stagger of her own heart. She smelled the clean soap of Alex's hands.

The doorbell chimed twice. Sarah looked up, then she jumped to her feet. It didn't occur to her to hang up her phone. By the time she was halfway across the floor, she'd forgotten she'd even been on it.

Alex took her breath away all over again. Sarah couldn't help but smile. "Welcome to Castle Gonzo, as Ellis calls it," she greeted him, thinking that he looked very handsome in his blue oxford-cloth shirt and khaki chinos.

Alex stepped inside and came to a halt, his eyes widening at the sight. "This is—"

"Not really what you'd expect," Sarah answered with a nod as she turned to follow his gaze. "I know."

Of all the decors she could have chosen, Sarah guessed

this was the last one her friends would have anticipated. Connie still looked for beads and Jimi Hendrix posters, but then Connie knew Sarah's parents. Ellis had said he wanted postmodern, and Randolph had begged for more color. But Sarah had known from the time she was ten what her house would look like, and it did.

"Sarah," Alex said with some awe as he stepped further into the living room where Oriental carpets covered dark hardwood floors. "Did anybody tell you that this is Phoenix?"

Right alongside him so she could get a whiff of that crisp scent of his, Sarah grinned. "Connie says that I'm the only person nuts enough to put an English country house in the desert."

Alex didn't look as if he totally disagreed. He couldn't seem to get over the whitewashed walls, exposed beams and tile fireplace. And that didn't even take into account the chintz furniture coverings and the French doors that led into Sarah's struggling garden.

To Sarah it seemed cooler this way, the dark tile and wood floors soothing after the harsh glare of the sun. She liked the flowers, the Regency period furniture, and the framed Pre-Raphaelite prints on the walls. To her it was peaceful, settled, comfortable. Nothing jarred in her house. Nothing surprised, and that was the way Sarah liked it.

"My mother says that I'm finally rebelling," she said.

"Against what?" Alex demanded, still looking around. "The circus?"

Sarah watched him as she answered, "The commune."

She loved to see the way she impacted on him. He turned on her and squinted a little as if to verify her statement, tilting his head as if to ease its way.

"You lived on a commune."

Sarah nodded. "Until I was sixteen. My parents were the original hippies—I, their little flower child. Our first family vacation was to Woodstock. Would you like a drink?"

"Oh, yes."

"You might want to sit down, too," she suggested diffidently.

He looked at the sofa as if expecting a rabbit to pop out. Even so, he eased himself down.

"I always wondered what happened to all the old commune people," he marveled, almost to himself as he settled back, eyes still to the traditional decor. "I guess they're forming design companies in the Southwest."

"Not all of us," Sarah said, and headed into her kitchen. "Beer or bourbon?"

"Beer. Where are your parents?" he asked.

"John's in Costa Rica building dams for the Indians," she said, reaching over to flip on the range before she burrowed into her refrigerator in search of Alex's beer. She found it instead in the freezer section, but evidently she hadn't put it there too long ago, because it hadn't solidified yet. "Blue is—let's see—last I heard she was in an ashram in Nepal. Then she goes back to Bangladesh."

"Blue?" he asked from the other room. "Your mother's name is Blue?"

"Not exactly June Cleaver," Sarah acknowledged, shoving the freezer door closed before anything fell out. "But she taught me a lot."

"Yeah," she thought she heard him mumble. "Fortune-telling."

"Beer," she announced with a broad smile as she returned. His legs crossed, one arm thrown over the back of the sofa, Alex filled her couch with a leonine grace. He looked so strong sitting there, as if nothing could hurt him. Immobile, implacable, with eyes so knowing and logical nothing should be able to trick him.

Still, Sarah knew that that wasn't the whole truth. It worried her on levels she couldn't name and stole some of her smile. "What about getting somebody else to do it?" she asked, dropping into her chair.

Alex looked over at her with a half frown. "I've been drinking beer since I was sixteen," he said.

Sarah didn't notice the humor that warmed his eyes. Waving away his jest, she leaned forward, her glass of tea still clutched tightly in her hand. "Don't you understand? This isn't a party game."

Taking a moment to pop the tab on his beer, Alex shook his head. "I thought we were going to talk about the business."

"I *am* talking about the business," she insisted. "How much do you think I can accomplish if you get yourself killed because you won't listen to me?"

"A comforting thought." When Sarah moved to object, Alex raised his own hand. "The warning has been given. Now, since I'm not going anyplace but back to Sunset Design in the morning, why don't you tell me what makes you think the company has problems?"

Sarah wanted to shake him. He was humoring her. She could see it in the patient set of his brow. She could hear it in the tone of his voice. Well, it would serve him right if he went out of her house and walked into a truck. Then maybe he'd believe her.

"If you do get killed," she threatened, "I get to put the inscription on the tombstone."

Halfway through his first sip of beer, Alex lifted an eyebrow. "What's that?"

Sarah smiled sweetly. "I was thinking of something along the lines of 'He wouldn't listen.'"

Alex laughed, a deep, throaty rumble of surprise. "It's a deal," he promised. "Now, let's get down to business."

Still, Sarah didn't want to move. There was more she needed to say, that he needed to understand. But she could see by the look in his eyes that he wasn't ready to listen. Throwing off a shrug, she popped back to her feet.

"Come on in the kitchen while I work," she suggested. "We can talk there."

Her kitchen was as homey as the rest of her house, with its red-tile floor and hanging bundles of dried herbs. She knew it wasn't as neat as it could be, but that was because she was cooking. And cooking, as Blue had often taught her, was akin to a drama, not a chore.

Sarah attacked her cooking in a style more like grand opera.

"Anything I can do?" Alex asked, slowing to halt behind her when he saw the pans piled on available surfaces and fresh foods cluttering up counterspace.

Sarah took a moment to try to assess. The pasta needed to go in, and the sauce was about to be put together. And the salad. Had she boiled the eggs?

"Would you like to make the salad for me?" she asked, still looking around the kitchen as if waiting for it to instruct her.

"Show me where everything is."

Sarah managed to unearth the lettuce and tomatoes and cheese, and discovered, after two false starts, that she did in fact have hard-boiled eggs, but she was having trouble remembering where she'd left the salad bowl. Alex chopped while she wiped up egg and looked.

"You said you had an uneasy feeling about the company," Alex said, tasting the tomato he was cutting and then following it with a sip of beer.

Buried deep in her cabinets, Sarah nodded. Then she remembered the pasta. Backing out, she headed over to where the water was trying to boil away.

"It's been creeping up for the past couple of months," she said, sliding the fettuccine into the water. "Nothing definite, and nothing we've been able to prove. Hector's getting pretty tired of my constantly coming down to accounting to double-check things." Staring at the range top without really seeing it, Sarah shrugged. "I don't know of any other way to do it. I even had Thaddeus install more safety backups on the computers, especially since I don't trust the things anyway. Have you seen the garlic?''

The sauce. She had to get it put together before the pasta finished. Reaching into the fridge, Sarah grabbed butter and cream and Romano cheese. And garlic. Just a little. But she thought she'd already taken that out. Brushing her hair away with a free arm, she turned back to her cooking island.

"The problem couldn't be in the plant in Virginia?" Alex asked, handing over the garlic from where he'd found it on a stool.

Sarah looked up, surprised. "Oh, thanks. I wonder why I put it there." When he passed the cloves to her, his hand brushed hers. A sweet tingle snaked up from his fingers, provoking a fleeting smile of surprise in Sarah. "No," she said, turning away, trying to think past the glow in her hand. "Virginia isn't the problem."

Cutting slabs of butter, she slid them into the pan and then pulled the flour over. Behind her, Alex returned to his chopping.

"Why not?"

Sarah shrugged. "I couldn't tell you. I just know. It's here somewhere...but my pepper isn't."

"I think you put it in the flour jar."

She looked. "Oh. Well, what do we do?"

"I checked with Thaddeus today," Alex admitted from where his pile of vegetables grew on the countertop. "And it looks like he's made things about as fail-safe as he can. He had alarms built in for unusual spending of any kind, and a good control schedule for inventory. He even changes the codes to get into the inventory and accounting programs once a week."

Sarah had never had a man in her kitchen before. Even standing with her back to Alex she could sense him there, like a wall of energy behind her, a sharp new scent in the house, an aura of strength. Stirring in the cream, she fought another smile and lost. She should be thinking about her company, and all she could focus on was the surprise of companionship, the seduction of electricity. He was distracting her, deterring her, and she was finding it more and more difficult to care.

"Is there anybody you suspect?" he asked.

Sarah almost didn't hear him. She was crumbling bacon and eyeing how many pine nuts she wanted to use, finding it difficult to focus on anything even so simple with her new discovery filling her. She was scooping up the nuts when his words sank in.

"Suspect?" she demanded, whirling around to find him facing her. "I don't suspect anybody."

Alex frowned at the nuts clustered in her palm. "I thought you were going to get me a bowl."

"Oh," she breathed, wiping hair out of her eyes and looking vaguely around. "Okay." Sarah bent to open drawers as she continued. "I thought *you'd* figure that out anyway. Can't you find problems with an audit?"

"Not necessarily without some kind of nudge in the right direction," he answered from above her, the knife making regular thunk-thunk noises on the counter. "It's rare for accountants to come across deliberate problems on a regular audit."

"But Ellis said you've ferreted out three, uh, embezzlers in the past year." Her voice had a little echo to it that made her want to chuckle. Alex sounded so far away, almost like a dream. A fantasy.

"Two of them were fingered by their co-workers. Another walked up to me the first day of a requested audit and turned himself in. Said he knew all along that we'd come for him. Embezzling is embarrassingly easy to do, I'm afraid."

Embezzling. Sarah hated that word. She hoped she'd never have to use it again. It implied distrust, deceit, maliciousness. The idea that somebody in her company could be intentionally doing that physically hurt Sarah. For a moment she paused, crouched on her haunches before the dim recesses of her cabinet, bothered by the dark.

"When did you first begin to suspect something?" Alex was asking, still chopping. "Was there a change in income or outflow recently?"

"No," she said, his question spurring her to continue rooting through her pots and pans. She was going to need the colander for her pasta. Pulling it out, Sarah stood to put it in the sink. "There wasn't anything different. That's the puzzling part. We're beginning to test new markets again, but we do that every so often so we don't get stale."

"New markets?"

The sauce. She'd almost forgotten to add the nuts...the nuts. What had she done with the nuts? "Sure," she answered, looking over the countertops for the nuts she'd set down somewhere. "We're looking at toys and computer animation systems for video."

Alex seemed to be watching her rather intensely as she ducked for a quick peek back along the area she'd just searched, to make sure she hadn't dropped the nuts there.

"Toys?" he asked. "Isn't that kind of a stretch?"

"No. We're thinking of designing something along the stuffed animal variety. We're creating new...Alex?"

"Yes?"

Turning on him finally, Sarah took a wave at her hair and frowned. "You didn't see where I put the nuts, did you?"

Alex never said a word. He simply walked over and slid open the cutlery drawer. There, nestled in an untidy little stack just shy of the cleaver were her pine nuts. Shaking her head, Sarah shot Alex a grateful smile and scooped them up.

"Thanks." Dropping them onto the counter, she drained the pasta into the colander. "Remind me to show you the

Snarkalump we've just put together. She's a real charmer.''

Pine nuts, a dash of nutmeg and the Romano. Sarah tasted the concoction and closed her eyes in contemplation. Once again her senses were unaccountably torn between the task at hand and the insistent tug of Alex's presence. It was as if he'd changed the color, even the texture, of the room. It was less placid, less pale—almost as if Sarah had decorated it to focus on the sharp accent Alex provided.

There was so much more to him than that accountant's temperament and athlete's body. He had a core that she could feel when she closed her eyes, pulsing away beneath his deceptive exterior. A heat, a fine, strong passion that needed release.

Sarah smiled secretly, her eyes closed, her tongue still preoccupied with the smoky taste of her sauce, her body singing in a way it hadn't in her life. And for a moment she did no more than savor the delicious sensations in her kitchen.

''Sarah?''

His voice sounded so puzzled. Sarah opened her eyes to see the bemused expression on his face. It made her smile all the more, provoking an urge to settle her hand against the hard line of his jaw. She didn't though. ''What, Alex?''

''What about the bowl?'' he asked.

''Oh,'' she said, looking around. ''Did you need a bowl?''

Chapter 4

Sarah didn't get much work done the next morning. When she closed herself in her office with Vivaldi and her tea, instead of dreaming up colors and shapes, all she could produce were eyes. Honey-brown eyes, the color of sunshine on brandy. Warm, patient, kind eyes that tended to frown when puzzled. And they'd frowned a lot the evening before.

They'd frowned when Sarah had kept forgetting to find the bowl for his salad, which she'd finally served from a pot, and then again when Sarah kept losing her ingredients and finding them in unlikely places. Alex had frowned when he'd heard about the commune and then again when he'd discovered her extensive collection of classical and Zydeco music.

Sarah liked Alex's frowns. A small gathering of lines between his eyebrows, they spoke volumes in polite silence. He wasn't rude about Sarah's eccentricities, and he didn't make fun of her like some people did. He simply seemed to be trying to comprehend her, like a physicist coming to grips with the theory of chaos. Those frowns meant that at least he was trying. At least he was still intrigued enough to ask questions and be surprised by the answers.

"If that's a premonition you're having, I hope I'm included."

Startled, Sarah looked up to find Connie leaning against the open door. "Oh, hi. I was just thinking."

"Uh-huh." Her friend sauntered in and plopped into the chair across from the desk, crossing her legs ankle to knee in a manner more reminiscent of school than business. "If that's thinking, I'd like to know what fantasizing looks like."

Sarah came very close to blushing. Instead she finally took her first sip of tea. It helped her escape her friend's sharp scrutiny.

Settling more deeply into the chair, Connie grinned. "I'm glad you finally remembered to hang your phone back up last night. I was close to calling out Phoenix's finest again, especially with all the doom and gloom you've been preaching lately."

Sarah winced. The incident had provoked another frown. "That would have been the last thing Alex needed. Especially since he was the one who found the phone."

Her statement was met with an arched eyebrow. "He was?"

Sarah nodded sheepishly. "He sat on it. I told him it wasn't a big deal."

Connie grinned like a pirate. "I *should* have called the police. Can you imagine what he would have said when they'd shown up?"

Sarah grimaced with the thought. "Thanks, Connie. You're a big help."

Connie considered Sarah a moment, her grin fading to bemusement, her head tilting to the side, her brown eyes concerned. Sarah knew what was coming even before Connie did. Still, she let her speak her piece.

"You're getting a little starry-eyed for only twenty-four hours, aren't you?"

"It's that thrill of danger," she retorted casually, her eyes on her teacup, somehow not even wanting Connie this close yet. Connie was her dearest friend, her family during those years when she'd had none, but Connie was also her common sense. Sarah was still savoring the newness of Alex Thorne in her life. She didn't want Connie to list the reasons why she shouldn't.

Danger. Alex. Thirsty. Drink.

Now what made her think of that?

"I'm enjoying myself," Sarah said, trying to ignore the bees of association that buzzed in her brain. "It's been a long time since I've done that."

Connie smiled. "Since Billy Peterson, junior year. Yeah, I know. Well, just remember what old Aunt Connie says. Look before you leap. Especially where men are concerned."

"How's the computer-animation system looking?" Sarah asked in a deliberate effort to change the subject.

Connie paused before answering, just to let Sarah know she wouldn't let her off the hook. "Like a dream. Thaddeus is composing psalms to it. We should have everybody checked out on it within a month...everybody except you, that is."

Sarah shook her head. "You know better," she said. "I get a headache just hearing you and Thaddeus talking about it. All I'd have to do is take it out for a spin once and I'd crash the whole system like a Formula One in the far corner at Indy. And then where would our investment be?"

"I've taken the precaution of insuring it against anything," Connie reminded her. "Especially you."

"For a nominal fee, I'm sure."

Connie rolled her eyes. "Nothing is nominal with that bunch. I know the process is revolutionary, but you'd think we're renting out the Stealth Bomber for a weekend jaunt."

Thirsty. Liquid.

"How does Peter feel about losing out our account to Datasys?"

Connie's shrug was offhand. "He tries not to let it get in the way of a good game of golf. Besides, he's dating me, not Thaddeus."

"When you guys decide to progress past sports and megabytes," Sarah said, "let me know. I'd love to have him over."

Connie offered a dry grimace. "And have you scare him off by telling him he's destined to bear my children? Not yet, thanks. Give the man a chance to get used to me, first."

Liquid. Thirsty. Drink.

Sarah was on her feet. "Where is he?"

Connie looked around. "Who?"

But Sarah was already headed for the door. "Randolph doesn't like him. I guess he didn't get him any tea."

With a reluctant sigh, Connie stood and followed. "Just once I'd like to be able to follow a conversation with you to its logical conclusion."

"There is no logical conclusion," Sarah goaded over her shoulder. "Didn't you ever read Samuel Beckett?"

Connie shook her head.

Alex couldn't keep his mind on business. He wanted to blame it on the heat. Between his size and his metabolism, he'd never been able to comfortably tolerate any climate too familiar with the words "arid" and "hot." By the time he'd left the hotel that morning, the temperature had already been hovering in the nineties.

He could look out the window and see the clean, dry

colors of the desert harsh against the white of the computer-room walls. It made him want to sweat, even in the climate control.

It made him think, surprisingly enough, of how cool the white had been in Sarah's house.

What an experience that had been, like a fast slide down the rabbit hole. He'd spent the entire evening struggling to keep up with her conversation and trying to justify the waterfall of words and ideas that bounced around the room like bright, fragile bubbles with the soft, quiet interior of her home.

Sarah had said that she'd decorated it for the child in her. She'd always yearned for the romance of an English country house, where flower gardens filled the air with scent and added color for the eye. Where the furnishings had been handed down for generations in the same family. The only thing that had been handed down in Sarah's family had been a recipe for zucchini bread, which she couldn't follow anyway.

She was president of one of the fastest growing companies in the Sunbelt, and she couldn't even follow the directions in that recipe. Sarah said she made all her meals up as she went along, sometimes trying to recreate dishes she'd tasted in restaurants and sometimes setting out on her own. If last night was any indication, the process was as much a surprise as the outcome. By the time they'd sat down to dinner, her kitchen had looked like an explosion at Spago's, but Alex had to admit that he'd rarely had such delicious food.

Then there was Sarah's garden. Alex looked out the window to see the silent wind dance through the wan trees. He ignored the computer readout in his hand thinking instead of the flowers so diligently planted and tended in Sarah's backyard: impatiens and oleander and begonias and geraniums, and any number of plants he didn't even recognize in a riot of color in the pallid landscape of summer. Quiet testaments to perseverance and inspiration from a woman who couldn't otherwise keep the same thought in her head for more than seventeen seconds.

He saw again the dreamy, guileless sensuality on her face as she'd stood before him in the kitchen with her eyes closed, smiling, as if savoring something delicious, as if hearing music he couldn't. He'd come unforgivably close to pulling her into his arms and forgetting the pasta and the premonition and the company.

"Here it is, Alex."

Alex looked up to see Thaddeus ripping another stack of paper from the printer. His hair seemed a little wilted this morning, and he was dressed all in black, like some circuit-riding preacher. Alex wondered how he could stand the clothes in this heat.

"Are you sure you want to hit the warehouse already?" Thaddeus was saying, his attention still on the printout he was gathering.

Hauling his briefcase onto the table and snapping it open, Alex nodded. "I might as well. It'll give Hector a chance to get his figures ready for me."

Thaddeus looked up. "Ready? What do you mean? We all just went through that stuff."

Alex shrugged. "He's trying to pull together this month's figures, too. Whatever Sarah thinks is going on may be new."

At Alex's words, Thaddeus sketched a quick sign with his fingers that looked as if he were warding off the evil eye. Alex allowed an eyebrow to slide north.

"I don't know that many superstitious computer jocks."

Thaddeus looked a little more uncomfortable as he handed over his paperwork. "Don't tell Sarah. I don't think she'd understand."

Alex shut the sheets into his briefcase and then turned to lean against the desk. "Voodoo only works on people who believe in it."

Thaddeus assumed a defensive position, his arms crossed tightly against his chest, his weight on one leg, his eyes furtively checking out his assistants where they bent over their keyboards on the other side of the room. Ever since Alex had proven that he was not only computer-literate but sincerely impressed with Thaddeus's own work with the company system, Thaddeus had warmed considerably. He now gave every impression of a man about to give sage advice to the newcomer.

"I'm not some ignorant native squatting by a camp fire," he objected, leaning close to Alex. "I'm one of the best hackers in the country. I'm telling you, man, by the time I was sixteen I could break into any defense department computer and rearrange firing codes if I wanted. I tapped into NORAD once, like in the movie. Only I just left a message and got out. They never caught me." Now he tapped his forehead, his message intense. "Because I'm the best, y'know? The smartest."

He was making Alex feel old. "And?"

Thaddeus leaned in closer, and Alex thought of every vampire movie he'd ever seen. "And, there isn't anything in any research computer I've ever tapped that explains Miss ESP Delaney. Nothing that tracks like logic. But I've seen it anyway. I've seen her get those little spells and go all white, and then something happened. I'm telling you, it's downright spooky."

"No," Alex disagreed with an easy smile, trying to dispel the young man's images. "The idea of your getting into the defense department computers is spooky. Sarah is just…different."

Thaddeus flashed him a sharp grin. "So was Dracula. I'm just telling you, I'm a lot more comfortable with facts and figures. Give me a good binary system and I'm like a pig in slop. This stuff—" shaking his head, he let his eyes roll "—it's weird, man. Too weird."

Alex did he best to contain his grin. "If you're so uncomfortable, why stay?"

It was Thaddeus's turn to grin, the wide, brash grin that said that he owned the world. "Opportunity, man. Opportunity."

"See? He *didn't* get his tea."

By now Alex didn't even flinch. Sarah breezed in from the hallway, her feet bare and her white gauze dress drifting around her like a vapor. She had yards of beads around her neck and wore an embroidered vest of some kind. Earrings that sounded like tiny bells tinkled in her ears. Alex couldn't help but smile at the picture.

Right on her heels was Connie, her classy Yves Saint-Laurent suit a perfect counterpoint to Sarah's gypsy charm.

"Good morning," Alex greeted them both.

Sarah pushed back her flying hair and shot Alex a smile. "Randolph forgot you this morning, didn't he?"

Alex fought the urge to look around.

"Sarah's been preoccupied with whether you got something to drink this morning," Connie explained, shifting her own weight in betrayal of her impatience.

Alex shrugged. Beside him, Thaddeus shot him a look that translated into *See what I mean?* Thaddeus was expecting another display of extrasensory sparks, Alex imagined.

"No, I'm fine," he said. "I was just headed out."

Connie motioned to his briefcase. "Kim said you were headed over to the warehouse. Did you get somebody to drive you?"

Alex shook his head and lifted the briefcase as a signal of intent. He didn't want to be deterred by another surprise luncheon date. "No. I got directions. I called over and they're expecting me."

Connie nodded. Sarah shook her head, her eyes unfocused again, as if listening.

"You sure you're not thirsty, Alex?"

Alex tried a smile. "No, thanks, Sarah. I'm fine."

She kept listening, but couldn't seem to come up with the right message. "Liquid," she murmured, rubbing two fingers against her temple. Giving her head a final shake, she flashed Alex a smile. "Oh, well. You're going to be back later?"

"Probably the end of the day."

She nodded. "We'll most likely be here. Make sure you check in."

Preoccupied with the sight of Sarah standing there barefoot and exotic, her eyes wide and unfocused and alluring, Alex swung past her before he could be tempted to stay.

"See?" Connie was saying. "You can be wrong. That means that some of the other stuff might be off, too."

Sarah couldn't seem to take her eyes away from the empty doorway. She heard the swish of the elevator doors and then the whisper as it whirred into its two-story descent from the computer area to the lobby. And she listened to the voice that had nudged her into wondering about Alex's hydration.

Liquid. Liquid.

It was still there, still strong.

"We have to get back up to your office, hon," Connie said, walking over to open the glass door. "I saw Mr. Willoughby waiting out with Kim when we flew down here. He's going to want to talk West Coast distribution."

"Fluid!" Sarah cried, swinging on Connie. "Not liquid, fluid. Oh, God, Connie!"

She ran for the stairs. Out of force of habit, Connie followed right along, her heels clacking on the cement as they swept into the stairwell.

"Sarah," she panted, trying to keep up. "What fluid?"

Sarah didn't even hear her. She was obsessed with the picture of Alex walking off the elevator and down the white-stucco-and-red-tile hallway, purposeful, unaware, unknowing. Opening the door out onto the sunlight. Pausing to face the heat, maybe looking up into the washed-out blue sky of the summer afternoon. Thinking of how hot the car would be when he slid inside.

Sarah ran faster, the skirt of her dress skimming her knees and whirling around behind her.

Hector was walking toward the elevators as Sarah banged out into the lobby. His eyes widening silently, he sidestepped her and stood to watch. A couple of designers who had been heading in the front door scattered before her. Sarah didn't even notice. She was frantically searching the parking lot for Alex.

The desert heat seared her as she stepped out into the sun. The asphalt burned her feet. She saw the metallic-blue rental car and ran for it.

"Alex!"

He was about to slide into the driver's seat. When he heard her calling his name, he came to an uncertain halt, his hand still on the door, one foot poised in the car.

"Sarah?"

"Alex, get out of the car."

"What?"

Connie pulled up even with Sarah and stopped her. "Get back off the asphalt, Sarah. Come on."

"The car, Alex," she insisted, stopping scant feet away, close enough to see the beads of perspiration on his face. "Please, I need to talk to you."

"Sarah," he objected, finally noticing her attire. "Your feet. You're going to burn yourself." He began to edge away from the car.

"Then come over to the grass."

"Alex, please just come talk to her," Connie asked, doing her best to drag Sarah off the shimmering parking lot.

With a half shrug, Alex shut the door and followed them.

"What kind of fluid does a car have?" Sarah asked the minute the three of them had reached the grass.

Alex frowned at her. "Fluid?"

She was scanning the car, trying to see, trying to envision something she didn't understand. "I'm not mechanical. Are you?"

For a moment his gaze followed hers. "Yeah, I guess."

She nodded distractedly and turned back to face the confusion in his soft amber eyes. "What kind of fluid is there in a car?"

Still trying to understand, Alex shrugged. "Brake fluid, power-steering fluid, water for the radiator. Window-washing fluid."

The light broke. "Brake fluid." She sighed with relief. "That's it."

Alex was staring at her. "What's 'it'?"

The nausea hit then, the waves of rejection that always accompanied the revelation, as if her body had to literally purge the warning. Sarah looked away from Alex, down to the spiky green of the grass. She concentrated on simple senses, willing away the revulsion, the exquisite pain of the near miss. She battled the shimmer of his face, the sense of balancing on a terrifying edge that could have wiped him away like a strong wind.

Slowly the real world reasserted itself. Sarah heard the sibilance of the sprinklers on the far side of the complex, the drone of traffic, the chatter of birds. The world rushed back into her tunnel and filled it, and the weight of it tilted her. She took great, unsteady breaths.

"I almost...missed you," she whispered, dread coursing through her, closing her eyes and draining the blood from her face.

"Sarah? Sarah, what's wrong?"

She felt his hands on her, his arm encircling her and holding her up. She heard Connie move forward out of long-honed instinct and then pause, uncertain.

"You think somebody tampered with his brakes?" her friend asked incredulously.

Sarah leaned into Alex. His chest was so solid. So substantial. Still assailed by the suspicion that she was perilously close to slipping from the edge of the world, Sarah placed her hands against him, settled her head against the hard planes of him and rested.

"I think somebody tampered with his brakes," she answered. "I bet if you looked, there's a puddle underneath the car."

She felt the disbelief stiffen him, imagined the puzzled frown creasing his forehead and almost managed a smile.

"Are you okay, hon?" Connie asked, stepping tentatively closer.

Sarah realized with a start that for the first time in ten years, somebody other than Connie had pulled her back from the edge. Someone other than Connie had retrieved the harsh edge of reality and braced Sarah against it. It should have felt more uncomfortable, more unsuspected. Yet Sarah had never felt so protected in her life.

"I'm fine, Connie," she said, and lifted her head away from the heady scent of Alex's warmth. "I'm just hot."

"Then let's get inside," her friend insisted, taking over from Alex. Still stiff with uncertainty, he gave Sarah up and followed as Connie led them back into the building.

"Do you want me to call the police?" she asked.

"I don't know," Sarah answered. Connie held open the front door, and the cool air washed over them. Sarah gulped in lungfuls of it to help offset the sweaty trembling.

"Sarah."

Alex had made it through the door and then stopped. Sarah and Connie turned back to him.

"I'll be up in a minute," he said. "I want to check this out."

Sarah's head shot up and her heart faltered. "Don't do anything stupid, Alex. Leave the car alone."

"I'm not going to drive it," he assured her, his hand returning to her arm. "I'm going to check the brake lines."

"We'll be up in the office," Connie informed him. When he nodded, Connie led Sarah into the building.

Randolph was waiting with tea. He dispatched one of the salespeople to handle the impatient Mr. Willoughby and kept a personal eye on Alex out in the parking lot. When Alex returned with the just-arrived Phoenix police in tow, Randolph showed them all in.

"Oh, Miss Delaney," the officer, Sgt. Valdez, greeted her with a smile. "Good morning."

By now back to business, Sarah abandoned here work and stood up in a friendly manner. Immediately she grimaced. For some reason the carpet was brutal against her feet.

Connie saw her look down at her feet and shook her head. "I keep telling you to leave your shoes on," she said, then betrayed herself with a sudden sheepish expression. "God, I sound like my mother."

"Are your feet okay?" Alex asked.

"Just a little tender," Sarah admitted, motioning everybody to chairs before reclaiming hers. She remembered now. The parking lot. She could feel a few blisters forming on the more tender skin, but it wouldn't do any good to confess. Not only Connie, but Alex, too, would probably end up chiding her. Curling her feet under her, she turned instead to find Randolph waiting in the periphery.

"How about iced tea this time, Randolph?"

Alex certainly looked as though he could use it. He'd probably be happier with a beer, as hot and bedraggled as he looked. There was a smear of grease on his once-crisp white shirt, and his hair was shoved back as if he'd been spiking his hands through it.

"Was I right?" she asked quietly.

Settling into the chair across from her, he nodded. "I wouldn't have even noticed the puddle."

"Mr. Thorne says that you think somebody's trying to threaten him," Sgt. Valdez suggested diffidently. He'd remained on his feet, but Sarah knew better than to insist on his comfort. She was well acquainted with the officer. A short, burly man with ruddy complexion and coal-black hair, he stood at attention, notebook in hand. Sarah also knew just how much she could admit to the officer. He was definitely of the American school of pragmatism. See it, feel it, believe it.

Sarah couldn't fault him. There were things she didn't want to believe until she saw them, either.

"I don't know if it's connected," she demurred, her gaze drifting toward where her fingers tested the cotton of her dress. "Mr. Thorne is here conducting an audit for the company, yes. When he left today for the warehouse, I saw a puddle under the car and...well, suspected that it was more than an oil leak."

To her left Alex stiffened just a little, but Connie sat back in perfect ease on the other side, her eyes comfortably on the police.

"Why do you say that?" Valdez asked.

"I'm...mechanical," Sarah lied baldly.

Even Connie had trouble with that one. So, unfortunately, did the officer. "Uh, Miss Delaney...no offense..."

"Mechanical," Connie broke in with a tight smile. "Not electronic. Sarah noticed the puddle when we went out to, uh, remind Mr. Thorne about something. He's probably more used to this kind of thing than we are, though. Maybe he made somebody nervous by showing up for an audit."

"Really," the officer murmured, chocolate eyes suddenly sharp as he assessed the people present. "You think something illegal's going on?"

Again Sarah smiled and hoped that the sick dread didn't show in her eyes. Again Connie did the answering.

"I certainly hope not. Mr. Thorne is helping us make sure."

Heaving a sigh of frustration, the policeman shut his book. "No likely suspects?"

Connie shook her head. "None."

The policeman looked as though he were all too familiar with the scenario. Few companies who caught embezzlers prosecuted them. It was bad for public relations. Valdez's expression betrayed his belief that this was already one of those cases. "Not much to go on, I'm afraid. The brake line could have been cut, but it's a hard one to prove. No injuries, no suspects, no certain motive…best I can do right now is take all the information and tell you to be careful."

"And call if somebody dies," Alex said with a wry grin, evidently equally as familiar as the policeman with the situation.

Valdez shot him a returning grin. "I'd settle for anything concrete. Just to be sure, I'll check to see if anybody saw anything suspicious out in the parking lot."

Randolph returned with the iced tea just as Valdez was leaving. Randolph went ahead and passed three glasses around and then confiscated the fourth for himself before heading out to his desk.

"Mechanical?" Alex demanded from where he leaned against Sarah's desk.

Back in her chair, Sarah giggled, taking a long sip of the chilled liquid to quench the parch in her throat. "It seemed the easiest way to explain things. Officer Valdez doesn't believe in hocus-pocus."

"He did seem to recognize you."

Crossing her legs and settling more deeply into her chair, Connie snorted.

Sarah shot her friend a delighted look. "My house is

also on Officer Valdez's beat,'' she explained to Alex. "I have some trouble remembering how to work my house alarm system.''

Alex raised a hand. "Say no more.''

There it was, that frown again, creasing his forehead, betraying his bemusement. But this time it was tempered by something more. Sarah saw the humor there for the first time, the resignation. And something else. Something she wasn't ready to label.

"Are you sure your feet are all right?'' he asked.

Why was Sarah convinced there was so much more he wanted to say? She met his gaze with her own, basking in the honeyed depths of concern, feeding from the sharpening emotions. His eyes seemed to soften for a moment, as if he could tangibly touch her across the room and soothe whatever it was that he saw hurting.

It unnerved her. She was used to the concern of her friends. She wasn't used to the singular focus of this man. She wasn't used to wanting to return her own attention solely to him.

But she did. Which was why she had to make the decision now and stick by it.

"My feet are fine,'' she said, tucking them even closer. "And you're going back to Denver.''

Chapter 5

Alex decided that he must have ESP, too, because he knew exactly what Sarah was going to say before she said it. Much to her dismay, it made him smile.

"I thought we'd already settled that," he said, rolling his glass in his hands enough to make the ice clink against the sides.

"No," Sarah disagreed, leaning forward for what she must have known would be a fight. "You just ignored me the last time."

Settling further back against the desk and crossing his ankles, Alex nodded. "Well, that's probably what I'll do this time, too."

First Sarah glared at him. Then she glared at Connie, who was still comfortably ensconced in her chair.

Connie just shrugged.

"He was your idea in the first place."

"But what if I don't know the next time?" Sarah asked Connie, because, Alex realized, she always tested her reality against her friend's pragmatism. "What if something happens to him?"

"He's standing right here," Alex reminded her gently.

Starting at his intrusion, Sarah turned to him. Alex was struck by the suffering in her cornflower-blue eyes. If he hadn't known better, he would have sworn that he'd really driven off in that car and run into a brick wall.

What bothered him was that, instead of using his common sense, which had always been his strong suit, he caved in to emotion.

The sight of Sarah hurting from just the supposition of his injury infused him with the most irrational urge to protect her. To soothe away the tight set to her eyes.

She'd known him for all of twenty-four hours, and yet she took responsibility for him. Alex decided that her shoulders were too fragile for that kind of burden.

Pushing away from the desk, Alex strolled over to seat himself directly in front of Sarah. "And if I go?" he asked, setting his tea aside. "What do you do then?"

"I don't know," she retorted instinctively, backing away a little. "I don't care. It isn't worth your life."

"So you're going to let whoever it is get away with it simply because they tried to scare me off?"

Her eyes swelled with unshed tears. "Yes!"

Leaning forward, Alex excluded everything but Sarah in his gaze. "No. I'm not leaving, Sarah. You might as well get used to it."

She was picking at her dress again as if she couldn't keep her hands still, the agitation shimmering from her. "I'd never be able to live with myself," she whispered, begging.

"Neither," he said quietly, taking her hand to still it, "would I." Then he smiled, trying his best to lighten her load. "I'd be kicked out of the benevolent order of accountants if I caved in to one half-baked attempt to scare me."

"Half-baked?" she retorted in outrage, stiffening in his grasp. "If I hadn't guessed—"

Alex held on, thinking how her hand felt like a frightened bird in his, struggling for flight.

"Sarah, think about that for a minute," he suggested. "From what I gather, you've impressed most of your staff with your magical powers. I can't imagine whoever did it wouldn't consider the fact that you might at least anticipate this, if not finger him."

"You don't understand, Alex," she argued, now passive in his grip as she fought to challenge his gaze. The two of them were insulated by their concern, each for the other. A wall of energy surrounded them, throbbed between them. Their eyes met only the other's, intense, certain, distressed. "What I have isn't a constant. I can't always tune in and see. My abilities are like…like lightning striking. Sudden, without warning or reason. I can't control it any more than I can control the weather. I can't count on it even being right. And everybody in the company knows that."

She leaned forward, closing the space, intent and anguished. "Alex, if I were so impressive, I would have known the minute I met you that you were heading for my office. I'd have known what it was that's wrong with the company. I would have known who sabotaged your car, for heaven's sake."

Alex didn't know how to reassure her. He only knew that he had no choice, hadn't since she'd first leveled those pleading eyes on him. He had to see this through.

"That's okay," he said in his best tone of nonchalance. "We're going to need more for a conviction anyway. As far as I've heard, premonitions still aren't categorized as physical evidence."

Sarah straightened, furious at his levity. Alex refused to let go of her hands. "People do these things without ESP all the time," he assured her gently, offering simple support when logic wouldn't suffice. "We'll just have to go back to doing it the traditional way."

"Which means what?" Connie asked.

Alex was almost surprised to hear her voice. He'd been so engrossed in comforting Sarah that he'd completely forgotten about Connie sitting alongside him. Giving Sarah's hand a final squeeze before letting it go, he straightened and faced the pragmatic eyes of Sarah's partner. "I need a ride to the warehouse."

From that moment on, Alex looked on all the employees of Sunset Design in a different light. One of them had sent him a very personal message, and it would be in his best interest to find the sender before he or she found him again.

There were a thousand ways to embezzle from a company. Padding inventory numbers, writing checks to phantom companies, including the dead and long-gone on payrolls. Simple computer gymnastics.

Alex had once seen the senior computer programmer in an international bank walk out with millions of dollars by skimming a penny from each of the bank's accounts. He'd seen a payroll clerk pocket checks of departed employees that same clerk had conveniently left on the company books. Since the line workers were mostly illiterate, the checks had all been made out to "Bearer."

First Alex checked the warehouse, which took two days. The warehouse crew were brash and hostile and went out of their way to make Alex's life difficult, but only because they were insulted. Not because they were crooks. From what he could see, the inventory matched.

Next on the agenda was a visit with Hector in the accounting department to go over the company's fiscal policies.

Controls were in place that should have prevented the easiest kind of embezzlement. All checks had to be countersigned by Connie, and a check could not be endorsed by the person requesting it. One person in accounts receivable took in the money, and Jill recorded and balanced it. From what Jill said, Hector and Ellis had set up most of the safeguards in the company, and they'd done a good job.

Everything looked squeaky clean, just as Sarah had said. But somebody had tried to make him a traffic statistic.

Alex could tell that Thaddeus had decided to like him. He could also tell that Hector wasn't as sure. He certainly had the attitude down right. As smooth as a marble floor, Hector spoke as if he'd been studying up on the book of yuppyisms. He really wanted the American dream, and Sunset Designs was his avenue.

Hector was working his way through an MBA with a minor in computer science and loved to wax eloquently about how he would bring the company into the twenty-first century. It seemed to be the one level on which he could communicate with Thaddeus.

But beneath all that gloss was a very careful, very suspicious man. Alex was sure Hector saw him as a real threat, since anybody from Hector's department was prime suspect in playing loose with company change. And that, in turn, would reflect on Hector's managerial abilities.

Alex was amazed when Hector invited him out to lunch. Nonetheless, he went. Some of his most interesting information had been garnered over burgers and beer.

"Nice car," Alex said. He supposed he could have been more surprised.

In the process of fitting key to lock, Hector flashed a smug smile. "Leather interior, Blaupunkt stereo, cellular phone. My present to myself."

The locks snicked and Alex opened the door. New-car smell wafted out into the desert air, making Alex wonder if Hector had a can of spray with the scent for when it got older. A shiny red BMW 735i. No real imagination, he thought as he settled into the seat. A big layout, though, right down to the car phone and CD player. And Hector liked his Armani suits and Gucci loafers.

"You really seem to be doing well here," Alex said.

"And I'll do better," Hector agreed, slipping the key into the ignition. "Sarah's a rising star."

"Sarah?" Alex asked. "Not Sunset?"

"Sure, both. I already have headhunters sniffing at me, even before they know me. It's Sunset. The company of the century, and all guided by a woman who can't even boot up a computer. Like the man says, it's a great country."

Alex maintained a passive attitude. "It almost sounds like Sarah's success is a fluke."

"No way," Hector disagreed, turning the car into traffic. "You're talking about a woman with six patents. She's a certifiable genius. She could just use a little baby-sitting."

Alex's attention was caught all over again.

"Patents?"

"Sure, didn't you know? She invented the Great Perpetual Motion Machine."

That took Alex's attention away from Armani suits and stereos. "The what?"

Surprised, Hector looked over. "Haven't you ever heard of it?"

"Sure," Alex admitted. "That damn thing drove me nuts in the malls last Christmas. Sarah invented it? She doesn't seem the type."

"That's the great thing about Sarah. You never know where she's heading next. She's invented a safer child car seat, a trauma table for hospitals and a new cloth-dying process. And now she's getting into computer animation? All I have to say is that the opportunity for personal growth is maximized. If you know what I mean."

Sunset Designs was getting more and more intriguing.

* * *

It had been a long day. Mr. Willoughby had been back for a finalized proposal on West Coast distributorship, and several ad agencies had made tentative forays into securing the services of the fledgling computer-animation department. A new linen account had come in, and Midcentral Airlines wanted something flashier on their logo—by tomorrow, and some time after lunch Sarah had lost her earrings. She wondered whether she was going to need glasses. She had a splitting headache.

Of course, there was also the matter of the sleep she hadn't been getting the past few nights.

She'd been lying awake in the dark, listening to the birds, the highway, the bugs out in her garden chirruping in tidal chorus. Listening for the next warning.

It hadn't come. The company had gone on as if nothing had happened. Alex had gotten himself dusty and crabby out at the warehouse and returned to closet himself in the accounting department without anything to report. Connie had provided Sarah with pragmatic patience and Randolph had served tea and schedule updates.

Sarah, alone in her office and then alone at home, had brooded. It was already wrong. She had too big a stake in all of this to be objective. How could she expect the sight to be clear? She strained for revelation when revelation only came uninvited. She ached for prescience as the future lay dark and silent.

Every time Sarah tried to focus on a direction, her attention skittered away, as if it had struck slick ice. Her vision shattered, dissipated, waned. Frustration mounted and opportunity evaded her.

Sarah wasn't sure what time it was. She'd holed herself back up after the last meeting to beat out a new airline logo and had somehow produced the new sheet-and-towel design instead. She liked it, too, a kind of swirling print in the pale Santa Fe blues and brick-red that reminded her of the sunsets out in the mountains. It was too bad she wouldn't have a place to put it in her own house, where flowers bloomed on her linen.

But that didn't resolve the Midcentral issue. And it didn't do anything about her headache. Finally giving in to a yawn and a stretch, Sarah slid the new design away and retreated to her couch and her afghan. Sometimes getting a quick nap released the inspiration.

Alex. She saw him the minute she closed her eyes. She heard his voice easing her fears as surely as his hands had supported her.

Strong hands. Callused hands. Gentle hands. Football players should have hands like hams and grips like vises. They should be as subtle as steamrollers and blessed with the brainpower of armadillos.

Accountants should be small and mousy and as dull as television golf.

Yet Alex was none of these things. He had eyes that expressed more emotions than most men possessed. He had arms that cushioned instead of imprisoned. He had a sly humor that defused tension and an anger that smoldered rather than exploded.

He had a history that tantalized beneath his civilized exterior, and he had a primal energy that Sarah instinctively recognized.

She should have been thinking of airplanes. Instead she conjured up wide shoulders, slim hips, long, powerful legs. She tormented herself with what she'd known and what she could only anticipate.

What kind of body lay beneath his tailored suits? What would it feel like beneath her fingers? Beneath her lips?

No wonder she couldn't keep her predictions in line. She couldn't keep her hormones under control, either. Just envisioning herself in Alex's arms sent her blood pressure climbing. Remembering the one kiss they'd shared stoked the fires even higher. If she ever got around to really fantasizing about what lovemaking with Alex Thorne would be like, she'd land on the floor with a stroke.

The creak of the office door broke in on her musings. Sarah was surprised to realize how it irritated her.

"I hope it's important, Connie," she warned without moving. "I don't want to interrupt a good fantasy for nothing."

"I hope it's about me."

Sarah wasn't sure about the stroke, but she did land on the floor. Pushing her hair out of her eyes, she looked up to find Alex standing inside her office. The light from the anteroom haloed him, handsomely outlining the very attributes Sarah had been considering in such detail.

No, no stroke. She could see just fine. And her imagination was working even better.

"All right," she challenged, hands on hips, legs still splayed beneath her, head up. "I might as well ask."

Leaning by one hand against the door frame, Alex tilted his head, a smile nudging the corners of his mouth. "Go right ahead."

"Is it hairy or not?"

It obviously wasn't what he expected. For a minute all he could seem to do was stare at her. "Uh, Sarah—"

"Your chest," she clarified with a sneaky smile of her own. "Do you have hair on your chest?"

He was staring again. "You *were* fantasizing about me?"

She giggled. "Well, I don't fantasize about Connie, and Randolph's gay. And I'm afraid I don't fancy juvenile computer wizards. Just the conversation would kill me. So…"

"Yes."

"Good. There are some things a woman needs to know."

"Are you having another premonition?"

"I don't know," she admitted, her eyes bright and her

chest suddenly tight. Settling herself more comfortably on the floor, Sarah flashed him her best smile. "But I'm certainly willing to try."

She should have felt at a disadvantage, sprawled at his feet like she was. Instead she felt...hungry. She couldn't keep her eyes off the clean cut of his slacks, the tight expanse of those shoulders of his beneath his shirt, the solid expanse of forearm exposed by rolled-up sleeves.

"Only if it has nothing to do with accounts receivable," he warned.

Sarah looked up to find his eyes in the shadows. It didn't matter. She could feel their heat, stirring chills in her, raising goose bumps.

"Do you know what time it is?" he asked, stepping on in.

Sarah took a look around. Out the window, Phoenix blinked fitfully beneath the trees and the stars struggled against the moon.

"I don't know," she admitted. "I lay down for a minute—" Returning her attention to Alex, she had to tilt her head back even further to find him. "Why don't you sit down?"

He took in her position. "On the floor?"

Sarah shrugged. "Why not?"

"I think I'd be more comfortable on the couch."

She grimaced at him. "Not into alternate experience, are you?"

Grinning, he approached and held out a hand. "*You're* the hippie," he reminded her. "I'm just an accountant."

For a moment Sarah couldn't move. Alex stood right over her, blocking out almost all the light, so that he seemed more a wraith than a man, a vision, a prescience...a promise.

Sarah shivered, the air that pulsed between them suddenly tumescent. They would be lovers. Not tonight, probably not very soon, but inevitably. He had just made that decision, and its force struck her like a physical blow.

Sarah didn't even remember taking hold of his hand. Suddenly, though, she was warm, warmer than she'd been in a long time—sweetened with a life she'd never realized she'd been missing. Alex pulled her to her feet, and she slid up against him. When he gasped with the sparks of their contact, she smiled.

They stood very still, Sarah's hand still in Alex's, her head back so she could look up into his eyes, her breasts grazing his chest. She felt his arm slide around her back, felt him draw her close. Saw the surprise in his eyes as he bent to kiss her.

Sarah's gaze held onto those eyes. Even caught in the whirlwind stirred by future needs and immediate desires, even as she felt the unbearably soft assault of his lips on hers, she sought the honeyed depths of his eyes beyond the shadow. She saw the impulse, the certainty and then finally, inevitably, the caution.

Alex's arms tightened around her. His fingers wove through hers. He coaxed his way past her lips and probed the soft, dark recesses of her mouth. Sarah held on to him. She invited him further, shamelessly, knowing now that she hadn't been wrong, that this was inescapable and right. She splayed her fingers against the crisp cotton of his shirt and longed to coax her own way past.

Groaning, Alex tightened his hold on her. His hands grew restless against her as his mouth covered hers with hungry demand. A heat welled from him, from the tips of his fingers as they strayed along her throat, from the solid wall of his chest where it met her aching breasts, from the steely length of his thighs where they fit against hers.

Sarah surrendered, sinking into it like a tired body into healing waters. She whimpered with the way that force leaped from him where he touched her, searing her skin and swirling deep into her to stoke her own heat. She arched against him, seeking warmth, the spark that crack-led between them and shocked her nipples to rock-hard little nubs.

But just as the heat from Alex's touch exploded in her, as the knot formed in her belly that she knew wouldn't soon go away, he pulled back. He straightened and dragged in a lungful of air as if he'd been close to drowning. And Sarah, even knowing now that it wouldn't ultimately end here, felt lost.

Before she had the chance to see the regret that would surely appear in those brandied eyes, Sarah settled her head against his chest.

"You're a little gun-shy," she nudged, her eyes closed. "Aren't you?"

For a minute Alex didn't answer. Still holding her close, he winnowed his fingers through her hair. Sarah wanted to sigh at the unconscious sensuality of it. She kept her silence, her own arms now around his waist, her ear to the ragged cant of his breathing and the trip-hammer thud of his heart.

"I'm very gun-shy," he answered, although this time in an apology rather than a challenge.

Sarah nodded. "I don't think I would have liked her."

She felt the rumble in Alex's chest and knew that his chuckle was one of surprise. "You're being a lot more charitable than I was."

Sarah smiled, assimilating the steady beat of his heart. "She didn't hurt me as badly as she did you."

She still felt his fingers weaving sparks through her, spilling a delicious lethargy she knew was already dangerous.

"She didn't hurt me," Alex said with a curiously sharp edge to his voice. "She made me grow up."

Sarah shook her head, her hair rustling against cotton. "No," she said simply. "She made you grow old."

Alex didn't seem to have an answer. He merely held on to her, his hand against her head.

"Aren't you hungry?" she asked quietly.

Alex stiffened before Sarah recognized the double entendre she'd just delivered.

"I'm talking basic food groups, Alex. Dinner."

"Oh. Yeah," he admitted, his voice less strained. "I am hungry. Matter of fact, that's why I came in here about four hours ago or so. Where would you like to go?"

She could hear his heart slowing back down. A good, athletic heart, untaxed by brief challenge.

"What hobbies do you have?" she asked, not moving, counting his rate already at the low fifties.

Alex straightened. "What?"

"Hobbies," Sarah insisted, moving her head so she could face him again. She was going to need a chiropractor soon. "You still keep in shape, I can tell. What do you like to do?"

Even in the shadows she could see the size of his scowl. "Dinner ranks right up there," he retorted in a low growl. "Wanna join me?"

Sarah chuckled. "You remind me of Connie."

"I hope not," he said. "I would have been kicked off the team after the first session in the showers."

Sarah laughed and the tension ebbed. It was time to pull away, to form an orderly retreat to companionship for the time being. She didn't mind so much when Alex smiled like that. Or even when he scowled like that, because it was playful.

"I mean you're both so focused. I bet you taught yourself to ride a bike without any help."

"When I was four."

Sarah nodded. "Connie knew what she was going to do when she grew up from the time she was three."

Alex lifted an eyebrow. "She knew she was going to work with you? She must be clairvoyant, too."

Easing out of Alex's arms, Sarah shot Alex her own scowl and went on a search for her shoes. "She knew she wanted to own a business. Connie's an army brat. I think it was her way of rebelling against *her* life-style."

"Connie's an army brat?" Alex echoed in astonishment. "You two must have been some roommates."

Sarah grinned from where she was rooting around beneath her desk. "With about as much in common as Thoreau and Rommel. Connie's mother says I ruined her daughter. But then, Blue says that Connie ruined me."

"It must have been a disappointment to your parents when you didn't follow in their footsteps."

She'd found her shoes. Easing the bone pumps away from the pig's protective backside, she slid her feet into them and turned back to Alex. "No," she disagreed with a happy shake of her head. "What crushed them was the day they found out I had a stock portfolio."

Alex actually laughed. "You?"

Sarah wrinkled her nose. "Don't be so smug. I'm quite good at it."

"All that fortune-telling, no doubt."

Now all she had to do was find her purse. "Nope. That has nothing to do with it."

From where he waited, Alex crossed arms and settled against the desk. "What are you doing?"

"My purse," Sarah answered from under the drawing table.

"Don't you think lights might help?"

"I always leave it in the same place. Then I swear it moves around on me."

"Uh-huh."

She was crouched close to the floor, checking out the mauve carpet for her mauve handbag in the dark. She didn't find it. She did find Alex. She tripped over him.

Alex's hands shot out to steady her. "I'm a little hard to miss," he objected. "Even in the dark."

Sarah straightened and fought the urge to nestle back against his chest again. She so enjoyed the feel of his hands on her arms, hands that were a little tighter than necessary, that telegraphed Alex's unsuspecting attachment.

"Sorry," she said, even though she wasn't.

Alex's smile betrayed arousal and frustration. "You should be," he said, thumbs rubbing slow circles into her shoulders. "My patience isn't what it used to be."

His patience wasn't what he was talking about. Sarah's eyes widened. She found herself easing closer again, seeking that heat, that life....

"Sarah, you'd better be here—"

Sarah whipped around like a shot. First she saw her purse on the file shelves by the door, where she was sure she never put it. Then she saw Connie.

Connie stood stock-still in the doorway, her mouth open, her eyes wide. She had a large bag in her arm, and the tempting aroma of garlic wafted into the room.

"Chinese?" Sarah asked hopefully, completely oblivious to the picture she and Alex presented, still much too close to each other, still flushed and anxious.

"I'm...sorry," Connie apologized, backing stiffly away. "I interrupted."

"I lost my purse," Sarah explained, waving an arm in airy dismissal. "Now, bring that back in here."

Still disconcerted, Connie looked down at the bag in her arms, then at Sarah and Alex. "Oh...I, uh, have a meeting. I couldn't get you at home and figured you'd forgotten to get there again. Thought I'd drop something off."

"Well, stay and share it," Sarah said, and turned to Alex for confirmation.

He'd added toleration and patience to the other emotions in his expression. "Your purse is on the shelf," he said, letting her go with a final squeeze only the two of them knew about.

Caught dead center between the delicious promise of garlic and the surprising loss when Alex took back his hands, Sarah flashed him an uncertain smile. "Thanks, I saw it. Now, I just have to hope my keys are inside."

Before Sarah could say anything more to Connie, her friend shoved the bag of food into her hands and backed out the door. Sarah stared, not sure what it was that was so suddenly wrong in the little room.

"Connie?"

Connie grinned. "See you in the morning. Don't get lost going home."

And without another word, she turned away from the office. Sarah didn't understand. She turned to Alex, to see the same concern in his eyes.

"I'll…uh…"Dropping the steaming bag next to her purse, Sarah headed out the door.

She caught up with Connie at the elevator.

"What's the matter?"

Connie stared, her posture stiff and uncomfortable. "Nothing," she obviously lied. "I have to go, that's all."

Sarah answered with an epithet she rarely used. Something about prairie litter.

This time Connie's smile was a little more honest. "I'm sorry," she apologized, flexing her stiff fingers and raking a few through her carefully coiffed hair. "I didn't have any business being so stuffy."

Sarah took a step closer, still not satisfied. But she didn't say anything. She knew she didn't have to.

Connie's gaze slowly returned to Sarah's. Sarah could see defensiveness, protection, confusion there. "I know you," Connie said quietly, a hand out to Sarah's arm. "You dive headfirst into everything you do without looking. It's dangerous."

Sarah tried a conciliatory smile of her own. "I've always had you there to warn me about the shallow places."

Connie shook her head. "I can't follow you in this

time," she warned. "You're on your own, and I'm afraid you're going to get hurt."

There wasn't any way Sarah could honestly satisfy Connie's concern. Her friend was right. Sarah did tend to jump in headfirst. She was in a position to get hurt. Badly hurt. But there was a certainty to her feeling about Alex that couldn't be communicated past her friend's worry. So Sarah reached out and gave Connie what she could.

"I can't say I'll be careful," she said honestly. "I can't say I won't be hurt. But I'll be all right, no matter what happens. It's a chance just like all the other chances we've taken to get where we are, and I think I'd like to take it. After all," she added with a sly grin, "you don't take any new ground without advancing."

At that Connie finally chuckled. She took back her hand and punched the elevator button. "Enough," she protested. "I know you've made up your mind when you start quoting *my* father. Just remember," she added, turning back for one last meaningful glance. "I'm there if you need me."

"I know," Sarah said with a final smile. "I love you, Con."

The door opened and Connie stepped in. Sarah knew she wouldn't know how to answer. She never did. Connie hadn't been raised by hippies to share the same words with friends that one would with spouses or lovers. Sarah did it without thought or prejudice. Connie was the closest thing she had to family, and she wanted her to always know that.

Raised by the Colonel and his brittle, correct wife, Connie still didn't know quite how to respond.

"See you in the morning," she said, and let the door slide closed.

Sarah shook her head and returned to Alex.

Chapter 6

For a long moment Alex didn't move from where he stood in the darkened office. He could hear the sounds of footsteps in the hallway and of traffic on the street. He could see the outline of desks and computers in the outer office. He could smell the faint perfume of Sarah against the assault of garlic from the bag. And he felt the heavy tension of Connie's surprise interruption.

Still, somehow, he felt disconnected. Unreal. It happened every time he was alone with Sarah. She drew him into the shadows with her smile and her bright, spontaneous excitement. She pulled him down, away from reality, away from sense, and let loose something in him that was better closed away.

Alex knew better. He'd been snared once, trapped as neatly as a fish in a net before he'd even recognized the calculation in his pretty wife's vapid eyes. He'd rued his capture quickly and paid for it at length. And yet, he was doing the same thing all over again, and he couldn't seem to make himself want to quit.

Sarah fascinated him. She was completely intuitive. She made him think of wood sprites, sirens, wholly sensual creatures caught between reality and imagination, able to dip their fingers into the well of dreams and pull one out whole. He thought of their fatal powers, their deadly allure, drawing men by their hands willingly to their deaths.

Damn. He dated pragmatic women, adults who walked carefully in the real world and debated it over drinks. He didn't tolerate bubbleheads anymore. He didn't take to flights of fancy. He'd made it a point not to after Barbi.

Yet here he was, mesmerized to a standstill by a woman who couldn't even keep track of herself, much less somebody else. A woman cared for by a host of adults, but who was oddly convinced that she was responsible for everyone around her because of whatever the gift was she thought she had.

Did he believe she'd really predicted the car situation? Probably not. She'd seen or overheard something and tucked it away. Like her purse, that memory was lost until someone had called it to mind. So much for the misty visions and unexplained feelings.

Besides, Alex was having trouble enough dealing with the tangible aspects of this attraction. He didn't want to have to consider what allowing hocus-pocus in would do to him. Intuition was something as simple as knowing a person well enough to anticipate him. Nothing more.

Nothing more.

"Alex? Are you still there?"

Alex started, looked up. Sarah stood in the doorway, little more than shadow and movement against the distant light. For a moment, for a brief moment, Alex thought to question her presence, to reach out a hand to test her substance. Instead, he shook away the fancies and approached.

"What was the matter?"

Sarah met his gaze, and Alex saw the light flicker across the blue depths like first sunlight on the sea. He found himself held still again, the memory of her body in his arms suddenly vivid. He could feel the sweep of her hair across his arm, the slender vibrancy of her against his belly, the surprising hunger of her mouth. And for a moment it was all he could do to keep from pulling her back into his arms.

He could still remember the moment he'd realized that they were going to be lovers. His body flushed with it. His imagination spun. His common sense went right into shutdown. With her woman's eyes, Sarah saw him too clearly. She threatened to unleash a part of him that best belonged tied down tight and secure.

"Oh, Connie's just being protective," Sarah assured him. "She's afraid I'm going to let you hurt me somehow.... Are you okay?" Sarah asked suddenly, stepping closer without bothering to flick on the lights.

At the last moment Alex reeled in his hormones and smiled. "I'm hungry," he said matter-of-factly. "I've been standing here smelling garlic and ginger and trying to decide if I really wanted to wait for you to come back before diving in."

Was it his imagination, or did Sarah relax? She stepped aside and turned back to where the bag waited. He guessed a moment passed. Reality intruded a little more.

Except that Alex couldn't keep his sense of fantasy at bay. He still half expected Sarah to have returned with holly leaves in her hair.

"You're right," she said, leaning over to peer inside. "It does smell great. Should we eat here, or at the house?"

"Here," he said a little too quickly. "I'd like to ask you a few things."

Sarah turned up to him. "You can't do that at my house?"

Alex answered by dipping into his pocket and rattling around for change. "Diet or regular?"

Sarah grinned her acquiescence. "You mean, harmful

chemicals or carcinogens,'' she retorted with a bright grin. ''Surprise me.''

Before Alex headed off to the soda machine in the lunchroom, he flipped on the lights. Just to be safe. In case she disappeared on him in there.

''I guess no one's come forward to confess.''

Alex shook his head while digging into a carton of Mongolian beef. ''Not that I haven't given them ample opportunity.'' Casting a careful glance across the table, he continued. ''You're willing to admit that somebody's doing this on purpose?''

''Doing what?'' Sarah answered in frustration. ''What would be worth killing a man over?''

''For some people? Pocket change. In this case? I'll be damned if I know.''

She looked up at him. ''You haven't found anything.''

''Not a thing. The warehouse crew thinks you're Mother Teresa and the accounting staff is sure you're Nostradamus. Everybody is on their best behavior, and I haven't found one thing out of the ordinary.''

''But something *is* out of the ordinary.''

Alex saw the pain in those soft blue eyes, the hurt of a betrayed child, and found himself wanting to lash out at whoever had provoked it. ''Something is out of the ordinary.''

It took Sarah a second to break the contact, as if she were drawing on him for some kind of sustenance. When she did, she dropped her gaze to where she picked desultorily at her dinner. ''What's your next step?''

Alex returned to his own food, unsettled by the unexpected sense of separation. ''I'm settling into accounting for a few days. Doing checks of receiving and shipping, payroll, that kind of thing. Then I'll do some quick checks on companies you deal with.''

''And if you don't find anything?''

He shrugged, his gaze back on her downturned head. "I'll do it again."

Sarah lifted her eyes. "What if—"

"I'm being careful."

With a frustrated huff, she slammed her plastic fork down. "Don't be stupid. A lot of careful people are...hurt"

"And a lot of companies are ruined by crooks. If you're so perceptive, Sarah, why can't you see that I'm not going to change my mind?"

That got a sheepish little grin out of her. "I can," she admitted, "but the feeling of danger keeps getting worse."

"In that case," he said. "You be careful, too."

"Me?" She seemed genuinely surprised. "These people are all my friends. I picked them because I connected with them."

"Connected?"

She blushed a little. "It's a Blue term. I just mean that I had to have a certain feeling—a kind of bond—before I could hire somebody. It's never failed me yet."

"I'm afraid that one of your friends has," he answered quietly.

Again Alex saw the bright pain and wondered how this self-absorbed artist could gather so many people in under her wing.

"It's so frustrating," she whispered, tears welling in her eyes, her hands restless. Climbing to her feet, Sarah paced over to the window and watched the thin line of lights that was the city. "I've tried so hard to see something."

"Is that how it works?" he asked, following to his feet, unsure of his place, his intentions.

She shrugged without turning. "It doesn't work any particular way," she admitted. "Sometimes I get a sense of something, like whether a person will make a good client. Or I see pictures. Like the time I saw Jared and knew he was going to marry Blue three months before he showed up on the doorstep. Then there are the times, like when I met you, I'm just…overwhelmed. Like being caught in a big wave with my head underwater. Those are the worst."

"You can't control it."

Sarah shook her head. "If I could, I'd be rich from the stock market." She offered a small chuckle. "Jill says that if I could get this thing to work right, I'd make a fortune for us both at the racetrack."

"Racetrack?"

Turning at the surprise in his voice, she nodded. "Sure, didn't you know? Phoenix has great racing. Greyhounds and thoroughbreds. Turf Paradise is just over on Bell." Stepping away from the window, hands deep in the pockets of her billowy cotton flowered skirt, Sarah grinned. "Unfortunately, I seem not to be one of those fortunate people attuned to the psyche of the horse. Or the greyhound."

Jill, Alex thought instead, sorting back through people. Accounts receivable. He'd have to check on her, too. And he'd have to get Sarah to talk a little more about her other friends. Offer unsuspected motives, opportunities, grudges.

Grudges, Alex thought with a mental shake of the head. Who could possibly have a grudge against Sarah? It would be like resenting springtime.

Nevertheless, somebody had tried to dismantle his brakes. There was at least one person with some kind of motive.

He got her to talk. Eased back into the couch, the lights off to better enjoy the show outside, Sarah offered information about her employees, praise for their work, sympathetic sketches of their lives, simple defenses for the people she trusted most.

There was Hal in design whose wife had cancer, and Maria in the secretarial pool who was putting herself and a brother through school. Sylvia, the sales manager who was the sole support of her single-parent household, and Joseph, a sales rep who was recovering from alcoholism.

All good people who had every reason to be grateful to Sarah. Any one of whom could have found themselves desperate for cash.

Alex ended up feeling like a heel. He listened to Sarah defend her staff like family, extolling and empathizing, and all he listened for was motive.

"What about Randolph?" he finally asked.

Lost in the jewel-studded night that danced outside her window, Sarah took a moment to look around.

"Randolph?" she asked, her eyes lost in shadow, her hair tumbled and shimmering. "What about him?"

"You said he's gay."

Sarah nodded. She wasn't making it any easier for Alex, who had never prided himself on his tact.

"Sarah," he said, "would he be a target for blackmail?"

It took her a minute to answer. A minute, Alex guessed, for the question to sink in. Suddenly she grinned.

"Do you mean does anybody else know?"

"Yes."

Sarah chuckled. "Only most of the legislative bodies in the United States. Randolph is an activist for AIDS funding. He helps run a hospice here in town."

Alex scowled at her delight. Sarah, a collector of people. A quiet champion without a cause. Wasn't there any dark underside to her motivation, he wondered. Any petty jealousy or prejudice or selfishness? She was so damn straightforward, so painfully honest and sincere. How could anyone take advantage of that? How could anyone deliberately hurt her?

Unfortunately, Alex had been out in the world long enough to know that there were people lined up for that kind of opportunity.

"He doesn't like you much," Sarah offered suddenly.

Alex saw that she considered him with tilted head and amused eyes. "Why?"

Sarah just shrugged. "He won't say. I think he's afraid you're going to hurt me."

Alex lifted an eyebrow. "Him, too? I seem to be a pretty popular guy all around."

Sarah offered a sly smile and an offhanded shrug. "Oh, I don't know. *I* like you."

He scowled. "Anybody else I should keep a lookout for?"

Sarah took a moment to think about it. "John," she admitted.

"John?"

"My father, remember?"

"Oh, yeah. The dam builder."

She nodded. "He's shown himself to be surprisingly protective, especially for a man who makes an appearance about once a decade." Her smile brightened again, impish and provocative. "But then, he's still out of the country. By the time he finds out about us, you'll be a daddy and I'll be designing from home."

Alex tried his best to quell the frustration at her words. "You see that, do you?"

She challenged him. "And a picket fence, and a boy for you and a girl for me. All that traditional stuff that made John cringe right up to the moment he left."

Alex didn't hear any regret. Any bitterness. He couldn't understand why. "Is that why you went to boarding school?"

"Oh, no," she said. "I went in when John and Blue headed off to save natives. They figured I should have some kind of structure to my life, since it looked like I was interested in more than natural foods and tie-dyeing."

"How often did you see them?"

"Since I was sixteen?" Sarah thought a moment. "Four times."

Alex sat stunned.

"No, that's not right," she amended. "Five. Blue and John came home for her wedding to Jared."

Five times. Five times in what, ten years? How could she survive neglect like that? How could she seem so outgoing and giving, when the people she'd relied on so much hadn't ever been there for her?

By adopting her own family, Alex realized. By vigorously defending the other psychologically needy. He thought of his own family, of the noisy holidays and the siblings always no more than a call away, of the months he'd spent locked in Lindsay's house and the strong bond that had tightened into steel with the tears and rage. He thought of his sister now, whole and happy, and how he fed on that like sunlight.

Damn. Sarah asked for no pity. She wouldn't have understood if he'd offered. Yet he wanted suddenly to hold her, to give her the security her parents had denied her with their frivolous affections.

"Well," he offered, struggling to pull something out from the story to praise, "at least their divorce was amicable."

"Divorce?" she asked. "Whose?"

Alex frowned at her. "Your parents."

"My parents were never divorced," she said simply. "Blue and John never got married."

"So explain it to me."

"Alex," Lindsay said with strained patience. "Why couldn't you wait a couple more weeks to have this crisis of faith? I can't really pay attention when this little beast is tap-dancing on my ribs."

"He'll play football."

"He will not. Are you sure you can't rely on cold showers a little longer?"

Measuring a short arc across the plush living area carpet,

Alex turned in the other direction, a hand raking through his hair. "It's not that. I'm trying to figure her out, damn it. She just doesn't make any sense."

"Why, because she can come out of a bizarre situation in one piece? Seems to me both of us qualify for that privilege."

"But we had each other. The family."

"And she did it all on her own. Why are you so scared of her?"

He turned again, walking faster, his neck corded with tension. "She's never had a real family. She was deserted when she was sixteen. She hasn't seen her parents more than five times since."

"She was raised in a commune, Alex, not Mayberry. Her definition of family might be slightly different than yours. Does that bother you?"

That stopped him. He really considered it, wanting to be fair. "No," he answered truthfully. "But I couldn't be as unconcerned about it as she is. Why?"

"Because when a person looks up stability in the dictionary, the name Thorne is next to it. I'd say she's done a hell of a job with what she's had."

Now Alex smiled, and it was wry. "Makes you wonder what we've really accomplished with all we were given."

"I know what I've accomplished," Lindsay retorted easily. "Swollen ankles, stretch marks and twenty-four-hour bathroom stops."

Sarah didn't sleep again that night. But it wasn't the threat to Alex that kept her tossing and turning. It was the promise of him.

Each step taken brought them closer. The certainty of it ballooned in her chest until she could hardly breathe. She was falling in love with him. She could see him fighting and had a feeling she knew why. But time and time again tonight his eyes had betrayed him. His hands had strayed toward her as if instinctively seeking contact, communion.

Sarah knew she perplexed him. Alex was such a logical man, and this wasn't in the least logical. The last person he should want to love would be a butterfly who couldn't seem to roost in one place long enough to taste it. Yet, she knew better. The more she spoke to him or basked in his smiles and scowls, she knew that she might be the butterfly, but he was the earth. Patient and knowing and solid, waiting for her, settling her and giving her rest. Alex would be the person who made her whole.

Throwing off the covers, Sarah bunched up a pillow and threw her arms over it, seeking warmth even on this hot night. She burrowed her face into the marshmallow softness and thought of the unyielding strength of Alex's chest.

The last person she would have imagined herself with. A football player. A man who for fifteen years spent his autumns butting heads and scrambling for a ball. A man who came away from that with regret and insight, who saw his life in terms of routines and rituals, but who never suspected the fires he had banked beneath his pragmatism.

What was it she had seen in his smile, the past that so colored him, that aged his eyes and steeled his resolve? Whatever it was, it had to do with his silent astonishment at her family. Alex had a completely different image of community than Sarah had been given, and much of it had to do with trials that had tested his steely determination. Trials that had hurt him, had strengthened him, had solidified his commitment.

Alex would never understand Blue and John and Jared, who had all traveled together after Blue and Jared's wedding. He would never fully comprehend what the life had been like when free love had ruled and children were community property. Sometimes Sarah missed those days when she'd run barefoot in the fields and been able to call upon any of twelve mothers. But there were other times when she envied Alex the normal upbringing that so formed him.

When Sarah had children, she didn't think she would give them to anyone else to raise. Neither would she send them away. And she would give them a father, one father, who would be as devoted to them as she.

It was comforting to know Alex would be that father.

"I'd make a lousy father."

Sarah took a look at the expression on Alex's face and laughed. "I guess that means you don't see the attraction of a Snarkalump."

"Attraction?" he countered, turning the lumpy ball of bright blue fur over in his hands. "I don't even see the face."

"Exactly," she said with a nod. "It's kind of like a Yorkie or an English Sheepdog. It's what makes them adorable."

"*Does* it have eyes?"

Sarah took the toy from Alex and lifted a section of fur. The hand-sewn eyes were more reminiscent of a basset hound's than a sheepdog's.

Alex settled for a small frown. "It'll probably make you a fortune. After all, I was the one who said that the Great Perpetual Motion Machine wouldn't last out the month."

"That's because you're too regimented, Alex." Resettling the fur, Sarah packed the Snarkalump back into its box and handed it over with another two. "For your nieces."

He rolled his eyes. "They'll be insufferable. Thank you."

"Do you need another yet for your sister?"

"Thanks, no," he retorted. "She prefers to play with toy soldiers."

Sarah grimaced. It was two days since they'd shared

dinner in her office. Two days in which Sarah had developed increasing difficulty in concentration. The staff had suspected premonitions. Sarah had to admit to herself that it hadn't been premonitions so much as visions. Fantasies. Memories of the taste and feel of Alex Thorne woven amid vague plans for the future.

Today she'd bumped into him in the accounting office when she'd wandered in the wrong door from the design department and remembered that she'd promised to show him the new toy line. It seemed more fun than coming up with a color scheme for Waldo's Restaurants, after all.

He smelled like soap, like citrus and cool breezes. Sarah wanted to close her eyes and take in the feel of him. But the gossip was already flying, and Sarah knew it didn't need any fuel. There was already an office pool going betting on whether Alex would win Sarah's hand or dump her in the dust, an image Sarah didn't particularly care for. Nobody would tell Sarah how the betting was split, but one look at each of her employees told the tale—the betting was heavily against her.

"Y'know," Alex was saying, bouncing the boxes a little in his hands as if weighing something. "Now that the Great Perpetual Motion Machine has been brought up, I've been meaning to ask you."

"I can get one of those for you, too." She smiled sweetly.

"Why didn't you tell me about your patents?"

Sarah shrugged, uncomfortable as always with that kind of thing. "You didn't ask."

Alex refused to retreat. "I would have thought a patent would be a pretty big deal. I'd think *six* would be cause for a media blitz."

"They were just ideas," Sarah defended herself. "I jotted some things down on napkins, I think, and Connie made sure I didn't give anything away."

"All of them?"

"No, the trauma table I did on one of those paper sheets when I was in the emergency room one time after falling off my bike. The table was too high to get up on, so I figured a way to incorporate a step stool and hydraulics."

Alex seemed capable of no more than a shake of the head.

"On a paper sheet."

She nodded. "They let me keep it."

He shook his head again.

"Sarah, there you are."

Both Alex and Sarah turned to see Thaddeus and Connie standing in the stockroom door, their expressions comically alike. Sarah didn't know whether to laugh or scowl.

"I'm stealing three Snarkalumps," she admitted, motioning to the boxes in Alex's hand. "Bribes for the accountant."

Connie swung a dry look in Alex's direction. "Enjoy them in good health."

"Cheaper than a cat," he retorted easily. "And you don't have to walk them."

It sounded as if Thaddeus swallowed his reaction.

"We're going to test-run the animation. Want to see a finished product?"

Sarah's grin flattened. "Are you going to explain it?"

"Put your fingers in your ears," Connie suggested. "It wouldn't look good if the company's president won't even look at her products."

"You know what computers do to me, Con." Sarah could see the polite bemusement on Alex's face. Of course, some of his best friends were computers. "I actually get headaches when Thaddeus explains how he programs. It frustrates me because I can't follow him at all."

"Computers only do what you tell them to."

"Computers," she retorted, "are relentlessly logical. I am not."

They had stepped out of the stockroom and now fol-

lowed Connie and Thaddeus toward the computer animation office. Sarah knew she was dragging her feet. She was
already nauseated at the anticipation of hearing them instruct her on how to program the images.

Rendering, they called it. One rendered a computer animation, and it was a process so complicated that one four-
second television station identification took them up to two
weeks' solid work. And they wanted her to understand it.

"If it makes you so crazy," Alex said as he matched
her slow step, "why introduce it? It's still your company."

"Because I have Thaddeus. I knew that he and Connie
would find the people needed to take care of the nuts and
bolts. If I gave them the image I wanted, I could hide in
my office until it showed up in three dimensions. It's a
spectacular tool," she admitted. "I just don't want to see
it work."

"You don't work with the computers at all?"

Offering a resigned sigh, Sarah looked up at Alex. "I'm
the only person in the office who writes letters on a type-
writer and submits expense reports in longhand. It's another part of being so very right-brained. I have no sense
of linear logic. I can't take point A to point C by way of
point B, and without that, I can't work a computer."

Alex, like all left-brained people, truly didn't comprehend. It was like the sighted trying to understand blindness,
except that the blind to them had a legitimate handicap.
The lack of logic seemed frivolous. "It just takes patience," he suggested.

"You were good at algebra," she challenged. "Weren't
you?"

"Sure."

"I flunked. I could tell them every answer to every question, but that didn't count unless I could come up with the
steps. I never could. It's like being dyslexic in a way."

Maybe "dyslexic" was a term he understood. Sarah saw
that he at least pondered it now. Maybe that was better.

"In that case," Alex said with a grin, "I guess I'd better not let you stop off in accounting and shut down my terminal before we head on to the demonstration."

"I'll go in with you and offer support."

They passed the news on to the other two and then dropped off at the door to accounting. Hector looked up from where he was working in his glassed-in office at the back. Jill, bent over receipts and logs, never turned. Other than that, the office was empty.

Sarah followed Alex over to where his notes were spread out on the desk and waited as he took his seat. The sun rode high outside the tinted windows, flattening an already colorless sky. In the distance Camelback crouched between them and the downtown area. Trees drooped in the afternoon heat. Traffic was picking up as rush hour approached. Sarah could hear it as a vague grumble, and thought how glad she was she didn't have to brave that. She had a car, but it suffered from neglect, since she walked where she needed to go.

"It really is a pretty place," she said, looking out to the clean lines of the horizon. "But it's hard to appreciate it from here. A balloon or an airplane…no, a balloon. It's quiet and solitary and close enough to see the landscape. It's too bad you can't use a balloon for an airplane logo."

Behind her, Alex pecked at the keyboard without answering. Sarah really didn't expect him to respond. If he was anything like Thaddeus, he'd keep only half an ear for her anyway while he teased that thing.

Besides, she was having quite enough fun thinking about Alex and herself alone in a balloon above the Superstition Mountains. Sarah and Alex and the wind, maybe a hawk swooping close as it cut arcs in the hot blue sky.

Not that they could really take a balloon out by themselves. Sarah didn't know the first thing about flying hot-air balloons, except that you put more hot air in to make it go up. So she guessed Randolph would have to come along, too.

"Champagne," she said quietly to the window. "And maybe some fried chicken. Does that sound like a lunch for a balloon ride? I think it sounds like fun. I thought we could go Saturday, if you're not doing anything."

"Well, hell…"

Sarah turned halfway around. "If you'd rather have something else, I can ask Randolph. He'd know. He's always taking the balloon up for sunset flights."

"No."

Now Sarah was facing him. "Why not? Don't you like heights?" Alex didn't lift his eyes from the screen as he kept punching keys. "Look at this."

Sarah scowled at him, but he didn't seem to notice. "What's wrong?" she asked without moving. She didn't even like to face the screen. All those symbols and numbers seemed to taunt her.

"I was going to print out this month's accounts according to company. What you do is—"

"Alex."

He heard the warning and looked up.

"I don't want to know what you do. Really. Is there a problem, yes or no?"

His frown dissipated with the wry smile that crept in at the edges of his eyes. "Yes."

"Do you need help?"

The smile broadened a little more. "Yes. Can you get Thaddeus in here? I think he'll know what to do."

"Fine," she said with a nod. "Just don't start talking loops and dot commands."

"How 'bout viruses?"

She was almost out the door when he said it. Sarah turned around, her chest suddenly tight. "As in you don't feel well, or the computer doesn't?"

"The computer."

Slowly she nodded her head. Sarah understood the theory of viruses. Someone had programmed in a command to sabotage the computer. Beyond that, she didn't want to dwell on any of it. The bright balloon of her fantasies shredded and disappeared.

"I'll get Thaddeus."

Chapter 7

Sarah sat hunched over her drawing board, a silver marker in her hand as she outlined the hunter-green title she'd just designed for Sunset Toys. They'd had a logo already, one almost ready for production, but Sarah liked these bright balloons better, the one with stripes of pink and purple and orange lifting in front of the others with big checks of green and white. The logo was whimsical and fun. Just the sight of it made her think of fantasies and escape.

Outside her window the night pulsed, and inside, Debussy swelled from the speakers. Sarah wiggled her toes in the thick carpet and brushed a free hand through her hair. When the door opened into her office, she refused to look up.

"No."

It took him a moment to answer. "You know what I want to ask?"

Sarah went on outlining, the strokes of the marker sure and swift and exact. "Why do you think I left? You're going to tell me that Thaddeus can't seem to fix the system, and do I want to call in somebody from the outside to assist?'' Now she looked up and knew that Alex could see her encroaching fear. ''Especially since Thaddeus might be the one who sabotaged it in the first place.''

Standing so solidly in the doorway, even with his tie loosened and his shirtsleeves hastily rolled up, Alex looked the picture of stability—of certainty. ''It's something you have to consider, Sarah.''

Sarah found herself wanting to run to him, to cower in the safety of his arms. ''I know,'' she admitted. ''But I can't have another outsider in this company. It would be too much.''

''And if it is Thaddeus?''

She offered an uncomfortable shrug, wishing she had more than the rationalizations she'd collected and dispersed the past two hours while she'd waited. ''The last time I was in there, Connie and Hector and Jill were helping. It can't be all of them, can it?''

''I don't know,'' Alex answered, coming closer. ''Can it?''

Sarah's head snapped up at that, her spine stiffening. ''No,'' she answered definitely. ''It can't.''

Alex's smile should have been amused. Instead, somehow, it conveyed sympathy. ''For the same reason the problem can't be in the Virginia plant?''

''Yes,'' she answered hotly.

Alex had reached the other side of the drawing board. His shadow fell over the balloons. For some reason, Sarah shivered. Like dancing on a grave, she thought distractedly, seeing the color sap from her drawing and wondering what it meant. Sunset Toys, the future of the company in shadow, in doubt? Maybe in trouble, and it was Alex casting the shadow.

Recapping her marker, she shoved the logo beneath the other papers piled on the table and stepped away.

''What do I have to do?'' she asked, still not comfortable facing the unyielding pragmatism in Alex's eyes. Make my problems disappear, she wanted to beg. Wave your strong, capable hands and take away the fear, the growing uncertainty that one of my friends is betraying me.

"What do you want to do?" he asked.

Stopping a few feet away, Sarah looked up at him. She knew he saw what she was feeling. She was hopeless at masking her emotions. His eyes shone in the scattered light from the arced lamp over her table. They were soft, like spring earth, as comfortable as steeped tea. Waiting, watching. Knowing.

"I want to run away," she admitted in a small voice. She was surprised when he smiled.

"Okay. Where would you like to go?"

Sarah tilted her head a little, trying to assess his intent, trying to brush away the tiny thrills of anticipation his invitation provoked.

"How can we?" she countered, trying for once to be the practical one. "The computer system is sick."

"And it has four doctors attending it who wouldn't miss us for a week."

Sarah sighed, feeling the weight of her own request, the series of events she'd set in order. Somehow it didn't help her to know that the person she was in effect accusing had initiated his own problems, had deliberately set out to hurt the company. Instead she felt that it was all her fault, born of her impressions, conceived with her unease. It was her fault that Alex was here, that he was in danger, that he would refuse to stop his search until one of her friends was exposed as a villain—or Alex himself was hurt.

Not for the first time in her life, Sarah wished her gift on someone else.

"Why don't you let me take you home?" Alex asked, taking her by the arms.

Sarah stiffened against the sudden desire to fold into him. "No," she said. "No, I don't want to go home."

"But it's late, Sarah," he objected. "And you can't do anything here to help."

Sarah looked up at him then. He was unconsciously brushing her arms with his thumbs, back and forth, gently, hypnotically. "Could we just drive for a while?" When he smiled, she felt the ground solidify at her feet. She felt her own weight ease a little.

"Where would you like to go?"

She grinned. "It doesn't really matter," she admitted. "I won't know where I am anyway."

Phoenix was an easy city to navigate. New enough to have wide boulevards, sensible enough to have a consistent street plan. Ten o'clock at night wasn't the time Alex would have thought he'd like to see the city, but he found that he was enjoying it.

The heat had died with the sun. A cool mountain breeze whipped in the window as they headed east through Scottsdale and past all the high-priced resorts that had been springing up. The sky overhead was clear, and the city sparkled like a new blanket of jewels. Alex could smell flowers of some kind on the night air and heard the restless rustle of palms.

Alongside him, Sarah leaned back against the seat, her eyes closed.

"How do you know where you're going?" she asked, not bothering to look.

Alex took a second to glance over at the distant columns and rowed palms of the Scottsdale Princess. Opulent and exotic, a far cry from the suburbs of Denver.

"Natural gift, I guess," he answered, heading instinctively for the mountains. He might not like deserts, but mountains were another thing altogether.

"I'm not completely directionally handicapped," she

defended herself. "I can get around Richmond blind-folded."

"Then why move?" he asked.

"Because I was outvoted. Connie and Thaddeus thought we'd do better in the Sunbelt."

Alex couldn't help looking over at her in surprise. "So just like that, you move?"

The streetlights flickered over Sarah's face. Seen that way, she looked even younger, childlike. Just ingenious enough to have said what she did.

"We *have* done well here," she retorted without opening her eyes.

Alex battled the instinctive frustration her words provoked. Who had let this innocent out on the streets? Who had told her she could be an adult when she couldn't even seem to make decisions on an adult level? It would surprise him if somebody *wasn't* stealing her blind. She was too trusting, too open, too impulsive for her own good. And there was always somebody out there ready to take advantage of that.

"Sarah—"

He glanced over to see that her eyes were open now. Open and smiling, and more knowing than he'd given her credit for.

"No," she said with new life in her voice. "They didn't take advantage of me. I'm perfectly content wherever I live. And Phoenix is as lovely as Richmond, only in a different way. So if it doesn't matter to me, what's wrong with deferring to the others? They're my friends." Now her smile broadened, and Alex knew she had him. "They're also the gears that put this engine into drive. It can't hurt to keep them happy."

"What if one of them is the one doing this?"

Alex felt her stiffen, saw the smile die. The night seemed to chill a little without it.

"I don't know." Turning back to the front, she pulled

a restless hand through hair that tumbled in the wind. "I won't know what I'll do until I find out what's going on."

They spent the next few miles in silence as the golf courses and Arabian studs slipped by, the city stretching out toward the hills beyond.

"Alex?"

"Yes?"

"What were you working on when the computer went dead?"

Alex hazarded another brief glance at Sarah and saw that her eyes were open and dark, facing the night like a personal specter.

"Accounts receivable."

Slowly Sarah turned toward him. "Jill?"

Instinctively he shrugged. "It's her department."

"And you think the breakdown was deliberate?"

"It sure looks like it."

"To keep somebody from looking at those records?"

"It would make sense."

Nodding, she looked away. "Who's capable of that?"

"I'd have to say damn near anybody in the office but you," he admitted. "You've collected quite a computer-literate staff."

"That's too bad."

"Yeah," he agreed, wishing he could somehow ease her dilemma. "I guess it is."

They weren't mountains like he was used to. These were more like hills dusted in chaparral and cactus. Even so, they lifted them above the city and silenced the night. Alex turned off onto a dirt road that twisted back toward Phoenix and shut off the engine.

Below them the lights in the valley spread out in a bath of glitter. The Southern Range blotted out the sky in the distance and the Superstitions ringed the night off to the left. Above, the stars mimicked the city for brilliance in a moonless sky, and behind them Granite Mountain was restless with night animals.

"This is beautiful," Sarah breathed without moving. "I don't think I've ever seen it like this."

Alex nodded, enjoying the light spring in her perfume even more than the clean desert scent wafting in from the windows. "Reminds me a little of the view of Los Angeles from Mulholland. Except that the air's clearer here. I wouldn't mind coming back when it's a lot cooler and doing some camping."

"You wouldn't think of living here?" she asked.

"I like being able to go outside during the summer."

"Oh, it's not that bad," Sarah argued. "After all, there's very little humidity. That makes it feel cooler."

Alex laughed. "A hundred and ten degrees is still a hundred and ten degrees. After growing up in Portland, Oregon, anything above seventy is heatstroke range. Especially for me."

Alex saw Sarah look over at him, her head tilted a little, the breeze from her window winnowing through her hair. She sat quietly, her hands for once still in her lap. "What's your family like?" she asked.

It took a minute for Alex to answer. He sensed something from Sarah, some need he couldn't name that solidified around that question. She asked it easily enough, as if seeking no more than passing conversation. But even so, he heard an echo. A distant sigh that seemed wishful.

The idea made him want to shake his head. Now *he* was hearing things.

Turning a little in his seat so that he could rest his back against the door and watch Sarah, Alex crossed an ankle over his knee and slung an arm over the seat. Sitting next to him in the soft darkness, Sarah looked once again ethereal, half real and half dream, with the starlight dusting her hair and the night protecting her. He refrained from reaching out to touch her just to make sure.

"My family?" he asked instead. "Middle-class. Pretty normal. My father is an engineer and my mother taught second grade. I have one older brother, Mark, who's responsible for the nieces. Another brother, Phil, who's in the air force, and the one sister, Lindsay, a psychologist."

"The pregnant one."

He nodded, grinning. "The very pregnant one."

"Tell me about her."

Alex again saw something in her eyes seeping out beneath the shadows. "What about her?" he asked.

Sarah shrugged, her movements small as if in apology. "You and she went through a lot together."

Alex opened his mouth and then closed it again. "Did Ellis tell you?"

Sarah's eyes were ghostly now, almost eerie in the dark. Alex felt a funny chill snake its way down his neck. He hadn't said anything about Lindsay; he knew it. It wasn't something he shared easily. But Sarah knew. He could see it in her expression. Not inquiry, but certainty. Understanding before the words were even out.

Alex didn't tell people about what Lindsay had gone through, because it was no one's business. All the same, he told Sarah. And when he told her, he felt somehow as if it belonged between them.

"Lindsay's the one who always tagged along after me. Dated my teammates in high school and harassed me into teaching her to drive. We were always pretty close." He realized he was smiling, the picture of his determined little sister filling his memory. "She was married before. Widowed. Her husband, Patrick, had a lot of problems, and Lindsay took them all on her shoulders. She's kind of like that. Patrick was killed in a traffic accident. Died in Lindsay's arms. She'd been driving." Again pictures assailed him, sensations he'd forgotten a long time ago. The shrill of the late-night phone call, the smell of disinfectant and blood in the emergency room. Lindsay, stark and shattered, her head bandaged and her hands shaking uncontrollably. The oppressive, hostile silence of her home those next few days. The fury and frustration and terror that mounted as she slipped further and further away.

"After all she'd been through with Patrick," he said, his eyes still back on Lindsay's grief, her guilt and despair, "she couldn't handle his death. We almost lost her."

He didn't realize Sarah had reached over until he'd stopped speaking, until he felt her warm hand on his arm. Alex looked down at the simple gesture, up again at the pain that must have been such a close mirror to the memory in his own eyes.

"That's what it was," she whispered, her eyes glittered softly. "I didn't know. It was horrible for you."

Settling his own hand over hers, Alex smiled, wondering at how easily he shared that private hell with Sarah. How comfortable it felt resting with her. Always before he'd brushed it off, distanced himself from it as if it hadn't hurt quite so much if he denied it.

But it had hurt. It had changed him. In the period of two months when he'd wheedled, cajoled and threatened Lindsay into hanging on to her life, he'd grown from a self-absorbed jock into an adult.

He'd outgrown Barbi and decided that he wasn't going to look back.

"Yeah," he agreed quietly. "It was. But it was worth it."

Sarah didn't seem to need any more than that. Alex could feel it in the tension of her fingertips. He saw it in the liquid emotion in her eyes. His own emotions rose and ebbed, as if called up and then drained from him. His memories danced between the darkness and the light, finally settling on the moment he'd stood up for Lindsay and her new husband, Jason, on their wedding day. Alex felt the old familiar tug of family affection that would never be spoken of in the Thorne household, communicated rather in gruff embraces and teasing, and knew that Sarah recognized it.

"Tell me about your family," he said in return.

For a minute Alex wasn't sure Sarah had heard him. She seemed to still be caught amid his words, unwilling to release his past just yet, unable to break the tie. Finally she took her hand back and used it to pluck at the folds of her linen skirt.

"My birth family," she asked, "or my celestial family?"

Alex grimaced. "I don't think we have time for that. How about just the people you ate dinner with on a regular basis?"

Sarah nodded, looking up as if to remember. "Well, that narrows it down to about forty."

"Forty."

She nodded. "Give or take a few. We ate on trestle tables. I helped prepare vegetables every night. We read passages from either the Upanishads or Thoreau before eating, and then sang after cleaning up."

"You really went to Woodstock?"

She nodded. "All I remember is being cold, wet and hungry. I kind of think of it as a refugee camp with music."

"How did you ever get from that to Zydeco music?" he demanded.

She grinned. "I never question the muse, Alex."

"I bet Blue taught you that."

She laughed. "No. Blue wasn't in the least musical. She was the quilter and herbalist."

Alex couldn't help but shake his head. He'd seen the tail end of the hippie era, touching its edges in high school, but he'd been too involved in schoolwork, too driven by football, to try to save the world. A typical self-centered, confused, frustrated teenage athlete.

"Is the commune still there?"

Sarah shook her head. "The last I saw of it, the land had been turned into a strip shopping mall. I haven't been back since."

"What about the people?"

She shrugged, the gesture a little stiff. "I don't know."

Alex kept his silence. He wanted to ask why, where had all those people gone who had sung with her and taught her and shaped her into the person she was. But something barred his way, some defense Sarah had erected with her hands where they lay clenched in her lap.

"Do you get together for holidays?" she asked quietly, her eyes straying to where she fingered the material in her lap.

"Holidays?" Alex echoed. "Sure. Whoever can, that is. What about you?"

Sarah smiled then, and it broke Alex's heart. She looked like a little child again, the girl who stood all alone at the edge of the crowd, too unsure of herself to join in.

"Blue celebrates Tet," she said, "and John prefers Ramadan."

"He's Muslim?"

The smile grew deprecating. "No. He just enjoys being singular. He has his chance now in Central America."

"What about you?"

She looked up with a wry grin. "Whatever strikes me," she said. "Since I don't have to check with anybody else's plans, it's easy to do."

"You don't have anybody else?"

Sarah shrugged. "Blue and Jared never had any children. I haven't seen my cousins since the various families reacted to the commune idea. I don't even think I'd recognize them."

"What about Connie?"

"She usually visits her parents. And, uh, we aren't comfortable in each other's company."

"What are you doing for Labor Day?" he asked, surprised at his own impulse.

Sarah looked up, her eyes dark and vulnerable. "What?"

"Labor Day," Alex insisted, fighting the urge to pull her into his arms and salve her isolation. "Or don't hippies celebrate that?"

Sarah's smile regained some of its sparkle. "Power to the people," she retorted. "Sure we do. I'm not doing anything, as far as I know. But I wasn't angling for an invitation."

Alex nodded, reaching over to take hold of her restless hand again. "You got one anyway. Lindsay's house for a barbecue."

"Pregnant Lindsay?" she asked. "Aren't you being a bit frivolous with your invitations?"

"By September she'll be dying for some company."

"I don't know," she countered coyly. "Do you think I'll get along with a woman who thinks I'm probably just another Barbi?"

Again Alex opened his mouth. Again he closed it. Sarah was smiling a sly, triumphant smile that told him she'd just won the round. He'd never mentioned Barbi's name to her. True, Ellis could have told her that. But he hadn't told anyone Lindsay's reaction to Sarah.

And Sarah had just told him.

Why did that make him feel so suddenly defensive? He wanted to ward her off, like Thaddeus with his evil-eye sign. Like Ellis battling evil spirits with chants and feathers. Sarah's sight endangered him, and it wasn't from guns and bandits.

But the attraction was stronger than the fear. Alex couldn't pull away.

"You're not a thing like Barbi," he countered easily. "You can count more than ten without taking off your shoes."

Sarah's bright laughter cleared the lingering past like a fresh breeze. Regrets and half-understood longings were swept away, and the night bubbled once again with her animation.

Alex stroked Sarah's palm with his thumb, thinking how very soft and small it was. How graceful. Alex had always thought of hands as tools, engineering marvels constructed for strength and dexterity. He'd never thought of them as artwork. But Sarah's hands were works of art. They danced, they soared, they sang in flight, their punctuation leaps and pirouettes.

They couldn't belong to anyone but Sarah.

"Hey," she said, suddenly squeezing his hand back as she straightened. "Did we eat dinner yet?"

Alex looked up at her. "What?"

"Aren't you starved?"

He didn't even think to lie. "Yes." And he knew that she understood he wasn't talking about food.

He heard her breath catch. He saw her eyes go a little wide. Her hand stilled in his and fluttered like a bird startled in its nest. His own body responded. Tautened. He felt it in his gut, a hot ache that coiled in anticipation.

"Alex—"

Before Sarah had the chance to object or ask, Alex kissed her. Leaning forward, one hand in hers, the other catching her along her jaw where he could feel the startled stumble of her pulse, he trapped her words.

She tasted like sunlight, like sweetness and warmth. Her mouth was pouting full with lips as soft as velvet. Her skin was smooth and fragrant. Alex curled his fingers into the hair that tumbled alongside her throat and stroked its silk. He tasted her soft groan and shuddered, his body anxious and demanding. Feeling her hand at his own jaw, he let go of the other. It lit against his chest and ignited a dark fire.

Alex reached for her, pulled her closer. Tremors ran

through her. A bird caught in a heavy hand, a flower in a hard wind, she seemed at once to quicken and die in his grasp. Alex fought for control. He tried his damnedest to reel in his senses.

But Sarah was so soft, so alive, her body responding even before she realized it. He could feel her breasts tauten against him, felt the nipples constrict through the light sweater she wore. Her fingers raked him slowly, like a cat kneading its claws. Her breath quickened into whimpers. Her lips opened to him.

So soft. He gathered her into him, easing around on the seat, fitting her more neatly against him. He kissed her cheek, her throat, her ear, soaking in the fresh-flower smell of her hair as it tickled his nose. He drew his hand along her shoulder, toward the throb at the base of her throat, lower. Sarah arched into his hand, lips parted, her breath fanning his cheek. Alex filled his hand with her breast, small and round and taut beneath the coarse cotton of the sweater. He felt her shudder, heard her gasp and knew that she was smiling.

And because of that, because she was happy, because he wanted her so badly that the hurt ricocheted through him like a high-caliber bullet, Alex let go.

"Dinner might not be such a bad idea," he murmured into the soft mass of her hair, trying to regain control. It had been a long time since his own body had betrayed him like this. A very long time since he'd considered trying to fold himself into absurd positions in the back seat of a car.

But that's just what he was doing now, and it wasn't fair to Sarah.

For a moment Sarah was silent. Still caught tightly in Alex's embrace, her cheek against his chest, she let her own breathing ease. "Are you sure?" she asked.

Alex wondered whether he'd hurt her. He lifted his head to see her swollen mouth, her languorous eyes and uncertain anticipation.

"Do you really want to tell our firstborn that we conceived him in the back seat of a rental?" he demanded, doing his best to smile. If Sarah was worth her salt as a soothsayer, she could tell just how much it took for him to be a gentleman. Even now his body clamored for release. For Sarah.

Sarah smiled back. "I wouldn't mind telling him we conceived him at the house."

Alex wanted to groan. Instead he lifted a finger and ran it down her nose. "Well, now, that's something completely different. Although, your friends are still back at the office trying to crack the problem."

Sarah couldn't have realized how wistful her smile looked. "They won't miss me. Seems to me we were going to have dinner anyway...."

His body bucked with the promise in her eyes. Damn. Alex was hanging on to his professionalism by his fingertips. He'd already lost his objectivity. One more look at those wide, wide eyes did it. Pulling Sarah into his arms for a last, serious kiss, Alex turned back to the steering wheel. "Not another word, or I'm going to run us into a ditch."

Sarah felt as if something had lodged in her chest and couldn't quite get free. She hadn't said anything to Alex since they'd started back, nor could she think of anything *to* say. The feeling of imminence was strong, a crescive anticipation that sent her thoughts flying and scattered her sense.

But was it the sight of just exhilaration? Sitting so close to Alex, watching the sure, steady movements of his hands as he guided the car back to her house and thinking of what those hands would be like on her, she couldn't tell. She had an overwhelming urge to giggle, to sing or move. Her body whispered to her. Her mind tumbled from possibility to improbability.

She'd felt it in him the minute he'd taken her into his arms. Heat, emanating from a source even he didn't suspect. Exhilaration, desire. His muscles sang like the rigging of a ship in rising wind. His jaw tightened so abruptly Sarah could almost hear his teeth grind.

Alex thought he knew himself. He imagined that he had a keen control over his body, over the less orderly preoccupations of his hormones.

But Sarah knew something Alex didn't. When Alex had taken her hand, had stroked her palm the way he would her body, she'd seen the surprise that hadn't yet appeared in his eyes. She'd heard the echoes of a cry that had yet to be voiced. She knew that he wouldn't recognize his own surrender until it had already passed.

It was with mixed emotions that Sarah opened the car door and stepped out onto her driveway. Equal parts anticipation and trepidation. Unholy exhilaration. Alex slammed his door and followed her across to the porch. Sarah sensed his tension, heard his quick tread and the shallow cant of his breathing. Her own wasn't much deeper. She fought off the urge to giggle. They both were probably going to hyperventilate before they even got inside.

Her heels clicking on the cement porch, she turned for her key.

"Oh, dear..."

Behind her, Alex slowed to a halt. "What's the matter?"

Sarah looked around, disoriented, still preoccupied by her body's rebellious reaction.

"My key."

"You don't have it?"

She looked back to the car, trying to think. "I must have left my purse at work." Just to be sure, she dug into her pockets, pulling from the deep folds of her denim skirt buttons and rubber bands and the watch she'd taken off to

wash her hands sometime earlier that day. And her earrings.

"Oh," she marveled, looking at them. "There they
are." They got set down on the porch along with her other
treasures. There were, however, no keys.

Alex couldn't seem to take his eyes off the growing pile
on the porch. "Those look like diamonds," he ventured,
motioning to where the earrings glinted up in the light
from Sarah's living room windows.

"Uh-huh," she nodded absently, following with two
business cards and a handful of sunflower seeds. "Connie
gave them to me for Christmas last year. To celebrate our
success."

Giving her pockets one last pat, she wandered off into
the yard.

"Sarah?"

"Just a minute." It had been Connie's idea to leave a
key there. Tucked into a little holder burrowed into the
planter she'd had built around her pine. Sarah just had to
remember which corner. She found it on the third try.

"I used to leave it under the mat," she admitted, stepping past Alex to pull open the glass door and slide the
key into her oak-and-glass front door. "But I kept taking
the mat inside to clean it and leaving the key sitting out
on the porch."

The door swung open and Sarah reached over to punch
in her security code to the alarm system. Then she returned
the key to its holder and the holder to its hiding place.
Alex waited on the porch right by where she'd left all her
gatherings.

Sarah had almost made it back to him when it dawned
on her.

"Uh-oh," she murmured, chagrined.

Alex looked up. "Uh-oh, what?"

She lifted her head to listen and then shook it. Sgt. Valdez wouldn't be happy. "Might as well just sit outside now."

Alex watched her sit down on the edge of her porch, the big door still open, light spilling out into the yard.

"Sarah, what are you doing?" he asked.

"Waiting. Have a seat." She was embarrassed enough already, without having to explain. He'd know soon enough, anyway—from the sounds of it, in about thirty or forty seconds.

"Well, at least pick up your earrings," he suggested, and bent to get them.

That was when the glass door shattered.

"What the—?"

Sarah heard a cracking noise from across the street somewhere. Alex whirled around with more speed than Sarah would have thought possible. Shards of glass tinkled onto her entryway and scattered over the porch. Sarah looked at the door and then at Alex, as if he could explain.

Instead, Alex jumped on top of her.

"Alex, really—"

There was another crack and Alex rolled them both off the porch into the flower bed.

"My geraniums," Sarah protested, struggling to get free. "Alex, get up before the police get here."

"Somebody's shooting at us," he whispered in her ear.

She instinctively tried to see. "What?"

That earned her another close inspection of the topsoil she'd spread. "Hold still. We have to get to some shelter."

"Shooting at us?" she echoed stupidly, thinking instead that he did have a hairy chest. It was tickling her nose where he pressed against her. His hand was on her head, and his arms were around her, shielding her from whoever was out there. "Well, they'll leave in a minute."

"What makes you so sure?" he countered. "Premonition?"

"No," she admitted to his pectorals. "When I opened the door, I punched in the wrong code."

Alex lifted his head just enough to get a look at her. "What code did you punch?"

Sarah did her best to smile. "One that said I was being held hostage."

Once Alex moved, Sarah noticed the flashing lights.

"All right, pal," the loudspeaker barked even as three more police cars screeched to a halt. "Let her up and throw out your weapon now, or you'll be breathing through your forehead."

Chapter 8

"Hey, you're Alex Thorne!"

Gritting his teeth in frustration, Alex did his best to ignore the gun barrel tattooing his temple. "Yes," he grated out, his face pressed close enough to the concrete to smell the dust in the cracks. "I'm Alex Thorne."

His fingers were laced behind his neck, and he was lying prone and spread-eagled on Sarah's sidewalk. Police cars choked the streets, and neighbors were already spilling out from nearby doors to watch the show. And just above his right ear, at the other end of the .357 that seemed far too friendly with his forehead, a young policeman was inspecting the wallet he'd just pulled from Alex's back pocket.

"Why would you want to hurt Miss Delaney?" he asked.

"Alex Thorne?" one of the other cops demanded, approaching. "I don't believe it. Stand him up, Phillips. I wanna see this."

Phillips retreated just enough to let Alex up.

"No kiddin'," the other policeman said in awe as Alex

did his best to straighten out a knee that had met with the corner of Sarah's porch on the way down. "We got us an all-pro here, boys. Why don't we see you on those beer commercials?"

Alex offered a wan smile. "Because crime pays so well," he said.

The gathering police laughed. The sergeant was looking way up at Alex, much as he might the Empire State Building.

"What happened?" one of them asked. "She punch in the wrong code again?"

Alex moved his hands just enough to remind his audience of his uncomfortable position. The sergeant who watched football immediately waved an at-ease and re-holstered his own gun. Alex brushed the dirt from his shirt. He had a sneaking suspicion he still had geranium petals in his hair from the fast dive off the porch.

"Roy Waller," the sergeant introduced himself with a huge smile, hand now outstretched. "Pleasure to meet you, Mr. Thorne."

"Alex," Alex amended, shaking hands with the bantam-sized officer. "I'm never formal with a man who has the power to strip-search me."

"So, what happened?"

"Sarah punched in the wrong code," he admitted, hand to his sore knee, his gaze swinging to where he'd left Sarah. "But just after she did, we were shot at."

Sgt. Waller was at immediate attention. "Shot at? Miss Delaney?"

Alex didn't even hear him. He had his back turned to the sergeant as he searched through the gathering crowd.

"It came from across the street," he allowed, eyebrows puckering. "I doubt they're still around, but you might find something."

"I'd sure like to hear that from her," the sergeant allowed, pulling out a notebook.

Alex was turning in the other direction. "So would I," he admitted. "Anybody see her?"

Several nearby heads lifted. Conversations faltered.

"Miss Delaney?" Sgt. Waller called as if that alone would bring her from the shadows. He didn't have any luck.

In the time it had taken the police to swarm all over Alex as if he'd walked out of a bank, Sarah had disappeared.

"Where are you going?" Sgt. Waller asked.

Alex threw open what was left of the storm door and stepped into the house. There was no knowing what Sarah would do. He could still feel the shock echoing in him, the bolt of adrenaline when he'd recognized the sound of gunfire. He'd been through this before. As far as he knew, Sarah hadn't. If she had any sense, she'd still be flat out in the flower bed, shaking like a new baby in the cold.

Not Sarah. She'd not only managed to get to her feet without anybody noticing, she'd slipped away. At least he hoped she had.

Glass crackled beneath his feet as he walked across the foyer. "Sarah? Where are you?"

Silence. She wasn't inside, either. Following on Alex's heels, Waller got a good look at the shattered glass and the bullet hole in the far wall. He was impressed enough to send his minions on a search of the lawns across the street.

"Valdez was telling us about his visit to the Sunset offices," Waller admitted, crouched down to get a better look at the bullet hole. "Think this had anything to do with it?"

Just the mention of the company sent Alex's head up. He knew where Sarah had gone. "Damn her," he growled, whirling around on his heel and heading back for the door. "She needs a baby-sitter."

"Hey! Where are you going?"

"She's at the office," Alex allowed, punching his way past the shattered storm door. Outside, lights still throbbed. A Minicam had joined the crowd, and the reporter was smoothing her hair before the magnesium lights. Police milled over the lawn. A few looked up when Alex stormed out the door. When they saw the look on his face, they instinctively backed away.

"At the office?" Waller echoed incredulously. "What the hell's she headed there for? It's dark."

"Knowing Sarah," Alex retorted blackly, "she didn't even notice."

"Wait," Waller objected, a hand to Alex's arm. "I'll take you. Phillips!" he yelled. "Secure the scene until I get back! Doesn't she know about leaving the scene of a crime?" he demanded as he tried to match Alex's stride and lost.

Alex just snorted. "Have you ever talked to her, Sergeant?"

"No. I've just heard Valdez talk about her. She's kind of a favorite around the squad room. You can always depend on her to liven up the day."

Alex snorted. "I'll bet."

The two of them swung into a cruiser and Waller edged them past the Minicam.

"Police were called out to this quiet neighborhood..." the reporter was saying. Alex saw her notice him and then recognize him. Her recital faltered to a stop, but before she could assimilate the new information, Waller had the lights and siren going and had cleared the traffic.

"So, why did she go to the office?" he was asking.

Alex thought the siren was loud. The last time he'd heard one this close, he'd been sharing the back of an ambulance with a couple of paramedics. He couldn't remember the noise being so irritating. But then, he couldn't remember much about that ride at all.

"Because she's afraid that the person who fired those

shots is a friend of hers," he admitted in a voice that was a little too loud.

Waller looked over in surprise. "Somebody at the company?"

Alex nodded, his attention on the green-glass-and-chrome building that was taking shape at the edge of Waller's lights as they turned onto Greenway Boulevard. "A group of them are at the office tonight working on a computer problem. I think Sarah wanted to make sure they're still all there."

Waller was definitely interested. "And if somebody's missing, you might have a suspect, huh?"

"We might."

They swung into the Sunset Design parking lot and screeched to a stop. Alex tumbled out before Waller had a chance to so much as switch off the engine. He wanted to know himself who would be there—or who might have just slipped away for food or rest or no reason at all. Would it be Thaddeus? Hector? Jill?

And if they had decided to try to slip back into the office without anyone noticing their absence, what would they do when they stumbled across Sarah as she hurried in with only their protection in mind? Alex went from a walk to a run.

She was standing with the security guard in the foyer.

"When?" she asked, disheveled and out of breath and whispery. Her small voice echoed in the marble foyer.

Alex wanted to shake her. He wanted to hold her. Without waiting for the sergeant, he stalked on into the building.

"Oh, they been gone a couple hours now, Ms. Delaney," the guard was saying. "Miss Connie was saying something about celebrating, but everybody else voted to go home."

Alex saw Sarah slump. He didn't know whether she felt defeat or relief. He felt frustration. Walking up behind her, he took her by the shoulders and swung her around. When he saw the hurt in her eyes, he realized how very afraid he'd been.

"Didn't anybody tell you never to walk off without letting somebody know?" he demanded, the fear metamorphosing into anger. The security guard flinched at the harsh growl, obviously uncertain whether to reach for his gun or not. Sarah, on the other hand, didn't seem to know what it meant to be intimidated.

"I'm sorry," she apologized, her eyes wide, her skin the color of old milk. "I didn't mean to leave you there like that, Alex. Really."

"Me?" he countered, incredulously. "I'm not talking about me. I'm talking about you wandering around in the dark within minutes of being shot at. You don't know that they weren't still out there someplace." He should walk out. He should damn well leave her to the police and all the trusty aides she'd collected over the years. Something was getting way out of control here, and Alex didn't like it.

Surprised, Sarah blinked up at him in a way that made him think of a baby animal caught away from its nest. Lost, troubled, uncertain.

"But they were shooting at *you*," she said.

"What makes you think that?" Waller asked on approach.

"Shooting?" the security guard echoed.

Alex couldn't take his eyes off Sarah, frustrated and furious and so relieved that he wondered that he didn't shake.

Sarah looked from Alex to the policeman. "Good evening," she smiled without moving from Alex's grasp. "Alex was with me."

Waller scowled. "We figured that out. Think you're ready to include the police in this little squabble now?"

"I don't know for sure it's about the company," Sarah objected lamely.

"Any other reason somebody would want to shoot Mr. Thorne, that you know of?"

Sarah and the security guard stared at Alex. Alex scowled. "Not in the past year or so, anyway," he said. "It's time to bring in the police, Sarah."

Even more tension went out of her, as if she were a balloon slowly deflating. "I know," she whispered. "But I hate to do it."

"In the past year or so?" Waller interrupted.

Alex decided not to dredge up old and unnecessary business. "Before we get involved in long explanations," he said, already feeling the trembling take hold of Sarah, "why don't we make a few quick phone calls?" It was all he could do to keep from shoving everybody back out of the way and pulling her into his arms. Damn her.

Sarah's head shot up. She was all set to object. Alex never gave her the chance. "They came a lot closer this time, Sarah."

"Okay," Waller agreed. "But I'm still going to find out about that year-or-so situation."

"It's not as interesting as it sounds," Alex assured him dryly, and guided Sarah over to the security desk where she could dial her friends.

"None of them live that far away," she demurred.

"Do you want the guard to get the numbers?" Alex asked, settling her into a chair.

"No, thanks. I know them all."

Alex shot her a sharp glance. "You know those phone numbers by heart?"

She shook her head, a hand instinctively up to brush hair from her forehead. "I know the numbers of everybody in the company."

"By heart?"

Sarah looked at him, and Alex saw the humor finally struggling to take hold. "Sure," she said. "Why not?"

And damned if she didn't.

"Connie?" she said brightly as if a policeman weren't standing over her shoulder taking notes. "Why aren't you here?"

The voice on the other end sounded just as happy, enthusing about whatever had gone on in Sarah and Alex's absence. Sarah nodded a couple of times, offered a few monosyllabic answers and promised to see Connie at work the next morning.

"The computer's fixed," she announced, hanging up. The life had disappeared from her voice. Alex could feel the tension of duplicity radiating through her. Sarah wasn't made for the double life. She should never have had to lie to her friends or ferret out traitors. But there should have never been a hole in her front door, either.

Alex hoped he was around when they finally did come up with the embezzler. He wanted very much to add his own small justice.

Thaddeus was home as well, and kept Sarah on even longer, extolling his own virtues. Unfortunately, they weren't as lucky with Jill or Hector. Neither answered.

"These people are all considered suspects?" Waller asked, scribbling away as Sarah hung up the final time.

"Nobody's considered a suspect," she objected miserably. "We haven't even found anything wrong yet."

Waller shot an incredulous look at Alex, who could only manage a shrug. "That's what I'm doing here."

"That's why you're getting shot at and sabotaged."

"It seems."

Waller nodded, and there was nothing hesitant about the opinion. "Then there are damn well some suspects someplace. Now, who besides these four?"

Alex looked down at Sarah. She looked up at him.

"Everybody," he admitted.

Waller sighed. "Is this a shorter story than the one about somebody wanting to shoot you?"

"Yes."

"Fine. We'll give it a run-through on the way back to the crime scene."

Sarah felt as if she were battling her way out of a fog. She was so tired she could barely sit up, and yet Sgt. Waller still refused to leave. Slurping at his third cup of coffee since setting himself up in her favorite armchair, the sergeant didn't seem to be in any hurry to finish his questioning. At the moment he was asking Alex about the previous sabotage, and Alex was patiently answering.

Seated alongside him on the couch, Sarah couldn't take her eyes off the front door. Especially at the hole in the front door, marking the exact spot where Alex's head had been before he'd bent down to get her earrings.

Her earrings. Oh, well, it looked as though she'd lost them again. Or maybe the dozen or so police technicians who had swarmed over her porch would find something. She really didn't care. Earrings didn't matter in the least when balanced against a life.

Alex answered some question and Sarah turned at the sound of his voice. He hadn't moved since they'd returned. He'd seated himself next to her and put an arm around her shoulder as if to shield her from the inevitable battering of police procedure. Protecting her, when he'd been the intended victim.

How could he be so calm, so authoritative and concise when he'd missed dying by inches? How could his anger have dissipated so quickly when it was her fault he'd been there in the first place?

Sarah felt weary, defeated. One of the people she'd trusted the most had tried to kill Alex. This had all gone beyond the company, beyond her or the trust they'd built up. This involved a crime so horrible that Sarah couldn't believe she wasn't able to somehow see it on the person.

But she hadn't even seen the danger. Completely submerged in the sensual delights of anticipation, she'd blithely led Alex right up to the porch and then provided the light to make him a better target. She hadn't had a clue, not a tingling or a murmur.

Why hadn't she insisted Alex leave like she'd wanted?

Why couldn't she do it now?

"You'll be hearing from the detectives a little later," Waller said as he drained his coffee cup and lurched to his feet. "But right now, you might as well get some sleep."

Sarah blinked at the officer, wondering whether he was joking. There was still glass on the floor and gouge marks from where they had extracted the bullet from her door, cups and saucers out and dusty footprints all over her rug.

She had just suffered a convulsion in her life, a shock that echoed along her nerve endings and whispered in the quiet confines of her house. Worse, she was responsible for it and didn't know how to prevent it happening again. And he suggested she sleep, as if the only thing she had to look forward to the next morning was exams.

"Maybe you'd have better luck," she said abruptly.

Waller swung around to her. "Pardon?"

She motioned to Alex. "Get him to go home."

Waller lifted an eyebrow. "That's what I just did."

"No," Sarah insisted, getting to her own feet, away from the solace of Alex's arms, away from the temptation to depend on him when it could hurt him. "To Colorado."

She was bringing Waller to a dead stop in the water. "But I thought he came here to help you settle your books. You want him to go?"

Sarah nodded. "Yes. Please."

Now Waller included Alex in his quizzical stare.

"Sarah thinks this will all get worse before it gets better,'' Alex explained without following suit. Comfortably sprawled back on her couch, with legs crossed and coffee mug in hand, he looked to Sarah as if he were settling in for the duration.

Waller buttoned his pocket back over his notebook. ''Probably will. Want some protection?''

''No,'' Sarah insisted. ''I want him gone.''

Waller squinted at her. ''Has he caused you any problems, Miss Delaney?''

''Oh, no,'' she said quickly. ''No. He's…well, it's just that I'm afraid he'll be hurt.''

Waller's only consolation was a shrug. ''Might happen. But I think he can take care of himself.'' He was turning away before Sarah could protest further when a thought stopped him. ''Which reminds me,'' he said, turning back. ''You were going to tell me a story, Mr. Thorne.''

This time Alex got to his feet. Sarah felt him close the space between them like a blanket of energy closing over her. It protected and nurtured her—and she was afraid of it, for his sake. The more she got used to it, the harder it would be to push it away.

''How about the abbreviated version?'' Alex asked. ''Sarah's beat, and I still have to get back to the hotel for an hour or two before heading back to her offices—'' he must have sensed her objection forming, because he turned on her with a scowl ''—whether she likes it or not.''

''Something I can check out would be nice,'' Waller agreed.

''My sister works for the Special Assignment Crime Task Force out of Denver. Little over a year ago, she and an agent named Jason Mitchell got involved with a case that put her in jeopardy. He hid her at my place while he closed it, but the bad guys found her.''

''And you?'' Sarah asked, plagued by a sudden impression of numbness, surprise, anger. Desperation.

''Let's just say I didn't help much.''

"That be the Esperanzo case?" Waller asked, eyes sharp. "Mitchell really put the nails on that guy's coffin."

Busying himself with a final sip of coffee, Alex nodded.

Waller nodded back with some satisfaction. "Couldn't have happened to nicer scum. I had a taste of the Esperanzo bunch down here, too. Sent Mitchell a personal thank-you note. You tell him for me when you see him, okay?"

"Happy to," Alex agreed.

"Her husband," Sarah said.

Both men turned to her.

"He's her husband, isn't he?" she said, sharp with the impression of hard, green eyes. Determination. Ferocity like a winter storm.

"Yeah," Alex admitted, the hand with the cup sagging a little in surprise.

Sarah grinned. "I can't wait to meet him."

Waller couldn't quite take his eyes off her. "So, does this mean he's staying?"

Sarah looked up at Alex and saw an equal determination. Not so hot, so visceral. Just as impenetrable. "Yes," she succumbed, feeling worse every time she did. "I guess it does."

"Good," Waller answered with a nod as he turned once again for the door. "Saves me from having to find him when I need him again."

"I'll be here," Alex promised.

"Here?" Waller asked, not turning back around again, his message implicit.

"I'm over at the Fountains when I'm not at Sunset," Alex amended.

Sarah let Alex walk Waller outside. She contented herself to collect cups and saucers and take them to the kitchen, considering the surprise revelations the brief conversation had brought. Trying to understand why that particular door should suddenly open up into a turbulent time in Alex's past when she couldn't manage to see what was in front of her nose.

It was so frustrating. And so frightening. Sarah wanted to protect him. She wanted to offer him half of what he offered her. Yet the wisdom she relied on as much as he did his mathematical tables was as faulty as a tattered gauze in a wind. Brushing close and then disappearing, never whole, never certain. Surprising when it failed, even more surprising when it didn't.

"How did you know?" she asked when she heard him step into the kitchen behind her.

"Know what?"

The tile carried his feet comfortably, the echo satisfying and whole. Completely against her will Sarah smiled to herself, even as she dipped soapy hands into the water to finish the dishes.

"Where I'd be," she said without turning, willing him closer, wanting to slake her thirst on the substance of him. "I'd only gotten there when you arrived."

"It made sense," he said gruffly. "As much as you make sense."

That did make Sarah turn around, because she knew something he didn't. "No," she disagreed. "It didn't make sense at all. I should have called, not gone over. I almost did, except that all those police were between me and the door."

"And you didn't want them to know what you were doing before you had a chance to do it," he scowled without much humor, the light in his honey-brown eyes more troubled than even he allowed. "You scared the hell out of me, Sarah."

Sarah shook her head, wanting him to see. "Don't you understand?" she insisted. "Connie wouldn't have known. Neither would Ellis or Thaddeus."

"Sure they would," Alex retorted easily. "Hell, Sgt.

Valdez probably would have known. It only took a minute to figure out where your first thoughts would be.''

Still Sarah shook her head. "No," she said, and knew Alex wouldn't allow her conclusion yet even if she could prove it to him. "For an accountant, you're a very perceptive person.''

Alex wasn't having any of it. "Accounting isn't just figures, Sarah. It's people, too.''

She smiled and swiped at her hair. "But it's mostly figures.''

Alex walked up then and lifted a hand to her forehead. "You have suds in your hair," he objected, wiping the moisture with gentle fingers. "Why don't you have a dishwasher like every other twentieth-century businesswoman?''

Sarah couldn't pull her gaze from his, basking in the sudden warmth of that sweet brown. The rapport, the last traces of gruff frustration, the growing wonder. "I like the feel of hot, soapy water on my hands," she admitted in a soft voice, her chest suddenly tight with his nearness.

Alex's eyes seemed to grow a little, his pupils dilating. Somehow nearness.

Alex's eyes seemed to grow a little, his pupils dilating. Somehow Sarah's own words hung between them like a promise rather than a simple admission. A plea that came colored with all the turmoil they'd survived this evening, from the moment she'd first courted Alex's sensuality to the moment she'd almost cost him his life. She couldn't help the words, the invitation that accompanied them. She couldn't stop it.

"We spend all our time distancing ourselves from the simple pleasures of the world," she said, hearing the breathiness in her voice and seeing its impact on Alex. "I bet you take showers, don't you?''

"Religiously." Funny, he sounded breathless, too.

Sarah nodded, never looking away, soaking in the heat

from his eyes like a summer sun. Suddenly, she felt small
and lonely and hungry. "I bet you'd be surprised by how
delicious it feels to sit in a hot, soapy bath for an hour or
so."

"We're not talking baths here, Sarah," he reminded her,
as if reminding himself, as well. "We're talking dishes."

"Soapy water," she amended. "Hot, soapy water. It
calms me. Soothes me. I like the slippery feel of it on my
skin," she admitted. "The scent. I soak in the water and
rub at my dishes and watch my garden, and all the problems of the world slip out of focus." Alex stood only a
foot away, tense, taut, radiating a sensuality that struck
Sarah like a tide. A hot, slow, pulsing tide that threatened
to suck her under.

"Soap," he echoed in a strained voice.

Sarah nodded. "You should try it."

He didn't move. Neither did Sarah. The water on her
hands evaporated, and the soap bubbles behind her popped
in the sudden silence. Sarah didn't even know she was
going to speak. Impulse and action were simultaneous and
sincere.

"Or you could make love to me."

Chapter 9

Alex didn't move. For a long moment he didn't speak. The insects chorused outside, and in the hallway the grandfather clock ticked away in the silence. Sarah never flinched, never prodded or excused. She merely waited, as taut as he, as hesitant. As torn.

And in the stillness that stretched until it threatened to snap like frayed nerves, Alex realized he couldn't do what she wanted. What *he* wanted.

It wasn't the desire in her eyes. He'd seen that before and understood it. It wasn't the suggestion in her voice or the temptation in her request.

It was the pain. The residue of what had happened that night. Alex saw the betrayal eating at her, saw the erosion of her safe, bright world and knew that it was security she asked for. Comfort.

And he couldn't offer it the way she asked.

He'd dealt with pain before. He'd held his sister through a depression so terrifying it had almost sent her through that mirror of madness. He'd beaten off her despair and held back his own loss when his knees had kept him from walking onto the field again. He'd survived failing to protect Lindsay when she'd been at physical risk. But this wasn't the same.

This wasn't a violent emotion. Nothing about Sarah was violent or passionate or desperate. She was composed of pastels and displayed her emotions the same way—in shades of fear, hues of joy. She still looked hurt, confused, like a child who couldn't understand the capricious world of an adult. She struggled with betrayal and couldn't grasp it, and it was Alex who felt the rage.

Standing there before him, she looked not so much the sensual nymph she could be but the loneliest, the most fragile person he'd seen. And Alex was afraid that his own surprising emotions would shatter her.

His hand shaking from the control he had to exert over himself, Alex reached out to stroke her cheek. "I don't think that's such a good idea right now, Sarah."

Her smile was tentative—at once relieved and disappointed. "You mean you're turning down the first proposition I've made in my entire life?"

Alex pulled her into his arms, soapsuds and all. "I mean that tonight's not the right time. You need sleep and you need a little security, and I'll be happy to provide them both. But beyond that..." He could only shake his head, fighting the surge of need, of desire—using all his legendary willpower to fight the turmoil her innocent request had unleashed in him.

Her head tilted back, sending her hair tumbling over Alex's arms, Sarah sighed. "And what about you, Alex? What do you need?"

Alex figured that Sarah should have felt what his body needed. It was certainly telling them both in no uncertain terms.

Why did his common sense shut down when he had her in his arms? He'd been ready to throttle her when he'd discovered that she'd run off tonight. He'd been ready to tear the person limb from limb who might hurt her. And here, filling his arms with the soft, frothy feel of her, he wanted to bury himself in her until the rest of the world disappeared.

Only one other time in his life had he been that short-sighted. Only one time had he given in, and look where it had gotten him. He had ended up alone trying to deal with the rage of loss by himself. He'd been flayed raw and left out in the wind. He'd risked too much.

"I need to get you to sleep and then find out what the hell's going on with your company," he finally said, the smile aching on his face.

Her smile grew. "You're lying, Alex."

He shook his head. "Give me credit for once not making my decisions based on hormones."

Sarah proffered a pout. "Leave it to me to fall in love with a practical person."

There was a lurch in Alex's chest. He tried to discount Sarah's words or their import to him. She was just being Sarah, talking off the top of her head, ready to believe in signs and portents. Even so, the words sounded unaccountably sweet.

"Next time make sure you don't get into elevators with strange accountants."

For a moment they stood there, soaking in the silence of the kitchen, the surprising comfort of isolation, the soothing cadence of matched heartbeats. Even the confusion seemed to ease a little.

"Alex?"

"Mmm-hmm."

"You can call about the baby now."

Still six feet under the smell and sense and feel of Sarah in his arms, Alex forgot to move. "Baby? What baby?"

He could feel Sarah smile against his chest. "The one they're naming after you."

Still he didn't understand. Alex couldn't quite pull his attention away from her, from the emotions that still warred in him like high winds.

Then, suddenly, as if the shell around him shattered, the answer hit him. "Oh, my God," he gasped, straightening to attention. "Lindsay."

He didn't even wait for Sarah's affirmation to head for the phone. Nor did he hear her, left behind, as she shook her head in gentle amusement.

"She's fine, you know."

"Why didn't you tell me?"

Sarah looked up at the distressed outrage in Connie's voice and set down her pen. It was still too early in the day. She hadn't gotten much sleep the night before, the sun was too bright, and she had a headache from having to sit in with Thaddeus on a demonstration of the video-animation equipment. She wasn't at all sure she wanted to deal with Connie right now.

When Sarah looked up, Connie came to a dead halt on the other side of the drawing table. "Oh, hon. You look like hell."

"Randolph already told me," Sarah admitted with a list-less swipe of her hair. Taking a final look down at the persistently blank sheet of paper on her drawing board, she finally gave up and climbed off her stool. Midcentral Airlines wasn't getting its logo today, either.

All Sarah could think of was loyalty and betrayal. Need and fear. Belonging and loneliness.

"Well, he was right," Connie said, walking up to take Sarah by the arm. Sarah followed her over to the corner without a protest. "Why didn't you call me? I could have been at your house in ten minutes flat. You shouldn't have been alone last night, for heaven's sake."

"I wasn't alone," Sarah admitted, sinking into the sofa

and curling her bare feet up beneath her. Her sandals stayed with the pig. "Alex stayed."

It took Connie a minute to find her voice as she settled herself in alongside and poured Sarah a cup of tea from the Wedgwood service Randolph had left earlier. "Was he a help?"

Sarah managed a smile. "He was a gentleman. I asked him to make love to me and he said no."

It was obvious that Connie wasn't sure how to react to either end of that statement. Consternation, alarm and relief all swept across her features in quick succession.

"You're right," Connie admitted, handing Sarah's cup across. "He is a gentleman. I'm not sure Peter would have shown such restraint."

"I'm not sure you would have let him," Sarah retorted with her first smile of the day.

Connie grinned. "True."

"I didn't even know," Sarah confided in her friend, her voice torn between confusion and misery. "He almost died, Con, and I didn't even get a warning."

"You had a warning," Connie reminded her brusquely. "You told him five times to go back to Colorado. I don't see why you should feel guilty because he doesn't see good sense when it's staring him in the face."

Sarah shook her head. "I know when there's going to be a flash flood. I warned you the time the train you were going to get on derailed. I told Hector when his wife went into premature labor."

"And you stopped Alex from driving on bad brakes," Connie finished for her, impatient with Sarah's uncertainty. "Stop being responsible for everyone, hon. It's a no-win proposition. Now, you wanna know what's going on here?"

Sarah remembered her tea and took a sip. "I guess."

Connie nodded, now all business. "The police detective called. He'll be here at eleven. I've set up interviews with everybody he requested—he requested damn near everybody, you know.''

Sarah shrugged uncomfortably. "I couldn't narrow it down.''

Connie's smile was proprietary. "What about the four of us who were maybe seven blocks away just before the shots were fired?''

"Come on, Connie,'' Sarah objected, then dropped her gaze to her cup, guilty and ashamed for what she'd feared the night before. "Besides, I…'' She couldn't quite bring herself to finish, to admit what she'd done.

Connie did it for her. "You checked. We'd already gone.'' When Sarah looked up, unable to keep the surprise and relief from her eyes, Connie grinned that old, brash grin of hers and took a long sip of her own tea. "For your sake, I wish we'd all still been stuck over that damn program. Unfortunately for all of us, Thaddeus managed to break through it about half an hour after you left. He really is a genius, by the way. We should pay him more.''

Sarah nodded, distracted by the enormity of the situation, by the tarry stain of duplicity, by the lingering envy at the sound of Alex's excited laughter the night before. "Okay,'' she said instinctively.

Connie shook her head and reached over to nudge Sarah's teacup in the right direction. "Are you sure you want to be here today?''

Startled from the morass she seemed to be caught in, Sarah looked up. "I don't want to be anyplace else.''

Connie sighed, the strain on Sarah's features now echoed on her own. "I'll have Randolph hold all your calls until the detective shows up.''

"Everybody except Alex,'' Sarah amended.

Connie smiled and Sarah remembered all those times Connie had cheer-led and refereed and conducted clandestine operations between Sarah and dates. "Everybody except Alex,'' she allowed, and got to her feet.

"Thanks, Con," Sarah said as her friend opened the door to leave. "I don't know what I'd do without you."

Connie turned one last time before leaving and bestowed one of her sharpest smiles. "You'd get lost on the way to the store, wander up into the mountains and become so intrigued by the shapes and colors that you'd starve to death with a stick in your hand scratching out designs in the dust."

After Connie left, Sarah tried her best to keep her mind on the problem at hand. She owed it to Connie and everybody at the company who was being interrogated and disturbed. She owed it to Alex so that he could get away before something else happened. But as hard as she tried, her gaze still drifted back to the sunbaked summer landscape and her thoughts to the evening before.

To Alex and his polite withdrawal.

What had changed his mind? She'd been so sure when they'd walked up to her house that he'd wanted to make love to her. She'd felt his defenses ease a little, tasted the stunning power of his arousal. His eyes had brimmed with it; his voice had rasped with it. The electricity had snapped and popped between them on the ride home, shocking careless fingers and igniting gasps. The promise of what would happen had stolen words and stretched minutes into agony.

And then the shots had been fired. Somewhere between that time and the moment she'd asked him to make love to her, he'd closed himself off again.

She'd seen her request slam into him, felt the residue hum through him like a live wire. He'd battled himself like a storm at sea and barely brought himself back under control.

Sarah would have loved to talk to Alex's sister. She wanted to know what his ex-wife had been like, what Alex had been like with her. Had he completely surrendered to her charm, opened himself up and exposed the hot core he now protected so closely only to have it violated? Had he decided that it was too much of a risk to ever do that again?

Was Alex, who had battled through all those years in professional football, who had survived his sister's crisis and the loss of faith from a capricious spouse, afraid of the emotions he'd locked away behind that neat button-down job of his? Was he afraid of something more, something intangible that Sarah couldn't quite get a finger on yet? Something, maybe even Alex wouldn't admit to, that he'd unconsciously recognized the night before?

And was it fair for Sarah to expose his vulnerabilities, when just by doing so she could put him in more danger? She wasn't wise. She was frightened and uncertain and overwhelmed by the sudden magic of Alex in her life.

How was she supposed to be able to know what would protect him? Why should she have to be strong enough to ignore her own needs for common good? She needed Alex. She needed his strength, his love, his wry eye on life— she needed the passion he had only hinted at. Sarah wasn't sure she had the courage to forfeit that.

Sarah was absorbed by the palm trees dancing in the wind outside when Randolph returned with a fresh pot of tea and some banana bread.

"The police didn't ask to interview me," he said without much inflection as he traded teapots.

Surprised, Sarah looked up. "Why should they?" she asked. "You weren't here last night."

Filling her cup and adding three teaspoonfuls of sugar, Randolph handed it over. Sarah could see something was wrong, but for the life of her she didn't know what.

"Randolph," she said, accepting her tea. "Are you upset because I don't think you're embezzling?"

His smile was light and fleeting. With eyes the size of a cocker spaniel's, Randolph was a heartbreakingly good-looking man. He also had the knack for looking like the only person left on earth who had serious thoughts.

"I guess I'm wondering if you don't think I'm talented enough to do it."

Sarah's headache swelled. "Sit down," she said, the most preemptive command she'd ever issued to Randolph.

"Sometimes I forget to say it," she said sincerely, reaching out to take his hand. "But there would be no Sunset Design without you. I guess I keep figuring that you know that."

Rather than lighten his expression, her words puckered his features into even more serious consideration. "Then will you take my word for something?"

Sarah didn't even have to think about it. "Of course."

When he lifted his eyes to her, Randolph looked like an archangel in a Michelangelo painting. Sarah couldn't help but smile.

"Alex Thorne isn't doing you any good here," he said abruptly, neatly erasing her smile. "Send him back to Colorado."

Sarah couldn't think of a decent objection. "Randolph?"

"You're not paying attention, Sarah," Randolph insisted. "Ever since he's shown up, he's been hurting you *and* the company, and I think you'll find that everything will be back to normal when he leaves."

"But the attempts on his life..."

He shook his head. "You trust my judgment. Trust me now. It's not us, it's him."

The white sheet of paper on Sarah's drawing table never was filled up that day.

Alex had been in a fairly good mood when he'd arrived at Sunset that morning. He hadn't slept at all the night before, stretched out on Sarah's couch and listening to her soft breathing in the next room. He'd ached without respite and spent too many hours ignoring the reasons.

On the other hand, he was an uncle again. Lindsay had given birth to a healthy nine-pound boy they had indeed named Alexander. After Lindsay had seen the size of the baby's head and shoulders, she'd claimed the resemblance was just too strong to ignore. She was healthy, happier than she had ever been, and Jason had been as tongue-tied over his child as a schoolboy with an idol.

And then Alex had waded back into the problems at Sunset. He hadn't been able to so much as find a handhold on them. Someone had deliberately sabotaged the computer system to keep Alex away from accounts receivable, and so far he couldn't figure out the reason, which was why he was so frustrated.

After nearly eight hours poring over printout, screen and calculator, he hadn't found a thing. *Nada.* Zero. By the time everybody else left the department, he had gotten as far as deciding to check something else out and come back to accounts receivable when he was fresh.

"You look tired."

Lifting his head, Alex took in the sight of Sarah standing in the open door to the accounting department. She was in slacks today, pink ones, with a kind of gauzy peasant blouse tucked in, some kind of fringed shawl at the waist and a chintz duster over that—and bare feet. Dangly earrings tinkled at her ears and beads fell from her neck in waves.

"Just frustrated. I can't find even a padded expense account."

He'd moved on to the files of companies Sunset dealt with. As he talked to Sarah, Alex punched them up, one after another, for a cursory look. His eyes burned and his attention was minimal now. He knew it was nearly time to quit.

Sarah walked in and perched herself on the desk just

out of view of the screen. "The police aren't any happier.
They say everybody has a motive, but nobody has a motive."

Alex flashed a quick grin. "Helpful." He scanned Dar-
row, Ltd. and then brought up Datasys. "Did they happen
to mention anybody's name in particular in connection
with last night?"

Something wasn't tracking, but he couldn't decide what
it was. Alex rubbed at his eyes and looked again. Still he
couldn't decide why the screen bothered him.

For her part, Sarah drew imaginary pictures on the edge
of the desk with a finger. "I wish more people had thought
to have good alibis last night."

Alex saw the frustration in Sarah's eyes. It made him
remember that it was Jill's department he'd spent investigating all day. "Jill didn't have an alibi, huh?"

Sarah sighed. "No. She said she wasn't home. But she
swears she wasn't here, either. Beyond that, she says she
can't tell us."

"What about Hector?" he asked.

Sarah took up exercising her toes at the end of outstretched legs and then got back to her feet. "Said he was
so wound up after working through the computer problems
that he took a long ride in his new car. His wife was asleep
by the time he got home."

Alex tilted his chair back and braced a foot against the
desk. "The seduction of a BMW 735. What do you think
about Jill?"

Sarah wandered over to the window and looked out.
"It's not Jill."

"You're sure?"

Sarah turned from the window, her eyes clouded and
resigned. "No. Did you find something in her department?"

"No," he admitted, looking briefly at the blinking cur-
sor that sat amid all the rows and columns of data. "There

wasn't anything. Which means that either I've missed it and have to go over it again, or I was deliberately steered in the wrong direction.''

Sarah was quiet a moment. Alex watched her, wishing he could offer her escape. Wishing he could soothe the strain in her small shoulders.

''What are you going to do?'' she finally asked.

He shrugged, contemplating the screen and considering his state of mind. ''Whatever it is, I'm going to do it tomorrow. I'm beat.''

Sarah turned back to the window. Alex looked up to see the late afternoon sun gild her pale hair and warm her skin. The night before when he'd checked in on her, the hall light had illuminated her sleeping features much the same way, making them younger, more vulnerable—making Alex feel old and tired and lonely standing in the dark.

''Balloons!'' she cried suddenly, spinning around.

Alex instinctively looked to the window. The clear blue Arizona sky was faultless and empty.

''No,'' she said with a little giggle. ''I mean let's go. Randolph's taking a sunset flight up today, and he invited me. Come along.''

That fast the life was back in her eyes, the sparkling invitation that was so deadly. Her hair settled at her shoulders like wind-swept silk. Her lips parted in a smile of delight.

''Please?''

Alex did his best to scowl past all the enthusiasm. ''I thought Randolph didn't trust me.''

''He doesn't,'' she admitted brightly. ''But he hasn't spent that much time with you, either. This could kill two birds with one stone.''

''Figuratively speaking, I hope,'' Alex amended dryly.

Sarah's smile grew as she closed the distance to where Alex sat. ''We can stop by for some chicken and wine and enjoy the sunset from the air. Come on, Alex. There isn't anything else you can do tonight. Celebrate your new nephew. Celebrate summer," she begged, setting her hands on his desk and leaning closer. "Celebrate life."

Alex scowled this time. "Hippies," he snorted. "Next you'll want me to go barefoot and wear beads."

Sarah giggled. "And grow your hair to your waist."

Damn it, she was infecting him, too. Suddenly he wanted to see her against the sunset, the breeze tousling her hair and the sun turning her hair into red gold. He wanted to take the computer and dump it into the nearest pit and walk away holding Sarah's hand and never look back.

Which was why she was so dangerous.

"One balloon flight," he agreed. "Accountants are only allowed so much fun," he informed her, shutting down the program and climbing to his feet. "It upsets their delicate systems."

Sarah snuggled close, her eyes bright and her arm threaded through Alex's as she guided him straight for the door. "In that case, we'd better make this good."

Sarah's voice sounded suspiciously smug. And Alex's chest went suspiciously tight just at the thought of it.

Chapter 10

Since a hot-air balloon rides wind currents, there wasn't much extra breeze. The air was still and sweet and cooling, lifting the balloon fast as the last heat of the afternoon rose off the desert. The sunset was lost to a band of muddy clouds that forecast some of the rare rain Phoenix was privilege to.

Preoccupied with the sea of collapsed material, a burner and a fan, Randolph had greeted Sarah like a partner and taken Alex's unexpected arrival with resignation. Now as they soared up over the edge of the Superstitions, Randolph relaxed a little and shared in the champagne.

Sarah was glad. She wanted Randolph's help and allegiance where Alex was concerned. She wanted as many friends as possible to help him. As much as anything, she wanted all her friends to like each other. Connie called it the one-big-happy-family syndrome.

"How long have you been ballooning?" Alex asked as he watched Randolph work the burner.

Randolph waited to finish a burn. Even after being up

with Randolph before, Sarah was still surprised at the noise
and heat every time he opened up the flame. It was like
standing next to a coke oven. Then, sudden silence, with
only the distant sound of sheep bells and one or two barking dogs drifting up from the desert to break through.

"I've been racing for about five years. Ballooning about
ten."

Alex nodded, took a considering sip of champagne and
a peek over the edge of the small basket. "Sure is a quieter
sport than football."

"More expensive, too," Randolph added, then offered
a dry grin. "Before you ask."

"You figured I would?"

Taking a moment to assess his drift, Randolph shrugged.
"It seemed inevitable, especially in your line of work."

Alex took another sip of champagne, his eyes steady
and noncommittal. Sarah could hear the gears mesh, could
almost see the calculations being formulated. Across from
him, Randolph was positioning himself, as well. It was as
if swords had met in the first clash of a duel.

"Well, since you want me to ask," Alex said evenly,
his tone doing nothing to ease Sarah's tension. "How
much would one spend on a sport like this?" The little
wicker basket didn't seem big enough or sturdy enough to
withstand the calculated mistrust that sparked like static
electricity.

"Let's just say that it's a good thing I'll never have
children," Randolph admitted, his eyes away to the hills.
"They'd probably starve. Of course, it's gotten better since
I've started competing. I'm sponsored now."

"By Sunset Designs," Sarah offered.

Alex smiled. "Of course."

In the end Sarah wasn't sure whether her idea had been
a good one or not. Randolph and Alex never did seem to
relax around each other. The ride was a success, such as
it was. The air cooled as the sun settled into the western

mountains and the first lights of Phoenix winked on. The rain held off, but tantalized with the faint smell of moisture on the evening breeze. The sunset sky shuddered with gold, with peach and hot corals and deepening blue beyond the curtain of clouds that still piled up at the horizon. And Alex and Randolph were so preoccupied with maintaining polite conversation that neither saw it happen.

It was just as well. Sarah had looked up again, wallowing in the rich, brilliant colors of the balloon against the sunset, wishing she could somehow suspend this moment longer, floating, aimless, almost content.

As she looked, the sun, which had been dodging in and out of the clouds for a few minutes, disappeared abruptly, casting a long shadow over the bright stripes that swept up toward the sky.

A shadow. A chill. A sudden terror.

Sarah gripped the sides of the basket, afraid of falling, afraid of dying. Feeling the awful stain of prescience dull her sight and dim her hearing. She felt the world shift, shudder and right itself, and still Alex and Randolph went on discussing lift ratios and wind velocity. She heard the future whispering in her ear, dread suspicions of disaster, and no one's head turned at the sound.

Sarah wanted out of the balloon. She wanted away from the sinking in her stomach. She wanted anything but the knowledge that she couldn't say for sure what it was she was seeing. She just knew that this sensation had struck twice, and that it had to do with her logo, with Alex and with some kind of danger.

For the rest of the ride, she sipped at the warming champagne and did her best to ignore her nausea.

When they finally bumped to a landing, Alex helped Randolph subdue the wilting balloon and pack everything away before he and Sarah headed home.

But Sarah couldn't really say that she felt a sense of victory, even a sense of relief. She'd felt undercurrents during the ride that had nothing to do with wind and found her best attempts at joviality met with polite smiles. And somewhere in the guileless blue of the desert sky, the future had lain in wait for her. By the time she leaned her head back against the headrest in Alex's rental, she felt exhausted and jittery.

"How about a swim?" she asked suddenly.

Alex looked over. "We just went ballooning," he reminded her. "After which I was going to drop you off at home and go back to the hotel."

Sarah looked over, wondering if he could see the sudden, surprising intensity in her eyes. The currents stirred, muddy and indecipherable, and Sarah was suddenly afraid of them. For once she didn't want to be left alone with her sight.

"After a swim," she said, and heard the slight note of pleading in her voice.

Alex must have heard it, too. Taking a brief look over, he searched out her expression with some worry. "What are you trying to tell me, Sarah?"

She couldn't. Sarah knew simply that the path she'd chosen for tonight was inevitable and that it felt like the only choice. The only right choice for them both, no matter what happened.

She knew how much she needed him, and that made her wonder whether what she was feeling was merely selfishness or truth.

"I'm telling you that I'd like a little time alone with you," she said. "Away from the computers and the police and everything." Sarah wondered if Alex realized why she watched the far distance instead of him as she talked. "And I don't think it would hurt you to unwind a little, either."

Outside the car, night had taken control. Darkness blotted out the scenery, melding mountain into anonymous sky and desert into oblivion. Only the city challenged. A cloud of lights flickered in the distance, and neon punctuated the free enterprise of suburbia. No relief out there, no quiet. Only the echoes of too many people, the murmurs of struggle and competition. Sarah could feel it like the pulsing of her own blood. She wanted respite. She wanted immersion.

"I thought that's what we were doing," Alex said, pragmatically.

Sarah offered a fleeting smile. "Except that you and Randolph still don't like each other."

Alex didn't insult her by denying it. "You can't make everything happy and bright, Sarah."

Sarah shouldn't have felt so miserable. "I can try."

For a moment Alex did no more than drive, one hand resting on the top of the steering wheel, the other tapping the outside of the car door in time to the music that wafted gently from the radio. The lights swept him in waves, riding up the set planes of his jaw, over his pursed mouth, darkened eyes and tousled hair. Sarah waited, unsure what she wanted him to say, unsettled by her own uncertainties, silenced by the surprising depth of her reaction to the sight of his features, sharpened again and again in profile.

"We'll stop by the hotel for my trunks," was all he said. It was enough to shatter the tension like ice over a thawing stream.

Sarah felt the current beneath rise in her, bubble free and take her in a strange giddiness. She recognized the passion of certainty and smiled with the wonderful anticipation that tightened in her belly. He was coming home with her. He was going to swim and then later, maybe take a turn in the whirlpool. He was going to relax. And Sarah, her instincts as sharp as any woman's when it came to a man, knew that this was the time she would have her decision from him.

She would set the stage with age-old precision and hope he would seduce her.

* * *

If this was the way Alex Thorne relaxed, Sarah was going to have to rethink her seduction plan. Taking a few extra minutes to make sure she looked just right in her aqua-and-black maillot, she'd stepped out onto her patio to find Alex already in the water. Swimming. Eating up the pool in strong rhythmic strokes that didn't so much as pause at the end of a lap.

Easing her way into water that steamed into the cool night air, Sarah watched him work his way back to the other end of the pool and realized how he worked off some of the aggression he'd once brought to the playing field. And if he didn't stop working it off so well, there would be no aggression left for her.

She didn't think to question her decision. In the back of her mind she knew that what would happen tonight would further complicate things when the sun rose in the morning. She even knew that she was casting yet more threads of involvement that might keep Alex where he could be in danger. But the moment he'd decided to come over, when Sarah had felt the rush of exultation at his simple statement, she'd known what his words had portended.

If she could only get him to quit swimming sometime soon.

God, she thought, watching his muscles ripple in the translucent lighting in the pool, he's so beautiful. Sculpted, each limb in perfect proportion, each movement as fluid as flight. His shoulders were tight and broad, the water sluicing along tendon and muscle as he reached for each stroke. His legs scissored effortlessly. Resting at the side of a pool she'd only used for lounging, Sarah admitted to herself that she could watch him swim for hours.

Except that she couldn't. Just watching him tightened the ache in her chest. Imagining those fingers cupping over her that way made her anxious. He was afraid of his strength, his intensity. Watching him, it occurred to her that maybe she should be, too.

When he reached the far side, Sarah slid under water. She could barely see him, his body all shadows and planes in the ethereal world of water. Holding her breath, her hands out at her sides to keep her in place, she smiled.

Alex never saw her. One minute he was slicing through the water, his mind deliberately on nothing. The next he ran into something solid. Something solid, but very, very soft. Sputtering and startled, he pulled to the surface, only to hear the bright music of a familiar laugh.

"Sarah—!"

"Did anybody ever tell you that you don't know how to relax?" she demanded, looking all the more like a nymph with the water beading in her hair and on her skin. A siren, maybe, was that the sea fairy? Rising from the oceans and luring sailors to their deaths? If she popped up the way she looked now, Sarah could do it. Even in the shadows Alex was sure he'd never seen eyes so blue, so big, so guileless. So lethal.

"If memory serves," he retorted, trying very hard to keep his eyes off the way the droplets slid along her throat, down the deep V neck of her suit and back into more shadows. "You invited me to swim. I was," he insisted, motioning behind him, "swimming."

"If you'd been on your feet," Sarah countered equally brightly, "that would have been a marathon. And I would have been sitting in the dust back at the two-mile marker."

"Well, then, what did you have in mind?" He shouldn't have asked it. Just the words opened some kind of door in him that focused on those water droplets, sliding, glistening, gathering on her skin. Disappearing into the warm cleft of her breasts where they strained against the bright Lycra of her suit. If he wasn't careful, everyone in the neighborhood would get a good idea of what he suddenly wanted.

Sarah, however, tilted her head to the side as if in serious consideration. Only the cagey sparkle in her eyes betrayed the fallacy. "Food," she admitted.

Struck by the urge to laugh, Alex rolled his eyes. "You should be the size of a defensive tackle, the way you eat."

Sarah giggled. "I am the size of a defensive tackle," she admitted blithely. Gesturing to her very enticing curves, she grinned. "This is an illusion. Smoke and mirrors."

Giving in to temptation, Alex tested some of those curves with assessing hands. "Smoke never felt like this." The suit was sleek and smooth, the waist and hips beneath it soft and small, fitting neatly in his hands. It was all Alex could do to let go.

He didn't regain his space, though. The cool night air chilled his wet skin, and the water soothed his torso. Sarah's breath drifted in soft clouds toward the invisible night. Her chest rose a bit more quickly and her eyes widened. Alex couldn't drag his gaze from them, suddenly suspicious that he was losing his balance. That blue was so hypnotic, so bright that it could blind a sane man and soothe a madman. Her hair glowed in the reflected light; the shadows trembled over it. Her skin glistened and beckoned. She smelled like wildflowers and chlorine, and Alex found the combination oddly alluring.

His own lungs seemed to work harder. His heart tap-danced as if he'd just done a triathlon instead of seven lousy laps. And deep in his belly, where he kept his dread and anticipation, something flared, but it was too soon to tell the difference.

He knew better. He had more control than this. He'd tumbled into a set of guileless blue eyes once and still wasn't sure he'd found his way out. He couldn't afford to do it again. If he considered making love to a woman, it should be done out of desire, not desperation.

But he felt desperate. He felt separate and cold and isolated, and all the warmth he needed stood so close he'd only have to reach out to claim it.

But he shouldn't.

"What kind of food?" he asked, knowing how strained his voice sounded and hating himself for the weakness.

Sarah seemed to startle at the sound of his voice. Her lips parted, closed. A little sigh escaped.

"What I'd like," she admitted in a curiously small voice, "is pasta. Lots and lots of white clam sauce and garlic bread."

Alex wanted to shake his head. He wanted to move free of her. All he could manage was a wry smile. "And of course you have a pasta maker."

Sarah grinned. "Of course."

"And by the time you're finished cooking, the kitchen will look like a mortar raid on an Italian restaurant."

How could she look so enticing merely by smiling? "Something like that." Her eyes were knowing, intimate.

"How about an apple or something instead?"

"Chocolate cheesecake," she said, brightening by degrees. "I made it the other day, so the kitchen's already clean. Want any?"

Alex couldn't help smiling back, wondering if chocolate really was a substitute for sex. If it worked, he might end up hogging the whole cheesecake. "Sure."

Food was very sexy to Sarah. She always liked how it was used in the movies, when lovers fed each other fruit or cake or candy. Food seemed to represent the exchange of primal needs, interlacing nourishment with sensuality, survival with pleasure.

Sarah especially liked the idea of a man licking her fingers as she slipped a morsel of food into his mouth. As a teenager she'd tried that once with a boy named Mark Walston only to get her nail stuck in his braces. Alex, she was sure, would be much more adept at something like that. If she could manage to talk him into it.

Her body still hummed with his nearness. She could feel his eyes on her as surely as the rays of the setting sun, branding her with their heat and suffusing her with light. He'd been so close, so very close to taking her in his arms again. She knew it. She could feel it, throbbing between them on the night air like heat off a hot street. And then, as suddenly as hard frost, he'd closed himself away again.

Which was where the food came in. Sarah padded back out to the yard, humming.

The insects were singing tonight. Off in the distance an owl screeched. Traffic murmured and the breeze sighed. The rain promised earlier had evaporated with nightfall, but a few of the clouds still chased a half-moon and mottled the stars. Out on her patio the flowers slept, their aroma heavy in the cool air. The palm rustled fitfully and water slapped against the walls of the pool. And stretched out atop the water as if suspended on aquamarine light, Alex floated on his back.

At first he was all shadow, like another specter of the night. As Sarah's eyes became accustomed to the change in light, though, she began to pick out features. His eyes were closed and his face relaxed. His arms were outstretched and his body still. Sarah thought of the temptation in her hands and smiled.

Then she saw the scar. New enough to still be pink, slicing his torso almost in half, like a saber wound, like a violation.

Numbness. Surprise. Terror. Fury.

Sarah didn't feel the plate slip from her hands. The crash startled her, brought a hand to her mouth. Alex stiffened at the sound, gained his feet with a splash.

"What happened?" he demanded, already looking for trouble.

Sarah's eyes were still on the scar, the memory. "Oh, Alex..."

The distress in her voice brought his head around.

"You didn't tell me."

He followed her gaze. "This?" he asked, motioning to the livid scar as if it were a tattoo. "Gallbladder. Bad surgeon."

"You were shot," she countered instinctively. "Three times." Stricken by the sense of blossoming pain, dimming consciousness, mortality, Sarah lifted her eyes to his. "You almost died."

Alex shook his head. Pulling his hands through his hair to force it back, he vaulted from the pool.

"I'm glad you weren't around when it happened," he chided gently, gathering her into his warmth. "I would have been a lot more worried than I was."

Her hand instinctively reaching for the flaw in his flawless physique, Sarah lifted her gaze to Alex. "Why didn't you tell me?"

His smile was protective. "What for? The only time this comes in handy is when I'm trying to impress marines and hockey players."

"But I can't get a handle on you," she protested, frustration suddenly welling in her, her head resting against his chest, where it seemed so warm and inviting. "I think I do, and then there's something else, something important. Every time I tell you to stay, I find out something else that tells me you should go."

"Sarah," he said, placing a hand beneath her chin and lifting it. "I'm not leaving. No matter what you say, or Connie says, or even what the governor of Arizona could say, I refuse to leave a job unfinished."

"You refuse to forgive yourself for letting Lindsay down," Sarah retorted instinctively as the fragile material of her vision fluttered again, revealing sights, emotions, choices. "You were protecting her. They shot you and took her, and you're still trying to do penance."

"Isn't that a little melodramatic?" he asked, his eyes too dark to be unconcerned.

"Is it?" she answered. "You think it was your fault, don't you? You should have somehow overpowered those men with their guns and saved your sister. And now you're in another situation where you think you can protect somebody, and you won't hear of leaving when it might save your life."

"I won't hear of being intimidated by somebody whose claim to fame is a fast finger on the keyboard."

Sarah saw him clench up with the memory, still only a year old, still more raw than the scar on his torso. The resolution to make this time different grated through him like the track of a rusty knife.

"I don't want to tell your family that you died trying to redeem yourself," she protested in a whisper.

His arms remained around her, his hands splayed across her back. His chest rose and fell erratically beneath her fingers, and his heart thudded. "That's not the reason," he said, his jaw like steel.

Sarah challenged him, dueled with the bronze in his eyes, facing him without flinching, even as she felt the strength gather in him. "Then what is the reason?" she demanded, her voice small and afraid.

A new light flickered at the depths of the metallic brown. "A reason?" he countered in a strained voice. "You want a reason?"

The air sparked between them. The night thrummed, and in the distance a siren wailed and keened. Sarah forgot to breathe. It took all her energy to remain steady before that new, unholy light and nod her head.

"A reason," Alex repeated in an amused little murmur. "Well, I have a reason for you."

His reason tasted an awful lot like a kiss. Sarah never

quite knew when she closed her eyes. She knew simply that one minute she was challenging him and the next she was surrounded by him.

His argument wasn't a gentle one. It was almost as if more than memories had been released when Sarah had touched his scar, as if the frustration and furious determination had somehow escaped alongside. Alex pulled her to him so tightly she couldn't breathe. His hands clutched at her, tangling in her hair and holding her to him. His mouth met hers with a bruising hunger. Sarah had asked for this. She had begged and cajoled and schemed. And when she finally met it, she was surprised.

His mouth was rapacious, nipping, sipping, plucking at her tender skin. He didn't wait for an invitation to invade, but sought her tongue with harsh strokes. Sarah gasped, sighed with wonder. She fought for balance, even caught tight in his grasp. She arched closer, his heat heady in the cool night. Stretched up on her toes, her head back before his assault, she admitted that no matter what she'd thought she'd orchestrated, Alex had surprised her. He'd taken it out of her hands and assumed control. And she was trembling with it.

"You want a reason?" he grated out, his mouth at her ear, his hand sliding up to cup a breast. "I'm bewitched. Damn it, I know better, but all I've been thinking of is doing this."

Lightning splintered in her with his hungry touch, the torment of his hands on her. Sarah's mind whirled with light and darkness and need. She opened her mouth and sipped at the water that slid over Alex's throat and drank at once his fire.

"I've tried so hard to stay away," he growled into her throat, spilling chills with his tongue. "Taken enough cold showers to drop the damn water table…."

Sarah nodded, panting, sinking into his touch. "I know…."

"Walked away when no sane man would…"

"I—" his mouth was working lower, tasting the upper swell of her breast and somehow sapping the air from her lungs "—know…."

Alex moved a hand just enough to slide a suit strap from her shoulder. Sarah bit her lip, curled her fingers into his back, lifted to her toes when her knees threatened to give out.

"I tried being mad at you."

She couldn't even nod. The evening air swept across her bared breast, cooling the moisture, tautening as Alex explored the nipple. She couldn't breathe, couldn't think, couldn't hold still. But she couldn't stand up, either.

"Alex—"

Somewhere in the depths of his hunger Alex must have heard the desperate note to her voice. Pulling himself together, he held where he was, his hand at her breast, his arm circling her waist.

When he lifted his eyes to hers, Sarah was halted by the volcano she'd unleashed. A molten energy, a voracious thirst that had only flickered in warning before, now glowed uncannily from his cat's eyes. And yet, still, the exquisite control to care.

"The whirlpool," she suggested breathlessly. "It's very…nice, and…I don't have to stand up."

Alex took a second to look over at where the water in the separate little pool steamed and bubbled in the shadows. Sarah saw the realization of how close he'd come to losing control stiffen him. Saw the recriminations pass without taking hold and the desire win out.

"Sarah," he managed, turning back to her, taking her into his arms. "I didn't bring a raincoat to this party."

A curious delight bubbled up in Sarah's chest. Her knees were still watery and her skin shuddered with anticipation. There was a melting in her belly that warmed her and a trembling in her hands. Even so, she giggled.

Outraged, Alex looked down at her. "This isn't something to joke about, Sarah."

"Oh, no," she agreed with a wave of her hand, unable to quite stop yet. "I know it isn't. It's just that I knew somehow you'd be the one to bring up the subject."

Alex was losing his patience again. "Is that a problem?"

"No," she insisted, lifting a hand to stroke his cheek. "It's so sweet. And so...left brain. It's all right," she assured him, lifting way up to deliver a little kiss of appreciation of her own, her breasts sliding up along his chest as she went. "I'm already taken care of, really."

His brows pursed. "You're sure."

Sarah smiled, happy and impatient and uncertain at once. "Next time it'll be your turn. This one's on me." Sliding deliberately back down, she held out a hand. "Now, it seems to me we're wasting some lovely moonlight."

Sarah loved her whirlpool. There had been many designs conjured in it as she'd drifted in the soothing rush of warm water. But it had always been a solitary pastime. As she stood before Alex, anticipating what her whirlpool would be like shared, she knew it would never be the same.

He wouldn't let her walk. Sweeping her up into his arms, Alex carried her past the shards of broken stoneware to the steps of the whirlpool and then slowly descended into the water. There was a seat, a ridge of tile that rimmed the edge and brought the water to Sarah's shoulders. Alex settled himself onto the seat and then eased Sarah down into his lap.

"I don't know what to do with you," he was saying, his eyes never leaving hers, his hands lifting once again to her hair. Wrapping his hands in it, lifting it from her neck, he brought her face to his. "You wouldn't know a wolf if he bit you."

Sarah wanted to move. She wanted to undulate against

Alex so that she could savor the slippery feel of water on him. Instead she let herself be kissed thoroughly and deeply. Her own hands were on his shoulders, shoulders like concrete, like tensile steel that bent with terrible pressure. She kneaded him, opening and closing her fingers like a cat sharpening claws in the sunlight, the sunlight that shafted deep into her belly and burned.

"You'd probably cook pasta for him and then he'd eat you up, just like grandma…"

At first the kisses were gentle, a greeting of wonder, an exploration. As Alex's grip tightened and Sarah surrendered, the kiss deepened, quickened. Their tongues parried and parted. Teeth nipped and tested. Soft groans of hunger mingled, and passion rekindled.

"I should walk away…while I have a chance.…"

Sarah felt Alex's hand fall again, felt it find her breast and knead it. She pressed into his touch, hungry and aching for him. She twisted in his hold so that she could arch against his chest, tormenting herself on the soft tickle of hair, on the sleek power of muscle. Her hands wandered, hungered. His hands commanded.

"I should lock you in your room.…"

Sarah gasped, her head back, as he nipped at her throat.

"You should shut up," she advised, as breathless now as he, "and enjoy your pasta."

He chuckled against her throat, a deep growl of pleasure, of surprise and hunger. Sarah pulled his head down to her. Alex swept the other strap from her shoulder and freed her breasts to the water. He slid a hand down her belly, over her thighs, her knees, his mouth still marking passage along her throat.

Sarah looked at her breasts, pale and full and glistening with water. She saw the golden tousle of his hair against her skin and the shadow of his hand beneath the water. She heard the harsh cant of his breathing and tested the set of his muscles. A whimper gathered in her throat. A fire crested in her belly and slid into her legs, following the path his hands had taken. As his fingers stirred the water that pulsed along her skin, she eased open her thighs to him. She stretched so that her breasts lifted from the water.

Alex cupped a breast in his hand, weighed it, caressed it. Pleasure tightened in Sarah. She fought for air. Her head fell back, her hair drifting in the water, her eyes to the night sky. She felt Alex take her breast in his mouth and she smiled.

Desire had been a fire in her. His tongue stirred it into conflagration. Sarah felt her legs melting, her limbs shattering. She clutched at him, rocked in his arms, hummed with the surprise of it. She begged him with her hands and her cries and her body, and he answered by slipping his fingers beneath the material of her suit and seeking out the fire he'd lit.

Abruptly Alex pulled away. Sarah stiffened, ready to protest, only to feel herself spun around to face Alex, to feel her suit slid from her and find herself fitted neatly straddling against Alex's hips.

His suit was gone, too. She didn't know how he'd done it. She didn't really care. Her body sang with the proximity. The water swept around them, and the steam dissolved the world into a dream. Alex wasn't smiling. His eyes were fierce and dark and hungry. Sarah shivered with the thrill of it. She fretted with waiting. She could feel his arousal against her, full and intimate, and instinctively eased against him. His body glowed in the soft lighting, the water glittering as it slid along his arms and down his chest.

Sarah loved Alex's body. But more, she loved his face, the handsome planes and steely jaw, the dark flavors of his mouth and the fire in his eyes. When she lifted her gaze to meet his, she found what she'd expected, and more. She found an incandescence, a hot, living ferocity that threatened to consume her. And knowing that it could, she smiled. She smiled and invited him to do just that.

From that moment grace was lost to hunger, finesse to desire. Alex let his hands loose on Sarah and she answered with her own. She writhed against him, moaning with the agony he incited, seeking more, seeking him. He gasped, growled, cursed as she tormented him. Lightning sparked and sizzled. The night air swept passion-heated skin and fanned the flames. The desert sang around them and the moon danced with the clouds.

And when Sarah began to splinter, her body coming apart at the magic Alex's greedy fingers stirred in her, he took her under the arms with hands as strong as passion and lifted her onto him.

She scrabbled at his back. She danced in his arms. She offered his soft, seductive mouth her whimpers and cherished his groans. Her body was full with him, taut and hot and anxious. Their bodies arched, sang, lifted into the night. Sarah's eyes flew open. Her head fell back. Her body convulsed around Alex and welcomed him home, and she cried out, soaring, spinning, singing in his arms. And even as she did, she felt Alex follow her, his hands clenching, clutching, his voice hoarse and surprised and awed.

Later, resting spent and sated in his arms, Sarah knew that she had finally seen the real Alex Thorne, the soul she'd so long suspected. Her practical, left-brained accountant had the steel of a general. He also had the fire of a revolutionary.

Chapter 11

"Oh, Sarah, you didn't."

Never bothering to look up from where she was working at her drawing board, Sarah scowled. "You're the third person who's said something like that this morning," she objected to her friend. "Am I *that* obvious?"

Flashing a wry grin, Connie stepped into Sarah's office. "Hon, the whole place can tell when you've broken a nail. This is just a bit more monumental."

Sarah didn't like the sound of that any better. "Could you please not make it sound so historic? I'm hardly an innocent."

"You're not exactly Sadie Thompson, either." Reaching the board, Connie leaned over it, her eyes avid. "So, how was he?"

Sarah went right on sketching, the idea completely formed and needing only expression for life.

When she didn't get an answer, Connie looked down. Then she moved around to get a better look.

"What's that?"

Sarah spared her friend a brief look. "Oh, a life jacket." She went right on drawing, close to completion.

Connie sighed. "A life jacket?"

Sarah nodded, lips pursed, eyes intent. "For airplanes. There was a thing on one of the shows this morning about how difficult it is to get into one of those life jackets the airlines give you. I had an idea..."

Connie looked stunned. "You never watch those shows."

"Alex does." It didn't occur to Sarah that this was a terribly odd statement. From the strangled noises alongside of her, it seemed that Connie thought it was.

"There, see?" Sarah said, motioning to her drawing. "Only the one strap, attached to everything. What do you think?"

"What was he like?"

Looking up from her sketch, Sarah blinked. "Who?"

Connie scowled mightily. "Alex. Are accountants as boring as their stereotype?"

Sarah could feel the blush build along her throat. "Hardly."

"Well?" her friend demanded, leaning in for the lowdown. "Defend his honor."

Facing Connie's renewed enthusiasm was unnerving. Sarah knew darn well that when her friend got that look in her eye, there would be no dissuading her. They wouldn't be getting back to the life jacket without some kind of news briefing. "I will give you," she offered, "one euphemism."

Connie scowled grandly and propped chin in hands. "Go on."

Sarah sighed. "You know how I describe my premonitions?"

Connie looked a little bemused. "Like lightning striking. Why?"

"Because, it applies to Alex, as well. And," she finished

with an unexpected giggle of delight, "last night I found out that lightning can strike the same place twice."

"Alex? What am I hearing about my friend Sarah?"

Startled by the sound of the familiar voice on the other end of the line, Alex straightened. "Ellis?"

"Damn right, this is Ellis. Ellis the avengin' angel if you been free with Sarah."

Leaning back in his chair, Alex raked a hand through his hair. The computer room was overflowing this morning with people training on the new animation system. Keyboards clacked and screens beeped and twiddled. Country-western music filtered from somebody's earphones, and one of the women was wearing sharp heels that clicked briskly across the floor. Alex wasn't at all sure he was in the right place to be having this conversation. As a matter of fact, he wasn't sure where this conversation *would* be appropriate. He had been trying so hard to sort out what had happened last night that he hadn't slept at all.

"I'm waitin', boy."

Alex winced. Ellis sounded much like he used to before trashing hotel rooms. "Did Sarah say something?"

"No, Sarah didn't say something."

"Well, she and I were the only two there last night. Where did you get your information?"

"A concerned third party—who thinks you might be using your less cerebral body parts to do your decision making, if you know what I mean."

Alex knew just what they meant—whoever "they" were. He'd spent the entire night wondering the same thing. After all the times he'd made it a point to walk away, all the cold swims and colder showers, why should he have picked last night to go into hormonal overload? What had it been about Sarah's eyes when she'd seen his scar that had broken his resistance?

"Seems to me," Alex said, rather than face the truth, "that you were the one so anxious to get me married off."

"Married is one thing," the voice threatened in no uncertain terms. "Taking advantage of a vulnerable woman is another."

Alex was all set to protest, the memory of Sarah's knowing smile hovering close enough to distract, when she wandered in the door.

He stopped, frowning at the difference he saw in her. She was a little mussed, her flowing linen dress floating around her calves like a breeze and her eyes wide and distracted. She made it several steps into the room before slowing to an uncertain halt and looking around, bemused. Without missing a beat, every person in the office pointed down the hall.

"Wrong office," they chorused with the precision of long familiarity.

Her eyes sharpened a little and she smiled. "Thanks," she acknowledged with a little wave, and walked back out the door. Barefoot. Humming.

Vulnerable as a kitten on a highway.

Alex couldn't quite deny Ellis's charge.

"Fine," he surrendered. "Come right over and push my face in. It'll be a pleasure."

Surprisingly Ellis did no more than chuckle. "Don't handle the guilts well, do you, boy? How's the company coming?"

Allowing a sigh, Alex sat back up and leaned his elbows on the desk he was commandeering from one of Thaddeus's assistants. The lack of sleep throbbed right between his eyebrows, and he rubbed at it with two fingers. "The police came and went. Sarah admitted that she wasn't sure she was going to prosecute the embezzler if that wasn't who was doing the shooting—I assume you heard about that, as well—"

"I did."

"The rest of the evidence is negligible. So I'm back on my own. Right now I'm rechecking the accounts receivable, and then I'll go back to the records of companies Sunset deals with."

"How much longer, do you think?"

"A day. A week. A year. Who knows? I'm not really breaking records here."

"Not those, anyway. Take care of her, man. She's fragile."

That was as much acquiescence as Ellis was going to give. He was probably the closest thing Sarah had to a big brother, and Alex knew all about how big brothers felt. There were times he still wasn't sure he wanted to admit how grown-up Lindsay really was. And Lindsay usually at least acted like an adult. Sarah meandered through her world as if oblivious to it. She tended flowers and drew pictures and couldn't remember to put on her shoes.

And she had the greediest hands he'd ever known.

"All right, Ellis," he gave in. "You've made your obligatory call. Now go back to your books and let me get back to my problem."

"Take care of yourself, too, my man."

Alex hung up the phone thinking that he was becoming sorely tired of everyone telling him to take care of himself. Most of all, he wished that concern would stop coloring Sarah's eyes every time she saw him, as if she were watching someone she loved with a terminal disease. He could take care of himself. He could take care of *her*. But he couldn't take much more of the worry in her eyes, the pervasive fear that melted the blue into a kind of sweet fire. It made him want to hold her, to shield her. It made him want to love her.

Damn. He knew better. He should never have given in the night before, should never have even agreed to sharing the pool with her. He was having trouble enough concentrating on his work without remembering how the concern in her eyes had transformed into vixenish laughter just with a kiss. How she'd seemed to brighten, deepen, sweeten with his touch. Her eyes, so ingenious and spontaneous, had suddenly glowed with a feminine power that still stunned him.

Alex could see her, wreathed in the spirals of slowly rising steam, her hair gleaming and her skin so soft it looked translucent, and he couldn't get over the idea that somehow she'd worked magic in that yard of hers. Reality had seemed to dissipate before his eyes, the worries and responsibilities and good sense suddenly the intangible in the misty night she'd created. Only sensuality and emotion had survived. The sweet slope of her breast, the bright cascade of her laughter, the instinctive choreography of her passion. The piercing torture of her concern for him.

Instincts. She lived on instincts and intuition, something Alex had never trusted. Immersed in the magic of her universe the night before, he had forgotten to question. This morning he remembered.

Get the hell out now don't make me do it don't make me do it

Startled, Alex pulled away from the keyboard. Where the hell had *that* come from? He'd been punching up some of the smaller files in accounts receivable when suddenly the message had appeared on his screen. A message that hadn't been there yesterday when he'd left. A tiny frisson of warning crawled up his spine. The warning was meant for him.

"Thaddeus?"

The redhead looked over. "Yeah?"

"Come on over here a minute, will you?"

It took Thaddeus even more time than Alex to react.

"Oh, boy. I hope that's a joke."

Alex shook his head. "I don't think so. What can we find out about it?"

Still facing the puzzling message, he shrugged. "The terminal where it originated. Time it was entered."

"Show me how."

It took them a few minutes.

"Alex?"

"Yeah."

"It originated here."

The two of them looked at each other. Alex hadn't moved from the room all day. Thaddeus had spent the majority of it fine-tuning the animation program with the staff. And whoever was threatening Alex had been in the room with them.

"This computer?"

Thaddeus shrugged. "A computer in this room. Alex, everybody in the building's been in here today."

"Was it entered today?"

"Nine-thirty this morning."

Nine-thirty, as everyone had milled around after Thaddeus's bells-and-whistles routine with the new animation program. Everyone. As much as he tried, the only one Alex could remember sitting at a computer was Thaddeus, who had finished the program alone.

Alex felt a small mental nudge, an urge to call out one particular name. He couldn't say why and didn't like it. He wasn't in the business of divining guilt like water. Until yesterday, he hadn't ever had the desire to.

Alex paused, lost for a fraction of a second in the past. Troubled by ripples of memory.

"Alex?"

Startled, he turned back to find the mysterious message once more taking up the screen in front of him.

"Yeah?"

"If you don't mind my saying so," Thaddeus said in a quiet voice, "that message sounds just a bit off balance."

His eyes on the frantic words, Alex couldn't help but

think the same thing. "Print it out for me, Thaddeus," he said. "And then don't say another word, okay?"

Thaddeus looked as if Alex had asked for the firing squad. "What are you talking about?" he demanded. "Aren't you going to do anything about it?"

"Sure," Alex promised him, wishing the message didn't nag at him. Wanting the lingering suspicion to disappear. "Catch the son of a bitch who wrote it."

"Don't say anything to Sarah," Alex suggested. "She wouldn't take it very well."

Thaddeus snorted. "She'll probably tell *you*. And then she'll do a Vulcan mind-meld with the computer and find out who infected it with bad vibes."

"Sarah?" Alex countered with a raised eyebrow. "Never. She hates computers."

Sarah was surprised to notice that the sun had gone down. She'd been immersed in her work, as usual, doodling with ideas and letting her mind drift toward inspiration. Randolph had stopped in a while earlier to check on her before he'd gone home, and Jill had asked if she'd like to go out to dinner. Thaddeus, infected with an unholy zeal over the new program, had spent the majority of the afternoon breezing in and out of her office, doing his best to reignite her headache.

The one person she hadn't seen that afternoon had been Alex. Thaddeus placed him in the computer department, where he was poring over reams of material and muttering to himself. Stretching out the kinks from her legs, Sarah smiled. She'd like to see Alex muttering to himself. He probably had that little frown between his eyes, the one that still showed up when she surprised him.

She loved him. The admission didn't stun Sarah. It seemed as natural as daybreak, warm and bright and alive in her. In a period of days, Alex had measured the emptiness in her life and filled it without even knowing it.

Within a matter of minutes, he had reawakened her as a woman.

Sarah lowered her eyes a little, still amazed at what had happened the night before. People had always accused her of practicing magic, but last night it had been Alex who had woven the magic. Just the brush of his gaze against her skin had dimmed the night. The strength in his voice, in his arms, had reconstructed time. Sarah had first fallen, and then floated and finally soared, and it had all been borne on the wings of Alex Thorne's passion.

He wouldn't be comfortable with it, yet, Sarah could tell. He'd been so quiet when he'd woken too far into the night to go home and Sarah had insisted on his staying. Breakfast had consisted of his watching the morning news reports with a bagel in his hand while Sarah watched him. It had been a careful truce, a polite withdrawal. Only Alex didn't realize that Sarah had no intentions of leaving it there. Sometime in the night, when they had showered and then shared her bed, fresh and clean and newly insatiable, she'd discovered a very definite taste for lightning.

She knew he was approaching before she even heard him. He stirred the currents before him, like a ship pushing through still water. Sarah brushed her hair back, setting her earrings to tinkling, and fought the blush the mere thought of him provoked.

It was nice to be in love, truly better than she'd ever hoped with half terror and half anticipation. As alive as she felt, Sarah was surprised she hadn't really tried it since college.

Of course, the way she'd felt in college hadn't been half as nice.

Her heart tumbled at the cadence of Alex's footsteps on the carpet. Her chest constricted and her smile drew a life of its own, perversely refusing to die. Sarah did her best to sit still, but by the time he opened the door, she was almost on her feet.

Then she saw him and faltered. "What's wrong?"

Startled, Alex looked up. "What?"

Sarah tilted her head, gathering impression. "You're worried about something. What is it?"

He scowled. "There's nothing wrong," he told her, pulling a hand from his pocket to furrow it through his hair as he walked in. "I'm tired. I'm seeing numbers when I close my eyes and hearing computer-generated music—which, by the way, is highly annoying."

Sarah couldn't help but smile. He did look tired. His shoulders were slumped beneath his snowy shirt, and his tie looked as if it had suffered a few yanks of frustration. Even his gait, usually so commanding, slowed.

"Zydeco," she said brightly.

Alex squinted.

Sarah giggled. "It sounds about as far from computer noise as I could get." Shrugging, she hopped off her stool. "I think that's why I like it."

She won a grudging grin from him. "Didn't Connie feed you yet?"

"You make her sound like my nanny."

Alex maintained an unrepentant air. "Zookeeper," he acknowledged, settling an elbow on the edge of her drawing board and leaning close for emphasis. "You could make a mint on tours through here just to see the exotic species. Did you know that your computer's being used to bet on horses?"

"Jill. I know. But it's personal."

Alex waved off the protest. "So's the program one of the sales staff has in to predict the end of the world. Do you know that you even have a keypunch operator who prays to her monitor the whole time she's working?"

Turning her back on Alex, Sarah bent to begin gathering together her paraphernalia. "Not to it," she told him. "For it. She thinks it's possessed by the devil, and that if she prays while she works on it, she'll stay safe."

There was a small silence of disbelief behind her. "I know this is a stupid question, but why does she still do it?"

Sarah straightened, one shoe in hand, to find a strained look on Alex's face again. "Because that's the trade the women's prison taught her."

"Of course."

Back down on her hands and knees to hunt up the other shoe, Sarah heard a heartfelt sigh escape Alex as he moved around to perch on her chair. "And you expect me to find the odd man out in this bunch," he objected wearily. "The way things have been going, I have the most horrible feeling I'm going to end up finding out that *I'm* the embezzler."

Sarah's head popped out from behind a couch. "That's silly."

Alex shot her a rather pointed look. "So is a company CEO playing hide-and-seek with her personal apparel."

Sarah checked under the couch. Nothing there but the pen she'd lost the other day.

"Where *is* Connie?" he asked.

Sarah popped up again and instinctively looked around. "I don't know," she admitted. "Haven't you seen her?"

"Earlier. I just figured she'd be here checking up on you, since it's almost ten."

That brought Sarah to a stop. "It is?"

She wasn't quite sure how to define the look in Alex's eyes, somewhere between amusement, consternation and dread. Was that what a man looked like when he fell in love? she wondered. It didn't seem nearly as nice as what women felt.

Her shoe was between the curtain and the window. The jacket to her dress was falling down the back of the bookcase. And when she turned around for her purse, she found Alex holding it out for her. Smiling, but not looking quite happy enough.

Slipping her shoes on, she skirted the outheld purse and dropped a kiss onto Alex's lips. ''Are you going to feed me?''

Again his expression shifted. Again there was a certain amount of consternation to be seen. ''Only if all you want is food.''

Sarah chuckled. Alex's words conjured up the night before, and it hovered between them, hot and intimate and sweet. Sarah blushed, her gaze slipping a little. Alex stiffened, quieted. The air between them shivered with remembered emotion, pulsated with banked desire. It was palpable, like a heavy breeze, like the smell of roses in a late garden. Like the swell of a taut silence.

''You frighten me sometimes,'' Sarah whispered honestly.

Alex's eyes narrowed in surprise. He went very still. Sarah knew it was what he feared himself.

So she smiled for him and lifted her hand, cupping his solid, square face. ''You woke something in me that I didn't even know was asleep,'' she admitted. ''Something I'm not sure I can control.''

She never took her eyes from his, the golden brown bathing her in its curious sunlight. Alex took her hand into his and then pressed it against his lips.

''I know,'' he said.

Sarah wanted to tell him to keep her hand, to never give it back or let it go. She wanted to always feel as safe and whole as she did right then.

''It's different than with friends,'' she said. ''Isn't it? You don't risk as much with friends. You don't open up as much.''

Alex's smile was crooked and sweet. ''You don't fall in love with friends,'' he told her. ''When you fall in love, you risk falling on your face.''

''Oh, well,'' she retorted with a silly grin. ''What's a scraped nose or two?''

Sarah had wanted support, declarations of undying love. What she got was a small shake of the head. "It hurts a lot more than that," Alex said, and she could feel the shattering loneliness.

She saw him walking away, making the choice that would return her life to its equilibrium, and wanted to cry out to stop it.

"Oh-oh, I'm going to have to stop checking up on you."

Sarah and Alex spun around to find Connie striding in the door, purse and briefcase in hand.

"No," she objected lightly. "Don't blush on my account. I've just been on a close encounter myself, so I'm not in the least embarrassed." Setting down her things on the bookshelf, she bestowed a wry smile. "Although maybe you should be. You two are putting a strain on the air-conditioning system, and it's only seventy degrees outside."

"You must have had a nice time," Sarah marveled at her friend. "You're heading into warp drive."

"I've been showing off our latest retirement investment," Connie admitted, then turned to take in Alex. "Did you know that our girl has done it again? I should thank you for not going home last night. You've inspired the Delaney Life Jacket."

"Life jacket?" Alex asked.

"Delaney?" Sarah asked, scowling. "Why not Sunset?"

Connie leaned against the doorway and considered Sarah with patient eyes. "What does the sun do when it sets?"

It took Sarah a minute to follow her train of thought. "It goes down."

Connie nodded, appeased. "Which is what we don't want the people who buy these to think they're going to do."

"Oh."

"What life jacket?" Alex insisted.

Connie threw a little wave in Sarah's direction. "After watching a piece this morning on airliner life jackets, our girl here decided to make a simpler one. The patent attorney is already salivating."

"Why Delaney?" Sarah asked. "Why not Mason?"

Connie took on a look of even greater patience. "Because you're the star, honey. Nobody connects Mason with anything but office memos."

Sarah still wrinkled her nose. "I'm not really sure if I want to see my name every time I look under an airplane seat."

Connie gathered together her paraphernalia. "Well, I have an appointment with an underused pillow." Stopping as she filled her arms, she turned to Alex, fixing a smile on him. "So, tell me. Does this mean I'm finally off the late shift? It's been playing hell with my social life, y'know."

"Connie," Sarah objected, "I told you you didn't have to always check up on me."

When Connie turned to her, she saw the sum of all their years together in her friend's suspiciously soft expression. "I'm the one who found your house," she said dryly. "I'm obligated to see that you use it at least every so often." Shifting her gaze a little, she considered Alex. "Are you going to take her home, or do I?"

"No," he said, the purse still dangling from his hand. "It's on my way."

Connie shouldered her own purse. "Well, see if you can watch something tomorrow morning on the common cold. I'd sure like a condo on Maui."

Sarah blushed. "Connie!"

But Connie was already out the door.

"She's a little wired," Alex commented, watching her brisk retreat.

"She's in love," Sarah said, retrieving her purse and preparing to follow. "I think she's even more excited by the life jacket."

Alex turned a bemused expression on her. "You really redesigned the life jacket?"

Sarah smiled. "You're really going to feed me?"

Ultimately Alex didn't get the chance to watch television at Sarah's the next morning. He didn't wake at Sarah's at all. He fed her and took her home, hearing the silence pile up between them in the dark as they approached her house. He wanted to make love to her again, to lose himself in the silk shower of her hair and drink in the little sounds of pleasure she made. He wanted to think he could open himself to a woman and feel safe. But it wasn't that easy. It never was.

So he pulled up to her house, ready to make his apologies—a long day, a headache, a call to Lindsay—only to find Sarah asleep beside him. Tousled, pouting, childlike. And he ended up carrying her inside—after digging her key out from underneath tree roots as he balanced her in his arms, that is—and putting her to bed. And then, astonished at how much he ached at the sight of her, he locked her back in and went on to the hotel.

Saturday morning found him at the keyboard in an otherwise empty office. He didn't mind; it was easier to get his work done. But his mind wasn't on work. As he punched up the companies Sunset dealt with, either supply or delivery, he thought of mistakes. As he scanned data and checked addresses and authenticity, he thought of opportunities.

Barbi had been a mistake. He'd invested everything in her, diving in headfirst only to find himself on dry ground. As naive as a love-struck kid, he'd done more than share, he'd bestowed, bequeathed. He'd given it all away before he realized he wasn't going to get anything back. And if that episode taught him nothing else, it should have taught him to be cautious, especially around blondes who made him feel protective and possessive.

Yet here he was preoccupied by another set of wide blue eyes. Here he was flagrantly courting disaster. No, he amended, he'd already gone past that. He'd made love to her. He'd surrendered to that guileless smile and irresistible passion, and couldn't think how to get free.

He wanted to back up, to regain his safe footing. But it was too late. He'd already tasted what it was that had been so exhilarating about falling in love the first time. When he'd made love to Sarah last night, he'd remembered how good it could feel to fall hard—and how very terrifying. He was falling in love with her and he didn't know what to do about it.

The first time he dialed her number, it was busy. Looking up at the clock on the wall, he saw that it was only about ten. Probably Connie checking up on any new inspirations. Doing his best to shake off the urge to try again, he turned back to the computer.

She wasn't really like Barbi, he reminded himself. Behind Sarah's distracted, seductive eyes hid a brain that sparked genius. Beneath that soft, slightly vague exterior lay a creation of whimsy and wonder. Alex couldn't imagine Sarah having enough focus to betray anyone, much less the man she loved. He couldn't imagine coming home to find her in bed with his oldest friend.

But he hadn't been able to imagine that of Barbi, either.

Alex was so distracted by contrasts and comparisons that he almost missed it. He'd been filing through each of the companies that Sunset did business with, checking the picture of each company against his own mental picture of legitimacy. Some he checked in directories, some he recognized from doing other audits in the textile industries. Some he made notes to follow up on. Then he reached one that brought pencil and eye to a halt.

It wasn't anything glaring. Nothing obvious or concrete, just an out-of-town address—and a date on which transactions commenced that corresponded neatly with the start of Sarah's "feelings."

Nothing. Perfectly kept records, goods delivered, payment made. All on time, all without comment or complaint, which in itself was unusual. But it wasn't that information that brought Alex to a halt. It was lack of data. An address, a phone number for questions, a name for addressing inquiries. No notes about sales visits or problems with the product. A curious flatness that was like a furnished apartment without personal touches. A neatness that sprang the catch on Alex's suspicion.

And the mailing address was a post office box. Perfectly legitimate, but also inescapably convenient for the felon. Post office boxes were favorite addresses for frauds. He'd seen this same data the other night and put the discomfort down to exhaustion.

Alex picked up the phone and dialed. The Los Angeles number was temporarily disconnected. He'd have to call Ellis and have him check up on things. But first, he'd call Sarah.

Busy. She really liked to talk. Alex brushed aside his own impatience and dialed again, rubbing at his chest.

"This better be life 'n death," Ellis growled in greeting.

"It's a lead," Alex answered, and was satisfied to hear Ellis scramble for coherency.

"Who is it?"

"I don't know," Alex admitted. "Who buys the computer programs at Sunset?"

There was a short pause. "It's always been Thaddeus," he said. "It's kinda like his religion, y'know?"

Thaddeus, the bright-eyed wonder boy who looked like Spike Jones. The wunderkind with a brash sense of himself and his capabilities. Thaddeus, who knew the progress of

Alex's investigation because he was so anxious to help. Alex really liked him.

"Ever heard of a company called Datasys?"

Another pause. "Wholesaler, isn't it? Connie once said they'd gone to them because they could come in cheap, what with Thaddeus there to set up the programs and teach 'em. You think it's Datasys?"

"I don't know," Alex admitted, rubbing at his eyes and unaccountably thinking of calling Sarah again. "I have a hunch."

"Oh, catching, huh?"

"An accountant's hunch, Ellis. That's different."

"Sure it is, boy. Sure it is. So, what do I do?"

"Check out Datasys on that fancy mainframe you have at the law school. I want to know who owns it and where it's licensed."

Ellis had a note of awe in his voice. "You really think this is it, don't you?"

For a moment Alex considered the information before him, the stark figures and data, and thought again of Sarah. "Yeah," he finally admitted. He was rubbing again, worrying at the weight that seemed to gather behind his breastbone. "I think we're on the right road. Call me when you get it. I have to call Sarah."

"Oh, man, don't burst the lady's bubble yet."

Alex hung up anyway. He suddenly wanted to check with Sarah, to find out what she knew, find out what she'd want to do.

He dialed Sarah's number again. Once more it was busy. He was in the middle of a string of oaths when he remembered the night he'd goosed himself on her telephone receiver. She'd left it off the hook again.

Frustrated, he looked up at the clock. Ten-thirty. He thought of calling the police, but then considered all the times they'd been there already. Her house was only a few blocks away; he'd go himself to satisfy his curiosity, ease the impatience.

Shutting down the computer, Alex stood and headed out the door. Damn her for a child. Couldn't she for once be responsible? He needed to talk to her about what made an innocuous-looking company suspect. He needed to ask who had authorization over what, who ordered the software, who gave approval for the money they put out on computerization. He needed to be there when she found out who it was who was hurting her, because he had to protect her.

The day was another scorcher, the heat slicing through his T-shirt and matting his hair. Even the air conditioning in the car didn't seem enthusiastic on the short ride to Sarah's. Alex took the corners a little too fast and screeched when he pulled the car to a stop in Sarah's driveway.

Her door was closed. Alex rang the bell, a hip against the newly replaced glass door, an eye along the neighborhood. Sarah didn't answer. He knocked. A couple doors down, a man watering his lawn did a little nonchalant eavesdropping. Alex pulled a hand through his hair and thought of going for the key. First he'd try the door.

It figured. She'd left it unlocked. If he did hang around, Alex was going to have to teach her a thing or two about personal safety. He pushed the door open and strode into the cool entryway only to find it as hot as the street. Alex faltered to a sickened halt.

"Sarah?"

The room was a shambles. Cushions were ripped. Windows were shattered. Books and papers covered the floor in ragged hillocks. The lamps were all broken, and the lovely old grandfather clock was gouged and scored.

Dread shot through him. Finally remembering to let go of the door, Alex stepped inside.

"Sarah!"

Chapter 12

The police arrived within minutes. Sirens screamed and the shudder of strobe lights strained the white walls. Even though he knew she wasn't there, Alex kept tearing through the debris.

This wasn't a burglary and it wasn't vandalism. This was a violation. Everything Sarah owned had been destroyed, her lovely antiques shattered, her prints slashed, her flowers uprooted and lying in untidy clumps over the lawn like piles of plague victims. Her bed had been ruined, the mattress ripped and the soft floral linens as mutilated as the real flowers outside.

A sudden, spilling rage took Alex. He heaved overturned furniture out of his way and clawed through the scattered papers. Panting, furious, frightened. Sarah wasn't home, and her house was a wreck.

It was Valdez who answered the call. Valdez the pragmatic, the rule keeper and protocol follower. Valdez, who stood in the living room as if he'd just witnessed a natural disaster.

When he saw Alex, he took an involuntary step backward. "Miss Delaney?" he asked. Behind him two more officers stepped into the mess.

"She's not here," Alex grated out. "No sign of her. I'd been getting a busy signal for half an hour and just figured she'd left her phone off the hook again."

Valdez looked around, almost at a loss. "No sign of foul play."

"What do you call this?" Alex retorted, chopping at the ruined room.

But Valdez shook his head. "I mean…uh, blood."

Alex paled even more. "No," he said quietly, raking a hand through his hair and looking around again. "No blood."

Valdez answered by turning on his backup. "You two get to the neighbors and find out why the hell nobody heard anything. Put out an APB on Miss Delaney. You know what she looks like."

"There was a guy out watering his lawn when I pulled in," Alex offered lamely, the rage sinking into frustrated impotence. "Maybe he saw somebody."

With a general nod, the two walked out, making it a point to close the door behind them. As if it could somehow offer some kind of protection now. Alex wanted to laugh.

The police again. Good heavens, now what could they be there for this time? It seemed she couldn't walk up the sidewalk anymore without running into a brace of blue uniforms.

"I'm sorry," she said, pushing open the door with her hip. "Did I trip the wrong code again?"

Sarah didn't even get a chance to set down the bags. Before she could turn back from shutting the door behind her, something very big barreled into her.

"Where the *hell* have you been?" Alex. He had his

hands on her shoulders—hurting her, he was holding on to her so tightly. He looked so angry that for the first time he frightened her.

"Alex?" she said in a very small voice, her bags crushed against her chest between them, the beautiful morning outside forgotten. "What's wrong?"

"I asked where you were," he demanded fiercely, giving her a little shake. "Damn it, you wander around like you're in a fog and just expect everything to be like a tea party. Don't you even lock the door when you go out, for God's sake? You just let anybody in here?"

Sarah was truly afraid now. Rage and frustration welled from him like hot poison. It washed over her, chilling her in its wake. Overwhelming her with its size.

"Alex, you're hurting me."

She might as well have slapped him. Her words stunned him into silence. Sarah saw it then, the surprise, the hurt, the spark of self-directed anger that had triggered all this.

"What's the matter?" she asked, dropping the bags without thinking about it, without hearing the fragile crush of eggshells at her feet. Her own hands came up, afraid now for him.

"How long have you been gone, Miss Delaney?"

For the first time Sarah realized that there was somebody else in the room. Sgt. Valdez. She was hardly surprised. He was usually the one stuck with sorting out her mistakes. Sarah was turning to answer him when Alex tightened his hold on her again, preventing her from moving.

"In a minute, Sergeant," Alex grated without taking his eyes from her, eyes that burned with a hundred raw emotions, every one making Sarah even more unsettled. "I'm sorry, Sarah. I should have known this would happen. I had a warning and didn't do anything about it."

"What would happen?" she asked, still seeing nothing but his eyes, his torment.

"What warning?" Valdez demanded beyond Alex.

"Someone came in while you were gone," Alex said to her, his voice as tortured as his eyes. "They did some damage."

Sarah felt the blood drain from her face. She knew the moment Alex's grip changed from controlling to supportive. When she turned to take in the rest of her house, he was there to protect her.

"Alex?" she said, her gaze traveling over the scope of destruction. "You do have...a wonderful sense...of understatement."

She couldn't help the catch in her voice. Tears crowded close. Shock stole her forward momentum. Devastation advanced like a cold mist that crept over the gutted cushions and slashed pictures.

Sarah tried to take in what had happened. She tried to understand that someone she trusted had done this to her. Yet it wouldn't quite gel. She couldn't do anything but mourn her small treasures, her silly little comforts that had grown so important over the years, first as she'd imagined collecting them, then when she'd actually discovered them waiting in a store or a flea market or an auction for her to find. Sarah couldn't move past the fact that her sense of stability foundered and was lost.

Then she looked up past the yawning ruin of her French doors to find her flowers. She never felt the tears.

"How long have you been gone, Miss Delaney?" Sgt. Valdez asked as gently as he knew how.

Sarah tried to pull her whirling emotions back into some kind of order. She reached out a hand to Alex, trying to regain a little of her security, and he wrapped an arm around her shoulders. She couldn't take her eyes from her flowers, dying out there in the sun, their color already dusty and faded.

"Sarah, how 'bout I get you something to drink?" Alex asked.

"Thank you," she agreed. "Tea would be nice."

But she couldn't let him go long enough to get it.

"What time is it?" she asked, finally turned to Valdez where he stood like a stiff-legged shorebird among her rubble.

"A little before eleven."

Sarah wanted to sit down, but there was nowhere to sit. No chair left unscathed, nothing. A sob escaped her and she let it.

"I think I left...around nine or nine-thirty. I walked." Looking over at Valdez, she sought reassurance. "You know."

"I know. You didn't see anything on your way out? Any strange cars in the neighborhood?" For a moment he dipped his eyes, escaping to his notes. It seemed to Sarah, though, that he was dodging away, uncomfortable. "Anybody you might have recognized?"

She could have taken the time to think about it, but she knew it wouldn't do any good. She never noticed things like that.

Flowers she noticed, and the crisp blue of the morning sky. The dusty browns and emerald greens of carefully tended lawns. The glaring, delicious whites of adobe against the desert morning. She might have exchanged hellos with neighbors—she usually did. She probably stopped long enough to play a little hopscotch with the Patterson girls over by the market. But she wasn't the kind of person to be distracted by something different. She had enough distractions of her own.

"No," she finally admitted on a sigh. "Nobody."

He gave a tentative nod and scribbled in his little notebook. "We're going to need to know if anything was taken."

"When she's ready," Alex said with such authority that he stole Sarah's attention. Valdez didn't think to argue.

"Nothing's gone," she said, turning back to Valdez. When he looked up with a certain amount of surprise, she offered a little shrug. "I'll check," she amended. "But I'd know by now."

"Come on into the kitchen," Alex suggested to her then, his hold purposeful. "You can sit there and we can talk."

Valdez immediately stiffened. "I think I'd like to talk to you about that warning, Mr. Thorne."

Alex nodded, his attention on Sarah. "In the kitchen."

Alex and Sarah made it there before Valdez did, because just then the lab crew arrived. Sarah caught their offhand greetings to Valdez as she walked out. The police took over her living room, and she escaped into her kitchen.

It was the same, only worse. The cabinets had been emptied, the refrigerator struck and left gaping like a wounded thing. The phone torn from the wall and the handmade little plaques and dried flowers and baskets ripped from the walls and strewn over the floor. And there was more.

Sarah stood before her wall, quiet and amazed. "They even knocked holes in my wall," she murmured.

There was a moment of uncomfortable silence before Alex answered. "No, they didn't."

Sarah turned to find him standing right behind her, a little awkward with embarrassment. "I did it."

Sarah's eyes widened and she took one more look at the three evenly spaced holes punched right through the wall-board.

"You?" she echoed in some astonishment.

Alex? Gentle, persevering, bemused Alex? Alex who had had the control to turn down her painfully abrupt advances for so long, who had been enough of a gentleman not to hurt her?

Abruptly the window opened again, as if the holes were the entry, and she heard a terrible, raw cry of frustration and grief. Heard another, years old, that sounded even worse, like the sound of a mortally wounded animal surrounded and finding no way out.

"I guess it's something I should have warned you about," he admitted as if hearing the same echoes.

Sarah shook her head and managed her first smile of the day. "You took care of Lindsay for five weeks when she couldn't take care of herself."

"And I destroyed her garage."

"And you never once touched your wife. You never even thought to hurt her."

Alex tried to get away with an offhand shrug. "I still had Dallas Cowboys I could take it out on."

Sarah wasn't sure why that should provoke sudden tears, but it did. She wasn't sure why his protestations should make her love him even more, or why the force of his fear and fury should have made her understand him better, but it did.

Not the destruction, not the betrayal or the blank wall of silence that met her attempts to see the culprit broke through her defenses. Not police in her house picking through what had once been her life or the feeling that she had somehow been violated.

Alex did it, with his gruff concern and his harsh frustration and the stark fear in his eyes. Alex, who had arrived to find her house a shambles and her missing, and had vented his impotent rage on her wall. Alex, who had no idea how wonderful he was.

Sarah crumpled into his arms, her sobs welling up. Her world dissolved into his embrace. His hands, which had bruised her with their intensity, now soothed. They stroked clumsily at her hair and patted her back. They eased her into his arms and settled her onto his lap when he sat. They provided safe haven and support and guided her to rest against him where the steady cadence of his heartbeat settled her.

Sarah never saw Valdez appear at the door or Alex's

silent glare of warning. She never saw Valdez retreat. She simply gave herself up to Alex's care and emerged stronger.

Moments later, Connie blew in with the detectives, Randolph and Thaddeus following close on her heels. Ellis called while everybody was being questioned. Every one of them hovered.

Connie looked as if her own child had been kidnapped. Randolph brewed coffee and tea and chided Sarah for not calling them right away. He acted as if he should have been the one to find the destruction instead of an outsider, as if Alex had no place comforting Sarah. Thaddeus brought the computer message with him and delighted in rehashing gory details with every detective he could find, especially those willing to share their particular expertise.

"Well, Alex," Connie finally said as they set about cleaning up some of the mess, "I'm glad you called us. Even though it wasn't quite the message I'd anticipated from you this early in the morning."

Standing at the bottom of her bed, Sarah thought of what it had held only two nights ago and couldn't even think to blush. She wanted to cry again.

"Can we do this later?" she asked in a small voice. It was like burying her family.

Connie shot her a sharp look. "Tell you what," she offered, wrapping her own arm around Sarah's shoulder. "Why don't I take you to my place for a nap and we'll let all this muscle finish cleaning up?"

Sarah was unaccountably alarmed by someone else touching her things again. Anyone else, even her friends. She wanted to sift through it herself, putting to rest her memories and gathering the courage to move on. But she wanted to do it later. Now it was all still too raw.

"No," she said, turning uncertain eyes on her friend. "I want to leave it. I want some time off first...please?"

Connie gave a reassuring squeeze and nodded, all common sense. "You bet. We'll leave somebody here to wait for the people to come board up and change the locks. Volunteers?"

"Happy to," Thaddeus offered.

Connie nodded. "Settled. You want to get some things to take with you, hon?"

Again Sarah had to summon her courage, because she had to tell her friend that she didn't want to go with her. It would be the first time she could remember ever challenging Connie's commanding good sense. If her life hadn't just been turned on its head and scattered about like the straw man in the wake of the flying monkeys, Sarah might have quailed a little longer. But her old points of reference were missing, her intuition cloudy and unsure. As much as she loathed to say it, the only person she could trust right now, the only person with whom she felt absolutely safe, no matter how much her brain reasoned otherwise, was Alex.

And she knew it was going to break Connie's heart.

Somehow Alex knew.

"Connie, maybe Sarah should come with me," he said diffidently from where he leaned against the wall. "I think she might benefit from talking to my sister."

Sarah felt Connie stiffen. "Your sister?" she demanded. "Whatever for?"

Sarah didn't give her a chance. "His sister's a counselor," Sarah said, locking eyes with Alex and reassuring herself with his solid support. "She deals with this kind of thing all the time. I think I would like to talk to her, Alex." She didn't mention the fact that Alex's sister was still in the hospital after giving birth.

Connie, however, had other arguments in mind. Dropping her arm, she faced off with Alex. "How safe is she going to be?" she demanded. "Can you promise to protect her? After all, you were the first one in line for this kind of treatment."

"I'll protect her," Alex answered without moving, without posing or posturing. He just leaned there, hands in pockets, eyes passive and quiet, voice even. Yet no one in the room would have questioned him.

Sarah felt the contest between Connie, born to protect, seasoned to support and provide, and Alex, whose instincts were still new. The air quivered between the two of them as old guard gave way to new.

Finally, in a sudden burst of sunlight, Connie grinned. The expression was as much acquiescence as warning. "Okay, kid. This is your big chance," she said brusquely. "I'm putting you in the game."

Alex's smile was slow and easy. "Thanks, coach," he answered. "I won't let you down."

Alex's suite was cool and quiet, living room, kitchenette and bedroom all done up in pastels and whitewashed walls. Outside, Sarah could hear the splash of the pool, the susurrous wash of a waterfall, and the periodic murmur of people wandering by the first-floor window, their conversation vacation-tempered.

The bed was a big one, firm and overflowing with pillows, and surprisingly enough when Alex steered her into the room and closed the curtains against the sun, Sarah snuggled right in.

He'd still been there later, when she'd started awake and when she'd drifted off to sleep again. He'd been in the periphery of her senses and the center of her dreams, his eyes always smiling and sure, his arms a harbor from the storms. And when she woke again to find the room hazy with late afternoon light, Sarah heard the murmur of his voice in the other room.

"You're sure," he was saying, and immediately Sarah heard the edge. There was an energy there, a decisiveness that brought her up from the pillow.

"I'm not in the mood for games, either, Ellis. You didn't see her house."

The lingering peace of sleep vanished with Alex's words. Throwing off the quilt, Sarah swung out of bed. Something else was happening, changing, ending. She could hear it in the clipped tones of Alex's voice. Dread and anticipation. She wasn't at all sure she wanted to know what was going on, but she knew she had to.

Alex looked up in surprise when she walked in. He was seated on the couch in his bare feet, his hair tousled from running his hands through it, the phone at his ear and a legal pad covered with scribbles in front of him on the table.

"Is that Ellis?" Sarah asked, swiping at her own hair to counter the effects of sleep.

Alex nodded and then listened. "He says his mama's recalling her feathers and entrails. Something about faulty equipment."

"His version of a security system," she admitted. "Ask him if you can get refunds on spells."

The mood eased for the few minutes it took Alex to get off the phone. Ellis passed along greetings and commiserations and dire warnings to housebreakers—something to do with *their* entrails. Alex chuckled and Sarah relaxed. When Alex hung up, Sarah knew she'd have to ask.

"Tea?" was how it came out instead. She knew she couldn't put it off, but she wanted to so badly.

Alex climbed to his feet. "I'll make it. You sit down."

Sarah scowled up at him. "Don't go all Randolph on me, Alex. I'm not as helpless as I act."

Alex reached out to draw her into his arms. "It's those damn eyes of yours," he protested. "They make you look like a Raggedy Ann doll that's been left behind."

Sarah scowled into the solid comfort of his chest. "I see."

His answering chuckle was deep and melodious against

her ear. "You'd bring out the protective instincts in Muammar Qaddafi."

For a few minutes they stood together, quiet, insular and content. Sarah drifted on his scent and the wash of his breathing. She eased down into his strength and found comfort, even though she knew that there would be monsters waiting when she opened her eyes again. For just that moment, the monsters were held at bay.

Finally Sarah collected her courage and stepped away. "What have you and Ellis been up to?" she asked.

Alex followed her over to the kitchenette and bent to pull a beer from the small refrigerator. "Solving Sunset's problems," he said quietly.

Sarah looked up, her breath caught somewhere beneath the big ball of dread in her chest. "You've found something?"

His eyes met hers without flinching—soft, sure eyes. Honey brown and sweet, knowing what she faced and what it would cost her. Assuring her that no matter what, he would be there for her.

"I think so," he said, the beer in his hand momentarily forgotten. "What can you tell me about Datasys?"

For a moment his question didn't register. Sarah had expected an identity, a crime, evidence. She hadn't been prepared to be led carefully in a direction that wouldn't be clear to her.

"What about it?"

Alex finally remembered his beer and turned his attention briefly to popping it open, the sound as sharp as gunfire in the quiet room. "Sunset went with the company just a short while ago, didn't it?"

Sarah shrugged. "I guess. I don't keep up with the computer stuff. It—"

Alex smiled. "Gives you a headache. I know."

Sarah lifted a hand to push at her hair again, but somehow it never passed higher than her mouth. She pressed it there for a moment, as if to keep the betrayal from spilling out. "Which is why that's where the scheme is. They knew I wouldn't pay attention."

"That you *couldn't* pay attention," Alex amended, leaning forward to her a little.

"But what about the others?" she asked, still not really wanting the truth. "They should have suspected something."

"People see what they want to see. Datasys was saving them money. It was the perfect setup for Sunset, because you didn't need the backup services of most software companies. You just needed the goods."

The little teakettle began to whistle, shrill and insistent, and Sarah turned to it. "And the new computer-animation package I wanted was so damn expensive, it seemed the perfect alternative."

"Ellis checked for me," Alex said alongside her. "There is no Datasys registered. What we think is that the software is coming in from the black market, bootlegged stuff."

"It did seem so perfect," she whispered, hovering over her tea like a shaman preparing for a ritual. "Especially with Thaddeus there. He was as excited as a kid...you know how he is about his own capabilities."

"Who found the company?" Alex asked.

Sarah looked up, stricken. Afraid. The ground was crumbling beneath her feet and she didn't want to look down.

"I don't know," she admitted, hanging on to the unqualified support in Alex's eyes. "I'm never in on those meetings." Briefly her gaze dropped with her admission. "I'm no good at it."

Alex wouldn't allow her guilt. Reaching out, he lifted her chin with his fingers. "And I can't invent life jackets," he retorted. "Come on, Sarah. You couldn't have known."

She shook her head, miserable. "I should have. I should have anticipated something."

Alex set his untasted beer down alongside Sarah's steeping tea and pulled her back into his arms. "And I should have told you the warning was left on the computer. My crime's worse than yours."

Sarah settled into his hold again. "Are we going to argue over who's more horrible?"

Alex nestled his cheek against her hair. "If you insist."

She sighed, capitulating. "Thaddeus," she said.

Alex didn't move. "What about him?"

"He's the one who orders the programs. Always has. He pores over those catalogues like a kid with the Sears Christmas catalogue."

Alex lifted his head a little. "Catalogues?" he asked. "You get catalogues from the company?"

Sarah pulled away enough to look up at him. "I think so. I don't know for sure. Thaddeus always has something he's pointing out to get. I never really look."

"I'd like to see one," he admitted, and then suddenly relented. "But that comes later. The order of the day is a little R and R."

Wishing she felt more resolved, Sarah shook her head. "We have to find out before anything else happens."

"We are," he assured her, running a finger down her nose. "Ellis is doing some more checking for me. I'll call the detectives and give them what we've got. Maybe we can track down the owner of that post office box the company uses and get some kind of name."

"I don't want to know," Sarah blurted out, ashamed and afraid.

Alex gathered her in closer. "I know," he said, brushing her hair back for her. "I wish it could be some other way."

She searched the depths of his eyes and found what she wanted. "Will you be there with me?"

He smiled. "All the way."

She nodded, as satisfied as she could be, as comforted. Still there was a knot of acid in her chest, a rot of betrayal. The gnawing trace of guilt told her she must have failed someone to have them turn on her like this.

"I'm so afraid," she admitted softly, as much to herself as Alex. "I can't feel a thing, and I don't understand why."

"What do you mean?" he asked.

Sarah lifted her head again, sought him out. "I touch their hands every day," she protested. "Ten times a day, all of them, Thaddeus and Jill and Randolph and Connie and Hector. Avarice is one thing, a cold kind of emotion. Subtle. I might understand that I couldn't detect that. But the anger that fueled the attack on my house should be a livid slash—a hot, living current that jumps out at me. And I haven't felt a thing. I'm too close to all of them," she finally admitted with a frustrated shake of her head. "I'm too afraid that one of them really is trying to hurt me."

"One of them is," Alex answered gently.

This time Sarah pulled away, turning from his honesty because she couldn't yet face it. "I know that," she said, then amended her words. "My brain knows it. The rest of me would rather keep going just the way I was."

She could hear Alex behind her, solid and supportive and patient with her denial. Knowing when to reach out and when to wait. And that was when she turned, the surprise finally reaching her.

"How did you know?" she demanded.

Alex didn't react. "Know what?"

Sarah tilted her head, amazed that she'd missed it, even through the morass of what had happened. "*You* were the one who knew something was wrong this morning," she accused. "Not me. I walked right in there without a clue. You drove over from work even though you had no reason to."

"Your line was busy," Alex protested, a sudden defense

appearing in his eyes, a stiffness reaching his posture. "I thought you might have left the receiver off the hook again."

"So you came over? Connie calls the police."

He didn't quite meet her eyes. "I'd had the warning."

"To you," she insisted. "All the attacks have been against you. But you knew there was something wrong at the house."

"Sarah," he warned dryly. "Don't look for things that aren't there."

Now she giggled, delighted that he couldn't see something so plain. "But I do that all the time," she protested, then leveled a finger at him. "So do you. You knew where I'd gone the night of the shooting when nobody else had a clue. And now this."

His gaze gathered consternation. "Sarah—"

"You're psychic, Alex," she protested. "I know it."

Alex reached for his beer then and took a good-sized slug. "I knew I was going to do that," he snapped.

"What's the matter?" she asked. "Does it worry you?"

"No," he answered with a tone of voice that should have brooked no argument. "Because *it* doesn't affect me. Have your tea, Sarah. I'm going to call the police and then we'll have dinner."

"Do you know what I'm going to say?" she teased.

"Yes," he said with great forbearance. "'Thank you, Alex. What a wonderful idea.'"

Sarah just smiled. "I'll go get changed."

He didn't smile back. "I'll call the police."

His attitude shouldn't have made Sarah happier. He looked much like a bear with a particularly uncomfortable thorn in its paw. But Sarah walked away humming nonetheless. She finally understood, and that made all the difference in the world.

Chapter 13

Who would have imagined? Alex Thorne, psychic. Pulling a lightweight linen dress over her head, Sarah found herself giggling. It was so wonderful, so…surprising. She'd been certain that he had been afraid of his emotions, of letting go. He'd been afraid of letting go, all right. Alex, who religiously observed the rituals of the left-brained adult, would never accept the fact that he was even a little psychic.

Sarah imagined that over the years he'd done quite a job of controlling that annoying little talent of his. He'd turned in the exact opposite direction, focusing on numbers and equations and logic to block out the very illogical fact that he could sometimes tune into other people.

He probably wasn't as acutely aware as she was. After all, Sarah had never had reason to question her gift. Blue and John had cultivated it as her right. But Alex, growing up in middle America with a body built for football and a brain that excelled in numbers, wouldn't have known what to do with the sudden flashes of insight he'd been given.

The logical decision would have been to simply tune them out. The problem was, of course, that when he really opened himself up to someone—like his ex-wife, someone like Sarah—his control slipped and the sight returned. It taunted him again, whispering at him when he wasn't paying attention, nudging him from sleep, too indistinct to identify, too persistent to ignore. It linked him so closely to the person he loved that he could anticipate them, could taste their emotions as well as his.

He could know, without realizing it, what was going on in their minds.

Alex was afraid of falling in love, because he couldn't control that kind of invasion. He couldn't separate it from the jumble of raw emotion that love was.

Sarah heard him talking to the detectives, his voice crisp and authoritative. Slipping into her shoes, she reached for a brush to take out some of the kinks in her hair. And she thought of how furious Alex would be when she wouldn't allow him to back off again. She smiled, as giddy and afraid as she'd ever been. As torn.

Sarah really wanted to talk to Lindsay after all. As close as Alex was with his sister, Sarah bet he could read her, could anticipate her. She bet that his ordeal with his sister's grief had been worse than even he admitted, because he hadn't just imagined her pain, he'd felt it. When Lindsay had been kidnapped beneath his nose, he'd suffered her terror as if it were his own. Sarah bet he'd never really questioned that connection like he would the ones that put him at risk.

Like women he could fall in love with, women who could take his secrets and torture him with them.

That, however, was not something to deal with right now. Sarah wasn't even sure she wanted to deal with her own sight right now. She wanted a quiet meal and a little conversation. And maybe later, they could go in search of another whirlpool.

"You're blushing," Alex noted when she walked out into the living room.

Sarah blushed even harder. "You're not supposed to notice."

Climbing to his feet, Alex assessed her with a twinkle in his eye. "Hard not to," he countered, "when it makes you look like you were just kissed."

Sarah slowed to a halt, a smile hovering and the fiery betrayal refusing to recede. "I wouldn't know," she said. "I haven't been kissed today."

"You haven't, huh? That's too bad. You look like you could use it."

"I could," she admitted with a rather plaintive sigh that belied the delicious acceleration of her heart. "I've had a hard day."

She hadn't meant to let it invade here. She'd wanted sanctuary, isolation, denial. Even so, the loss of her home bled into her expression. She could tell by the reaction in Alex. His eyes softened and his shoulders slumped a little as he approached.

"We'll take care of that later," he said, knowing without admitting it, even to himself—especially to himself. "Together. But tonight we're going to pretend that you and I are the only two people in the world." Lifting a hand, he cupped her cheek, his touch warm and gentle and heartbreakingly solid.

Sarah tried to grin, leaning a little into his touch. "Except the waiters," she amended. "I don't want to do any work."

"And the cook."

"And the man with the violin who strolls among the tables playing gypsy music."

Alex shook his head. "Sarah, this is Phoenix. The nearest gypsy is in Bucharest."

Sarah's heart lifted as she met Alex's gaze with renewed

life. "Mariachis then," she bargained. "Trumpets and guitars."

Alex rolled his eyes and wrapped his hand into her hair. "You are a glutton for punishment."

She must have been. She didn't protest the whole time he was kissing her. In fact, she didn't even mind. When he lifted her face to his, she went. When he bent to taste her lips, she wrapped her arms around his neck and held on tight.

The sweetness of his touch seeped through her like sunlight. The dark flavors of his mouth surrounded her. His arms swept her up and his hands held her to him. Sarah folded into him, her body melting very agreeably, her breathing stumbling right behind her heart and her feet losing touch with the ground.

And there in Alex's arms, she found her sanctuary.

"Dinner," he murmured into her throat.

Her breath escaping in something that sounded like laughter, Sarah nodded. "I think I can already hear the trumpets."

Alex chuckled back and shook his head so that his hair tickled her cheek. "I can't seem to say no to you."

"Good," Sarah gasped when his tongue found the soft shell of her ear. "Then maybe after dinner, we can go in search...ah, of a whirlpool."

Abruptly Alex's head came up, a wicked glint in his eye. "*That's* what you were blushing about," he accused, still holding her tight.

Sarah's answering smile was coy and knowing. "You must be psychic," she marveled.

That was all it took to get Alex out the door.

Sarah was being much too docile. Alex couldn't get comfortable, knowing that at any minute she'd jump back on her latest favorite subject about him and ESP. Showed you what psychics knew. She probably saw it in all her friends, the way some people saw satanic verse in all rock music. Maybe it was a little lonely being the only witch on the block, and she was looking for some company.

Not Alex Thorne, thank you. He had enough to deal with without playing with Ouija boards and floating tables. He was an accountant, not a channeler. Trances were for people like Sarah, one foot on the ground and the other in the ethereal plane. Nobody would think twice about it. In fact, they'd probably be disappointed if she didn't profess to at least some kind of eccentricity. CPAs, on the other hand, were not valued for their prescient powers. At least, not unless it had to do with changes in the tax law, and so far Alex hadn't had any inclination in that area.

Not that he had anything like that at all.

Except for Lindsay. But that was natural. She was his sister; they'd been through a lot together. Of course, he'd have a special bond with her. Anything else was out of the question.

Now Sarah sat across from him with quiet assurance in her eyes, waiting to spring...gathering momentum to accuse. As if he didn't have enough on his mind already.

As if he weren't distracted enough with the lead suddenly turning up, and the destruction of Sarah's house and the possibility of one of her friends being the culprit. And Sarah, wide-eyed and alive, her skin like warm milk, her eyes glittering like sunlight on water. Her conversation breathy and bright, as if they'd just met that day over drinks and decided to wander on in to eat.

Sarah, who needed to be protected and led like a puppy, who deserved to be secure and happy. Sarah, who needed love more than she knew and gave it without accounting. Who touched the world like one of her flowers, bright and fragile and fleeting.

Sarah, who was not Barbi. Who demanded more from him than Barbi had ever known how.

The comparison conjured an image. A raw autumn day,

the sky a flat, hard gray and the wind torturing the leafless trees. End of season, almost the end of his career. It was in sight by then, his knees constantly complaining, his times slowing. The seasonal depression hit, following him home from the play-off loss that had ended their chance at another bowl.

The depression was deeper this time, gnawing, troubling. Steering him without his realizing, building in him like a head of steam, like a load that got heavier and heavier, as if somebody had been piling bricks on his chest, one by one.

A load that refused to go away, that had been growing brick by heavy brick all season long until it brought him home on that cold, lonely day. That last day...

"Alex?"

Startled, Alex looked up to realize that Sarah had just called his name.

"I'm sorry," he apologized, plagued by the memory of the old weight. "What did you say?"

Sarah smiled and Alex couldn't think what had reminded him of Barbi. "I asked if you wanted the rest of your dessert."

He looked down to see the half-eaten cake on his plate and shook his head. "You're going to eat that, too, huh?"

Sarah reached right over. "You keep eating like that," she accused, "you're going to waste away to your last two hundred pounds."

Right then she looked like a precocious little girl, all laughter and games. Alex knew that she would return to the matters that worried her, but for now she'd decided to put them away. Totally without his permission, he felt his own mood shifting in her wake, as if she were a clean breeze tugging at him.

"How do you do it?" he demanded, fingering the stem of his wineglass instead of the inside of her wrist, which was what he was thinking of fingering.

Puzzled, Sarah looked up. She had a little smear of chocolate icing at the edge of her lip. Reaching over, Alex wiped at it with a finger. Sarah smiled and tilted her head, considering.

"Do what?" she asked, her eyes already knowing.

Alex motioned to the detritus of her once-sizable meal. "Recover so quickly."

Sarah looked down at the plates and then back at Alex. Her small shrug was eloquent. "It will all return in its time," she admitted. "But for tonight I've decided to escape." A disconcerted smile tugged at the lips Alex had just touched. "I think that for right now, I'd rather fall in love."

Alex let his eyebrow convey polite skepticism. He was glad Sarah couldn't touch the sudden squeeze in his chest or hear the stumble of his heart at her words. "That easy, huh?"

"With you, it is." Unaccountably, her smile grew a little wicked. "But then, I don't have a Barbi to keep comparing you to."

Alex had no business laughing at that. For some reason he did. "Sarah," he mourned, "someday you're going to learn to be honest and forthright."

Sarah answered him evenly. "You wanted to know."

Alex didn't know where to go from there. He ached for honesty of his own, but didn't know what that was. Except, after spending the night with Sarah, Alex hadn't been able to sleep on his own. He was nagged by the most uncomfortable feeling that he'd lost his choices long before he'd taken her into his arms.

Alex had always held control. It had been as much a part of him as his mathematical brain and agility on the field, and he'd only surrendered it once. Only once. And after Barbi he'd learned to never surrender himself again. But now, as he saw the seductive life in Sarah's eyes, as he considered her rare enthusiasm and sweet sense, he was tormented by the need to lay down in her arms and give himself up to her.

It wasn't so much that he hurt, but that for too long he'd felt nothing at all. He'd closed himself off from that with his logic, with his control, and thought himself better for it. He'd suffered with Lindsay and died a little because of Barbi. It had sent him running for cover.

Now, though, warming himself in the incandescence of Sarah's spirit, he knew he didn't want the dark again.

Around them the restaurant hummed and clinked and tinkled with activity. Waiters skirted on silent feet and women smiled. The piano player had started his set out in the bar, desultory notes cascading from the high, pale ceilings.

Within the island of their table, there was silence. Not a taut silence, but a full, throaty silence of comfort, of belonging and possibility. A silence that pulsated with promise.

Without words Alex courted Sarah. He let his eyes dance with hers, his brandy like late sunlight settling into the sea of her blue. He offered a slow smile that carried the crescive exhilaration in his chest. When she smiled back, her answer complete and enticing, he reached a hand across to hers and captured her.

Her fingers were warm and small, hesitant creatures that took captivity with a flutter. Her palm was silky and receptive, curving a little against the slow stroking of his touch. Her wrist betrayed her, the pulse jumping erratically at his approach.

Alex never released her eyes, commanding them to him, consuming them. He'd never seen such a wide expanse of blue, even the sky seeming small and confined compared to her. He'd never touched a hand that tingled with such life. She was like a force, like the sunlight or the wind that shouldn't be restrained, shouldn't be controlled. She should be praised and cherished and nurtured.

"I'm not that fragile," she whispered, somehow understanding what he thought.

Her words opened something in him, some hidden place that he had locked carefully and, he'd thought, permanently. Alex felt that locked door open a crack, creaking with disuse, jealously guarded all this time against being breached.

He recognized a new warmth, a glow like a desert sunrise seep in, clear and strong and bright, and knew somehow that it wasn't all his, that it was more. It was Sarah's. But even so, it belonged to him.

His hand tightened instinctively as he fought the hint of new emotion that buffeted him. He sat perfectly still, not hearing the persistent clamor of the restaurant, not recognizing the Beethoven from the piano. It was all he could do to hold himself together before the confusing tide that threatened him.

He straightened, tried his best to withdraw. But Sarah wouldn't let go. She held his hand and smiled, and seemed as young as birth and as old as eternity as she watched him.

"I love you," she said, still holding on. Waiting, watching, understanding.

Alex tried to answer. He wasn't sure what he wanted to say. He knew she wasn't asking for an answer. She was giving it, explaining as much as she knew how. But Alex had no explanation. He had no reference to mark this new invasion, this tumble of emotions that threatened to overwhelm his own.

He was seeing into her soul as surely as if it were his own, and the sensation pulled away his balance until he felt as if he'd fall.

Pain. He felt it sneak in under the rest, a child's hurt of loss, an adult's grief of betrayal. Like low clouds, dark and tangled, sour on the mind, igniting a like pain in him that anyone should suffer such treason. Hurting when all he wanted to feel was pleasure.

"How 'bout a walk?" he asked, needing room.

Her smile was spontaneous and delighted. "There's a moon out," she agreed.

Sarah tread carefully. She and Alex strolled down along the patio terraces, listening to the rustle of the palms and the steady wash of the waterfall. The night sky arced in milky moonlight, and the breeze ruffled the water of the pool. Alex had an arm around her shoulder and his head down, and Sarah held her breath.

She knew, but she didn't. She'd never been taught to fight what was happening, never thought to question it. She couldn't imagine the turmoil in Alex's mind as he battled between instinct and emotion. She knew only how she wanted it to come out.

"At least you're not being smug about it," he said abruptly.

Startled, Sarah looked up to see the steel in his jaw, the strain lines across his forehead. She could imagine his eyes, lost in shadow, their brown cloudy and troubled.

Instinctively she squeezed his hand. "It's too much of a responsibility," she assured him quietly, the tension eating holes in her chest.

So much hinged on these next few minutes. So much of her. Her life was teetering in precarious balance, its only reality right now the man who held her hand. She needed him to understand, knew he had the capability, but wasn't sure whether he really, in his heart, wanted to.

It wasn't a matter of courage. Courage was beating back his sister's depression with his bare hands, walking away with grace and dignity from the sport that he loved like a woman. Courage was facing the problems of Sunset day after day when his life was threatened.

This was the left brain battling the right. Common sense

warring with possibility, a possibility Alex would never have consciously acknowledged. This was a weight that, once accepted, might never again be lifted, a duty and a burden. Sarah knew.

It wasn't a frivolous thing she accused him of. It wasn't something he could ignore when he wanted, something he could give back when he got tired of it. If he truly opened himself to his sight by loving her, he would have to face all its implications. He would have to face it day after day for the rest of his life, sharing Sarah's life as exquisitely as he felt his own—more, if he loved her. If he felt toward her anything like she felt for him.

He was a storm brewing, a convulsion of emotion and denial. It buffeted Sarah like a strong wind, and she ached to ease it for him. She yearned to tell him it would be all right, when she knew that it wouldn't, really. He wouldn't just have her love. He would have her pain and her frustration, her impatience and anger. When they finally found out who was cheating the company, only Alex would really know how she felt.

Alex's head jerked up. He stopped in his tracks and turned to Sarah. She saw his eyes, dark and defensive and surprised, and knew that he'd felt her sudden pain of betrayal. Without hearing the thoughts, he'd touched the emotion.

"I'm sorry," she apologized, not sure whether she really was, wanting soul mates but never wanting them to share the bad parts. "I don't know how to close off from you."

Sarah was afraid Alex would turn away again, that he would try to escape into his shell. Instead, he faced her. Sarah held her breath. Her heart stumbled, righted itself and went on. She couldn't see past the emotions that skittered across the surface of Alex's eyes like tattered clouds skirting the moon.

He took her by the arm. "You scare the hell out of me," he rasped, his hold almost as fierce as that morning.

Sarah refused to flinch before the turmoil in his eyes. "I'm really not Barbi," she whispered, aching for his eyes to clear, to see his sweet smile take hold.

He didn't smile. Instead, he crushed her to him, his head down, his arms tight, his voice tortured. "I know that," he admitted. "I know."

Sarah wrapped her own arms around him, wanting so much to offer some kind of comfort, to convey the love that swelled in her as she thought of the steel in Alex's determination, the gentleness in his hands. As she thought of the life he'd denied himself because one woman had betrayed him.

"What did she do to you?" Sarah demanded, accusing the other woman, condemning her for what she'd done to so vibrant a man.

Alex shook his head, his hold fierce, his heart thundering in Sarah's ear. "I knew," he admitted, his words harsh and abrupt. "That was it. I *knew*."

Like a cancer eating at him; uncertainty, dread, shame. The growing realization that his wife was deliberately hurting him. Worse than the mere suspicions Sarah held about her friends, more desperate, more inexorable. Sarah understood; she sagged beneath the weight he must have carried without having understood it.

"I love you, Alex," was all she knew to say to counteract it. "I love you."

He pulled away long enough to tilt her face to him. It was then, unbelievably, that Sarah saw the smile. Darker than it should be, less free, but there nonetheless. Wondering and amused and glad. "I know."

And then, slowly, deliberately, he bent to kiss her. Sarah sighed, answering with her lips, with her arms and her hands. Her body swelled in anticipation, hummed with welcome. Her frustrations and fears fled before Alex's gentle assault.

He surrounded her, his arms a haven, his mouth greedy

and delicious. He'd sipped at bourbon with dinner and it lingered, smoky and sweet on his tongue. He plumbed the depths of her mouth and nibbled at her lower lip. Sarah stretched up to him, her body seeking the solid planes of his, her breasts already aching and anxious. She felt lifted and free, shot with chills and sweetened with a slow, dark heat that spilled before Alex's hands.

"Oh, Sarah," he whispered against her, his beard chafing and his hands taut, "what are you doing to me?"

Sarah couldn't withdraw. She reached up to him, her hands topping his shoulders, her cheek nestled against his. He seemed the only warmth on this cool evening when the moon silvered the night and the desert wind chilled her skin. Alex was the only life, and Sarah sought him.

"I'm falling in love with you," she murmured back, her heart now a stumbling runner. "I told you."

"You're making me do things I don't want to do," he accused, sounding more breathless than upset. "You're making me fall in love with you."

Sarah backed away enough to look up into his eyes, her own filled with as much ingenious question as she could, even though she knew exactly what he meant. "You don't want to fall in love with me?" she asked.

He scowled with the gruff exasperation that she so delighted in. "I'd rather be audited by the IRS."

Sarah chuckled, resettling herself enough to widen his eyes a little. "You'd probably have more fun," she agreed sagely.

"I'd sure as hell have more peace," Alex countered, his voice a little tighter as her breasts brushed against his chest. His one hand moved, almost as if of its own accord, searching out her breasts where they were trapped against him. Sarah felt him snake up against her, his fingers reach the soft fullness and hesitate. She moved again, an instinctive undulation that brought her right into his grasp.

He faltered. His breathing stumbled a little. His eyes

narrowed. But his hand stayed, closed, captured. The night paused, suspended in anticipation. Even the distant rustle of the restaurant seemed to still. Blue eyes locked with golden and hoped. Golden challenged, the cool moonlight stirring something surprisingly hot in the depths. Alex's hand opened, then advanced, his fingers tipping Sarah's nipple in fire.

She gasped, the contact jarring her, splintering something in her that tasted suspiciously like control. His eyes held her, pored over her and brought her to a halt in his hands. The smile that grew on his features lifted her again.

"I think I'd like to go back to the room," he said simply.

Sarah managed to tilt her head in question. "The room?"

Alex nodded. "I believe it's my turn for responsibility," he countered, his sane words a sharp contrast to the rasp of urgency in his voice, "and unlike some others, I don't carry it around in my wallet."

The sun broke through and Sarah grinned. She wanted to giggle, to sing, to fly. She wanted to soar right into Alex's arms and find her freedom there, too.

"Besides," he added with deliberate meaning. "The whirlpool's well within view of the entire hotel."

She was air. She was light and sweetness and life. Alex pulled her into his arms and filled himself with her, drinking in her sighs and capturing the dance of her body. He plundered her mouth and trapped her against him with his hands, winding them in her hair and not letting go. He crushed her against him, starved for her softness, for the faint scent of morning that surrounded her.

His own body took control, drowning out the questions with his need, silencing the turmoil with the maelstrom her hands stirred. Alex ached. He groaned with hunger, strained against it, knowing that he couldn't stop any more than she could, hoping only that he could wait.

She surprised him again, this flighty creature of the twilight, this fairy child who didn't seem to live in the real world. Passion welled from within her, hot, seething hunger that stunned him with its ferocity. Alex had called her a woman of pastels, seeing and feeling the world in shades. He'd been wrong. Here in his arms, she writhed, she whimpered. Given Alex's encouragement, she stoked his fires with hands that seemed insatiable.

The moments fused into sensations. The courting of lips, the silk of hair tumbling around his arms and sweeping his cheek as they fell together onto the bed. The whisper of material as it brushed together, as it parted and fell to the floor. Murmurs, words exchanged on sighs and groans, hearts thundering in syncopation as hands sought and surprised.

Desire flared suddenly and then coalesced, thickening like molten steel. Stretching across his belly and searing his groin. Sarah's hands stirred it, deepened it. Her lips quickened it.

Alex tried to hold back, to savor and praise. He couldn't. His hands fled on, intoxicated with the velvet-soft feel of her skin. His body shuddered with her torment. He drank the salt from her passion-dampened skin and sated himself on the button-hard arousal of her nipples. And when he knew he couldn't wait, he dipped his fingers into her and found her full and weeping and hot for him.

It cost everything to turn away from her even for a moment. When he returned, her arms were open and she was smiling. Her eyes were wide, languorous, a summer's sky. Her skin glowed and her breasts taunted. And Alex, afraid and amazed and struck by the power of what Sarah offered, entered her arms. He wove his hands into her hair and pulled her mouth back to his. And then he eased into her.

She surrounded him, so soft and warm, so welcoming.

She arched against him, pulling him deeper. Whimpering, tossing, she wrapped around him and began the dance.

Alex fought for control. He groaned, a growl of pain at waiting, at the torment Sarah was igniting with her lithe body. He could feel the shivers gather in her, heard the shudders, suddenly saw the surprising storm that swept her as he stoked the lightning in her. He felt the tide sweep her, inside and out, her fingers raking at him for purchase, her cries breathless and pleading. She clamped around him, pulling him home, tumbling, flying, shattering him with her surprise.

The storm reached him, broke in a fury as he plunged deeper, deeper, dancing with her, mingling his own groans with hers, crushing her softness, her fragile, sweet softness to him, wanting her impossibly close and knowing she couldn't be close enough, disappearing within the wind and then tumbling back slowly to the ground.

They were still wrapped in each other's arms, cooling in the night air, quiet with contentment, when the phone rang. Alex wanted to ignore it. He frankly never wanted to move again, to leave Sarah even that much. She still held him, and he nestled against her hair.

"Alex—"

He didn't move. "If we ignore it, it'll go away."

It didn't. The phone went right on ringing, as if having heard Alex's challenge.

Again Sarah moved, enough to lift her head. "I could probably reach it from here."

Alex sighed. Moving nothing but his arm, he found the phone.

"Hello?"

"Alex? Are you all right?"

Alex couldn't believe it. He wasn't sure whether he wanted to laugh or curse. "Trust me, Lindsay," he growled with meaning, "I'm just fine."

"I've been calling you all day, damn it. Something's

been wrong, hasn't it, and you haven't told me because of the baby. Damn it, Alex—''

He shook his head and handed over the receiver. ''Here,'' he suggested. ''I think she'd like to talk to you. I'll be right back.''

By the time he climbed back into bed, the two women were talking like sorority sisters. He might have known it.

''Now—'' Sarah smiled a little while later when Lindsay had been pacified and the receiver replaced ''—where were we?''

The phone rang again.

Alex looked at it as if it were alive, sure it was malevolent.

''Are you going to get it?'' Sarah asked, barely able to keep a straight face.

''No.''

But he did anyway.

''Alex, are you okay?''

Alex groaned. ''Ellis, if you had any idea what a ridiculous question that was, I'd be in a neck brace.''

''Congratulations, my man.'' He sounded like he really meant it. ''I knows you is gonna do the right thing by her. Ain't dat right?''

The street-boy accent was one Ellis reserved for on-field intimidation. It sounded almost as impressive over the phone. Only a few hours earlier it would have aggravated Alex. He didn't like being pushed, even by good-intentioned friends. After what had happened between Sarah and him, though, he found himself smiling.

''That's a fact, Bubba,'' he retorted easily, his mind and eyes on Sarah, his decision made before he asked the question. ''Now, why did you decide that I needed to be awake at this hour of the morning?''

''Because I have some new information for you.''

Alex tried his best to keep the sudden tension to himself. ''Uh-huh. Will it wait for the sun?''

"What? You tellin' me after all this, you don't wanna know?"

"Not right now."

Ellis took a moment to enjoy his pique. "You don't want to know."

"Ellis," Alex suggested evenly, his voice much too calm for the new storm encircling in him. "Call me in the morning."

Without another word of explanation, Alex hung up. Then he took a moment to call the desk and have them stop further calls. The two calls had gelled something in him, some suspicion that had hovered closer all evening, and Alex needed to deal with it. He needed to face it and name it. And he needed to do it alone with Sarah, without intrusion of the company or friends or family.

"So," Alex said, turning back to see Sarah watching him, her hair tumbled and her eyes bright and welcoming. "Where were we?"

"What's happening?" she asked, her eyes concerned.

Alex smiled. "I'm falling in love," he told her, slipping down to take her into his arms. "Any objections?"

Her eyes widened. "That simple?"

Alex would never lie to her. "Nope. Do you mind?"

Her smile was wanton and guileless at the same time. "Not as long as you show me what I can do to help."

Alex was afraid. He couldn't call it anything else. But he couldn't do anything but try. "Oh," he said with an answering smile. "I think I can do that."

Chapter 14

Sarah didn't sleep. Even after making love again, slowly, deliciously, eye-to-eye and graced with the music of Alex's praise, even after curling into his arms and listening to the gentle rhythm of his sleep.

The future was closing in on her. She could feel it rising in her like a tide, stifling and surging at once, terrifying and wonderful. Deep into the night when the world had slept and moonlight died, Alex had allowed himself to love. He had told Sarah about Barbi, what it had cost him to walk in one fall day and find his wife in his bed with another man. What he had lost, what he had sacrificed.

He hadn't made any promises. Sarah knew it was too soon for that. He was still having trouble trusting, accepting. Where Sarah was sure, so sure she wanted to sing and laugh and dance, she knew she had to be patient with Alex. He'd spent an awful long time tempering his passions to suddenly let them free again. He'd distrusted his instincts too long to simply change his mind.

Normally Sarah would have been patient. She could

have waited as long as Alex needed and more for him to reach his decision. But this wasn't normally. This was when Alex was in danger, when somebody was out to hurt him for helping her. This was when she wasn't supposed to trust anybody around her even though that went against all her instincts. Sarah didn't know how to be patient when possibility crowded in so closely, when happiness and grief could wear the same words.

It would be soon. The certainty of that roiled in her like acid. Alex had yet to make a decision that would steer him away from the danger.

Sometimes Sarah could forget all that, losing it in the immediacy of his smile, or shoving it away when she couldn't face it. But it always returned, stealing in on her sleep or surprising her when she wasn't paying attention.

Alex was more at danger now than ever, and it was her fault.

"Are you sure you want to go over there this morning?" he asked from the other room.

Standing by the sitting room window, Sarah looked out on the bright morning. "I have to face it sooner or later."

Last night had been so wonderful, so full of promise and anticipation. This morning the rest invaded, as it always did. Dear God, but she wanted it over.

She never heard him approach. Standing right behind her, he settled his hands on her shoulders. "Later's just as good as sooner."

Sarah couldn't face him. She kept watching a little boy splash out in the pool. "I don't suppose it would do any good to ask you to leave for a while?"

"Not any more than the other thirty times you asked."

She turned then, accepting his embrace, his comfort when he was the one in peril. "It won't go away, Alex. I can't make you safe."

He dropped a kiss on her head. "I'll be fine, Sarah. I promise."

"You'd better be," she retorted without much heat against his chest. "Or your sister's going to be really mad at me."

He lifted a hand to her hair. "She likes you, y'know."

That made her hurt even more. "I like her, too." Sarah didn't want to have to call her with bad news. She didn't want to hear any kind of pain in that woman's voice. Please, God. Please.

Sarah straightened. "Can we go now?"

Alex's eyes were soft and patient. "Only if you kiss the cleaning crew."

She did, much more enthusiastically than the union demanded.

Connie and Randolph beat them to the house. Sarah was glad Thaddeus had opted to spend the day at a long-planned seminar in Las Vegas. After listening to the evidence against him the day before, she didn't really want to face him. She didn't want to believe that the same man who had revolutionized the company could be stealing from it, too.

Sarah needed to keep busy, so it was just as well the house was still a shambles. Her friends kept up a steady stream of conversation, and Alex appeared time after time when she needed him, holding her or taking her hand when the scope of the destruction became too much.

A little before eleven, Alex made a phone call from the bedroom. When he came out, he excused himself for a while and left. Sarah knew what he was doing, knew it had to do with the company and Thaddeus. She didn't ask him where he was going. She told him to be careful and kept on cleaning.

Time collected, massed, filling the empty silence of her house with dread, marching toward the morning when she'd have to face her friend and accuse him. When she'd have to know why he'd not just stolen but tried to hurt her.

Alex returned in the afternoon, weary and wilting a little. Nobody looked up from what they were doing when he came in. By that time the house appeared to be almost healed. Sarah was sitting cross-legged on her living room floor, sifting through a pile of books and knickknacks to see what was salvageable. Across from her, Connie did one last circuit with a broom, and Randolph was reassembling enough furniture to get by for the time being.

Alex brought sodas with him and passed them out. Then he leaned against the wall, sipping.

"Connie," he said in a carefully even voice, "who buys your computer programs?"

Both Connie and Randolph came to a sudden halt. Sarah went right on sorting, certain that she didn't want to hear this.

"Thaddeus," Connie answered as if Alex should have known better. "Why?"

"Was he the one who suggested you go with Datasys?"

Sarah held her breath.

Connie thought. "I guess," she admitted slowly, propping her can on the end of a table. "We were all in a meeting at the time. It was when we decided to go with the new animation software to update our computer. We knew it was going to be expensive...Randolph, do you remember?"

Randolph looked very uncomfortable. "Thaddeus," he admitted. "Why?"

Alex rubbed the condensation from the can, his eyes on his work, brows drawn. "The computer software you've been getting has been bootlegged."

Connie froze. "Oh, God."

Randolph looked over to Sarah, but she was still facing her book, her hands trembling.

"Poor Thaddeus," Connie said. "He was so excited

about finding such a cheap company. He'll be crushed when he finds out somebody's scamming him.''

That brought Alex's head up. "Some of those programs were bootlegged through Sunset's computers," he said.

Now the silence was complete. Sarah closed her eyes against his accusation. Her heart died a little. Her throat stung. She thought of Thaddeus, brilliant, madman Thaddeus who made evil-eye signs behind her back and turned her imagination into reality, and still couldn't believe it.

"But the catalogues," Connie protested. "I've seen them."

"Printed on your desktop publishing system," he acknowledged. "Did Thaddeus have free access to the building?"

"We all do," Sarah finally answered, her head up, her eyes glittering. "All the officers have their own keys. Any one of us wanders in and out of that office all the time."

"Even *I* have a key," Randolph admitted, instinctively gathering the wagons against the accountant.

Sarah wanted to smile. She wanted to cry. These were her friends seeking to protect each other.

"What do we do?" Connie asked, her voice stricken and small. "He isn't even in town today. He's at that seminar up in Las Vegas."

"I'll talk to him," Sarah said.

She felt Alex object before he ever said a word. She turned on him, for once the one who wouldn't be challenged. "I'll talk to him first thing tomorrow," she repeated emphatically. "Then we can call the police if we need to."

Taking a telling look around the room that still bore the marks of destruction, Connie couldn't agree. "Sarah, what if he—?"

Sarah swung on her friend. "This is Thaddeus we're talking about, Connie. He's my friend, and I owe him a chance to explain. We'll talk to him in the morning."

For a moment the tableau held, uncomfortable, uncertain. Unbelievably, it was Randolph who broke the tension.

"I've had enough slavery for one day," he announced, deliberately setting down his can and facing Sarah with his big, sad eyes. "What about a balloon ride?"

Sarah turned to Alex. "What about it?"

She saw a frown cross his face, felt the hesitation in him like a horse breaking gait. "I'm afraid I'll have to bow out, Sarah. I'm waiting to hear from Ellis again. You go, though."

Something warred between them—hesitation, denial, fear. Fear for each other, she for his life, he for her happiness. Sarah knew that Alex felt himself her tormentor, no matter that she'd asked him to do the job. His success had upended her carefully constructed universe, and Alex hurt for her because of it. And he knew it would only get worse.

And Sarah, terrified of the mists that still crawled around in her subconscious, could only think of how she'd brought Alex to danger.

But Thaddeus was out of town. Alex would be all right if she left with Randolph and Connie. He needed to talk to Ellis, and he needed to do it alone, without Randolph's accusing eyes or Sarah's pain.

Still, Sarah didn't want to leave him.

Thaddeus. Sweet, mad Thaddeus.

Alex crouched down before her, a hand to her cheek. "I know," he said softly. "But it'll all turn out okay, I promise. Remember that it wasn't to hurt you. If it had been, you would have been here when this happened. He waited, though. He's only angry at me, and I can live with that."

There was something in his eyes, Sarah thought, some knowledge that escaped her. She desperately wanted to reach in and tap it. Her world was whirling about her, its logic and order tumbled, day now night and the seasons scattered. The one thing she'd tried to build with her company, the sense of family, of worth and sharing and generosity, had been poisoned.

Sarah needed Alex's strength now, his sanity. She clung to the certainty in his eyes like a toehold on a high cliff. She soaked in the love that only the two of them could feel throb in the still air.

Finally she managed a smile. "While we're up, I'll look for a place for us to build a house," she teased. "All alone in the desert."

"Desert?" he countered with a crooked smile. "Oh, no. The Denver Chamber of Commerce is waiting to tell you how much you'd like creating near the Rockies."

"We only have so much daylight left," Connie reminded them dryly.

Sarah looked up at her friend and grinned. "What do you think, Connie? Would you like to learn to ski?"

Connie scowled, the previous few minutes still telling their toll on her features. "Right after I find another computer genius who can communicate with you. Now, come on and let Alex finish his work."

"You'll be here when I get back?" Sarah asked him.

Alex smiled and her world settled a little more. "I'll say 'hi' to Ellis for you."

His parting kiss was long and deep and rich with memories of the night before. Sarah wished she could have enjoyed it more. She just couldn't stop thinking about Thaddeus. About what would happen in the morning, and how it might affect Alex.

Alex didn't wait very long. The minute Connie's Audi rounded the corner, he turned back for the phone. But he didn't call Ellis. Not yet. He had other business to take care of, business about Thaddeus.

Thaddeus, the wizard who had broken the security codes in school and then left with only a taunt. Thaddeus, who thought Sarah was possessed and yet understood her enough to transfer her designs to computer animation.

Thaddeus, who had been brilliant enough to break into the Landyne's computer and pull out the new animation program whole, who had printed up his own manuals and catalogues.

Thaddeus, who had shown Alex how to find out when and where a computer activity had originated, and then left his own out in plain view to be found.

Alex didn't spend much time on the phone. When he got off, he headed out on a chore of his own, knowing how much time he'd have before Ellis did call back, knowing that Sarah would be upset with him. At this point he knew he had to risk it. There was a brick on his chest, and he only knew one way to prevent it getting heavier.

If he was psychic, if this was what it was like all the time, he didn't like it much.

His head said that Sarah wasn't in personal danger yet. The latest attack had been against her, but she'd been at a safe distance. Like a child destroying its doll instead of its mother. Besides, Sarah was with both Randolph and Connie. That kept her safe no matter what.

Alex went on his errand anyway, his suspicions crowding out his reason, the feeling of running out of time propelling him.

The phone was ringing when he walked back into Sarah's house. Alex checked his watch, just to make sure. Ellis was early. That was either very good news or very bad. It was all coming together now, and Alex found himself growing more unsettled than ever with the outcome.

"That you, Bubba?" he asked, receiver to his ear as he checked the fridge for anything salvageable. He was hungry.

"Alex? Is that you? Where have you been?"

Alex forgot the refrigerator. He forgot his stomach.

Something was very wrong. The weight had just multiplied.

"Connie?"

"I don't know what to do. I just can't believe it, and now he's up alone with her—"

Alex straightened, ran a hand through his hair and closed his eyes. "Connie, slow down. What do you mean he's up alone with her? The three of you aren't back on the ground?"

Her voice was tight and frightened, at the edge. "The three of us didn't go up. Only Randolph and Sarah. Oh, Alex, I didn't know. I'm sorry. It was Randolph all along, and I sent him up alone with her."

"Randolph isn't going to hurt Sarah," Alex said quietly, his eyes opening again, their color suddenly cold and flat. It was all changed now, the dynamics thrown off. "What do you mean it was him all along?"

"I was so mad," she gulped, as if words were air. "I wanted to know how the hell Thaddeus had pulled that over on us. I told Randolph I'd pick the two of them up, but that I should check on something at work...and I found it. In *his* desk. In Randolph's desk when I went looking for keys. He's been working with Peter. They've been siphoning the stuff straight from Landyne all along. The two of them, when I thought Peter was dating me for my sexy body." The laugh wasn't pleasant. "He was playing perimeter guard. What are we going to do?"

Again Alex checked his watch. "When were you going to pick them up?"

"What if he knows?" Connie demanded. "What if he realizes I found the note from Peter? Alex, I left Sarah up *alone* with him!"

Curiously enough, Alex felt very calm. Purposeful. Connie's words gelled his suspicions, his uneasiness. He knew now what had happened and what he was going to have to do. He knew that he wouldn't let Sarah down. He just had to get to her in time.

"There's something else," Connie admitted in a rush. "I kept...I kept a gun in my desk since this has all started. A .38." She took a breath and hurried on. "It's gone, Alex. It was there Friday when I left. I couldn't find it today."

"Do you want to call the police?" he asked.

"He'll see them," she protested harshly. "Alex, anything could happen if he thinks he's caught. Look what he did to Sarah's house."

"Then we'll be there. Where were you going to meet him?"

"Where you guys landed when you went up. It's a spot he uses a lot."

"All right," Alex agreed, checking his watch again, thinking and shoving back the rising tide of impatience. He had to do this right or Sarah would be hurt. He had to keep his head. Even so, the next few minutes roiled in him like acid. "Give me a few minutes. I'll swing by the office and we'll go in your car so he doesn't suspect anything. Let's keep this real low-key, Connie, and everything will be all right."

"No police," she reiterated. "We can do this ourselves."

"Just you and me, Connie," he agreed. "Now, let's get going."

Randolph had been right. The sky was a robin-egg blue with fleecy clouds ringing the horizon like an old man's hair. Sarah tilted her head back and savored the music of the mountains below, cherishing the brief reprieve. Alex and Connie waited in Phoenix, and Thaddeus waited in Las Vegas, but for the moment she had freedom. She had sunlight and hot breezes.

Thaddeus. She still couldn't come to grips with it. Her

mind skittered away from him, the truth too painful to approach. Sarah wanted so much for the culprit to be someone she didn't know, some faceless stranger who hadn't brought her meals and driven her home on rainy days. She wanted it to be someone she could have foreseen.

She wanted to at least feel resolution now that they had Thaddeus's name. But she didn't. She still felt churned up and uneasy and afraid. She wanted to get to Alex and make sure he was all right. She wanted to slip into his arms and reassure herself.

"You're a genius, Randolph," she murmured, hands clutching the wicker, head back to the sun.

"Nothing like a little aerial jaunt to escape the pressures," he offered alongside her. "Are you really thinking of moving to Denver?"

At that, Sarah opened her eyes to find his serious. "I don't know," she admitted. "What would you think about it?"

She expected concern from Randolph. What she got was a careful shrug and a glance out over the hills. "I'd like to think you wouldn't dump the lot of us for a set of big shoulders."

Sarah squinted at him, surprised. Unhappy. "You really think I'd do that?"

Again the shrug. "Love is blind, sweetie. I mean, look at Jill and Hector."

For a moment, only the creak of the basket could be heard. "What about Jill and Hector?"

Randolph shook his head. "I didn't think you knew. Jill wouldn't say where she was the other night, because she was with Hector. They've been…*with* each other a lot lately."

Still Sarah had trouble with his revelation. "Jill and Hector?"

Randolph nodded, eyebrows raised in evidence of his opinion. "Like I said. Love is blind."

Hector. Stringently, upwardly mobile Hector threatening his marriage with pudgy, uncertain Jill. And Jill attracted to the superficiality of Hector. Sarah couldn't believe it.

"How did you find out?"

Randolph just shrugged, and again his expression was curiously eloquent. "I seem to be a safe repository for female anguish."

Sarah looked away, out over the clean, crisp hills, to the future and the past. "I thought I knew all of you. I thought we could trust each other."

A hawk skirred the currents, sweet and sharp and free, and Sarah watched him. He soared straight up past the balloon, right into the sun. Sarah saw stripes of green and yellow and pink. She saw the pallid blue, the burning sun.

And suddenly she saw the shadow.

The shadow that wasn't there, that had fallen on her drawing and settled over her flight with Alex. The warning. The omen.

"No..."

Her hand came up, holding in fear that squeezed at her lungs and drowned out the breeze. Sarah heard the hawk screech and thought of someone falling. Someone dying.

The world tilted. A cracking echoed off into the hills and Alex's face betrayed surprise. His own hands came up, holding in his life, clutching to his chest, flying. Flying, falling, failing.

Falling. Hurt. Now.

Move, Sarah.

"Alex!"

She didn't even feel Randolph's hand on her arm at first. Her eyes were wide and staring, unable to look away from the scene her gauze had just lifted to reveal. The dust brown of the desert, the cactus spearing the sky like accusing fingers. The blood, so red, so livid against the wan colors. The gasp of Alex's pain.

"Sarah, what's wrong?"

Randolph was shaking her, gentle hands holding her up, cushioning her.

"Sarah!"

"Randolph, it's Alex," she gasped, turning, trying her best to focus. The terror had struck as sharp as glass, shattering her calm, freezing her, flaying her with haste. "We have to get to him now. Something's wrong."

"What do you mean?" he demanded. "He's at your house. Sarah, we can't get there from here."

"No," she insisted, shaking her head, grabbing hold of her friend. "He's coming to meet us. He's coming here, and we have to stop him."

"Who's going to hurt him, Sarah?"

"I don't know," she groaned, straining to see, unable to. Only feeling the blood drain from Alex even before it blossomed on him.

"Where?" Randolph asked.

Sarah pointed, certain even though they could see nothing beyond the hills. "Hurry, Randolph, please."

"All right," he agreed. "I'll try. Now, you settle down, Sarah. Take a sip of that water or something. We'll get there when we can."

"We have to hurry," she persisted, bending away, answering Randolph's suggestion. Water would be good. She felt so hot. So dry, so frightened.

Reaching for the jug of water, Sarah bumped into Randolph's shoulder bag, the one in which he kept his maps and glasses and calculator. It tipped, spilling a map and a book on ballooning. Holding the gallon jug in one hand, Sarah bent back down to right the bag.

"Don't worry about it," Randolph said, his attention on the flame above his head.

Sarah didn't hear him over the sudden, roaring burn. She

tried to push the map in one-handed with no success. Dropping the jug, she reached back down.

Randolph's hand was there to stop her. "Don't," he objected.

Sarah straightened, the bag already in her hand. Randolph yanked it away, almost upending it again.

"I said don't," he said, setting the bag by his feet. "I'll take care of the maps."

But it was too late. "Randolph," Sarah said, looking up at him with sudden hesitance, "where did you get a gun?"

Chapter 15

It was all Alex could do to sit still. His chest felt like a barbecue pit. His stomach knotted and he was sweating. He wanted to move or pace or talk. On the surface, though, he maintained the calm that had soothed Connie's agitation after it had taken him almost a half hour to reach her.

He seemed to be carrying it off, because the farther out into the hills they drove, the quieter Connie grew. Connie had asked Alex to drive and then had sat in silence, her hands worrying over the purse she always carried and her attention ahead, as if it could somehow hasten their journey. She never once looked away from the road.

Alex saw, though, that her knuckles were white where they gripped the leather, and her jaw was working faster and faster, until it looked as if she were demolishing gum. Alex decided to keep the silence as long as she did.

Hurry. Hurry. Time's running out.

He heard it, as if Sarah's voice were singing in his own head. He felt the stampede of seconds, the drain of sand from the hourglass. He saw the thing she had feared loom in the distance like a gathering storm cloud.

Alex didn't know what it was, not like Sarah would have. He just felt it building in him, brick by heavy brick. He and Connie were driving to the point of resolution. Of truth. They were headed toward a confrontation that Sarah had already seen. Only Alex saw something else. He saw now that Sarah was in danger, too.

He didn't know how. This time he didn't question it. He just measured the acid that built, the weight that accumulated, and knew that he didn't have much time left to protect her.

Hurry.

"She's not going to understand at first," Connie suddenly said as if continuing a conversation. "Sarah's so trusting. She won't believe it's Randolph. She couldn't believe it was Thaddeus."

"It *wasn't* Thaddeus," Alex offered with a quick look over at her drawn features, wishing his voice didn't betray his tension.

Connie didn't even seem to hear him. "It'll take time, I know. It'll take some hard work, but she'll pull through okay. She always has."

Alex wrapped his hands more tightly around the steering wheel and glanced out over the empty sky. "Looks like we're still early."

"It has to work out all right," Connie insisted. "It just *has* to."

"She'll be fine, Connie," he assured the woman. Connie started a little, as if she'd almost forgotten he was there.

"I know she will be," she said with a tight smile. "I'll be there for her. Just like I always am."

They were about five miles shy of the landing point when Connie suddenly straightened. "Turn left up here."

Alex looked over at her and then at the unmarked turn

that led back into the hills. "Where?" he asked. "We're not anywhere near the spot."

"I know a shortcut," she insisted, pointing now. "Turn there. We'll save time."

"We have plenty of time," Alex assured her. "You're asking me to turn five miles short and head north on a dirt road. I don't think it'll help."

"No," she argued, shaking her head. "We don't have time. Now, turn."

Alex really didn't expect it. Not like that anyway. He was turning to challenge her yet again, to make sure he got the directions right, when he felt a nudge at his waist. A cold nudge.

"I said turn," Connie ordered, and shoved the gun harder against him.

"Hurry, Randolph, please!"

The air was getting cooler. Far below, the hills were corrugated cardboard. Randolph turned from his propane gauge. "If I go any higher, I'll run out of fuel, Sarah."

"No, you won't," she insisted, leaning over the side to get a better look. "We're so close I can feel it. But in another few minutes we'll be too late. You said the winds will carry us faster if we're up higher."

Randolph looked down, checked his gauges and opened up the burner. The roar spilled into the basket like the belch of a dyspeptic dragon, and the balloon soared higher into the clear sky. The earth shrank away, and the distant hawks circled in silence. But Sarah saw more. She saw the glint of a vehicle and knew it. She felt the anger even this high, heating in her chest and forcing tears to her eyes. She knew the terror of frustration, when time compressed too quickly and the way was too long, when the future rushed up to meet the present and she drifted, unable to do anything to stop it.

"Connie, no," she moaned, tortured. "Don't do it."

"Pick that gun back up," Randolph commanded. "I carried it for protection, and you're going to be protected."

"She won't hurt me," Sarah protested in a strangled whisper, her eyes focused far below.

"You don't know that," Randolph retorted hotly. "She's gone too far, Sarah. None of us know what she's capable of."

But Sarah couldn't listen to that. Her best friend. Her family. Her mentor. The ground crawled by and Sarah could do no more than worry at the picture of Alex in her mind. Alex hurt, dying. Alex shot by her best friend, and Sarah impotent to stop it. She knew somehow, even without seeing what was happening, that only surprise would save Alex. Only silence until the very last moment.

"Come on, Randolph," she pleaded. "Work some magic with this thing."

Connie knew how to hold a gun. Now she had it trained on Alex with both hands, eyes as steady as her hold. Alex thought she was sweating. *He* sure as hell was.

They were standing alongside the bend on the side road, where the tan sedan had come to a rest. The hills rose close north and south, blocking them from view from the main road.

"Sarah will never forgive you if you shoot me," he said, putting his hands carefully raised, as he stepped away from the car. Praying for time.

"Sarah will never forgive *Randolph*," Connie corrected, lifting the gun enough to let him know that she wasn't going to let him get away with anything. "When Sarah goes to look for you, Randolph will come with me. And, later, the police will find you both. Randolph couldn't take the duplicity. Couldn't live with himself after what he'd done to you. It'll seem like he killed himself, too. And old Connie will be left to clean up the mess, just like always."

"Is that what you want?" Alex asked, checking for any

kind of cover. The ground was sere, the chaparral scarce. A few saguaro cacti pointed skyward, but they didn't offer much to stop a bullet. He'd have as much luck rolling under the car.

"That's the way it has to be," she assured him, a curious fire now in her eyes. "I like Randolph, but we can do without him. And you, you've tried to ruin everything I've built.... Sarah will depend on me even more now, because I'll be there when you're gone...she's always depended on me."

"How did you do it?" Stall. Keep her talking. Let her ramble on about whatever she wanted. All Alex needed was a little time, and a lot of luck.

How the hell did he keep getting into situations like this? Accountants weren't supposed to end up facing a gun, and here he was on his second visit.

"Do what?" Connie demanded, stepping closer, her elegantly cut slacks and blouse strangely at odds with her purpose.

"Set up the phony company. Did you have Peter help you?"

"Him?" She didn't seem amused, even though she laughed. "He had no idea what was going on. The security at Landyne is a laugh. I was into their computers after our third date. I was pulling off their programs in another week. The master manuals came right from the storeroom."

"Why?"

"What?" She *was* sweating. She lifted a hand away to wipe at it, evidently not as nonchalant about killing face-to-face as computer theft.

Alex made a shrugging motion, his shoulders beginning to shriek in protest, his gut churning, his patience lost. *Come on. I'm running out of time here.*

"Why did you do it? The money?"

"For Sarah," she said. "She wanted the new animation

program. And you know Sarah, she just doesn't think of things like cost and budgets. She's like a little girl with her nose pressed up to the toy shop window. So, I got her her toy.''

''And found out how easy the rest was.''

Now Connie was amused. ''Thaddeus really ended up thinking it *was* his idea. We could have ended up saving thousands if you hadn't butted in...if you hadn't *changed* everything!''

The gun was beginning to waver. The venom was spilling over, eerily lighting her eyes and tightening her face into a mask. It was all Alex could do to hold still. To wait.

''If it hadn't been me, it would have been somebody else,'' he countered quietly. ''Somebody would have uncovered the fraud.''

''But they wouldn't have made Sarah fall in love,'' she hissed, leaning forward with her outrage. ''Sarah had us before. She had her *friends*. She didn't need you to come along and make her...make her *dissatisfied*! She didn't need anybody but us until you *seduced* her. Randolph was right.''

Alex was trying to keep eye contact, to soothe. Connie was building up a head of steam, the kind that could demolish the interior of a house. The kind that could pull a trigger.

Come on.

Then he saw it. Sinking straight out of the sky like a brightly painted stone. Silent, streaking at them like a bulbous arrow right between the row of hills.

''No,'' he whispered involuntarily. Not yet. Not now.

Connie didn't see. She didn't hear. Alex couldn't believe it, but she didn't know that a hot-air balloon was just over her shoulder.

''Now, Denver,'' she was ranting, the gun dipping in rhythm to her vitriol. ''Just what were we supposed to do when she went traipsing off after you? What would have become of *me*? After all I've given to her?''

Alex tried to ignore the balloon. He could feel its approach in his chest, piling up with the bricks, stifling his breathing, tripping up his heart.

''Are you listening?'' Connie shrilled. ''Answer me, damn it! What was I going to do when Sarah quit to have your babies and join the damn Junior League? What were all of us going to do?''

She lifted, sighted, wiped away the sweat.

''Connie, don't!''

Sarah's voice shattered the moment. From one second to the next, the entire fabric of tension was torn. Control burst like an overblown balloon.

Connie's cry of rage was guttural, hoarse, primal. She faced Alex, knowing Sarah's voice and realizing what it meant. Shattering, crumbling, spinning over the edge of control. The balloon was ten feet from the ground, shooting at a point to Alex's left. Sarah was already trying to climb out.

Alex saw her and involuntarily moved toward her. He fully expected Connie to come after him. She didn't. Pulling the gun with her, she whirled toward the balloon.

''No!'' she screeched. ''No, you can't!''

She pointed the gun at Sarah.

Alex didn't think. He didn't have the time to even warn Sarah or notice the sudden throb of lights over the dusty landscape. The minute he saw the gun start to move, he threw himself at Connie. He was midair, stretched out as if he were reaching for a long pass, when the gun went off. The impact spun him around. His hands reached for the thud that had taken his breath away. His legs buckled and he fell.

''Alex!''

Sarah tumbled out of the basket, even though it was still

five feet in the air, and she hit the ground running. Alex had crumpled into a ball on the ground, blood staining the dirt. Sarah screamed his name and screamed it again. She didn't see the loose gun or Connie scrambling to pick it up. She didn't see the police cars pulling off the main road beyond the hills. She just saw Alex, bleeding, his life soaking into the arid land.

"No, Sarah, please," Connie begged, crawling toward the gun, scrabbling in the dirt to get beneath Alex where the weapon lay. "Leave him alone. Leave him alone."

Sarah couldn't see for the tears. "Alex," she sobbed, reaching shaking hands out to him. "Oh, God, Alex."

She pulled at him. He rolled free of the dirt, his eyes squeezed shut, his breathing a rhythmic grunt.

The gun glinted in the afternoon sun. Connie reached for it. "Let him go," she demanded, lifting it. "Let him go, now. He's wrong..."

Sarah didn't even hear her. She just saw the sudden pallor on Alex's skin, saw the blood that stained his shirt. "Please be all right, Alex," she pleaded, trying to gain the composure to help him, afraid of what she'd find. He wasn't answering her and his breathing didn't seem any easier. She didn't know whether he was dying or not. "Oh, God, please, Alex."

"Sarah, *listen* to me," Connie sobbed, pushing at her.

Sarah looked up, seeing something that she didn't recognize, a poison that had been so deep in her friend that it had been unnoticed. She sobbed, lost, frightened, angry. "Get away from me," she demanded in a voice that echoed from the hills.

Connie flinched. "It's *his* fault," she insisted, turning the gun on Alex.

Sarah didn't think. She jumped to her feet, wanting to be between the gun and Alex, fighting something she didn't understand. "You hurt me," she accused, deathly cold and flushed. Raging when she never had before.

"You hurt people I love. How could you?" Stepping forward, one step at a time, one step away from where Alex lay helpless behind her.

"For you," Connie objected, the gun still pointed squarely at Sarah's chest, bobbing with Connie's anxiety, unstable as she. "Don't you understand? You never deal with the real world. How the hell can you understand what I have to do to protect you? What I've *always* done?"

"Connie, how could you?" Sarah demanded, the only thing she seemed able to say.

Connie lifted the gun even higher. "You don't know. You still don't know." She gripped it with her other hand, lined it up to Sarah's face.

Sarah froze.

She heard the roar behind her. Connie flinched, faltered. Sarah thought to charge. She never got the chance. Crouched and howling with fury, Alex barreled into Connie like a defensive tackle.

The gun skittered away into the rocks. Connie flew back and landed in a crumpled heap. Alex faltered to a halt, doubled over and gasping.

"Son of a—" wrapping his arms around his chest, he dragged in a breath "—bitch. I think my ribs are broken." With that, his strength gave out and he ended up on his knees.

Sarah knelt by him, trying her best to pull everything together. "Alex? You're not dead?"

Still facing the dirt, Alex managed a grin. "No, Sarah. I'm not. But the Phoenix police are going to be mad about their equipment."

Sarah couldn't stop the tears. They spilled over, stained the dirt alongside the blood that still oozed from between Alex's fingers. She tried to stop her hands shaking long enough to check Alex's wound. She tried her best to be controlled and helpful. All she could end up doing was shiver and sniffle.

"What equipment? What happened? Oh, Alex, are you all right?"

"You sure do know how to put on a show, boy. You think next time you could give the police better directions so we can save you in time?"

Sarah looked up, stunned, to see Ellis towering over them. Alex was still rocking back and forth, his arms around his chest. Behind them, Randolph was battling the balloon into submission with the help of a couple of police. Several more had arrived to retrieve Connie and the gun.

"I'll...remember that," Alex answered his friend.

"I bet you even ruined that fancy tape recorder they taped to all your chest hair, huh?"

In explanation, Alex pulled up his shirt. There, taped to his sternum, was a small square plastic-and-metal box: a small, square, badly dented box. Slashing along from it toward Alex's right side, a long, deep gash bled steadily.

"Impressive." Ellis admired it, then bent to help Alex up.

Sarah couldn't move. "You knew?" she asked, her voice very small, the tears dissolving into little sobs.

Ellis flashed her a smile. "He ain't my accountant 'cause I like his suits, little girl."

Sarah was watching Alex though, where he stood with Ellis's help. "You knew?"

Alex shook his head for her. Then, holding out a hand, he smiled. "I had this...feeling," he admitted.

Sarah's eyes widened. She climbed to her feet without using Alex's hand and faced him again. "You did, huh?"

He settled one arm around his chest and took her hand with the other. "Sgt. Valdez doesn't believe in funny little feelings, did you know that?"

Stunned, quiet, Sarah nodded. "I know."

Alex nodded back, squeezed her hand. "It's sure a good thing I do."

Sarah couldn't take her eyes from him. "You do?"

Alex's eyes warmed, brightened, opened like a sunburst. Sarah felt their kick all the way to her toes, filling her, lifting her, settling her, surrounding her when she needed it. "I do. I thought you and I could talk about sharing some...feelings."

"Right after you explain everything to the man," Ellis objected with a suspicious smile.

"He has to go to the hospital," Sgt. Valdez said in his best authoritarian manner as he strode forward.

Alex never looked away from Sarah. "Meet me there later?" he asked. "I think we have some negotiations to settle."

Sarah smiled, feeling the burden begin to lift for the first time. Filling herself with the relief in his eyes and his heart. Sustaining herself on the love that emanated from him like heat from the sun.

"As soon as I get Connie settled," she answered.

"Are you kiddin'?" Ellis demanded instinctively.

"She's her friend," Alex reminded him. "Sarah has to make sure she's all right."

Sarah smiled for Alex in silence. *I love you.*

He smiled back. *I love you.*

Sarah knew then that both her premonitions had come true. There was a lot she had to deal with. Connie's actions lay like ashes on her tongue, weighed like grief in her. She would have to understand that and get by it. But she had Alex to help her. Alex to help share the burden. And Alex to share the future with, as well.

As premonitions went, she figured she'd still come out ahead.

Alex was right. Sarah had to admit that she loved the Rockies. Where Phoenix was spare and almost stark, the mountains outside Denver were green and deep and rich. Fragile wildflowers nodded in the field, and blue spruce shadowed the hill behind the Mitchell house. A stream chattered in the shadows at the back of the property, and bare gray rock shouldered into the sky.

It was Labor Day, and the Mitchells were having a barbecue.

"You really got him to admit it?" Lindsay Mitchell was asking.

Her attention equally divided between the baby in her lap and the sight of Alex lounging in a nearby chair talking football with his brother-in-law, Sarah smiled. So this was a family. This was how Alex had been raised, how he celebrated his life and marked his seasons. She had to admit she liked it. She liked it a lot.

"The psychic ability's been there all along, from what he's said," she told Lindsay. "Alex just didn't understand it. All I did was give it a name."

Lindsay's chuckle was delighted and mischievous. "I bet he bucked like a mule at the idea."

Sarah couldn't help an answering chuckle of her own. "He considers it the ultimate insult to suggest that a CPA is psychic. I've been instructed not to 'bandy about' the information."

Lindsay's laughter was full throated and delighted.

"That sounds like trouble," Jason announced from where he was sharing Alex's beer.

Alex snorted. "They're talking hippie stuff. Ignore 'em."

Sarah kept her smile. Her gaze was on Alex's namesake, a bright-eyed little thing with a ferocious grip and a lusty set of lungs. The owner, so far, of a train set, football, baseball, glove and Snarkalump, all compliments of his godfather.

Sarah remembered the babies back on the commune—chubby, placid things passed from hand to hand and slung on hips when work was done. She never remembered experiencing such delight when one fixed its astonished smile on her.

"Sarah," Alex warned without turning from his conversation. "You're getting a little too interested."

Sarah looked up. "Have you ever thought about it?"

She didn't notice Jason and Lindsay follow the half conversation with no little interest.

"Not till we decide where we're going to live, I won't."

Sarah smiled, satisfied. It was easy access to Alex's pride, his melting adoration of his nephew and namesake, his surprise at his new paternal feelings. It wouldn't be long before the need for his own child met hers.

"You still haven't decided?" Lindsay asked, her expression betraying perfect understanding of what Sarah and Alex had alluded to.

Her finger caught firmly in little Alex's grip, Sarah shook her head. "The company's voting on it this week. They liked the Denver proposal, but they are all pretty settled in Phoenix."

"Have you replaced Connie yet?"

Sarah nodded, still unable to talk about her friend without the pain. "We voted on that last week," she admitted, trying her best to smile. "Randolph has taken over the duties. He's a natural, you know. Besides, he knows more about what's going on in the company than even Connie did. And Ellis is staying in town for a while to clear things up."

Sarah felt Lindsay's hand on her arm and understood the other woman's empathy. She heard the question before it was asked.

"Connie's...uh, still not doing very well. We asked that she be able to stay near us in Phoenix so we could all be there for her. Especially since her parents don't care...still, they said yes."

Sarah never heard Alex approach. The baby fluttered in her lap, his arms waving and his mouth working up to a wail of impatience. The firs sang with a breeze, and birds chattered. Sarah's sight was inside though. Deep in where the hurt and betrayal and guilt still lived.

"Whose fault is it?" Alex asked gently to remind her, his hand on her shoulder, his strength surrounding her.

"No one's," she answered as she always did, not quite believing it yet, but hoping she would soon. Lifting a hand, she placed it over Alex's, holding him to her, securing herself with him.

"So, tell me," Lindsay spoke as she stood to scoop up her son before he got a chance to make good his threat, "if the company votes to stay in Phoenix, what happens to you two?"

Sarah looked at Alex, waiting for the little frown to appear. It did, right between his brows, betraying the lengthy negotiations that had taken place on that very subject.

"We're considering several options," he admitted. "The only thing we've agreed on so far is the marriage part."

Lindsay grinned. "Have you guessed Sarah's surprise yet?"

Now Alex was really scowling. Plopping down into the chair Lindsay had just vacated, he actually harrumphed. "You mean about the wedding plans? No. It probably involves standing buck naked in a stream somewhere and chanting mantras or something."

Sarah laughed, the joy bubbling up as it always did near Alex. She squeezed his hand and held on tight. "There are better things to do naked in a stream," she assured him. "I was thinking more along the lines of a visit to Portland."

Alex frowned again, puzzled. "Portland? Why?"

Sarah shrugged, savoring her little surprise, anticipating his reaction. "I thought we'd be married in the same church as your parents. We could have all your family there."

Alex's eyes widened. He went very still. "And all the Sunset people," he answered, a smile breaking over him like sunrise. "You're sure?"

Sarah nodded, losing Lindsay and the baby and the rustle of the early evening meadow for the golden sun in Alex's eyes. "I'm beginning to like this tradition stuff. Do you mind? I see us getting matched rocking chairs and a front porch."

"And Thanksgivings at the house...wherever that's going to be."

"And a boy for you and a girl for me."

He smiled for her, a private smile that betrayed all that was kept between them, and it filled Sarah like sweet dawn.

"You still see that, do you?"

Sarah tilted her head. "Sure. Didn't I tell you? And a white picket fence."

"Do you also see what I'm thinking right now?" he asked, his eyes suddenly languorous and intimate. Neither of them saw Lindsay ease away. Neither heard Jason join her or the screen door close.

Sarah's eyes were only on Alex's. "Something to do with that stream, I think."

"Wrong," he disagreed, his fingers testing the sudden throb at her wrist. "The other part."

She saw the hunger rise in him, sparking in the honeyed depths of his eyes. She felt the energy leap from his fingers.

"The mantra?" she asked anyway, loving to tease him.

He didn't even smile. "You only get one more guess."

Sarah wanted to squirm with the sudden heat. "Oh," she whispered with a slow nod. "I see. Is this going to happen soon?"

Alex's smile was enough to make Sarah sigh. "Almost immediately, I'd think."

Just as he said it, Sarah saw it. Late sun dappling them

in light, a breeze whispering across flushed skin. Murmurs and sighs that danced amid the rustle of leaves. And something more. Something that made her smile.

"You know," Alex amended, his voice husky. "It is hot out. Maybe that stream wouldn't be such a bad idea after all."

Some premonitions ended up being more fun than others. As Sarah let Alex pull her to her feet, she had the feeling that this would be one of the best.

* * * * *

Dear Reader,

When I was a child, I had an imaginary friend. My friend may have shown up in my life because I was an only child, with a great deal of time on my hands. I learned at an early age to keep myself entertained, and I have a hunch my friend was the result of those times.

My imaginary friend and I would have great conversations. We seldom argued, and he was great company. But as time passed and I grew older, he drifted away, and I soon found my companions between the covers of many, many books.

However, I never forgot my imaginary friend. He was someone I could talk to, share things with, someone who kept me company in the dark, and who I knew loved me very, very much.

That fantasy came back to me in the form of this book. It was one of those what if? kinds of things. What if we really could communicate with others in our heads? And what if we didn't know who our mental friend was? And what if?

I was off and running with my story.

And sometimes late at night—even now—I sometimes wonder if maybe my imaginary friend wasn't just a figment of my imagination, after all. What if?

Annette Broadrick

MYSTERY LOVER

Annette Broadrick

To Sherye Ritchie,
who creates a world of beauty wherever she goes....

Chapter One

Jennifer Chisholm opened her eyes in surprise and glanced around her living room. She must have fallen asleep while watching television. She couldn't decide what it was that had awakened her. Sam, her fourteen-pound tiger-striped cat, had made himself comfortable by draping himself across her as she lay on the couch. One outstretched paw rested softly against her cheek, the rest of him covered her to her knees. No wonder she'd slept so comfortably. She'd been sleeping under a fur coat—a living fur coat.

The low tones from the television drew her attention for a moment. The actors in a black-and-white movie, filmed more than fifty years ago, cavorted across the screen.

What time was it?

The rhythmic ticking of her clock was the only other sound in the room. She glanced to where it hung over her rolltop desk in the corner. The hands faithfully pointed out to her that it was ten minutes past two o'clock in the morning.

She had gratefully stretched out on the couch at nine in order to watch one of her favorite television shows before going to bed. Jennifer's day had been hectic. Her days were generally hectic when Mr. Cameron was out of the office. He'd been gone for almost a week now.

Jennifer was thankful that tomorrow was Saturday. She would have a couple of days to recuperate from her busy schedule. Hopefully he would be back in the office on Monday.

"I'm sorry, Sunshine. I'm afraid I miscalculated this one."

That was what had awakened her. Chad was contacting her. Jennifer's eyes widened. Her surprise wasn't due to the fact that she was suddenly hearing something when there was no one there—she was used to that. What had caught her off guard was that she hadn't heard from Chad since she'd told him off several months ago. There was only one person who referred to her as Sunshine—one person who didn't have to communicate with her by phone or in person.

When she was a small child she had referred to him as her invisible friend. The adults around her had been amused and a little sorry for her. An only child was often a lonely one. No doubt making up an invisible friend made life a little easier to handle.

Jennifer had never been able to convince anyone that she wasn't making him up. In time, she had stopped trying.

"Chad! What's wrong?" Her voice sounded loud in the room, but she hardly noticed. She could feel his agitation and pain, something she'd never felt with him before. Something was wrong—drastically wrong.

She tried to sit up, but Sam's weight on her chest seemed to hold her pressed against the sofa and cushions.

"Nothing that you can do anything about, I'm sorry to

*say. I just wanted you to know how very special you've
been to me all these years.''*

Jennifer had never heard him pay her a compliment before. She had once told him that he only came into her life
to bully and irritate her, and he'd never denied the accusation. Now he sounded so full of regret...as though he
were telling her goodbye.

Once again she tried to sit up. Pushing against the sleeping cat, she said impatiently, ''Would you get off me, darn
it? You must weigh close to a ton!''

Jennifer felt a jolt as her remark reached Chad just before he said, *''I apologize for disturbing you at this hour.
I should have realized....''* He seemed to fade away.

''Don't leave, Chad!'' she said rapidly. ''I was talking
to Sam.''

''?''

''My cat. Don't you remember? I've had him for several
years.''

''I had forgotten the name.''

''Please tell me what's wrong. You seem different,
somehow.'' She stood up, concentrating on the voice in
her head.

*''That's not important. I just wanted to let you know,
Sunshine, that I love you very much.... I always have.''*

Chad loved her? The irritating, teasing, invisible friend
of her youth actually loved her? Jennifer couldn't believe
what she was hearing.

''No, you're not dreaming.''

That was a perfect example of why she found him so
irritating. She found it most uncomfortable to have someone who could monitor—and offer unasked-for comments
on—her thoughts. But Jennifer had to admit that the past
few months had been very lonely without him.

He'd been such an integral part of her life for so long
that she hadn't realized how much she would miss his

presence. If she'd known, she would never have yelled at him, ordered him to get out of her life and to leave her alone.

He had done just that.

Now he was back and she knew something was seriously wrong.

"What is it?"

"I didn't mean to upset you. I just needed to—"

"I'm going to be much more than just upset if you don't tell me what's wrong."

"I walked into a trap, I'm afraid. Well laid, I might add. They knew me well enough to know my curiosity would keep me following them until they had me."

"Will you kindly tell me what you're talking about?"

"It's too late to go into it. It's never been important for you to know what I do for a living. It's not important now. I just wanted to tell you I love you and hope life showers you with the blessings you deserve."

"Chad, please tell me what's wrong." She waited for a moment but got no response. "Chad?" There was no answer.

Frustrated beyond belief, Jennifer sank down beside Sam once more and stared unseeingly at the television.

How could he do this to her: check in to say goodbye and then leave again?

If she could just once get her hands on him she'd—

But that was the trouble. She had never laid eyes on him.

Dropping her head wearily on the back of the sofa, Jennifer tried to clear her mind. Chad had a way of getting her emotions stirred up. He was good at that. He always had been....

Jennifer couldn't remember exactly how old she was when Chad had first made his presence known, but she knew it was some time after the automobile accident that had changed her life. Her mother, upon being questioned, had said Jennifer was just past five years of age when the accident had occurred. Jennifer remembered very little about it and often wondered if what she knew was what she had remembered or what others had told her later.

After several days in the hospital following the accident, her father had died, leaving her mother to find a way to support herself and Jennifer.

No one was to blame for the fact that Jennifer had trouble making friends. She was shy and often stood on the sidelines and waited for someone to include her in their games.

As she grew older, and her mother allowed her to go home alone after school, she returned to an empty apartment where she waited for her mother to get off work.

Jennifer had grown increasingly despondent in the months following the accident. Until Chad spoke to her one day....

Jennifer had stood looking out the window of their Oceanside, California apartment, yearning for the days when her mother had been home and would take her to the beach. Jennifer loved to play on the beach and to watch the waves as they came rolling in to touch the shoreline.

Now her mother had so little time for her. Jennifer had no one anymore.

"You have me, Sunshine."

Jennifer glanced around the room. There was no one there. She glanced at the television but it wasn't on.

"Who said that?" she finally asked softly.

"I did."

"Who are you?"

There was a brief pause before she heard, *"Chad."*

Jennifer started walking through the apartment, looking behind doors, vaguely aware that although she was hearing someone, the messages seemed to come from inside her head.

"*They are,*" he confirmed. "*I'm sending you thought messages.*"

"Do I know you?" she finally asked, puzzled.

"*It's enough that I know you, Sunshine. I just wanted you to know that I'm here. You don't have to feel lonely.*"

"Are you real?"

"*Real enough.*"

"I mean, you aren't my guardian angel, are you?"

She could feel his amusement. "*Something like that, maybe. But I'm very much a human being.*"

"How old are you?"

"*Oh, I'm very old. Almost ancient.*"

Jennifer didn't doubt that at all. How many people could talk to you in your head? She'd never known of anyone who did that before.

She asked her mother about Chad when she got home. Unfortunately her mother had too much on her mind to really tune in to Jennifer's questions and absently replied that she supposed everyone had a guardian angel, and she was pleased to know that Jennifer's angel went by the name of Chad.

Of course her schoolmates made fun of her. Jennifer discovered that she didn't care. Probably they were so busy they didn't even hear their angels talking to them.

She could always hear Chad.

But by the time Jennifer reached her teenage years, she discovered that Chad was far from being an angel.

"*Why are you mooning over that picture of a movie star?*" he asked one day.

Jennifer glanced around, embarrassed to be caught gazing with longing at her idol's photograph. Then she realized she hadn't been caught. It was Chad.

"I'm not mooning."

"Of course you are. Why do you think someone like him would never notice you? You have a very nice figure."

"I'm skinny."

"No, you're not. And stop worrying about the size of your breasts. They're just fine."

"Chad!"

"Did I say something wrong?"

"I just wish I could see you as clearly as you seem to see me."

"You probably could, if you concentrated. All it takes is practice."

She had taken him at his word. Jennifer never managed to pick up anything to do with his appearance, but she had learned to contact him whenever she wished, which proved to be a little unsettling for him on one occasion.

"Chad! Mother said I can't go with Sue and Janey to the show tonight. You know that isn't fair. What can I tell her to convince her I won't get into any trouble if she'd just let me go?"

She waited for a few moments, but didn't get an answer.

"Chad?"

"Not now, Jennifer. I'm busy."

He'd never been too busy for her before. They'd been conversing for years now. He'd helped her with her homework, explained algebra to her so that she finally understood it. Why, Chad had always been there for her.

"Busy? Doing what?"

What she received then was something akin to a groan. *"Thanks a lot, Sunshine. You just blew that one for me!"*

"What did I do?"

"My dear, sweet, innocent child. There are times when my mind is on other things and I don't need the distraction."

"Are you with a girl?" she asked suspiciously.

"I was. I'm afraid my lack of concentration at a crucial moment offended her."

"Oh, Chad. I'm sorry."

"Believe me. No sorrier than I am."

She didn't know what to say. Jennifer had forgotten why she had flounced into her room. The idea that Chad had a life totally unrelated to hers had never occurred to her before. She had always taken him so much for granted.

Several days passed before she attempted to contact him again.

"Chad?"

"Yes?"

"Are you busy?"

"What's up, Sunshine?"

"Oh...nothing much. I was just wondering about something...."

"Uh-oh. Now you're curious. I was afraid of that."

"Would it be possible for us to meet sometime?"

"Possible, but not practical."

"Why not?"

"Because I don't live in Oceanside."

"Oh!" She had never given his residence any thought either. "Where do you live?"

"Why do you ask?"

"Because I'd like to get to know you better."

"What do you want to know?" Before she could say anything she felt his laughter. *"Whoa, whoa. Wait a minute. Some of those questions are indecent. And no. I don't look anything like your favorite television hero."*

"How old are you?"

"Much too old for a little girl like you."

"Are you married?"

"No."

"Do you intend to get married?"

"Maybe."

"When?"

"Maybe I'm waiting for you to grow up."

"What good will that do, if I don't know who you are?"

"Ah, but I know who you are and that's what counts."

"You mean you've actually seen me?"

"Of course."

"When?"

"Whenever I come to Oceanside."

"Where are you now?"

There was a hesitation. *"I travel around considerably. Part of my job."*

"What's your job?"

"If I thought you needed to know, Sunshine, I'd tell you."

"You can be so irritating. Did you know that?"

"Now that you mention it, you aren't the first person who's pointed out that trait to me. Perhaps I should work on it."

"Perhaps, nothing." Jennifer was walking home from school and realized that more than one person passing her had given her a strange look. She supposed she did look a little peculiar, walking down the street arguing with someone who obviously wasn't there. "Are you serious about waiting for me to grow up?"

There was a long pause and she thought he wasn't going to answer her. *"No. I'm not serious, Sunshine. I guess I was just trying to be irritating, as usual. My life-style isn't conducive to a marriage arrangement, I'm afraid."*

"Oh." Jennifer could feel the depression settling through her.

"But I'll always be here for you, no matter what. Don't forget that."

"How will I ever explain you to my husband?" she said, attempting to convey a lightness she didn't feel.

"You won't have to. I would never intrude when you

didn't need me. Once you're married, things will be different.''

''I don't want to lose you, Chad.''

Jennifer could still hear herself repeating those words. Even when she'd gotten so angry at him, she hadn't really meant for him to take her so literally and to drop out of her life.

Chad was special. They had a very special relationship.

Now he was in some sort of trouble. If only she could figure out something she could do to help him. She'd do anything.

''Anything?''

''Chad! You're still there! Yes. Tell me what to do.''

''I've been thinking....''

''Yes?''

''You are my only contact with the world right now. My abductors figured all the angles but that one.''

''Your abductors! You mean you've been kidnapped?''

''More or less. They aren't holding me for ransom, though. They just don't intend for me to show up again.''

''Could I call the police or something?''

''I'm working on that. Why don't you get some sleep while I think through my plan a little more thoroughly. Let me know when you wake up. Surely there's some way we can utilize our special communication.''

She laughed. ''I'd love to. You've done so much for me. Now it's my turn.''

''We aren't playing games here, Sunshine. These people mean business. I really walked into a hornet's nest with this one. Now, go get some sleep.''

Jennifer checked the door to be sure the chain was on and the lock secure, turned off the television and snapped off the lights. He was right. She would have to get some rest. If Chad felt he could wait until morning, then she'd try to get a few more hours of sleep.

She had a hard time quieting down her mind once she crawled into bed with Sam curled up behind her drawn-up knees. After all these years, she now had the chance to meet Chad in person.

Chapter Two

By nine o'clock the next morning Jennifer was driving her five-year-old Toyota toward Las Vegas.

For the past five years Jennifer had been living and working in the Los Angeles area. She was pleased with her job, her apartment and her life-style. To be more precise, she was content to stay in the shallows of life, never tempted to seek out the depths and excitement that others seemed to crave. Chad had a lot to do with her way of thinking. He had spent many hours talking to her about some of the trouble young women could get into if they weren't careful, especially if they were trying to prove something, to either themselves or other people.

Jennifer realized she didn't have such a need. She was content to be who she was and live her own rather unexciting life.

Therefore, this would be her first visit to Las Vegas.

Jennifer wasn't particularly looking forward to arriving there. Her attitude could be traced back to the fact that Chad had been less than forthcoming about what he wanted her to do.

Following his instructions, she had immediately hopped into the shower as soon as she awakened, quickly donned her clothes, then contacted him.

He immediately responded.

"How are you?" she asked, more out of concern than politeness.

"I feel a little groggy, but that's to be expected," was the reply.

"Have you been drinking?" she asked, surprised.

"No. But I got a fairly hard clout to the head last night."

"Oh."

"They've made it clear that I have offended their sensibilities by being so nosy. They have a very physical way of showing their displeasure."

"Who are 'they'?"

"I can't give you a positive ID at the moment, Sunshine. Are you still willing to help me?"

"Oh, of course. What do you want me to do?"

"Go to Las Vegas."

"Las Vegas? What are you doing there?"

"I'm not in Las Vegas. I want you to contact a man there for me. You'll have to see him in person and he's tough to reach. I would say almost impossible, as a matter of fact. But you've got to try. He's the only one who might have an idea how to find me."

"Who is he?"

"His name is Tony Carillo. He owns the Lucky Lady Casino."

Jennifer could feel her heart leap in her chest. "You want me to go find a gambler?"

"I'm not concerned with his personal habits at the moment, Sunshine. He's the one who can help me."

"What do you want me to tell him?"

"Wait until you get to Vegas and I'll tell you."

"Chad! Must you be so mysterious?"

"*At this point, yes. You don't have to do this if you don't want to.*"

"I didn't say that. Of course I'll go."

Jennifer found a small bag and gathered a few of her clothes and cosmetics. No doubt she'd be gone the entire weekend.

The day was going to be another hot one, Jennifer decided soon after she left the apartment. But then, what could you expect in August? If she'd ever thought about going to Las Vegas, which she hadn't, she was sure she would have picked a cooler time of the year.

Jennifer could not get rid of the tight knot of excitement that seemed to have formed in her chest. At long last she was going to find out more about Chad.

He had reluctantly told her that Tony was an old friend of his and if anyone could get him out of his present precarious situation, Tony could.

What Jennifer also realized was that Tony could tell her a great deal about Chad that she had always wanted to know.

Jennifer faced the fact that rushing to Las Vegas to help Chad was the most exciting thing that had ever happened to her—which certainly seemed to make a statement about her life.

Actually, having Chad in her life was the only exciting thing that had ever happened to her. After a very careful poll among her classmates while she was growing up, Jennifer had discovered that she seemed to be the only person blessed with an invisible friend.

She had quickly learned not to discuss him with anyone, and what else, after all, did she have to talk about? Jennifer hadn't been interested in dating because she never knew what to say. She didn't care anything about cars and that was what most of the boys talked about.

So she had spent many hours talking to Chad about things she was interested in, things she had read about in books, or magazines. She had known he was much older than she was and had a great deal more experience with life. Yet he had always been very patient with her, willing to discuss any subject she brought up.

Jennifer smiled to herself, remembering how he had dealt with her questions about sex. Now that she thought about it, those questions should have been asked of her mother, but whenever she broached the subject, her mother had seemed embarrassed and Jennifer had allowed her curiosity about the subject to drop.

Chad had been much more matter-of-fact. She had been lying there in bed one night, thinking about some of the stories she was hearing at school, when Chad had spoken up.

"Don't believe everything you hear, Sunshine. It could get you into trouble."

"If you think that I would do something like that—" she started to say indignantly, when he interrupted.

"Of course you will…at the right time and with the right person. But sex isn't something to be experimented with, like a toy. The act of love is all tied up with our emotions. When it's used only as a tool to convince people around us that we're adults, we can get hurt and hurt many others as well."

They had talked long into the night, and by the time Jennifer fell asleep she felt as though she had graduated from childhood.

His lessons had stuck with her through the years. Although she had dated once she moved to Los Angeles and began working, she had never been tempted to prove anything with anyone. Nor had she met anyone with whom she wished to share such intimacy.

Perhaps she wasn't the type to marry. She certainly

didn't draw second looks in a crowd. Jennifer had always been disgusted that she'd stopped growing when she was only a couple of inches over five feet. Although she had often been told that her eyes were her most striking feature, whenever she looked into the mirror all she could see were wide blue eyes staring back. Even her hair wasn't a real color. She wasn't quite a blonde, nor was her hair dark enough to be considered brown. Jennifer thought of herself as an almost person. Almost average height, but not quite, almost blond, but not quite, almost attractive...but not quite.

Not that it mattered to her, she reminded herself firmly. She was content with her life. And now, she was doing something for Chad that would help to repay all the wonderful things he had done for her through the years. She smiled at the thought.

Eventually her mind made its way to her job, and for the first time, she felt a little uneasy. Jennifer hadn't given a thought to whether she would be back home in time to go to work on Monday. If not, she wondered what she should do.

Jennifer had taken a secretarial course as soon as she completed high school. It had been important to her that she be independent as soon as possible. Her mother's health had never been good and Jennifer wanted to relieve her of the burden.

She could have stayed in Oceanside but preferred to get away, to make new friends, to experience new things. Her new life would have been very lonely if she hadn't had Chad.

Surprisingly enough, Jennifer made many friends at the school, and when one of them mentioned that the Cameron Investigation Service was looking for stenographers, she and two of the other graduates had applied.

Jennifer had been surprised at the size of the place. She

wasn't sure what she had expected, but certainly nothing on the scale that met her eyes. The receptionist sent her to the personnel director, who tested her and had her fill out the necessary applications. The director explained that Mr. Cameron managed to keep several stenographers busy transcribing the reports he dictated.

C. W. Cameron had built quite a reputation, so Jennifer was told, as an insurance investigator. Although he was out in the field quite often, he kept in touch with the office and oftentimes called in and dictated on the machines that were set up to take telephone transcriptions.

Jennifer had been working there for almost five years and she thoroughly enjoyed her job. She had been Mr. Cameron's administrative assistant for several years now, handling as much as possible for him when he was out of the office, doing the preliminary investigations of cases— the tedious, time-consuming research that went with that sort of investigation—then turning them over to him to follow up the leads she uncovered.

They worked well together and he paid her quite well. Jennifer felt it was unfortunate that Mr. Cameron was such a cold, unfeeling individual. Perhaps it came with the job, or something.

After all the years she had worked for him, he still insisted on calling her Ms. Chisholm. In this day and age of immediate first names and instant friendships, C. W. Cameron was a throwback to another era.

He wasn't all that old, either. Jennifer had gotten a glimpse of his insurance file once, which stated his age as thirty-seven. He didn't look that old, until you gazed into his eyes. His eyes seemed to have too much knowledge about people and their behavior.

Some of the women in the office teased her about working for him, since he was single and more than a little handsome, with his tawny-colored hair and sherry-colored eyes. Jennifer shivered a little. He might be attractive, but he was too cold a person to ever attract her.

Jerry was more her type. She had been dating him occasionally for almost a year now. She really enjoyed Jerry. He was relaxed, easygoing, fun-loving, and did not pressure her to deepen their relationship. Too bad she couldn't combine the personality of the one man with the brilliant mind and incisive intellect of the other one. What a combination that would be.

Jennifer suddenly remembered that she had a date that night with Jerry, and she had totally forgotten about it. He would be over to pick her up and she wouldn't be there. How could she have been so absentminded? When Chad had contacted her, everything else had flown out the window.

She would have to call him and explain as soon as she got to Vegas. Explain what? Jennifer had never been able to find the words to tell Jerry about Chad. At first, it hadn't been important. They had been casual friends, neighbors until Jerry had moved to be closer to his new job. Occasionally he would have her over to eat popcorn and watch television. Once in a while she would prepare a meal for them and they'd go see a movie. After he moved, they spent less time together, but he still called to see how she was doing and to talk about his job.

Jennifer had never stood him up before. Surely he would understand that something unexpected had come up that changed her plans.

By the time she reached the outskirts of Las Vegas, Jennifer was tired and hungry. She hadn't wanted to stop and eat, which was a good thing. Crossing the desert hadn't given her much opportunity.

First things first. She would find a restaurant, eat and call Jerry.

He answered on the fourth ring.

"Am I interrupting anything?" she asked.

"Oh, hi, Jennie. I must have fallen asleep. Couldn't figure out what was happening at first."

"Things must be tough on the job these days, huh?"

He laughed. "No. Just resting up for our big date tonight."

"That's why I called, Jerry. I'm afraid I'm going to have to cancel."

"Is there something wrong?" She heard the concern in his voice.

"Not really. A friend needed some help this weekend and I volunteered."

"Where are you? I keep getting all kinds of background noises."

"I'm in a restaurant."

"Oh. Well, I'm sorry I won't see you tonight. I've been saving all kinds of things to tell you."

"Look, why don't I call you next week? We can check our schedules and pick another time, okay?"

"Sure. No problem. Well, you take care. I'll talk to you later."

Jennifer hung up and walked out to her car. The desert heat caused her to wish she'd worn something besides her jeans and shirt. One of her halter tops and a pair of shorts would have been more appropriate.

"Not in a casino, Sunshine."

"Oh! There you are. You pop up at the most unexpected times."

"I told you I'd contact you once you got to Vegas, didn't I?"

She shrugged and realized that that wasn't much of an answer. "Okay. I'm here now. What next?"

"I want you to go into the Lucky Lady Casino, go all the way to the back. You'll see a sign that says Manager's Office. Whoever is there, tell them that you need to see

*Tony Carillo. That you have a message from Tiger and
that you have to see him personally to deliver it."*

"Tiger?"

"That's right."

"And he'll know what I mean?"

*"Sunshine, this isn't going to work if you're going to
question and analyze everything I tell you to do. Are you
with me or not?"*

"Of course I'm with you. I wouldn't be here if I
wasn't."

*"No need to get testy. All right. The Lucky Lady is on
the Strip. You shouldn't have any trouble finding it."*

She didn't.

Now that the time had come for her to do something,
Jennifer felt her heart begin to race in her chest. She had
never before realized what a coward she was. There
seemed to be no adventure in her soul. No doubt there
were many people who would enjoy the mystery and in-
trigue of what she was now doing. But not her.

"You can back out anytime."

"Oh, shut up," she muttered. A couple coming out of
the casino glared at her as they passed. "I'm sorry, I
wasn't talking to you," she tried to explain. They point-
edly looked around the area. No one else was around. Jennifer knew her smile was a little weak as she shrugged and
hurried on in.

"I thought I taught you better manners, Sunshine."

She kept her head down and tried not to move her lips.
"This is not the time to go into my behavior, Chad. I'm
doing the best I can at the moment. I'm just not used to
this sort of thing."

*"That's what I've been trying to tell you. You've limited
yourself too much all these years. You need to reach out
and stretch your potential to its maximum."*

"Right now all I want to do is find Tony Carillo."

"May I help you?" The beautiful young woman sitting at the desk in the manager's office asked Jennifer a few moments later.

"Yes. I'd like to see Mr. Carillo."

"Do you have an appointment, Ms.—"

"Chisholm. Jennifer Chisholm. Uh, no. I'm afraid not. Would you tell him that I have a message for him from— uh, er—Tiger?"

"Tiger?"

Jennifer could feel the heat in her cheeks as she determinedly kept her gaze on the woman in front of her. "That's correct. I'm supposed to deliver it in person."

The woman picked up the phone on the desk and dialed. Then she spoke quietly into the receiver. She waited, obviously listening to something, then responded and hung up the phone.

Her gaze was filled with speculation when she glanced back at Jennifer. "There's an elevator across the lobby. Push the top button. Someone will meet you to show you his office."

"Good work, Sunshine. You passed the first hurdle."

"What do I do next?"

"Wait until you meet Tony, then I'll tell you."

"What's the matter, don't you trust me?"

"Yes. I just want to make sure they aren't giving you the runaround."

Jennifer stepped off the elevator onto plush carpeting. A young man about her age stood there waiting. He grinned. "You're here to see Tony, right?"

She nodded her head.

"This way."

She followed the man down the hallway and into a well-decorated office. A secretarial desk was on one side, and what looked like a word processing unit was carefully covered. There was nobody in the office.

The young man tapped on another door, then opened it. Motioning for her to enter first, he waited until she passed him, then quietly closed the door behind her. She was now alone with the man Chad called Tony Carillo.

His office appeared to be the size of Jennifer's entire apartment. She looked at the ornate wall hangings and furnishings with awe before her eyes turned to the man who had gotten up from behind a massive desk and started toward her.

He looked to be in his mid-thirties, and was of medium height, with dark hair and eyes. He held out his hand to her as he approached.

"I'm afraid I wasn't told your name, young lady," he said with the hint of a smile. "The only information I got was that you have a message from Tiger."

"Jennifer. Jennifer Chisholm. I was told to—"

"Ahh. So you are Chad's Jennifer." He took her hand and held it between both of his. "Yes. He has chosen well."

"Chosen?"

"What I meant to say was that I've heard many things about you and am delighted to meet you at last."

"You know Chad well?"

He laughed. "Extremely well. We grew up together in California."

"Oh."

"So what can I do for you? You said you had a message from him."

"From Tiger."

"Right."

"You mean Chad and Tiger are the same person?"

"Yeah. It was a joke because we always hung around together. You know...Tony—the Tiger." His smile widened. "That was probably before your time."

"He's in trouble."

Tony's smile disappeared. He led her to a sofa and they sat down. "What sort of trouble?" he asked with a frown.

"I'm not sure. He said he walked into a trap."

Tony gazed out the window and she could tell that he was thinking. Finally he turned back to her. "Where is he?"

"He didn't say."

"When was the last time you talked with him?"

"Well, you see—"

"Tell him late last night."

"Late last night," she managed to parrot.

"Uh-oh. Then something must have turned sour at the last minute. He thought he had them for sure."

"You talked to him recently?"

"Yes. He's working on something for me."

Jennifer gave a quick sigh of relief. "Oh, good. Then you can help him."

"Not if I don't know where he is. I know who he was dealing with, though. Max can play rough."

Jennifer wished she knew what more to say. Never had she felt more helpless.

"Tell him that I'm somewhere in southern Utah, in the mountains. I'm in some sort of shack. I haven't seen anyone since they dumped me here last night. I have a hunch no one is going to bother to see if I'm eating. There's nothing here."

Jennifer repeated Chad's words. When she finished, Tony stared at her in confusion. "I thought you just said you didn't know where he was."

"Well, I didn't. I still don't. That isn't enough information to find him, is it?"

"It's a hell of a start, let me tell you. Max, the man I've been hoping to get enough evidence on to take to court, owns property in southern Utah. Before we had this falling out, he took me up there hunting a couple of times. I think I know exactly where that shack is.''

"*That's a relief, Sunshine. Looks like you've managed to get me some help.*"

"May I go with you to find him?" she asked.

"*No!*" Chad replied quickly.

"I can't see any reason why not. I'm sure you're anxious about him."

If he only knew. After all this time she was finally going to meet Chad face-to-face.

Chapter Three

Sunshine, I don't want you involved in this. Let Tony do what he has to do. You go on back to L.A."

Tony had left his office, telling her to wait while he made some arrangements, so Jennifer was alone.

"Chad, I want to know that you're all right."

"I will be. Just as soon as Tony gets here."

"I want to help."

"You already have. Now go home."

"No."

After a moment of silence, he replied. *"Sunshine, I know that you want to see me. Believe me, it isn't necessary to our relationship."*

"Maybe not as far as you're concerned."

"Didn't you tell me you no longer wanted me in your life?"

"I was angry at the time."

"But you were right. I was trying to run interference for you, trying to make your life easier for you. No one can do that for someone else. I need to keep my distance and allow you to live your own life."

"And make my own mistakes."

"*Exactly.*"

"If you hadn't warned me, I would have made a very bad one."

"*And by warning you, I almost destroyed our relationship.*"

"You could never do that. I just overreacted."

She had been been at work one afternoon when her boss had returned from lunch with one of his clients.

"Ms. Chisholm," C. W. Cameron said, pausing in front of her desk, "I'd like you to meet Larry Donahue. Larry, my assistant, Jennifer Chisholm."

For a moment Jennifer could only stare at the man who held out his hand. He could be the very same man whose photograph had hung on her wall when she was a teenager—her movie idol. The same flashing smile, shining blue eyes, the same rumpled black curls falling across his forehead.

"Jennifer, did he say? I'm so pleased to meet you. C. W. tells me you're invaluable to him."

Her eyes quickly met the unsmiling gaze of her employer. He had said that about her? Mr. Cameron was a man of few words, and those were seldom complimentary. Of course he had always been prompt with her raises and Christmas bonuses, so he must be pleased with her work. She smiled at the incredibly sexy man in front of her. "I enjoy my job, Mr. Donahue." She glanced at her boss, then turned her gaze to the man standing beside him. "I'm happy to hear that Mr. Cameron is pleased with my work." Her employer's expression didn't change. He nodded his head in acknowledgment of her words and waited for his client.

"I'd enjoy seeing you again, Jennifer. Would you be interested in having dinner with me tonight?"

Jennifer was taken aback by the blunt approach of the

man in front of her. "Oh! Well, I, uh—" She glanced at her boss but could not read anything in his expression. Meeting the pleading gaze of the other man, she smiled and replied softly, "I'd like that."

Larry's grin caused a quiver to run through her. "Great. Why don't I pick you up when you get off work? We can go from here."

"I'm not sure when I'll be through tonight and I'd much prefer to go home and freshen up first."

Larry shrugged. "No problem. Let me have your address. I'll pick you up, say, around seven-thirty, if that's all right?"

She smiled and nodded, delighted with the man and his obvious eagerness to get to know her better. After writing down her address, she gave it to him.

Larry turned to the man beside him and stuck out his hand. "I really enjoyed our meeting, C. W. I'm sure if anyone can get to the bottom of this mess, you will."

Jennifer watched C. W. Cameron give Larry one of his rare smiles. "I appreciate your confidence. I'll be in touch with you in a few days."

"Fine." He left the office, giving Jennifer a quick salute that she found enchanting.

"You've made a conquest," her boss said quietly.

She searched his face for some clue as to what he was thinking.

"Do you mind that I agreed to go out with him?"

He raised his brows and shook his head. "What you do on your own time is none of my business." He glanced down at the stack of mail in front of her. "Is there anything there I need to see this afternoon?"

"Oh, yes, there's a couple of things I wanted to check with you—"

He turned away. "Bring them in," he said, striding through the door to his office.

She picked up the stack of mail and shook her head. She had never known anyone to be as distant with people as her employer. They had known each other for several years and yet they had nothing but the business in common. It was just as well, she supposed. He was a fair employer, treated her well. What more could she ask?

A little warmth, maybe? A little personal interest? Something more than his usual "good morning," or "I'll be back later," or "I'll be out of town for a while." She wondered if he ever really saw her as a person, or whether he thought that she had arrived along with the rest of the office equipment—with a serial number tattooed somewhere on her body.

What difference did it make? She had a date that night with a man that had stepped out of her dreams. This could be the beginning of a beautiful relationship. Jennifer smiled as she followed her boss into his office.

She was singing as she got out of the shower that night.

"What's put you in such a good mood, Sunshine?"

"Oh, hi, Chad." There were times when she was definitely glad that he couldn't see her, especially now, when she was drying off from the shower. There was something to be said for their type of communication. "I have a date tonight."

"I've never known you to be this excited about seeing Jerry."

She laughed. "You're right. I met someone new today. His name is Larry Donahue."

"Are you talking about the real estate developer?"

"I don't know. He's hired Mr. Cameron to do some investigative work for him."

"You have no business going out with Larry Donahue."

Slowly Jennifer straightened from drying her legs. She reached over and pulled her robe off the hook from behind the door. Sliding her arms into the sleeves, she carefully tied the sash before saying anything. Somehow she felt more prepared to do battle when she wasn't bare.

"I know that you're concerned about me, Chad, and I appreciate that. However, I'm a big girl now. I can pick and choose my own dates."

"Come on, Sunshine, don't be that way. I didn't mean to offend you. But that man is a womanizer. Besides making money, his biggest ambition in life is to see how many women he can coax into bed with him."

"How can you say that about someone you don't even know?"

"Because I do know him. In addition, I know his type."

"Well, he seemed very nice to me and I agreed to go out with him. I'm certainly not going to greet him at the door with the news that my invisible friend has forbidden me to go out with him."

"Just be careful, will you please? For my sake?"

"What do you mean, for your sake? What business is it of yours?"

"Remember when you used to call me your guardian angel?"

"That was many long years ago, before I discovered you were far from being an angel!"

"You allowed me to protect you then, Sunshine. Don't push me away now."

Jennifer began to blow-dry her hair, effectively drowning out anything Chad might try to say. When it was dry, she quickly put on her makeup, touched up her hair with the curling iron and went into the bedroom.

Larry would be there soon and she still hadn't decided what to wear.

"Nothing too enticing."

"Chad, I don't even have anything enticing! Would you leave me alone?"

"Just be careful that you don't give him the wrong impression about you."

"Fine. I could have worn my nun habit if I hadn't just sent it to the cleaners."

"Very funny."

"You're being ridiculous, Chad. You're worse than a father."

"I know. That's what I've tried to be—the father you lost, the older brother you never had...."

Jennifer felt ashamed of herself. "Chad, you have been everything I've ever wanted in a best friend, and believe me, I appreciate all that you've done. But I'm a big girl now. You've got to let me grow up."

"I know you're a big girl now. Why else do you suppose Larry Donahue is interested in you?"

She found one of her favorite dresses, made in a soft peach color, and quickly slid it over her head. It had long full sleeves, a scooped neckline, and from a fitted waist flowed into a full skirt that ended mid-calf.

"All right, Chad. Are you satisfied? This dress would fit in very well at a PTA meeting."

The doorbell rang and she hurried to the door without waiting for a response.

Her evening with Larry Donahue turned out to be delightful. He treated Jennifer like a princess. She realized midway through the evening that Chad's warnings had made her nervous and at first she'd been a little tense. However, Larry could not have treated her with more kindness and consideration. After dinner they went to two different clubs to dance, and by the time he took her back home Jennifer felt as though she were floating several inches off the ground.

Of course she invited him in. That was the only polite thing to do. After making coffee they sat and chatted on her sofa. Knowing that Sam might annoy him, she had even had the foresight to put the cat in her bedroom and close the door.

Larry had made several suggestions during the evening of other things they might enjoy doing together, so she knew he planned to see her again. Jennifer could see nothing wrong when he leaned over and kissed her. He wasn't pushy, nor did he make her feel this was the first step to a well-planned seduction. It was a get-acquainted sort of kiss and Jennifer responded appropriately.

"Don't forget what I told you, Sunshine. Be careful."

Jennifer's mind suddenly snapped back into awareness from the floating bliss Larry's kiss had provided. How dare Chad interrupt her at this point in the evening! He'd never done anything like it before.

She forced herself to concentrate on the words, *Go away, Chad.* He was always so good at reading her thoughts. Surely he'd get that message.

Larry must have felt her stiffen in his arms because he drew back slightly.

"I've enjoyed this evening so much, Jennifer. Thank you for spending it with me."

"I've enjoyed myself very much, Larry."

"I don't want to overstay my welcome," he said with a charming smile. "May I call you?"

"Of course."

She walked him to the door. He stood there looking down at her for a moment. "You are so beautiful. I can't understand how you've managed to stay single."

Jennifer laughed. He sounded sincere enough, but since she looked in the mirror every day, she knew what she looked like. Perhaps he did have a way of exaggerating things.

Larry slowly pulled her into his arms and kissed her. She relaxed against him.

"Has he mentioned his wife and three children yet?"

Jennifer's eyes flew open and she gasped. That was a low blow. Even Chad couldn't stoop to such a thing.

"What's wrong?" Larry asked, puzzled when she jerked away from him.

"Do you have a wife and three children?" she blurted out suddenly.

He looked a little taken aback at the timing of her question. "As a matter of fact, I do, but I'm not sure why you should bring them up at this time."

She stared at him in disbelief. The same charming smile, the flashing eyes, the black curls tumbling across his forehead. He didn't even seem concerned that she had asked. For a moment, too many thoughts were racing through her head for her to say a thing.

"I wasn't trying to keep them a secret or anything. I assumed that C. W. told you I was married."

"No, he didn't."

"Oh. I take it that makes a difference to you."

"It certainly does. I'm sure that it makes a difference to your wife, too."

"My wife and I understand each other very well. There's no problem where she's concerned."

"Well, I'm very much afraid that there's a problem where I'm concerned." She opened the door. "Good night, Mr. Donahue."

He shook his head, puzzled at the abrupt change in her behavior, and walked out the door.

After carefully closing the door behind him, she slumped against it. What a letdown to what had been a beautiful evening.

"He was right, you know. You really are a beautiful woman—inside and out, Sunshine."

Jennifer straightened and wished that Chad was standing in front of her. She would dearly have loved to throw something at him.

"Why would you want to throw something at me? What did I do?"

"As if you didn't know. You ruined a beautiful evening for me."

"How could I ruin it?"

"You know very well what you did. Every time he kissed me, you made some sort of a comment."

"Oh, did I? How rude of me. I'm really very sorry."

"Sure you are. You knew exactly what you were doing!"

"Well, not exactly. But whenever your thoughts go a little hazy and syrupy I know something is going on."

Jennifer stormed into her bedroom and was greeted by Sam, who protested his recent incarceration.

"And I don't want to hear anything from you, either!" she exclaimed, reaching around and unzipping her dress. When Sam continued to bemoan her unfair treatment of him she eventually sat down on the bed and scooped him up in her lap, stroking his long coat and wishing she could think of something to put Chad in his place.

"Hey, Sunshine, I really am sorry if I upset you. That wasn't what I meant to do."

"Wasn't it? It seems to me that ever since I first met you, you've been telling me what to do, how to do it, when to do it and what not to do. Frankly, I'm sick of it."

There was no response.

"And that's another thing. There's no way I can argue with you. Whenever I try you just clam up and disappear and I can't reach you."

"You always reach me, Sunshine. Sometimes I just don't choose to answer."

"That's what I mean. I can't argue with myself."

"Good point. Think about it."

Jumping to her feet, Jennifer dropped Sam on the bed.

"I am sick of you, do you understand that? I wish you would just go away and leave me alone!"

"Do you really mean that?"

"I wouldn't have said it if I didn't mean it." She waited for a reply but there was nothing more. After a few minutes she said, "Chad?" There was no answer.

So he had taken her at her word. She was glad. She wasn't a child anymore and didn't need a guardian angel or whoever he thought he was being.

Now Jennifer stood in Tony's office, looking out the window. Chad had never contacted her again. Not until last night. She had missed him. Missed his sense of humor, his teasing and tantalizing, missed his caring about what happened to her.

Now she had a chance to meet him and she wasn't going to let the opportunity slip by. She grinned at the thought. He was obviously a captive. There was nothing he could do but stay where he was until they came to get him. She could hardly wait to see his face when she walked in.

Over the years, Jennifer had speculated on Chad's looks. He would give her no help at all. It was amusing, really, how her image of him had changed through the years. As a child she pictured him as old, with white hair and kind-looking eyes. By the time she was a teenager he began to get younger in her eyes. After all, some of their discussions had been very open and frank. Somehow she couldn't see a kindly looking, white-haired gentleman telling her some of the things Chad had told her.

And now, she found herself treating him as a contemporary and an equal. Of course she loved him. How could she not love him? He had been so many things in her life. He'd been there for her, no matter what. But she had to admit that she felt a little peculiar about finally meeting him face-to-face after all this time.

She was glad that Tony was going to be along.

The office door opened and she turned around. Tony stood in the doorway. "You ready to go?"

She nodded.

"I borrowed a pickup. It won't be the smoothest riding vehicle, but we'll need the four-wheel drive once we get up into the mountains."

Jennifer followed him out of the room.

"I forgot to ask if you've eaten," he said as she passed. "Yes."

"I think we'd better stop off at a convenience store somewhere and pick up something to take with us. There's not a whole lot between here and where we're going if we should get hungry or thirsty."

Poor Chad. She could imagine how he must be feeling, stranded out in the middle of nowhere, recovering from a head wound, without food. He hadn't said anything about water. She wondered about that.

They didn't waste any time at the store and were soon on the road. For the first several miles they were quiet, each lost in his and her own thoughts. Eventually Tony said, "I'm sorry we had to meet this way, Jennifer, but I'm glad that we finally have a chance to get acquainted after all this time. I'll admit I didn't recognize you from the first time I saw you."

She looked at him in surprise. As far as she knew, she had never seen this man in her life. "When did you ever see me?"

He glanced around briefly, then returned his eyes to the highway. "The same time Tiger did, when you were in the car wreck."

"The car wreck! Mother said I was only five when that happened."

"I know you were just a little thing. I felt so sorry for you."

"You and Chad were there?"

"Yes. We had been down in San Diego that day, just a couple of kids, really. I'd borrowed my dad's car and we'd gone down to see who we could impress, you know the kind things guys will do."

She smiled. "Not really, but it makes sense."

"We'd decided to stop and eat in Oceanside—Tiger knew a girl that lived somewhere around there and he was trying to figure out which house she lived in, so we were driving up and down the streets when we saw the car that came barreling around a corner and plowed into the one you and your family were in. God, it was awful...as I'm sure you remember."

She shook her head. "I don't remember much about it at all."

"We were the first ones there. It happened on the edge of town. There weren't many houses out that far. The guy that hit you was hurt bad, we could tell. And your mother and dad were pinned in the car." He shook his head. "I'd never seen anything like it. Tiger told me to go for help and he stayed there, trying to see what he could do. When I got back, I found him sitting beside the road holding you. He told me later you had been knocked unconscious in the back seat and when you woke up you became hysterical. He managed to get you out. So he sat there and held you until the police and the ambulance came."

"I never knew that."

"He was really upset, I can tell you. When they got your parents out and took all of you to the hospital, he insisted we follow. We stayed there at the hospital and waited to hear how you were doing."

"My mother told me my injuries weren't serious."

"That's what we found out. He worried about you later, though, when he heard that your dad didn't make it."

So her guardian angel had been a teenage boy when he first met her.

Tony continued to reminisce. "I remember that until we graduated from high school he would still go back down there and check on you."

"He did?"

"Sure. Don't you remember?"

How could she tell him that she didn't even remember what Chad looked like? She had no memory of him whatsoever.

"I know that he seemed interested in how I was doing," she said cautiously.

"He was. He used to talk about you all the time. The things you were doing, what you were learning in school. He was always so proud of you. I used to tease him about waiting around for you to grow up."

She glanced at him sharply. "He said that to me once."

"Then what's he been waiting for?" He gave her a glance from the corner of his eye. "You are certainly as grown-up as he could possibly want now."

Jennifer could not control the blush that she could feel flooding her face. "He admitted that he was only teasing me."

"You notice that he's never married anyone else, though," he pointed out in a wise tone. She glanced over at him and he winked.

No, she hadn't known that Chad wasn't married. She couldn't help feeling pleased at the idea that perhaps he had been waiting for her.

Then another thought struck her. "Are you married, Tony?" She would hate to have a jealous wife misunderstand her leaving town with Tony.

"I was. Unfortunately for me she found someone she wanted more, someone who wasn't spending all his time trying to make a living." He shrugged, but she could see the hurt that was still there. "I'm surprised Tiger trusted me with you, come to think of it. He's always telling me

I have a terrible attitude toward women. Can't imagine why.''

She smiled. "Obviously you're his best friend. Otherwise he wouldn't have sent me to find you."

"You're right. We go back a long way. When I called him and told him that a former business associate was trying to hassle me, he agreed to check it out for me. Neither of us thought it would turn out to be anything like this."

"What does Chad do?"

He looked around at her in surprise. "Don't you know?"

Jennifer had already accepted the fact that Tony did not know how she and Chad communicated. It was strange to think that she was closer to Chad than anyone in many ways and yet they were still strangers. She didn't want to have to explain their relationship to Tony, not if Chad hadn't already done so.

She tried to find a way to phrase her response that would not make the relationship even more confusing. "Chad is a very private person." Tony nodded his head. "Whenever I hear from him he chooses the topics we discuss. He doesn't like to talk about himself."

"That's Tiger, all right. He's always been that way. Something of a loner. When we were in the Marines together we'd—"

"Chad was in the Marines?"

"Sure. We decided to go in right after we got out of high school. Why?"

"He never told me."

"Oh. But he stayed in touch, didn't he?"

"Yes."

"That's kinda odd, him not telling you. He always knew what you were up to. Maybe your mother wrote to him or something. When we were stationed overseas he spent a lot of time talking about you.''

Jennifer was having a tough time trying to put everything she was learning from Tony into perspective with what she already knew about Chad. He had lived a full and active life all the time he was in touch with her, and yet had never given her a hint of it.

She almost cringed at some of the childish questions and concerns she'd had back then. He had been so patient with her, kind and full of a sense of caring that had eased her over the rough spots in her life.

Oh, Chad, do you have any idea how much you mean to me?

''*Obviously not enough to do what I ask. I thought I told you to let Tony come get me.*''

Jennifer tried to disguise the sudden start she gave when Chad responded. She shifted on the seat and glanced at Tony. ''I think I'll try to catch a nap, if you don't mind. My day started out fairly early,'' she explained, trying to sound nonchalant.

''Good idea. Once we get off the main highway, the road is going to be too rough for you to do anything but hang on!''

Jennifer closed her eyes and willed herself not to speak out loud. *Chad? Can you hear me?*

''*Of course I can hear you. What I want to know is why you aren't halfway back to L.A. by now?*''

You know why. I wanted to see you.

''*Has it ever occurred to you that perhaps I don't want to see you?*''

Please don't be that way. Did you really come to see me when I was a child?

''*Tony and his big mouth. Yes, Sunshine, I used to drive down there on a regular basis.*''

Then why don't I remember you?

"Because you never saw me. I used to sit outside the school and watch you come out. You were such a sad little thing for a long while, but there was nothing I could do to help."

But there was! You started talking to me.

"Yes. I realized that night of the accident when I tried to calm you down that I could pick up your thoughts—all your fear and terror. While I sat there holding you I not only talked to you, I tried to send you my thoughts to calm you. They seemed to help."

I don't understand why I can't remember.

"You were just a baby. I don't think you'd even started school at that time. Later, whenever I thought of you, I discovered I could pick up on what you were thinking."

Have you ever been able to do that with anyone else?

"No. But then I've never tried. Like I've told you. You're special."

So are you.

"Come on, Sunshine, don't try to make me some sort of romantic hero. You wouldn't even like me if you knew me."

How can you possibly say that?

"Because you have an image of me as someone very gentle. I'm not a gentle sort of person."

You are with me.

"I know."

She smiled slightly and drifted off to sleep.

Chapter Four

Tony was right. As soon as they turned off the paved road, Jennifer woke up.

"Road maintenance is a little slack in this area, wouldn't you say?" she managed to get out while bracing herself against the dashboard of the truck.

Tony chuckled. "I warned you."

"So you did. How much farther do we have to go?"

The sun had set and the evening light was rapidly fading. Tony flipped on the headlights, then glanced at his watch. "I haven't been here in a few years. It seems to me we have at least a couple of hours of this before we get there."

"No wonder Chad felt bruised and shaken."

"You know, I've been meaning to ask you. How did he manage to call and let you know what had happened to him? It doesn't really make sense, anyway. If he was going to contact anybody, why you? Why not me?"

Now what do I say? she asked Chad. There was no response. *Chad... Chad! What do you want me to tell him?*

"*That's up to you.*"

"Thanks a lot!"

"What do you mean?" Tony asked, surprised at her tone of voice.

"Oh! For, uh, thinking that he should have called you instead of me, of course. That wasn't very kind of you."

"Maybe not, but it makes sense. Why didn't he call me anyway?"

"Maybe he'd run out of quarters."

"Besides, that place is so primitive, I can't believe there's a phone for miles."

"Maybe it has a ham radio unit and he got someone to relay it over a phone somewhere."

"I suppose. I can always ask him when we get there."

If we ever do, she thought, knowing that she was going to have bruises all over her bottom by the time they arrived, not to mention on her arms and legs.

"*I tried to warn you.*"

"I know."

"You know what?" Tony asked. "Is there something wrong?"

"Not really. I suppose it's from being alone so much. I have a habit of talking to myself."

Tony shook his head. Jennifer knew he was beginning to wonder about her. She looked out the window, trying to hide her smile. Tony obviously didn't have too good an opinion of women anyway. She doubted if it would improve staying around her.

"I take it you live alone?" he asked after they had bounced along in silence for a few miles.

"Sort of. I share an apartment with a five-year-old cat named Sam." She would no more consider that she owned Sam than that he owned her. They had a workable relationship where each understood the other. Sam allowed her to feed him, pay his rent and keep him entertained. In turn, he looked after her, pointed out when she stayed out too late or tried to get away with oversleeping in the morning, and made judgments on any of her friends who happened to drop in.

"I thought about getting a pet, but I'm not home enough to look after one."

"Sam's been a lot of company to me. Since I don't travel much, he's never been much of a problem. This is the first time I've ever gone off and left him for a weekend."

"Aren't you afraid he'll get hungry?"

"Oh, no. I left him plenty of food and water. That's never the problem. He doesn't like being left alone. He's learned to tolerate it during the day, since he knows I have to work. But he gets very irritated when I'm out all evening. I have a feeling he's going to be irate by the time I get home."

"You know, there really wasn't any reason for you to come out here with me, once you let me know where he is."

"That's what Chad said," she muttered under her breath.

"Did you say something?"

"I was just agreeing with you. If I'd known what the roads were going to be like, I might have given more serious thought to returning home."

She turned her head to look at Tony and a brief flash of light caught her eye. She stared out the back window.

"Something wrong?" he asked.

"I thought I saw a light flash behind us."

Tony glanced up in the rearview mirror and they hit a particularly deep hole. Jennifer almost hit her head on the ceiling of the cab. "Sorry. I don't dare take my eyes off the road for a second. What sort of a light?"

She continued to watch out the back window. "I'm not sure. Could there be another car coming this way?"

"There could be, but it's rather hard to believe." He was quiet a moment. "Unless it's the same person or persons who brought Tiger out here and left him."

Jennifer discovered a knot in her chest that was making it difficult for her to breathe. She had no idea what she was getting into, but this wasn't her idea of a fun evening at all.

Tony cleared his throat nervously. "You know, this really isn't my style. I mean, I can handle myself all right in my own environment, but getting out here in the Great Outdoors—Well, Tiger's able to handle anything, anywhere. But not me."

"He wasn't able to handle this particular situation or he wouldn't be stuck out here."

"Don't rub it in, Sunshine."

"Keep watching and see if you catch a glimpse of that light again, okay?" Tony asked, continuing to concentrate on the road in front of them.

They were silent during the next hour, each watching the road—Tony the front, Jennifer the back. Twice she thought she saw a flicker of light, but the curving roads didn't reveal much.

"Not much farther now. I bet Tiger is going to be glad to see us."

Jennifer had been growing more and more tense. She didn't know how she was going to react when she saw Chad for the first time, particularly since he had made it clear that he didn't want her there. She was sorry she had insisted on coming along. After all, he had as much right to his privacy as she did to hers.

The light hadn't appeared in several miles and Jennifer decided that if it had been a car, the car had long since turned off, turned around or reached its destination.

"Ah hah!" Tony exclaimed with a sound of satisfaction. "He's got a light on, waiting for us." He pointed across a wide ravine and, perched on the side of a steep slope, she saw a small cabin with a dim, flickering light in the window.

"Are you sure that's the right place?"

"Fairly sure. Of course, we have several more miles to go to wind behind the ravine and get over there, but we're almost there."

By the time they pulled up in front of the cabin, Jennifer was shaking. As soon as the truck stopped, Tony jumped out of the cab and hollered, "Hey, Tiger, it's me—Tony."

The door of the cabin opened and a man stepped through, caught in the glare of the truck lights. Jennifer had no trouble seeing him very clearly.

He was tall, over six feet, with thick brownish-blond hair that was tousled. He wore khaki pants tucked into combat boots and a red-and-black-plaid shirt. The sleeves were rolled up to above his elbows, emphasizing his muscular arms. He stood there in the light, his hands resting casually on his hips and waited patiently for them to join him.

Jennifer could not seem to make herself move from where she sat inside the truck. Frozen, she continued to stare at the man who had been such an integral part of her life for the past twenty years.

Snatches of intimate conversations they had had came back to her and she cringed. How had she dared to be so open with him? He knew everything there was to know about her—her thoughts, her dreams, her ambitions.

She knew nothing about him. Most particularly she hadn't known that Chad was also the man she worked for, C. W. Cameron.

"You might as well get out of the truck, Jennifer, now

that you're here," Chad said in a voice that clearly carried to where she sat.

How could he have done this to her? She continued to stare at him in shame and disbelief. There was no way she could have known. C. W. Cameron was nothing like Chad. Absolutely nothing.

She would never forget the first time she had been introduced to him. She had worked for his company as a stenographer for almost three months. Of course she had caught glimpses of him as he came in and out of his office, but that was all.

His assistant, Marlene, had recently announced her engagement to a man from Chicago and was happily making plans to move. Everyone had been wondering who would take her place. There was a chance someone might be promoted. Then again, they might look for someone outside the firm to fill the position.

When Jennifer was called into his office, she wasn't sure whether to be pleased or not. She hadn't been out of school long and probably had the least experience of anyone there.

C. W. motioned for her to sit down in the chair across from his desk. Timidly she perched on the edge of the chair. She glanced down to see what he was reading and saw her name on the folder. He must have gotten her file from personnel.

He glanced up without smiling. "I apologize for the delay in this meeting, Ms. Chisholm. I generally get acquainted with all of my employees within a few days after they arrive."

Jennifer forced herself to relax. So. She wasn't here to be interviewed for a new position. This was just a delayed welcome-on-board type of meeting.

C. W. continued, "I'm afraid things have been a little

hectic lately and my schedule has not gone as smoothly as I would have wished.''

Jennifer didn't know what to say, so she sat there with her hands clasped together in a death grip, trying to look relaxed, intelligent and at ease.

He glanced down at her folder, then back at her. ''I notice that you made very high grades at the business college you attended.''

''Yes, sir,'' she admitted shyly.

''I'm curious to know why you didn't go on to college.''

She looked at him in surprise. ''There weren't enough funds for that, I'm afraid, and it would have put an even greater burden on my mother. I needed to go to work as soon as possible.''

''Have you thought about taking night courses?''

Again she looked at him in surprise. He was treating her more as a counselor would than an employer would.

''I'm not against that, of course. I just don't have a particular field I would be interested in pursuing.''

''I see.''

She could almost hear him thinking ''no ambition.'' Perhaps that was true. She enjoyed her work and was quite content with it.

''You've done a remarkable job since you've been here, Ms. Chisholm,'' he offered quietly.

''Thank you.''

''I have noticed, though, that when you transcribe my dictation it does not come back to me in the same form in which I dictate it.''

Jennifer tried hard not to show how his comment affected her. She had tried to make only the revisions she felt absolutely necessary.

''You seem to feel the necessity to correct my grammar and my sentence structure from time to time,'' he pointed out in a dry voice.

She forced herself to meet his bland gaze, but she could read nothing. The golden eyes seemed to look right into the most vulnerable part of her being.

"Tell me, how did you hear about this job?"

Jennifer was surprised at the sudden change of subject.

"A friend at school mentioned that the agency was looking for stenographers. So I applied."

He continued to sit there, waiting, as though she had more to say. Jennifer had never seen a man who could be so still. His hands rested on the desk in front of him and she covertly studied them. They were large, strong hands. He was a large, strong man.

"Had you ever heard of the agency before? Or of me?"

She glanced up at his face again, startled by his questions.

"No, sir."

"You don't have to keep calling me 'sir,' you know. I may look old enough to be your father, but that's not quite the case."

The personal remark unnerved her, just as their whole conversation had done. She had never known anyone like him and didn't know how to respond to the man.

"Are you always so quiet?" he asked.

"When I don't have anything to say," she admitted.

He smiled and she was amazed at how the smile softened his harsh features. The smile quickly disappeared.

"I'd like you to begin working closely with Marlene for the next few weeks and learn her job before she leaves us, if that's agreeable with you."

Jennifer gasped. "Me?"

He glanced quickly over her shoulder, then his gaze pinned her to her chair. "I believe you're the only other person in the room. Why? Do you see some problem?"

"I, well, I, uh, no, not exactly. I mean, I don't have

much experience and—'' She couldn't think of anything else to say.

"I realize that. What I also realize is that despite your rather tender years, you show a great deal of initiative, intelligence, ability to grasp a new situation, willingness to work—in other words, all the attributes I want in an assistant. Do you want the job?"

Dazed, she stared back at him. Did she want the job? Did she want to work closely with this man every day? She knew so little about men. *Chad? What should I do?*

There was no answer. Chad was good at that. He might spend time with her going over her options, but he never made up her mind for her.

"Mr. Cameron, as you may well guess, this comes as quite a surprise to me." She searched for the right words. "If you don't mind, I'd like a day to think it over."

He watched her for a moment, then said, "Ah, yes. I did forget one rather important piece of information—your salary." He named a figure that doubled what she was presently making. "That's a beginning salary, of course. As you progress and take on more responsibility I will see that your raises reflect your increased worth to the company."

He stood up and she immediately got to her feet. "Perhaps you're right, Ms. Chisholm, to want to think this offer over. I will be waiting to hear your decision."

Jennifer barely remembered leaving his office and returning to her desk. She worked the rest of the day with no idea of what she was doing. Thank goodness the transcriptions of tapes had become so routine by then she could manage without her total concentration.

As soon as she got home that night and greeted Sam, who was still little more than a kitten at the time, she said, "Chad? I really need to talk to you."

"Go ahead, Sunshine. Talk."

Jennifer gave a sigh of relief. There were times when she couldn't get in touch with him, and she'd been afraid that tonight of all nights he wouldn't respond.

Kicking off her shoes she sat down in her favorite chair with a sigh.

"I got a terrific job offer today, Chad. I need to talk to you about it."

"I thought you just started a job."

"I did. It's the same place, only a different position. A much higher position. I'd be working as Mr. Cameron's assistant."

"Isn't he the fellow who runs the place?"

"That's right."

"Who is he?"

"What do you mean?"

"I mean, what do you know about him?"

"Not all that much, really, except for office gossip. He's single, attractive—"

"And that's why you'd go to work for him?" She could almost hear the disgust in his voice.

"Of course not. I'm not even sure I want to work for him, actually."

"What's the problem?"

"The problem is that I don't know that much about men. I don't remember my father that well. I never had any brothers. The boys I knew in school were more friends than anything. I think I'm a little afraid of him."

"You mean you think he'd chase you around the desk?"

She thought about that for a moment. "No, I don't think so. He doesn't seem to be the type of person. If he were, I'm sure the office staff would know about it. There's never been any talk about his personal life."

"Then what's to be afraid of?"

"He's so stern, so rigid. All business. He doesn't ever seem to relax."

"*Maybe he's busy.*"

"I'm sure he is. I understand his dad opened the agency some years ago and when he was killed his son came home to run it." She got up and wandered into the kitchen and poured herself a glass of apple juice. "I'm sure that wasn't easy for him to do."

"*Probably not. What had he been doing before then?*"

"Nobody has ever said."

"*I'm afraid I don't quite understand what you want from me, Sunshine.*"

"I'm not sure, either. I think I'm afraid of failing. The job has so much responsibility attached to it. I'm not sure I can handle it."

"*Your boss must think you can or he wouldn't have offered you the position.*"

"I thought of that. I just don't know how he can tell so much about me. He doesn't know me at all."

"*Maybe he's a good judge of character.*"

"What if I let him down?"

"*But if you don't try, won't you be letting yourself down?*"

"I suppose. I hadn't thought of it that way."

"*Only you can decide what you want out life, you know. Nobody else can do that for you. If you're content working as a stenographer, if you don't want to learn anything more, then be the best stenographer you can be, and be happy doing it.*"

Jennifer was quiet for a few moments. "I guess I've still been blessing my opportunity to get a job as soon as I finished school. I hadn't looked any farther down the road than that."

"*Now you're being challenged to look down that road to your future.*"

"Yes."

"*Well, for the record, I believe in you, Sunshine. I know that you can do anything you decide you can do.*"

"Thank you, Chad. What would I do without you?"

"*You'd do just fine and you know it.*"

The next morning she went into the office and told Mr. Cameron that she would be pleased to work as his administrative assistant.

Jennifer sat there in the truck, watching the two men talking. Slowly she opened the door and crawled out of the cab, already feeling the bruises on her backside. When she approached the two men they stopped talking and turned to her. Tony smiled, obviously pleased that they had found his friend. Chad, or C. W. Cameron, she wasn't sure how she was going to be able to think of him from now on, stood there waiting, watching her expression, revealing nothing of his thoughts to her. He never had. Only Chad had done that. Chad. She felt such a sense of loss that she almost crumpled with the pain. Chad, her lifelong friend, seemed to be gone. In his place stood the cold, aloof and distant man she had worked for all these years.

She didn't know what to say.

C. W. Cameron suddenly smiled, a warm, relaxed smile that caused a feeling of light and energy to flood over her. He took a couple of steps toward her and enfolded her in his arms. Holding her close, he laid his cheek on the top of her head. "You finally found me out, didn't you, Sunshine?"

Chapter Five

Jennifer's ear was pressed hard against Chad's chest and she could feel the heavy thumping of his heart inside. She had never been so close to him before, never felt the strength of him.

Raising her head she looked into his eyes. They were guarded, but there was a hint of emotion that she had never seen before. "How are you feeling?" she managed to say. Her voice sounded weak and trembling.

"I'll feel better once we get away from this place. If you hadn't arrived, things could have gotten a little desperate. There's nothing to eat up here and the nights get a little cold, even in August."

"Did you have some water?"

"Yes. There's a well."

Tony spoke up. "We've got food in the truck. I don't see any reason to hang around here, do you?"

Chad glanced over at him. "No, I don't. Especially if you think you've been followed."

The three of them started for the truck, but Chad hadn't

let go of his grip around Jennifer. He had tucked her under his arm, his hand clamped against her waist, holding her to his side.

Jennifer clambered into the truck quickly and sat in the middle. The men hastily followed, slamming their doors. Tony had automatically slid behind the wheel again, leaving Chad to sit beside her. Because of the floor shift, Jennifer found herself plastered against Chad's side. His arm was draped on the seat behind her. She wriggled, trying to place some distance between the two of them. His hand fell on her shoulder, effectively pinning her to his side. *"You're fine, just where you are."*

Of course. He still knew what she was thinking. He had always known, even when they were working together. Never by any hint had he given away his extra knowledge of her. She wondered how he'd managed.

"It wasn't easy, Sunshine, believe me."

She darted a glance in his direction, but he wasn't looking at her. Instead he had leaned forward and was digging into the sack at his feet. "Ah, food." Reaching down into the sack he pulled out a plastic-wrapped sandwich. With a grin he handed it to her. "How about opening this for me, would you? I'm short of hands at the moment."

Since his left hand was curved around her shoulder and he gave no indication that he would ever move it, she recognized that he preferred their current position over eating, despite how hungry he was.

Without saying anything, she unwrapped the sandwich and held it out to him. He seemed to inhale it. She reached down and found the six-pack of soda they had bought and without asking, opened one of them for him.

"Thanks," he muttered, taking a long swallow and exhaling with a sigh.

"What do you think is going on?" Tony asked.

That was what Jennifer wanted to know, but she had a hunch they were concerned about two different subjects.

''The way I figure it, your friend didn't appreciate all my questions. I was sent out here on a wild-goose chase.''

''Where did they force you off the road?''

''I don't know. I've never been out here before. It was long before we left the highway, though,'' Chad replied. He began to massage Jennifer's neck and shoulders, his fingers pushing and kneading the stiff muscles. They hit a sudden bump and he held her against him for a moment, then eased his grip and began to stroke across her shoulders again.

''I didn't see any sign of your car.''

Chad sighed. ''I'm not surprised. I didn't have a chance to remove the keys. There were three men in the car. Only two brought me up here. My car will probably turn up abandoned somewhere.''

''Do you think they intended to let you die up here?'' Jennifer asked.

''Who knows? I didn't make any friends when I hit the first guy. That's when I must have gotten clobbered from behind. By the time I came to I was in the back seat with a pistol aimed at me and we were on this road. My biggest fear was that one of the holes in the road would cause that pistol to go off. You can bet I stayed as quiet as possible.''

Tony laughed. ''Actually, you look a hell of a lot better than I expected. I can remember some of the scrapes we used to get into when—''

''Yeah. Me, too, Tony. But I'd rather not go into them at the moment.''

Jennifer felt his gaze rest on her profile but she refused to look up at him. He still didn't want her knowing any more about him than he could help, which she found extremely annoying, under the circumstances. He knew everything about her.

"Not everything, Sunshine."

She forced herself not to answer him out loud. Tony didn't need to know what was between them. *Why didn't you ever let me know who you were were?*

"How could I? Remember, it wasn't my idea for you to come to work at the agency. It took me a few weeks to overcome the shock of finding you working for me, and another few weeks to decide that despite everything, you were the best employee I had."

She remembered now that he had questioned her on her choice of coming to work there. At the time they were having a high turnover of employees. Since then, the problems had been worked out and the work force was much more stable.

"People still move away and have babies. That's the norm for the working world these days," he continued.

If you didn't want me working for you, why did you make me your administrative assistant?

"I didn't say I didn't want you working for me. I said it was a shock. Like I told you, despite our relationship, you were the most suited for the position. The personnel director suggested you to me, although I had already recognized how well you edited my tapes as you went along."

I thought you were upset about that.

"I was more amused than anything. You have such a keen mind. You constantly amaze me. You might be shy in other areas, but when you know you're right you do what you have to do."

I am not shy.

"Of course you are. You rarely date."

Whose fault is that? she demanded, glancing up at him out of the corner of her eye.

Chad had been eating another sandwich while she held his soda. Now he took it from her, deliberately trailing his fingers across hers.

"I never stopped you from dating. You and Jerry seemed to have a good relationship."

A friendly relationship, that's all.

"What's wrong with being friends?"

Not a thing.

"Are you still blaming me for telling you Larry Donahue was married?"

Of course not! She thought back for a few minutes. Wait a minute. You're the one who introduced me to Larry.

"Right. But I didn't expect you to date the man just because I introduced him to you."

Then why didn't you say something there in the office?

"Because we don't have that sort of relationship in the office."

Jennifer grew quiet. So much had hit in the past hour that her head was still reeling. What was going to happen to her now? Nothing in her life was going to be the same again.

"That's the way life works, Sunshine. Nothing ever stays the same. We wouldn't want it to, now would we? That's part of our growth pattern—to learn, to gain wisdom, to expand."

I was perfectly content to leave things the way they were.

"Oh, were you now? Who was it who insisted on coming up here to finally meet Chad? Who was so gleeful that you had found me in a position where I had no choice? You wanted to know. Now you do."

Now I do, she repeated a little sadly.

"And you're disappointed." Chad shifted. She could feel the long length of his leg pressed against hers. Since he had taken the can of soda out of her hand, it was free. She could almost feel the hurt that he was experiencing at the thought that she was disappointed to learn his true identity. She shifted her hand until it rested on his thigh.

Not disappointed. Shocked is more the word. When I think of the times—

"*Don't think of them.*"

How can I possibly forget them? You listened patiently while I carried on and on about how cold and unfeeling my boss was. You must have had a tough time not revealing how amusing you found me.

"*I wasn't amused, Sunshine. I could feel your frustration with the situation. Unfortunately, what you were dealing with was the real me out in the business world.*"

Nonsense. You are not cold and unfeeling. You are warm and caring and— Jennifer caught her breath as the memory of his earlier words came back to haunt her. He had told her that he loved her. He had told her that he had always loved her. Chad loved her. That meant that C. W. Cameron also loved her. She was dazed by the thought.

He sat quietly beside her, refusing to comment on her most recent thoughts. She was almost grateful.

The two men began to talk and Jennifer gratefully tuned out their conversation. Her mind was in such turmoil. In all the years that she had tried to guess at the type of person Chad was, she would never have pictured him as a no-nonsense businessman, brisk and efficient.

Jennifer let her head rest wearily against his shoulder. Too many things had come at her too quickly for her to take them in. She allowed her eyes to close, enjoying his solid warmth beside her. She would have to think about everything later.

By the time they reached the smoother surface of the highway, Jennifer was sound asleep in Chad's arms.

Later Jennifer vaguely recalled being lifted and held close and a sense of movement, but that was all. She had been so tired. And why not? She'd made the drive from Los Angeles, plus the additional one into the Utah mountains. She'd been bounced and bruised and she had met her lifelong friend in the flesh, which had been traumatic, to say the least.

The next thing she knew was that she was lying in bed, the covers tucked cozily around her.

"Sunshine? Are you awake yet?"

Drowsily her eyes opened. She was in a strange room. Rolling onto her back she saw that she was in a hotel room. The drapes were closed and there was very little light in the room. Bewildered, she sat up and the covers slipped to her waist. Only her scraps of underwear kept her from being totally unclothed.

"Chad!"

"Ah, so you are awake. Good, I—"

"What did you do with my clothes!"

"?"

"And don't play the innocent with me."

"If you will look on the chair in front of the window, you will find them neatly folded and waiting for you to put on."

She saw them just where he described.

"Oh."

"Did you bring any others with you?"

"Yes, but they're in the car."

"And the car is—?"

"Parked in the Lucky Lady's parking lot. You had no right to take off my clothes, Chad."

"No right? Come on, Sunshine. You sound like some Victorian lady. You wouldn't have rested in those jeans and you know it. Are you afraid I took advantage of you while you slept?"

"Fat chance."

She could feel his amusement. *"Would you like to meet me for brunch? Several of the casinos around town put on an excellent spread."*

Jennifer tried to see what time it was, but it was too dark.

"Almost ten."

That late! And she had to get back to Los Angeles. After all, she had a job to do and—Her job! Suddenly she remembered all that she had learned the previous day.

"Are you afraid I'll fire you if you don't get back to work in time?"

She didn't know what to think. Never had she been so confused. "I'm going to take a shower. I should be ready in about half an hour."

"Fine."

She hopped out of bed and went into the bathroom. Everything in the two rooms was clean and of the highest quality. The hotel had thoughtfully provided shampoo and deodorant as well as a shower cap if she didn't want to take time to wash her hair.

Jennifer had no choice. She felt grimy after the dusty ride on the back roads yesterday. The hot water felt wonderful beating down on her and she forced her mind to relax and enjoy it. She had time enough later to try to figure out what to do with all the new information she'd just received.

Eventually she faced that she would have to leave the security of the shower. Wrapping her dripping hair in a towel she stepped out of the tub and started drying off.

"Sunshine?"

She kept drying. "Are my thirty minutes up?"

"No, but I brought your suitcase in for you. Do you need anything out of it?"

Her suitcase—with her toothbrush, her hair dryer, her— "Where are you?"

"In your room. Where else would I be?"

Hastily she draped the large towel around her and jerked open the bathroom door. Peering around the corner she saw her suitcase on her rumpled bed and Chad sitting on the chair by the window.

He had obviously spent a restful night. His hair appeared slightly damp from the shower, and his clothes looked fresh. Today he wore a pair of Levi's that fit him embarrassingly well, and a white, long-sleeved shirt that once again had the sleeves turned up above the elbows. He was sitting stretched out in the chair, his legs extended and crossed at the ankle. Today he wore moccasins. His elbows rested on the high arms of the chair and his hands made a steeple under his chin.

She had never seen C. W. Cameron dressed in anything but three-piece business suits that effectively concealed his well-developed body. Nothing Chad had on today hid much of anything. The top three buttons of his shirt were open and she could see the soft golden hair revealed there.

When her gaze met his eyes she saw that he was amused at the long study she was giving him. He hadn't been wasting his time, either, obviously enjoying the view as she stood there with a towel wrapped under her arms and hanging to mid-thigh.

"How did you get in?"

"I have a key, why?"

"No reason, I guess. Thank you for getting my clothes for me."

"My pleasure." The way he drawled the words and the look he had on his face as his eyes continued to wander from her towel-draped head to her bare toes made her grab her suitcase and hurry back to the bathroom.

She could hear his laughter through the closed door.

Jennifer did not find the present situation particularly amusing. To think that all this time she had been working for Chad and he had known...

She saw her wide-eyed expression in the mirror and almost groaned out loud. How could he?

That time two years ago when she had gotten so angry at Mr. Cameron, she had almost quit. In fact, if it hadn't been for Chad insisting she simmer down before making any decisions...

Of course he'd been right. No one should make decisions when they were angry. A person wasn't really thinking when angry. But oh! How she had wanted to quit. He had been so arrogant, so rude.

He'd also been putting in long, grueling hours, and he'd had several clients come in demanding immediate help. At the time she had not seen the situation from his side. All she knew was that he was demanding impossibly long hours from her. Yet he'd been there working right alongside her.

What would have happened if Chad hadn't calmed her down and she'd given notice? Would she have been any happier anywhere else?

The answer was no, of course. She enjoyed her work. She found it challenging. Now that she recalled that particular incident, she remembered that she was surprised the next day when Mr. Cameron had asked her to go to lunch with him to discuss some business matters that he preferred not to have interrupted by the constant ringing of the phone.

They had sat for two hours while he discussed the present crisis in the office. He had asked her advice on how to handle the sudden influx of business, and he had listened when she made a few suggestions. Before long, each of them was coming up with ideas built on the other's suggestions. By the time they returned to the office Jennifer had totally forgotten that she had seriously considered resigning. He had stopped in front of her desk while she put her purse away. When she sat down he was still standing there.

"Thank you for a very valuable lunch, Ms. Chisholm.

I hope we can get some of these ideas working for us immediately. They should help the wear and tear on our nerves.''

She smiled at him, aware of the strain in his face. "I hope so, too, Mr. Cameron."

No sooner had she gotten home that night and been greeted by Sam when Chad had gotten in touch with her.

"Well, Sunshine? Did you resign today?"

"No, of course not."

"Why do you say, 'of course not'? Didn't you tell me last night that you no longer wanted to work for an arrogant, rude, bullying slave driver of a boss and that you weren't sure you'd even be able to stay for the two weeks necessary to work out your notice?"

"I overreacted."

"You mean he isn't any of those things?"

"He's tired, Chad. Really worn out. The poor man has been trying to do the work of three people. I think I convinced him today to hire at least one more investigator, possibly two, to help with the work load. He's seriously considering it."

"What a difference a day makes. Yesterday he was arrogant and rude. Today he's a poor man."

"You can make fun of me all you want. Once I calmed down, I realized that I only saw what was happening to me, what I was going through, how mistreated I was. Today, he gave me an opportunity to look at it from his point of view. He's never asked more of me than he's asked of himself. In fact, he generally puts in longer hours than I do, since he's out in the field so much as well as in the office digging through the piles of paper alongside of me."

Now as Jennifer put on the finishing touches of her makeup and made sure her slip didn't show under the dress she had hastily packed, she realized how many times she and Chad had discussed her relationship with her boss.

How embarrassing. No wonder he as her boss had no trouble understanding her. If only she'd been given the same opportunity. But she had, actually. As Chad he had explained his position as much as he could without revealing his identity. He had given her an opportunity to see inside of him, to share his thoughts and feelings.

Jennifer placed her hand lightly on her breasts, where the tiny butterfly fluttering seemed to have started. She and Chad had been much more intimate over the years than other people. They had never shared a physical intimacy, but that seemed almost superfluous to what they already had.

She knew he loved her and was there for her, just as he had known when he had contacted her that she would do anything to help him, no matter what it was. They had experienced a true union of their innermost spirits by the long-familiar exchange of their thoughts and feelings.

How could she say she didn't know the man sitting out there waiting so patiently for her? She knew him as well as she knew herself.

And she loved him with a depth of feeling that almost shook her with its intensity.

Jennifer opened the door and stepped out into the room. Chad had his eyes closed and he opened them when he heard the door. She knew that the dress she wore was the same color as her eyes. It was a simple cotton sundress that she generally wore to the beach or to go shopping. Not wanting to take much time with her hair, she had combed it back from her face and let it wave to her shoulders.

Chad never took his eyes off her as he slowly came to his feet and walked over to her. She could smell the light scent of his after-shave, and she realized how familiar the smell had become to her over the years. Many times, before she looked up, she had known when he'd returned to the office by that special scent.

Now she carefully explored his face with her intent gaze—his thick brows that almost met across his nose; his deep-set, hooded eyes, that seemed to glow with a secret fire of their own; his nose, that looked as though it had been broken more than once; his high cheekbones and square jaw. She saw the honesty and integrity stamped on his face, the experiences life had tossed his way, how little joy he had found so far, and how little he really expected to find.

Jennifer went up on tiptoe and slid her arms around his neck. "Oh, Chad, I love you so much," she whispered with trembling lips as she placed them on his firm, well-shaped mouth.

Chapter Six

Chad put his arms around her as a drowning man would grab a life preserver. They clung to each other, his mouth parting hers and taking possession as though he had spent years of dreaming about the opportunity. No one had ever kissed Jennifer that way before. She had been used to gentle, friendly kisses.

There was nothing gentle nor particularly friendly about what he was doing at the moment. Chad was making his claim to her clear. He lifted her in his arms and carried her back to the large stuffed chair he had recently vacated and sank down without ever losing contact with her mouth. His tongue searched and explored her mouth—lightly tracing the slightly uneven line of her teeth, coaxing her tongue to meet his in a playful duel. It was as though he had waited forever for the opportunity to get to know her as well physically as he knew her mentally and emotionally.

His hand rested at her throat. When he began to explore the contour of her face with his lips, placing tiny kisses in a careful row, his hand slowly inched downward until it rested on her breast.

Jennifer had never experienced so many intense emotions at once. She was shaking with reaction. Never in her wildest imaginings did she expect to feel so on fire. Everywhere he touched a combustive flame seemed to flare up between them. She shifted restlessly in his arms.

He clamped his arm around her waist. "Be still," he said sharply.

Her eyes snapped open. That was the least loverlike command she'd ever heard.

"I'm having all I can do to hang on to my self-control as it is, Sunshine," he advised her with a rueful grin.

Jennifer wanted to disappear in a puddle of embarrassment. Of course she knew all the clinical details regarding sex, but at the moment she hadn't been thinking about those facts.

Hastily getting to her feet, she straightened her dress and attempted to smooth her hair where his hand had ruffled it only a few moments before.

"I suppose we should go get something to eat," she managed to say while trying to steady her breathing.

He grinned. "I suppose we should," he mimicked softly. "Otherwise, we might not leave this room for the rest of the day."

She whirled away from him in an attempt to hide the expression on her face. How could she tell him that she wouldn't mind at all spending the rest of the day in bed with him?

"Why, Sunshine, I'm shocked to hear such lascivious thoughts coming from your pure and chaste mind."

Oh, no! She had forgotten how clearly he could read her mind. Turning to face him, knowing that her face must be a lovely shade of fiery red, she said, "Stop it, Chad. I can't seem to block you out of my mind the way you do me. But don't you dare tease me about my thoughts, do you understand?''

He stood up and faced her from across the room, his smile gone, his expression serious. ''I'm sorry, Jennifer. I wasn't making fun of you, please believe me. I was trying to lighten the volatile atmosphere, if possible. You see, this is why I knew a relationship between us would never work. Everyone needs their privacy, even from their closest loved one. I don't want to destroy what we have in the hopes of having more.''

Picking up her purse and pocketing the room key, Chad handed her the purse and opened the door. ''I want to make love to you very much, but not at the expense of everything else we've always shared. I won't ever sacrifice that, do you understand me?''

He closed the door and politely guided her down the hall, his hand resting lightly at her waist.

Jennifer realized that she seldom heard him call her Jennifer. She had always been Sunshine to him—or Ms. Chisholm. For a shocked moment she felt a loss so intense she could scarcely comprehend it. What would it be like never to be called Sunshine again? That had been a very special name between them that no one else had ever known.

She understood what he was saying to her. Their physical response to each other was astonishing, like wildfire racing before the wind. But she wasn't willing to give up their unique relationship in order to experience the full expression of their physical love for each other.

When they reached the lobby of the hotel, Jennifer recognized that they were next door to Tony's casino. A blast of hot air hit them when they stepped outside.

''Do you mind if we take your car? Mine hasn't been found yet,'' Chad said, as though nothing out of the ordinary had happened between them.

Jennifer nodded, her thoughts still engrossed in all the

discoveries she'd been making—about herself, her beliefs, and about Chad.

They made idle conversation over brunch. Jennifer had never seen so much food at one time before.

"Haven't you ever been to Las Vegas before?" Chad asked later, sipping his coffee.

"No. It isn't the sort of place you'd visit alone."

"True. Maybe we should plan to stay another night and I'll show you around."

She glanced down at her dress. "I'm afraid I didn't bring anything dressy to wear."

"That's no problem. We can always find something here, if you'd like."

Jennifer grinned. What better way to see Las Vegas than with your best friend? Add to that the fact that he was also your boss and was giving you permission not to be at work the next day and she could find nothing in his suggestion to complain about.

"I would love it." She stood up and held out her hand. "I can hardly wait to get started. Let's go."

He laughed at her enthusiasm, and for a moment Jennifer stared at him in astonishment. She had never seen C. W. Cameron laugh. Never. She had seen an occasional smile, but that was all. Now he looked happy and relaxed. She was amazed at the transformation.

Hugging his arm as they went out the door, Jennifer decided to make that day the most special day of her life. She knew without consciously acknowledging it that they might not have many of them together.

Chad must have made a similar resolution. Never had Jennifer seen C. W. Cameron so relaxed before. His smile came easily as she took him on a tour of the stores, modeling the most outrageous and the most demure outfits for him. She found that she enjoyed making him laugh or catching him by surprise.

As a joke she tried on a flame-red dress that molded her curves, leaving a long length of leg showing. Hastily digging in her purse she found some hairpins and gathered her hair into a rather precarious topknot on top of her head. Casual curls fell in front of her ears and along the nape of her neck. Thankful that her heels were high enough to effectively show off the dress, Jennifer sauntered out of the dressing room to where Chad waited.

Later she wished she'd had a camera trained on his face when he saw her. He did a perfect example of a double take. He was sitting in a chair and she ambled over to him and leaned down, knowing the top of her dress would fall open.

"You look a trifle bored, cowboy. Care for a little action?" she said in a low voice.

His gaze zeroed in on the front of her dress, then bounced up to meet hers. Jennifer thoroughly enjoyed watching the color wash over his cheeks, then recede.

"I don't think that's quite, uh, you, Sunshine," he said in a strangled voice.

She straightened, running her hand from her waist down to her thigh. "Oh, I don't know. Just feel this material. Isn't it something?" Gently picking up his hand where it was clenched on the arm of the chair, she placed his hand on her thigh.

Chad jerked his hand back as though the dress had been as hot as its color indicated.

"What are you doing?" he asked in a gruff whisper.

"Trying to find something to wear for tonight, honey," she drawled, trying not to laugh.

"Well, that won't do at all."

She assumed a disappointed air. "Oh, that's too bad. I always thought that red was definitely my color."

Without looking at him Jennifer sashayed back into the dressing room. She was chuckling as soon as she reached the small cubicle. Curious to see if she could, Jennifer tried to focus in on his thoughts, in a way similar to what he said he had done with her years ago.

All the time she was taking off the red dress and trying on the next one, she concentrated. Slowly she began to pick up his amazement and confusion at her behavior, as well as his embarrassment.

What's the matter, cowboy? Can't you take a little teasing?

"Is that what that was?" he responded promptly.

I always wondered how I'd do as a dance hall girl.

"You'd be a sensation. However, I don't think my heart could handle much of that."

You'll like this one much better, she assured him.

He did. The blue-green material shifted color like the ocean on a sunny day. The dress fit her snugly to the waist, then flared to a swirling skirt that emphasized her trim legs.

She felt his sigh of relief when she walked out. Her smile was impish. "Is this better?"

"Much," he said with conviction.

After paying for her purchase with her credit card they were soon back on the street.

"Tony asked us to drop in this afternoon if we had time."

"I'd love that." Jennifer recognized that no matter what they did, she would love it. She enjoyed being with Chad, getting to know the physical side of him. C. W. Cameron was still very much in evidence, but the shock had worn off and she was catching glimpses of the Chad she knew and loved beneath the gruff exterior of her employer.

When they reached the ornate lobby of the Lucky Lady, Jennifer paused and looked up at Chad. "Why don't you go on up while I stop in the rest room for a moment?"

"Would you like me to wait?"

She shook her head, still a little shy with him. "That's

not necessary. I need to freshen my makeup and it will probably take a few minutes. But I promise not to be too long.''

Chad leaned down and kissed her softly on the lips, disregarding anyone who might be watching. ''I'll see you upstairs, then.''

When Jennifer sat down in front of the mirror, she hardly recognized the glowing woman in front of her. Her hair seemed to have a vitality all its own, her eyes sparkled and glittered, even her skin seemed to have taken on a special glow. Love was the best beauty aid going, she decided with a grin.

Hastily renewing her lipstick and powdering away the shine on her nose and forehead, Jennifer left the ladies' lounge and started toward the elevator. Before she realized what was happening, two men, one on each side of her, took her arm and propelled her through the front door of the casino and into a waiting limousine just outside the door.

''Wha—? Wait a minute. What are you doing?'' The car pulled away from the curb and quickly joined the traffic along the Strip.

''Don't worry, lady. Nobody's going to hurt you,'' one of the men said. She glanced around the car. Jennifer had never seen so much luxury in an automobile before. The driver wore a uniform and cap and the men on either side of her were in dark suits and wore sunglasses.

Chad!

''What is it? Where are you?''

I don't know where I am or where I'm going. Two men just grabbed me as I started toward the elevator and they're hauling me away in a luxury car.

''Who are they?''

I have no idea.

She could feel his fear and anger wash over her, and she almost flinched away from its intensity.

"We're not going to hurt you, lady," the man repeated. "Our boss wants to see you."

"Who is your boss?"

He looked at her without expression. In a flat tone he replied, "He'll tell you, himself."

"Where are you now?"

I don't know. We just passed the Tropicana and seem to be heading out of town.

"Don't worry, Sunshine. I'm right behind you. What does the car look like?"

Uh, it's silver. She glanced around. *Has some sort of antenna on the trunk.*

The car picked up speed once it left the town area. Jennifer didn't want to give away the fact that they might be followed, so she forced herself to continue looking straight ahead. There wasn't much to see. Occasionally there would be a house enclosed in a high fence. Most of them had swimming pools, which Jennifer didn't find too surprising. The desert was a good place to spend time in the water.

They made a sharp right turn onto a smaller road that took them farther from any other signs of houses. Eventually they pulled up in front of a heavy gate. The driver spoke into a small hand-held mike and the doors slowly opened. As soon as the car passed through, Jennifer turned around and watched the gate close. The gate was the only break in a tall, stone wall that seemed to encircle a multi-acre area.

After following a winding road for several minutes, the car eased to a stop in front of a sprawling, one-story home in adobe and red tiles, that was designed for Southwest living. The home was beautiful but Jennifer wasn't in the mood to stand around and admire it.

She was escorted with a great deal of courtesy into the house and was thankful for the air-conditioning that greeted her at the double-doored entrance. One of the men showed her into a large room, which had one wall of glass and overlooked a giant swimming pool. The water looked very inviting.

The sound of ice tinkling in a glass caused her to turn around. A middle-aged woman holding a tray of drinks smiled and said, "I brought you something to drink."

Jennifer smiled. "Thank you." She walked over to the tray, which had been placed on a round coffee table. There was quite a selection to choose from. She poured herself some iced tea from a pitcher, added lemon and sipped the liquid absently.

"Where are you?"

Behind a massive stone wall. Did you ever see the car?

"I got a glimpse, but that's all. Did you turn off the main road?"

Yes. We turned right, just past a white, two-story house on the left that had a cyclone fence. Did you see that?

"Damn. Yes. I passed it a few miles back. Who's there?"

No one at the moment.

"Try to stall them until I get there."

Chad! There's no way you can get onto the grounds. The wall is massive.

"I'll check it out. Just be careful. When you have any more information, let me know."

She wandered around the room, sipping her tea and enjoying the objets d'art that spoke of expensive tastes. Jennifer couldn't believe her attitude toward what had happened. At first she had been startled, then frightened—until she had made contact with Chad. After that, she had calmed down. She knew she wasn't in any danger. She had been treated with courtesy and kindness at all times, except for having been whisked out of the Lucky Lady by a couple of strangers.

Plus she had a great deal of faith in Chad's ability. Jennifer had to admit that she was curious as to what was going on. She had a hunch she'd be told eventually.

When a man walked into the room, Jennifer was ensconced in a comfortable chair, gazing out at the garden surrounding the pool.

"I'm sorry to have kept you waiting, Ms.—" He paused, waiting for her response.

Jennifer's gaze returned from the garden and made an inspection of the man standing before her. He lacked several inches of being six foot, but he made up in girth for his lack of height. She had to admit that his excellent tailoring did its best to conceal his obesity. Her eyes wandered to his face, which was as round as his body, and met a pair of black eyes that seemed to have seen everything in the world and would no longer be surprised at anything else they might see. His gray hair was thinning badly, despite his attempts to disguise it.

Without getting up, she said, "Jennifer Chisholm," in a quiet voice. "And you are—?"

"Max Taylor. You may have heard of me."

"Yes, Mr. Taylor, I've heard your name before. Are you responsible for my sudden visit here?"

He laughed, obviously amused at her attitude. "Yes. This is my home."

"Is this your usual way of getting company when you're bored, Mr. Taylor?" she asked before taking another sip of her drink.

He sank down into a chair opposite hers with a sigh. "Not usually, no. I'm just tired of Tony's games, that's all."

"And what do I have to do with Tony's games?"

"I'm not sure. That's what I intend to find out."

"Why me?"

"Because you're the only woman Tony's been around lately. I figured if I brought you out here, he might be willing to talk to me. Up until now, he has refused my calls."

She nodded her head sagely. "I see. I'm supposed to be your calling card, is that it?"

He grinned. "I suppose you could put it that way."

"Obviously you don't know Tony very well. He doesn't care for women."

"Now, wait a minute. I've known Tony Carillo for years. You aren't trying to tell me that he's—"

"Uh, no, Mr. Taylor. That isn't what I meant. He's a little bitter at the moment, that's all. Obviously you have mistaken me for his girlfriend. I'm not."

"But you managed to see him yesterday when no one else has been able to get to him in months. He's holed himself up in that casino and refuses to talk to anyone."

"If you could talk with him, Mr. Taylor, what is it you would want to say?"

"That's between me and him."

"Okay."

They sat there for a few moments in silence. Jennifer once again began to admire the beauty of the garden.

"I figure Tony should be trying to call me any time now," Max finally muttered.

She glanced around and smiled. "Don't count on it, Mr. Taylor. Your men were so slick at whisking me out of the casino no one knows where I went."

"But Tony will miss you and begin asking questions."

"Hardly. Tony doesn't even know me. The only reason I saw him yesterday was to find my—er, boss, C. W. Cameron." Jennifer began to put some things together. "Do you by chance own some land and a small cabin in southern Utah?"

He looked at her suspiciously. "So what if I do?"

She shrugged. "I just wondered. That's where Tony and I found Mr. Cameron last night."

Max suddenly sat up straighter. "You mean that man that was nosing around—You mean Tony sent him to—Are you telling me you found that place?"

"I wouldn't presume to tell you a thing, Mr. Taylor. Nor would I want to point out to you that kidnapping is a federal offense." She took another sip of her tea and returned her gaze to the beauty of the outdoors.

"Who is this Mr. Cameron?" he demanded.

She turned her head. "I told you. He's my boss."

"What was he doing snooping around me?"

"I don't know. You'll have to ask him."

"What does that mean?"

"Just that he'll be here demanding some answers from you before too long. Hope you have them for him. He can be very demanding." She sighed. "A very difficult man to work for, I'll admit." Her limpid blue gaze met his. "But the job does have certain compensations."

For a heavy man, Max Taylor moved with surprising agility. He strode out of the room and she could hear his voice calling someone as he stormed down the hall.

Idly she wondered if she'd hurt his feelings. Here he was being such a kind host. Oh, well. Maybe he'd have to find someone else to make friends with.

"Sunshine?"

Oh, hi, Chad. My host's name is Max Taylor. He knows Tony and seems to feel Tony is avoiding him. He's also the man who owns the cabin in the mountains where we found you.

"Damn."

Where are you?

"I've found the place. I was hoping that I wouldn't have to storm it, though."

*I can ask him to let me go. He seems a very accom-
modating fellow.*

"He's anything but that, believe me. He's ruthless.
That's why Tony got out of the partnership with him. He
doesn't like the way he runs his business."

Oh. Jennifer had a sudden hunch she shouldn't have
been baiting the man.

"What did you say to him?" Chad demanded.

*Oh, nothing much. Reminded him that kidnapping was
a federal offense.*

"That's great, Sunshine. Nothing like reminding him
that he's in deep water now." He was silent for a moment.
"You aren't even scared!"

*No. This is kind of fun, you know? Nothing very exciting
has happened to me my whole life. Now in one weekend
all kinds of things are happening. Maybe you should let
me come out in the field with you more often.*

She wasn't sure, but she was almost certain that what
she felt was a groan in response.

"Sunshine?"

Yes?

"Please don't antagonize the man. I've got to get in
touch with Tony and see if he can shed any light on this."

*Good idea. He said he expected Tony to call now that
he had his girlfriend.*

"What!"

*Yes. That's why he had me grabbed, to get back at Tony.
Isn't that amusing?*

"I don't find a damned thing funny about any of this.
Why should he think there's something going on between
you and Tony?"

*I suppose because I was shown up to see Tony yesterday
when I first arrived. No one else has been able to get
through to him.*

"I told you that."

Yes, I know. So now Max thinks Tony and I are sweethearts.

"Maybe we can use that. Just sit tight, Sunshine. I'll be in touch."

She smiled. "I know."

"Who are you talking to?" Max demanded, as he stomped back into the room.

"No one."

"I heard you talking to someone. Are you bugged?"

She glanced down at the sundress she was wearing. "No. I just have a habit of talking to myself. That comes from living alone too long." She looked at him and smiled. "Is there a chance I could go lie down somewhere for a while? I didn't get much sleep last night."

Max eyed her suspiciously. She met his gaze with a very innocent smile. Abruptly he turned, motioning her to follow. The hall they followed was spacious and long. Eventually Max paused and opened a door. The drapes were pulled and the room was in cool shadows. As luxurious as the rest of the house, the elaborate decor seemed to imply that whatever was troubling Max, it wasn't the lack of money.

She nodded her head. "Thank you, Mr. Taylor." Closing the door quite gently in front of him, she heaved a sigh of relief and went over to the bed. Slipping off her shoes she stretched out on the bed. "Okay, Chad. I've taken myself off to a bedroom for a nap. That should keep me out of trouble."

There was a long pause. She wasn't sure he had heard her. *"Good idea,"* came back distractedly. *"I'll see you soon."*

Obviously his mind was on other things, such as how to get her out of Max Taylor's home. She turned, snuggling her head into the pillow. She wasn't particularly worried. Chad could do anything.

Chapter Seven

A soft tap on a nearby door brought Jennifer from a deep dreamless sleep. She forced her eyes open, dismayed to find herself in a room she didn't remember. Jennifer wasn't used to traveling. She was used to waking up in the same bed day after day. Yet for the past two days every time she had opened her eyes she was in a strange environment.

Another tap sounded on the door. "Ms. Chisholm?"

Max Taylor. The past few hours suddenly came back to her. Hastily sitting up, she ran her hand through her hair, trying to bring some semblance of order to it.

"Yes?"

The door opened and the man stepped through the doorway. "Your friend Tony has just called. Obviously you have not been aware of his regard for you. He asked me to meet with him and to bring you with me."

"Oh." She slid off the bed and stood up, feeling around for her shoes with her feet. "He isn't coming out here?"

"No. We're to meet him in town."

After putting on her shoes Jennifer found her comb in

her purse and quickly ran it through her hair. Then she followed Max out the door.

Once again she was escorted to the limousine, this time by her host. Silently they rode back to town.

Chad?

"?"

We're on our way to meet Tony. Are you with him?

"Yes."

I love you.

A feeling of love and warmth swept over her and she smiled. Who needed the words when she could feel so much expression from his emotions?

They eventually pulled up in front of a luxury high-rise condominium that overlooked a golf course. There was enough daylight left for Jennifer to appreciate the view before they went inside and rode up to the top floor in an elevator.

Max acted as though he'd been there before. He guided her down the hallway and paused in front of an unmarked door. Pressing a button, he stood back and waited.

Tony opened the door. Pulling Jennifer into his arms, he gave her a quick hug, then stepped back, still keeping his arm around her waist. "Come in, Max," he said politely. After he closed the door he leaned over and whispered in Jennifer's ear, "I'm sorry about all of this, honey. Tiger has been ready to take me apart limb by limb for the scare."

"No problem," she said with a smile. "Where is he, by the way?" She glanced down the hallway.

"Straight ahead." He motioned for her to go ahead of him.

The hallway led into a large room that overlooked the city. Max was already standing there, waiting for them, when they walked in. So was Chad.

He strode over to Jennifer and looked down at her. "You okay?"

She nodded.

He glanced up. "If it's all the same to you two, we're leaving."

"Sure, no problem," Tony responded. "Max and I will probably be tied up for some time."

Max looked stunned to see the woman he had assumed belonged to Tony walking out with another man. Jennifer guessed that he was probably coming to the conclusion that he hadn't figured things out quite right, after all.

Chad didn't say anything all the way down in the elevator. Neither did Jennifer. When they reached the street, Jennifer looked up and said, "Now, what?"

He motioned to her car. When they got inside, he said, "I don't think it's a good idea to stay in town any longer. Would you mind driving home tonight?"

She smiled. "Not at all."

"I'm staying here. I've still got to find my car. Tony said he could probably find out from Max where it is."

He began to drive toward the Strip.

"Do you have any idea what's going on?"

"Tony's been filling me in, but there's no sense in getting you involved any more than you already are. That's why I want you to return home." He glanced at her. "Will you do that for me?"

She nodded. "Whatever you say."

"I'd looked forward to taking you out tonight. Maybe we can do it some other time."

"Maybe we can."

"Jennifer?"

She continued to stare straight ahead. "Yes?"

"Are you going to tell me what's wrong?"

"Just let down, I guess. I don't know."

"A lot of things have happened in the past forty-eight hours."

"Yes."

"You still aren't sure about me, either, are you?"

She glanced at him in surprise. "Of course I'm sure of you. I would trust you with my life."

"Thank you. But how are you going to feel about working with me now that you know who I am?"

"I'm not sure."

"We've got to take this one step at a time. Can you understand that?"

"Yes."

"Do you believe me when I tell you I love you?"

How could she not believe him when her mind was filled with his images, his feelings and thoughts? "I believe you."

He was quiet for many long minutes. "You need time to think it through."

She couldn't disagree. Jennifer no longer knew what to think or feel. She was confused, and being around Chad at the moment was only contributing to the problem.

Chad pulled up in front of the Lucky Lady and got out of the car, leaving it running. She got out and walked around to the driver's side. He stopped her before she sat down. She stood by the door, leaning against the car. He leaned over and kissed her very softly on her lips. "Drive carefully."

"I will."

"Let me know when you get home."

"Okay."

"Tell Sam hello for me."

She groaned. She'd forgotten about Sam. "If he's speaking to me by then."

Chad touched her cheek with his forefinger, tracing a

imaginary line along her jaw, then up to her lips. "I'll be back as soon as I can."

Jennifer suddenly remembered all the work waiting for him when he returned. It was hard to remember that when she'd left the office on Friday her boss had been a distant and aloof employer to whom she gave little thought after office hours. She shook her head, bewildered at the changes that had come about so quickly.

As though he could no longer help himself Chad drew her closer and kissed her. She could feel his heart's heavy rhythm in his chest. Jennifer realized that he didn't want her to leave him. She got a brief flash of them in bed together, and she could feel her body beginning to respond.

Chad abruptly let go of her and stepped away, his eyes refusing to meet hers, but not before his body, as well as his thoughts, had given him away.

Jennifer slid into the car and closed the door.

"Don't forget, Sunshine. I want to know the minute you get home."

She nodded, refusing to look at him. One more look and she would wrap herself around him and beg to stay with him that night. Yet, that was what they were afraid of. What would happen once they made love to each other? Would it destroy the closeness they shared? Did they dare find out?

She knew Chad wasn't ready to test that part of their relationship. She wondered if he ever would be.

While Jennifer made the long, lonely drive back to Los Angeles, she finally recognized what she should have seen sooner. Chad had no intention of letting their relationship go any further. If he had, he would have told her who he was before now. She was beginning to understand why he had tried to talk her out of finding out who he was.

Chad had felt safe in the role he was playing in her life. He knew what she did in her time away from the office.

He worked with her during the day, so was able to spend time with her.

If Chad had his way, they would continue their relationship as it now was, with her added knowledge of who he was.

Could she be content with a life like that? Not knowing the full physical intimacy of a relationship? Granted she hadn't been tempted to explore much before now, partly because she had never felt that pull with anyone. However, now that Chad had kissed her, had held her and had allowed her to discover how much he wanted her, Jennifer knew she was going to have difficulty coming to terms with not being able to fully share her life with him.

By the time Jennifer reached her apartment she was exhausted. She had only a few hours to sleep before it was time to get up and go to the office. There was no question but that she had to be there, now that she knew he wasn't going to be.

She barely got into the apartment before a flying ball of fur landed on her shoulder. "Sam! You scared me." He began to nuzzle her cheek and neck, telling her how miserable he'd been without her. He had begun to feel abandoned and was too pleased to see her to be upset.

Jennifer carried him into the bedroom along with her small bag. "I'm home, Chad."

The reply came back immediately. *"Thank God. Any problems?"*

"Not a one."

"Sam okay?"

"He seems fine. Very glad to see me, as a matter of fact."

"Probably did him good to be on his own for a while. He'll appreciate you more."

"Could be."

"Try to get some sleep now, Sunshine."

"When do you think you'll be back to the office?"

"I'll have to call you when I know something definite."

"Love you, Chad," she said sleepily as she climbed into bed and curled into her pillow.

"Sleep well, Sunshine. You've had a rough weekend."

When the alarm went off Monday morning, Jennifer had the curious sensation that she had dreamed her entire weekend. Was it really possible that C. W. Cameron was also her friend Chad?

By the time she had been at the office for a few hours the events of the weekend had been shoved to the back of her mind, and she found herself racing to stay abreast of the new paperwork and phone calls that came through with persistent regularity.

It was sometime after four o'clock and Jennifer had long since lost track of the number of calls she'd answered when the phone rang once again.

"Mr. Cameron's office."

"Ms. Chisholm?"

Jennifer's heart seemed to leap out of her chest. She had no trouble recognizing the deep voice on the other end. Nor did she miss the aloof tone and the name he had used. "Yes, Mr. Cameron?" She couldn't control the slight quiver in her voice.

"Is there anything happening that I need to know about?"

Funny you should ask, she thought dryly. "Several things came in the mail today that will prove helpful with some of your investigations." As she had done so often in the past years, Jennifer quickly summarized phone messages, information from the mail and interoffice communications. He gave her instructions, delegated some of the work, took down some numbers and told her he would be in touch.

"Uh, Mr. Cameron—?"

"Yes?" There was nothing but professional politeness in the tone.

"When do you expect to be in the office?"

"Hopefully the latter part of the week."

"Have they recovered your car?"

There was a moment of electrified silence, as though she had said something shockingly intimate. She waited, not knowing what else to do, but she got the definite impression that she was infringing on his privacy.

Jennifer had almost decided he wasn't going to respond at all when he said, "Yes. I have my car." A statement of fact, no more. He wasn't going to say when he got it, or where it had been, or if it had been damaged. And he had made it clear that it was none of her business.

"Oh. Well. I'm glad to hear it."

"Was there anything else?" he asked impatiently.

"No. I believe that was all," she said slowly.

"I'll check in with you in a day or two."

"Fine." Jennifer carefully put down the phone. The rest of the office was busy. No one had thought anything of the phone call she had just received. Just the normal communications between the boss and his assistant. That was the problem. It had been too normal. He had totally ignored everything that had happened over the weekend.

Jennifer spent the rest of the day concentrating on carrying out her employer's instructions. Carefully typing up his comments, she attached a sheet of paper to the front of new files she had set up, then placed them on the desks of the other two investigators.

By the time she was ready to leave the office, Jennifer was proud of what she had accomplished that day. Driving home she made the startling discovery that no doubt that was the reason Chad had reverted to the C. W. Cameron she knew. He valued her work as his assistant. He didn't want to cause anything to change that, even if he sacrificed a possibly closer relationship.

Once again, Sam seemed to be pleased to see her when she got home. She was glad someone was.

After dinner she tried to watch television, but couldn't keep her attention focused long enough to follow what was happening.

Finally, she could stand the silence no longer. "Chad?" She waited a few moments but got no response. "Chad. Can you hear me?" Still no answer. Again, this was nothing new. For the past six months she had not communicated with him. He was making it clear to her. The only reason he had contacted her on Friday was because he had no other recourse if he wanted to get out alive. She had served her purpose.

Jennifer didn't even realize she was crying until the tears began to drip off her cheeks. Nothing had really changed since last Friday. And yet, everything had changed. Jennifer had been given a glimpse of what her life could be with the man she loved. She also knew that he loved her. He hadn't been able to conceal his feelings from her.

But C. W. Cameron had made the decision not to do anything about his feelings. And he expected her to accept his decision.

During the coming weeks Jennifer tried. She put Chad out of her mind every time something reminded her of him. She put everything about her weekend in Las Vegas to the back of her mind, determined to wait until the pain was less before allowing herself to enjoy the few memories she had of being with him.

C. W. Cameron followed the same schedule as he had before. He spent a few days in the office, catching up on paperwork, then was gone again. Never by word, look or action did he give her any indication that he saw her as anything but his assistant. He treated her with aloof courtesy and distant kindness.

Jennifer wasn't at all sure she was going to be able to survive his courtesy and kindness. As the weeks went by, she felt less and less like eating and it began to show. Several of the women at work teased her about her new diet.

C. W. Cameron neither noticed nor cared.

Eventually her resistance dropped and she came down with the flu, missing several days work. He called once to see how she was feeling, but only as her boss concerned about her welfare.

During those days of fever and pain, of sleepless nights and drug-filled days, Jennifer realized that she had accepted his decision as final. Who did he think he was? Why did he have the right to step into her head and heart whenever he pleased, then blithely walk away when he became too uncomfortable with the situation?

By the time she woke up one morning, weak but clear-eyed, Jennifer knew that she was not going to give up without a fight. And the man she worked for had already taught her something about fighting, fair or otherwise. If one didn't work, she'd try the other.

She waited until she was able to get back to full production on the job, which took some time. Jennifer was disgusted at herself for allowing her body to become so weakened. She had more self-respect than that. In order to fill some of her lonely evenings she joined a health club and began to work out after she left the office. She met several people who came in regularly at the same time as she did and they began to visit back and forth while they worked on the machines.

Jennifer was pleased with her body's response. As she gained her weight back she began putting it on in all the right places. There had been nothing wrong with her body before, but now it looked even better.

She also discovered that she had much more energy. No longer did she drag home and fall on the couch exhausted after a day of hard work.

However, the biggest change was in her attitude to her employer.

"Good morning, Ms. Chisholm," he said one morning after having been out of the office for two weeks.

Her smile was warm and welcoming, filled with sparkle. "It's good to have you back," she said. Her tone was filled with such a loving quality that he glanced around to see if anyone else had heard her. No one seemed to be in the vicinity.

"Are these my messages?" he muttered, avoiding her gaze.

"Um-hmm," she said softly.

She watched with interest as a darker color spread over his tanned cheeks. "May I get you a cup of coffee?" she asked pleasantly.

His eyes darted to her in disbelief. In all the years they had worked together, she had never offered to bring him coffee before. He nodded abruptly. "Thank you," he said, striding into his own office.

She paused in the doorway of his office when she returned with his coffee. *I'm so glad you're back,* she said to him silently. *I've missed you.*

He never looked up, but she noticed his grip tightened on the pen he was holding. She set the cup down on his desk. "Do you need anything else?" she asked quietly.

He shook his head, refusing to look up.

Chad had heard her, she knew that. Whether he answered her or not, he had not tuned her out, which gave her an idea for another experiment.

She knew many things about this man, things she hadn't

consciously realized. A person couldn't trade thoughts with another person for years without learning about them. Jennifer had also learned quite a lot about him the weekend they had spent in Las Vegas. That knowledge could be put to work to help her convince him that they deserved the chance to see if they could make a relationship work.

Jennifer had a vague glimmering of what she had in mind, but didn't have the knowledge to fulfill it. As soon as she got off work that night she went to the public library and checked out several books on sex. When she noticed the expression on the librarian's face, Jennifer just smiled and explained, "Research."

For the next couple of weeks Jennifer read several sex manuals, studied pictures and received a crash course in all the sensual arts. She found herself blushing more than once but reminded herself that all of this was perfectly normal and natural between two people who loved each other.

She loved Chad. She knew that Chad loved her.

Now all she had to do was to convince him to give their relationship a chance.

Chapter Eight

Jennifer planned her strategy carefully. For this to work at all, she wanted Chad in the same town, at least. So she had to wait until he returned from his latest trip.

In the meantime, she continued to treat him with warmth and friendliness whenever he called in, amused to note that he had become even more aloof with her efforts. Whether he was calling from out of town or was in the office, she was open and amiable with him.

The day he came in from the Midwest he looked tired and discouraged.

"How was your trip?"

"Rugged," was his only reply. He went into his office and sank down in his chair, staring at the papers in front of him with dismay.

"None of those are emergencies," she said, following him into the room. "May I make a suggestion?"

He glanced up at her warily, an expression to which she had grown accustomed during the past few months.

"Why don't you go on home?" she asked as though he

had responded. "It's already after three. There's nothing here that can't wait until tomorrow to be dealt with, after you've had a good night's sleep."

He leaned his head wearily against the back of his chair. "That's the best idea I've heard in a while," he admitted.

"You've been working too hard."

His eyes met hers and she immediately knew what he was thinking. *"You know exactly why I've been working so hard."*

She was sure he wouldn't appreciate her acknowledging that she had picked up his statement. Instead, she said, "I have another suggestion. You might want to do what I do after a long, hard day."

"What's that?"

"I go home, fill my bathtub with warm water, pour myself a glass of wine, light a candle and sit there in the tub, sipping on the wine, and let my mind go blank. I try not to think of a thing. Just sit there and relax. It's amazing how much it helps. I sleep a lot better, too."

"I haven't been getting much sleep lately."

She steeled herself from responding that she knew. Because of her feelings for him, she had been able to tune into him more and more over the past few months. She knew how unhappy he was, how confused, and how determined he was not to do anything to cause her to quit her job and leave him entirely.

Chad had decided that half a loaf was better than nothing. He was wrong and she was determined to prove that to him. Half a loaf was a compromise that wasn't necessary or even wise. They deserved much more than that, and she was willing to go to great lengths to prove that to him.

He straightened in his chair. "I believe I may follow your suggestion." He glanced down at the stack of telephone messages in his hand. "You're sure these can wait until morning?"

"Positive."

He stood up. "Then I think I'll take your advice."

She stepped back so that he could pass her, but not far enough that he didn't have to brush by her as he passed. She felt him flinch.

Yes. He was vulnerable. But then, so was she. Love created vulnerability and it was all right, so long as the other partner didn't abuse it. That was what she intended to show Chad, if he would just give her a chance. Their deep feelings for each other were nothing to run away from, but something to run toward.

Jennifer made sure she left at five o'clock and went directly home to her apartment. There was no stopping at the health club tonight, no visiting with her friends. Instead, she did just what she suggested Chad do. She filled her bathtub with water, poured a small glass of wine, put a quiet instrumental recording to play on the stereo, lit a candle and, after stripping off her clothes, slowly lowered herself into the warm and soothing water.

Quieting her mind she began to tune in to Chad. He was quiet, as though asleep. That was all right. He needed his rest. She spent the next hour soaking and relaxing, and silently rehearsing.

By the time she had something to eat and was ready for bed, Jennifer was shaking with stage fright. So much depended on how she did this and how he responded.

She turned out the light and crawled into bed. Forcing her body and mind to relax, she began.

"Chad?"

"?"

"Are you asleep, love?"

She got a sense of drifting clouds and cool breezes. He was very relaxed, but she didn't think he was asleep.

"I was just lying here tonight, thinking of you, and decided to picture you here in bed with me."

She felt an electric vibration sizzle between them and knew beyond a doubt that she had his attention. She smiled to herself. "I see you lying next to me, your head on my pillow...."

She felt his energy surge, then retreat.

"I love to pretend that you're in bed with me, Chad. It makes my life less lonely. Are you tired of being alone, Chad?"

There was no response, but she knew she had his attention.

"If you were here I'd lean over and kiss you, very softly, on the lips. Your lips feel so good to me, Chad. I love their firmness, and the fullness of your bottom lip. If you were here, I would touch my tongue to its surface, and lazily taste your mouth."

She waited, but got no response.

"If you were here in my bed there would be no need for either of us to have on any clothes. I would want to feel your body pressed against mine."

"*!*"

Jennifer smiled. "I wouldn't want any covers on us, either, and I would want a light on, so that I could see you...just as you could see me. I would want to touch you, explore you with my fingertips, to get to know your body as well as I know mine, to place my breasts against your chest and feel the soft downy curls on your chest brush against me."

"*Jennifer!*"

"Yes, Chad?" she responded.

"*Would you cut that out?*"

"What's wrong, Chad?"

"*Not a thing. Not a damned thing.*"

"I'm sorry if I bothered you, love. I know how very tired you are and how much you need your rest."

Silence.

"I'm sure you're used to having a woman in bed with you. It doesn't mean a thing."

More silence.

"It's different with me, though. I've never wanted to go to bed with another man. Only you. Only you, Chad. I've been waiting years for you. I used to lie in bed at night and try to imagine what you looked like, but I never could. Now I know. I can see your muscular body, your strong, handsome features, I can feel your soft, thick hair through my fingers, and smell the tangy scent of your after-shave. I can feel your—"

"Why are you doing this?"

"What do you mean? Loving you?"

"Are you trying to make me lose my sanity?"

"Of course not. I love you, Chad."

"You don't know what you're talking about."

"Oh, but I do. You've given me a chance to come to terms with the Chad I grew up with, and the man I've known as my boss for five years. I no longer glamorize you, Chad. But that doesn't mean I love you any less."

"I'm not interested in a physical relationship with you."

"Oh? You really surprise me, Chad. As long as I've worked for you, I would never have guessed you preferred—"

"Damn it, Sunshine, you know better than that."

"You really had me fooled, you know. The way you kissed me, the way you touched and caressed me—"

"It's a good thing you aren't here right now, you know. I would show you my sexual preferences fast enough!"

She grinned. "Is that an offer? Give me your address and I'll be right there. Wait, I'll get a pencil." She lay there quietly, waiting for a response.

"Don't bother. I am not going to give you my address. You are not coming over here. You are going to leave me alone, do you understand me?"

"Very well. You come in very loud and clear. Can you hear me all right?"

She could feel his frustration, irritation and thwarted sexual desires all tangled in a whirlwind of emotion. The cool, unflappable C. W. Cameron might be able to hide behind that calm facade with everyone else, but he had given her an open pathway to his heart when she was too young to appreciate what he offered. Now there was no way he could close her out.

"Sunshine...I'm tired. I've had less than four hours' sleep in the past fifty-six hours. I'm beat. Will you please just go away and leave me alone?"

"Of course I will, love. Why don't you turn over on your stomach and relax. Just pretend that I'm there massaging the tense muscles in your back and shoulders. Feel my fingers glide over those muscles, and smooth away all of the aches. Feel my—"

"Jennifer Chisholm, that's enough!"

She lay there quietly in bed, grinning from ear to ear. After a few moments she heard, *"Sunshine?"*

Jennifer didn't answer.

After several more minutes went by, he said, *"Sunshine, I'm sorry. I don't want to hurt your feelings. I just want to be left alone, okay?"*

Jennifer turned over and snuggled into her pillows. Not bad for the first night's work.

She was on the phone when C. W. Cameron walked in the next morning. Without looking up at him she handed him three calls that had already come in for him, while she continued to speak into the phone.

When she hung up, Jennifer went back to the coffeepot

and got two cups of coffee. Without saying anything, she placed one of them in front of him and sat down in the chair across from his desk.

He glanced up from the mail in front of him.

"Did you sleep all right last night?" she asked.

"No, thanks to you," he muttered.

Jennifer was delighted. That was the first time in the office that he had allowed their two separate lives to come together. It was a start.

Over the next several weeks Jennifer set up a loose schedule of contact with him. When he was out of town she would idly let him know when she went out with friends after work. He didn't need to know how many were in the group. If he thought she was on a date while she commented on what was happening around her, that was his choice.

Her purpose was to let him know that she wasn't wasting away without him; that she had a full and busy life and that she was happy with her environment. At the same time she let him know she missed him and wished he were there to share some of those good times with her.

He never responded.

Jennifer refused to become disheartened. She couldn't expect to break a twenty-year habit in a couple of months. Time was on her side. Actually, she knew that whether or not he would admit it, Chad was on her side, too.

It wasn't that he didn't love her. He was afraid of the commitment. Nothing new about that. Almost every magazine she picked up had an article or two about men and women who were afraid to make a commitment. She could understand and appreciate where they were coming from. If she hadn't grown up with Chad in her life, she would no doubt feel the same way. But because of Chad, her life was different.

Her commitment was made. That commitment had begun years ago when a teenage boy reached out to her in her loneliness and sorrow and tried to ease her pain.

Now it was her turn to reach out and ease his loneliness and sorrow.

He'd been back home from one of his trips two days when she sent him a message late one night. Jennifer was lying in bed and had been thinking about him. Focusing her thoughts to project to him, she said, "I wonder what it's like to sleep with someone, to actually share a bed. Are you used to sleeping with anyone, Chad?"

"What sort of crazy question is that?" was his immediate response.

Good. Many times he ignored her. She must have gotten under his skin with that one.

"That's not crazy. You're thirty-seven years old. I'm sure you haven't spent all that time in bed alone."

"You might be surprised."

"I lie here at night and pretend you're here with me, but since I'm not sure whether you're used to sleeping on your back or your stomach, or whether you'd curl up to my back or perhaps I'd curl up to yours..."

No response, but she felt his reaction, knew he was visualizing them together.

"I don't think I'd want to sleep in anything. Not with you here to keep me warm. You certainly do have a way of doing that. Every time you've kissed me my temperature has gone up a few notches. I can just imagine what it would be like for your hands to touch and explore me, to—"

She felt a very heated response, but no words.

"Good night, Chad. Pleasant dreams."

Actually Jennifer had discovered that her plan had somewhat backfired. She was finding that her sleep was filled with dreams of Chad and some of the books she had read came to life with her and Chad as eager participants.

She would wake up and find herself trembling, oftentimes aching with need. The mind and the imagination
were the most erotic part of the body. Jennifer had absolutely no doubts on that subject.

And she wasn't going to be able to continue the torture
she was putting them both through. After one particularly
graphic evening, Jennifer ended up crawling into a cold
shower for several minutes before going to sleep.

So much for trying to use their unique communication
abilities to convince him they belonged together.

To make matters worse, once she managed to fall asleep
she had slept so heavily she did not hear her alarm go off.
Eventually Sam was able to get her awake by tromping up
and down her back and meowing until she opened her eyes
and saw the time. There was no way she could make it to
work on time.

C. W. Cameron was already at his desk, with his cup
of coffee, talking on the phone when she came in. That
was the first time since she'd been working there that he
had beat her in. Of course it was also the first morning she
had been late.

He glanced up when she walked into her office, nodded
and continued to talk while she hastily put her purse away
and sat down. The mail was piled high on her desk and
she automatically started sorting it, wishing she'd taken
the time to swallow a couple of aspirin tablets before she
left home.

Jennifer felt defeated. She had been so hopeful that in
some way she would reach the stubborn, lovable, opinion-
ated, tenderhearted, irritable, adorable man she loved.
However, at the moment she was at a loss as to what to
do. Nothing worked.

For the first time Jennifer faced the fact that she might
need to quit her job. If she accepted that there would never

be anything more between her and Chad than their working relationship, she wasn't sure she could continue.

Jennifer heard her employer hang up the phone but she didn't look up. When he suddenly spoke in front of her, she jumped.

"Leave that and get your purse."

The words were quiet but there was no doubt in her mind that he meant every word. She looked up at him, horrified. Granted, she had been considering leaving the agency, but she needed time to find other employment. Besides, how could he even consider firing her for being late, when it was the first time in all her years of working there?

His expression gave nothing away.

Are you firing me? she thought in a rush.

"No," was the equally quiet answer.

Jennifer got up and reached for her purse. He held out his hand as though for her to precede him. They paused at the receptionist's desk. "Ms. Chisholm and I will be out for the rest of the day. Please take our calls and tell whoever asks that we'll both be in on Monday."

The look of astonishment on the receptionist's face probably mirrored Jennifer's own expression. Chad had never before asked her to go anywhere with him. As a matter of fact, he hadn't asked now.

Trying to keep up with his long stride, she hurried beside him. When he noticed that she was almost running to keep up with him, he slowed his pace somewhat and politely took hold of her elbow. They stopped beside his car.

The sporty lines of his Nissan did not look in any way damaged, she thought as he unlocked the door, then held it open for her.

Jennifer settled in, made sure her safety belt was fastened and waited for him to explain where they were going. And waited. And waited.

When he pulled into the airport she glanced at him in alarm. "Are you going out of town again?"

He waited until she had gotten out of the car, made sure both doors were locked, then took her elbow once again, motioning her toward the terminal. "*We* are going out of town."

"But where?" She glanced down at the neat suit she wore. "I don't have anything to take with me."

"You won't need anything," he assured her blandly.

He kept walking past the ticket counters and toward the gates. They went through the security check in silence. When he stopped at one of the gates and gave his name she heard the announcement of the last call for the flight leaving for Las Vegas, Nevada.

Once again he ushered her through the gate and down the passageway to the plane. He gave their boarding passes to a smiling steward, who pointed out their seats. After making sure she was strapped in, he pulled some papers out of his inside coat pocket, unfolded them and began to read.

"Is Tony still having problems?"

He continued to read for a moment, then reluctantly raised his gaze to meet hers. "Not that I am aware of."

Clearly he wasn't in the mood to talk. Well, quite frankly, neither was she. Her head was pounding, her heart was racing, and she didn't understand what was going on.

They were already in the air before Jennifer realized this was her first flight. She'd been too confused and mystified to give it much thought.

Since Chad had given her the seat by the window, she spent most of her time looking out. Jennifer was determined not to give him the satisfaction of pleading to know what was going on. He paid her salary. If he decided to take her away from the office on one of their busiest days, she supposed that was his business.

Forcing her mind to quieten, Jennifer continued to stare out the window until she fell asleep. She woke up as they were making their final approach to land. Now she had plenty of time to worry about how well the pilot knew how to fly, if all the mechanics had been alert when they checked over the plane, and if anyone would think to notify her mother if something happened to her.

Chad obviously knew his way around an airport. Within minutes he had stopped to pick up the keys to a rental car and they were quickly outside.

The weather was much nicer in late October, Jennifer noted with something like relief. She started to make a comment along those lines to Chad when she caught a glimpse of his face. The aloof, thoughtful expression did not remind her of a man who was interested in passing the time by discussing the weather.

Jennifer waited to see where they were going.

Her first surprise was that they didn't go on the Strip. So they weren't going to see Tony, she decided. Her second surprise was when they parked near a very official building downtown and Chad escorted her into the courthouse and down the hall to the license bureau.

Her knees almost buckled when he explained to the clerk that they were there to get a marriage license.

Chapter Nine

The normal busy office sounds of the license bureau made a soothing background for Jennifer's thoughts, which could best be described as chaotic. She had assumed that the reason for their trip had something to do with the agency. By the time she could find some order to her thoughts, the clerk was asking rapid questions.

Jennifer answered them in a daze. Chad's composed answers further rattled her. After the money was handed over, Chad took the license and escorted her from the room. By the time they reached the hallway Jennifer had managed to find her tongue.

"Chad, wait!"

He looked down at her with no discernible expression and waited.

"We need to talk about this. I mean, you never—I didn't expect—We haven't—"

He held up his hand like a traffic cop at a school crossing. "You don't have to marry me if you don't want to, Jennifer. No one is forcing you. If you'd like, we can catch the next plane back to L.A. and—"

"I do want to marry you, it's just that—"

He took her arm and began propelling her down the corridor. "Then we shouldn't keep the judge waiting. He only has a few minutes between court hearings."

When she came out of the courthouse some time later, Jennifer felt as though she couldn't get enough air in her lungs. She felt as she had as a child when she had ridden the carousel—no matter how tightly she hung on, they were going around so fast she could scarcely catch her breath.

Once again they got into the car, only to drive a few short blocks. They pulled up in front of the Golden Nugget casino and hotel. The marble and gold trim glistened in the sun. She looked at Chad in total bewilderment. He assisted her from the car and handed the keys to the waiting attendant.

Once inside Jennifer stared around the lobby in awe. The place looked like her idea of a palace. Chad had gone over to the reservation desk, where he signed in and was handed a room key.

He took her arm and escorted her to the elevator.

When they reached their floor and started down the hallway Jennifer began to fully realize what had just happened. She and Chad were now married, and like any eager bridegroom he was rushing her to a hotel room.

Chad, rushing to get her in bed?

She glanced up at him but as usual could read nothing from his expression.

Chad? Not by a flicker of an eyelash did he betray that he heard her. Instead, he opened the door and motioned for her to precede him. The room was large and exquisitely decorated. Jennifer walked over to the window and peeked out. She heard the door close with a soft but definite thud and turned around.

Chad shoved the bolt through the door, then turned

around. He reached up and began to loosen his tie as he slowly and deliberately paced toward her.

"Now, then. You may have to help refresh my memory as to what it is you want me to do to you." His coat came off and was tossed onto a chair. His tie soon followed and he started on the buttons of his shirt. "I believe the first thing was for us to be without any clothes, in the daylight, with no covers...so we could enjoy the sight of each other."

Jennifer felt a sudden need to retreat. Unfortunately her position by the windows precluded that, unless she wanted to be so undignified as to try to crawl out the window. With her luck, it was probably sealed. She put up her hands in a calming gesture. "W-wait a minute, Chad. I think we should talk about this."

"Talk? Haven't we done enough of that over the past...how many weeks has it been now? I can't remember when my sleep started to become interrupted with graphic descriptions of what you and I should do in bed together." He sat down on the side of the bed and quickly removed his socks and shoes. Standing once again, he unfastened his belt, unzipped his trousers and stepped out of them.

Jennifer could only stare at the man in front of her. Of course she had seen men stripped down to the barest of essentials. She'd been raised in Southern California, after all, and had spent much of her youth on the beach. But she had never seen C. W. Cameron in that condition. He could easily have caused quite a commotion on any beach.

Once stripped of the civilized clothing, Chad looked like a warrior. There wasn't an ounce of unwanted flesh on him. His broad shoulders and chest rippled with well-trained muscles. The navy-blue briefs he wore couldn't disguise his masculinity nor the well-developed muscles in his thighs.

Jennifer could only stare at him.

Barefoot, he padded over to her, reminiscent of some jungle cat silently stalking its prey. She took a deep breath and tried to release her tension along with the air. The exercise had worked in her aerobics class. She was willing to try anything at this point.

He paused in front of her, then began to systematically remove her clothes. Her hands came up to stop him.

"Is there something wrong?" he asked blandly.

"I just think we need to—"

"So do I. But it's more fun not to have clothes in the way."

"I mean, I think—"

"Ah, but this isn't the time to think, Sunshine. This is the time to feel, to enjoy, to experience." He tilted his head slightly, looking for the fastener on her skirt. He smiled when he found it and watched with enjoyment as her skirt fell to her ankles, leaving her standing in her teddy, hose and heels.

"Not bad at all," he commented. "I should have remembered my camera." He shrugged. "Can't remember everything, I suppose."

He took her by the hand and led her to the bed. Gently pushing, he lowered her to the bed and began to remove her hose.

Jennifer pushed his hand away. "I'll do it!" She removed her shoes and hose and she sat there, staring at Chad with something close to fear on her face.

Reaching behind her, he pulled down the covers to the bottom of the bed. Then he scooped her up and laid her on one of the pillows.

Chad stretched out beside her, turned on his side so that he faced her and propped himself up on his elbow.

"Now, then, it looks to me as if we still have on too many clothes, but I suppose they will take care of themselves."

Jennifer had always thought the teddy she wore to b feminine and dainty. She had never noticed how little th lace bodice actually concealed. There was more flesh tha lace.

The same with the bottom half. Cut high on her thigh the silk and lace did more revealing than concealing. Sh must have leaped several inches when Chad rested hi large hand on her abdomen.

"Why don't you just relax now? This is what you'v been dreaming of and talking about for weeks now. Lik Cinderella, your dreams are now coming true."

"Uh, Chad, before we go any further—"

He jackknifed up in bed. "You're absolutely right. just isn't the same, is it? You kept insisting we would d this without any clothes." He reached over and slipped th tiny straps of her teddy off her shoulders and quickl pulled it down over her waist and thighs, knees and ankle

Jennifer frantically felt around for the covers.

"No, no. None of that now," he said, smoothly slidin his briefs off his hips.

Jennifer quickly averted her eyes from his body. He gaze met his and she saw the heated look of desire shinin from his eyes. She blinked. He might be making a gam of this, but there was no mistaking that his intentions wer serious.

Closing her eyes, Jennifer tried to think, but it was n use. He was too close. She could feel his heated bod brushing against her, smell that tangy after-shave that wore, and when he leaned over and lightly touched his lip to her, she could still taste the flavor of his favorite mint

This, then, was exactly what she had fantasized all thes weeks. With her eyes still closed Jennifer tentative reached out and touched his face, her palm resting on h cheek. He quickly turned his head and placed a kiss in h palm.

She slid her hand up through his hair. Jennifer loved the
el of his hair—the clean crispness that still had a faint
ent of the herbal shampoo he used. Blindly she lifted her
outh to his. He accepted her offering with a gentleness
at eased the constriction that had been in her chest since
e had first awakened that morning.

This was Chad—Chad who had spent a lifetime teasing
d provoking her, Chad who knew her better than anyone
se in the world, Chad who had taught her so much—
ho was about to take the next step in her education.

Somehow his knee seemed to belong there between her
ighs. It rested very comfortably there, and Jennifer be-
me used to its solid weight pressing her gently into the
ft mattress.

There was so much she wanted to learn about him. Jen-
fer began to trace the line of his shoulders and arms with
r fingertips, barely grazing the surface. She felt a chill
n over his skin where she had touched. She smiled.

Later her fingers tangled in the soft hair on his chest,
d she explored the path of curls as they nestled entic-
gly around his nipples. Feeling bold and venturesome,
nnifer placed her lips on one of his nipples and felt the
lt to his body.

Following the path of hair on his chest, she noted that
narrowed at his waist and swirled around his navel. She
uched her tongue lightly to the slight indentation there
d once again felt his body respond.

She continued her exploration by running her fingertips
wn his thighs, feeling the hard muscles lightly covered
a dusting of blond hair. He had such a beautiful body.
e felt as though she had been invited to feast at a sump-
us banquet and wasn't sure where to start.

Before she could decide, Chad seemed to have other
as. He pulled her back down beside him and he began
kiss her—long, mind-drugging, consciousness-removing

kisses. No longer tentative, they made a claim on her
coaxing and beguiling her to follow his lead.

Jennifer idly noted that her arms were wrapped tightl
around his neck, holding him as securely as he held he
Her hands could not stay still. They roamed restlessl
across his broad shoulders, following the slight indentatio
of his spine as it made its way down his back. He fe
wonderful.

When Chad's mouth finally slipped away from her
Jennifer drew in some much needed air. She felt as thoug
she were about to faint from excitement. Then she discov
ered why his mouth had slowly made a path of kisse
down her neck. He was inching closer to her breast, whic
was cupped in his large hand.

His tongue darted out and touched the pink tip, causin
it to contract and harden. Then his lips slowly surrounde
it. Jennifer had never felt such a sensation in her life. He
whole body seemed somehow to be connected with tha
small, dainty tip. She felt an inner tugging, deep inside, a
though a dam had been opened, and moist, hot sensatior
leaped and swirled in her depths. Her bones and muscle
seemed to liquefy, and she had a sudden picture of hersel
lying on the bed beside Chad, turned into melted honey.

Taking his time, Chad eventually moved slightly so tha
his mouth could taste the other breast. His fingers lightl
played with the tip of the one he'd just abandoned a
though to soothe it while he was gone.

Jennifer discovered she was gasping as though ther
weren't enough oxygen in the room. Her skin seemed t
have a life all its own as it rippled under his touch.

Time and place seemed to disappear. They had drifte
into an uncharted world with no landmarks for Jennifer t
grasp and identify. Surprisingly enough, she wasn't afrai
because Chad was right there with her, every step of th
way. He led her, yet he never rushed. He introduced he

new sensations, but never coerced. And by the time he lifted his weight so that he was above her, Chad filled her vision and her mind with his presence.

Here was the culmination of everything she had hoped for, everything she had dreamed of. Chad was offering his love, his very being to her.

She accepted his gift as she accepted his body, so that they could share this ultimate union—the one final but necessary step to complete all that they were to each other.

Jennifer realized that they had shared this ecstasy before, many times—the intermingling of their thoughts and feelings and their love. Only now they were allowing their bodies to express themselves in a similar fashion.

The act of love. What an appropriate name for such a beautiful commingling of bodies, minds and spirits. To be able to express oneself in this most intimate of ways seemed to be the ultimate blessing given to human beings. They became one in the most literal sense of the word; whole, complete and perfect in their union.

Jennifer didn't remember falling asleep, but when she woke up hours later the room was dark and the covers were pulled up around them both.

She lay in the curl of Chad's body, while his arm and leg effectively held her closely to his side. Well, that answered another question about how they would sleep, Jennifer decided with a grin.

There was no reason to get up, although she recognized that she was a little hungry. Chad slept heavily beside her. Her mind flitted back over the past several hours. She still couldn't believe it. She and Chad were married. She was now Jennifer Cameron. Mrs. C. W. Cameron.

Of course Chad wasn't his real name. She had seen his legal signature many times. Charles Winston Cameron. He would always be Chad to her.

Jennifer wondered what all of this would mean when

they returned to Los Angeles. They had never talked about
marriage before. She had no idea where he lived, nor if he
had family living. She knew his father was dead. Did he
have any brothers or sisters?

Her eyes widened when she thought about her mother.
Although they talked on the phone on a regular basis, she
didn't see her mother as often as she'd like. Now she was
going to have to come up with some way to explain her
sudden marriage to her boss.

That was going to take some fast talking, she knew. Her
mother had been full of questions when Jennifer was first
promoted, no doubt hoping that something might come of
the closer association with an eligible bachelor. Jennifer
had wasted no time in setting her mother straight. Her
description of C. W. Cameron had caused them some hi-
larious moments.

Now she had to find a way to explain to her mother.
She wondered if she could start out with, "Say, Mom, do
you remember my invisible friend, Chad, I used to have
when I was a child? Well, I married him."

Somehow that didn't have the right ring to it. How
about, "Say, Mom. A funny thing happened at the office
the other day. I looked up at cool, aloof Mr. Cameron and
fell madly in love with him. He admitted he felt the same
way, so we—"

Nope. That didn't really get it, either.

Maybe—, "Mom, I met this tall, good-looking stranger
one weekend when I was in Las Vegas. No, Mom, I don't
go to Las Vegas as a rule. Honest, Mom, I'd never been
there before in my life. Really, Mom—" So much for that
idea. She'd never get past the first sentence.

"You know, Mom, love is a funny thing. You never
know when it's going to hit you. It's kind of like a disease.
That's it, an incurable disease. And you look at a person
and see them totally different. Well, one morning when

vent to work I looked up and there was Mr. Cameron and discovered the love of my life.''

The trouble with anything she might say was that no matter how she explained that she had suddenly married er boss she knew her mother would immediately suspect ennifer was on drugs.

She sighed. No doubt she'd come up with something hen the time came. Her eyes drifted shut. She really was red. She couldn't remember the last good night's sleep ne'd had. Jennifer smiled, thinking of the nights she had retended that Chad was curled up to her back, holding er close. Her imagination hadn't been able to come close provoking this sense of total bliss....

The next time Jennifer awoke, she was more aware of had's touch than anything else. He must have awakened ad found her in his arms. His mouth seemed to be quickly nemorizing her body and his hands were doing things to er that must be banned in Boston.

Jennifer responded with the newfound knowledge she'd iscovered about herself—she enjoyed, very much, the hysical side of their relationship. And she was learning omething new all the time.

For the next two and a half days the newlyweds didn't ave their room. Food was delivered and quickly con-med. When they weren't eating or sharing a friendly ower, they were in bed—either asleep or making love. There was very little conversation that weekend.

Chapter Ten

All good things have to end sometime. Jennifer had hear that phrase all of her life, but to tell the truth, she'd neve given it much thought. Since there hadn't been many goo things that had happened to Jennifer, she'd never learne how and when they ended.

Her brief honeymoon was different. If she could hav wrapped the memories and taken them home with her, sh would have, to savor and enjoy over and over dow through the years. Unfortunately, life didn't work that wa

They caught an evening flight back to Los Angeles. Je nifer had long since let go of her need to ask question She was quite content to follow Chad's lead at the m ment. She'd found nothing to complain about so far in h plans. Adopting a wait-and-see attitude was not only di ferent for her, but fun as well.

C. W. Cameron had never been one for small talk, s she wasn't surprised that he had little to say to her no He could no longer hide the possessive gleam in his ey when he looked at her. She rather liked that possessiv gleam. Jennifer had a hunch that if she took the time to look in a mirror she'd see a similar gleam looking back at her.

What a weekend. Chad had requested toothbrushes—everything else had been provided by the hotel when they got there. Obviously clothes had not been a problem. They merely put on what they had worn on Friday. Luckily Jennifer had had the foresight to hang up their clothes so that they didn't look too wrinkled.

Her hair had been something of a problem. Without a drier it had dried naturally, allowing the natural wave to have its way. She had managed to subdue it with some pins she had in her purse. Anyone looking at the two of them in their sober suits would assume they were business associates returning from a meeting.

And what a meeting that had been!

Jennifer glanced down at her bare hands. He hadn't given her a ring. When had he had time to get one? She wasn't sure when he'd made up his mind to marry her, but had a hunch it was during the last sleepless night they had both spent when she'd been so explicit in her fantasies.

He had an amazing memory, come to that. He had done everything she had ever suggested in her wildest fantasies, plus some things she had never read about in Masters and Johnson. No wonder he could say he hadn't slept with very many women. When did they have time to sleep?

Jennifer glanced at Chad from the corner of her eye and noted a slight grimness around his mouth. Perhaps it was normally there but she hadn't noticed it during the past two days. His lips had been anything but grim.

After arriving back in Los Angeles Chad guided her to where they had left the car. His experience at airports and in airport parking lots was understandable—and welcome.

Jennifer was curious to know where he intended them to spend the night. She would need to go home and feed

Sam. Poor Sam. She'd also need clothes for work tomorrow. However, he might prefer staying at his place. She would wait and see what he suggested.

However, his suggestion was the last thing she expected.

They pulled into the office parking lot and Chad parked next to her car. For the first time since they left Las Vegas he turned around and looked at her fully. Jennifer felt a sudden premonition that she wasn't going to like what he had to say.

She didn't.

"I'm going out of town early in the morning. I need to go home and pack. I should be back by the end of the week. That should give us time to decide what to do about our marriage."

She stared at him, stricken by the lack of any emotion in his voice. "What do you mean, what we should do about our marriage?"

Chad ran his hand through his hair. "This isn't really the time to discuss it."

"I agree," she said. "We should have discussed it before we got married. However, we didn't, so it looks like now is the time."

Chad leaned his arms on the steering wheel and rested his chin on them. She'd never noticed his profile before. The clean, strong lines intrigued her. This man of the many different personalities intrigued her. If she ever figured him out, she would probably be able to write a book about him. There was no one else around like him.

"You made me angry," he finally admitted to the windshield.

She thought about that for a moment. "So you married me as punishment?" she asked.

"You have been slowly driving me out of my mind for months with your lovemaking fantasies. I couldn't take them anymore."

Jennifer didn't know what to say. She sat there, staring at him.

"You've been a part of my life for too long, Sunshine. I couldn't take advantage of you. I knew exactly how you felt about sex and lovemaking. And why not? I helped to instill those values in you. Yet you had pushed me past my limit of tolerance. So I married you. I didn't feel I had a choice."

"You married me so you wouldn't feel guilty about making love to me?"

"Yes."

"I see."

"But I don't like being manipulated. Nobody does. You took something special that we shared, something so unique that I have never been able to explain it in words, and used it against me. Okay. You won. I'm not sure what it was you wanted but if it was to make me want you so much that I never seemed to be able to get over aching for you, then you accomplished what you set out to do."

He never looked at her. His entire conversation was directed to the windshield in front of him. She might not even have been in the car with him for all the notice he gave her.

"I decided to solve both our problems. By marrying you, I felt it was acceptable for me to make love to you, something you have obviously been determined to have happen."

"But you don't want to be married to me."

For the first time he looked around at her. "If you would stop and think about it, I don't lead a life that is conducive to marital harmony. I'm gone more often than I'm here. I put in long hours at the office. I don't have the time nor the energy to work on a relationship...with you, or anyone else."

As far as that was concerned, Jennifer hadn't given

much thought to marriage, either. She enjoyed her life, her freedom and her ability to do whatever she wanted.

"Why does marriage have to change anything?" she asked in what she hoped was a reasonable tone of voice.

"It just does, that's all."

"It doesn't have to. Look at it this way. Nothing that we like about our lives has to change. You travel, I have my time to myself. But when you're home, we're together. What's wrong with that?"

He thought about her suggestion for a few moments. "What about children?"

"You made very sure that we were protected this weekend. I think that's a choice we can make. Who knows? Maybe you'll get tired of traveling one of these days. Stranger things have happened, you know."

He shook his head. "I think we need some time to think about it. I'll see you later on this week."

So she was dismissed, just like that. Jennifer got out of his car with all the dignity she could muster. Marriage ceremony or not, she felt that she had just participated in a wild, weekend fling that he regretted now that it was over.

She wasn't sure how she felt at this point. There was a blessed numbness that seemed to have wrapped around her.

Without saying another word, she got into her car and drove away.

This time Sam didn't let her off the hook for going away and leaving him alone. He had run out of food, although there was still some water left. As far as that went, he could go on a diet and it wouldn't hurt him any.

But his angry greeting seemed to be all Jennifer needed. She closed the door of the apartment, looking around to see that nothing had changed. Not a thing. Only her. She had changed and she knew she would never be the same again.

Chad had been right. She had exerted pressure on him, unfair pressure, to get him to acknowledge how he felt about her. He had acknowledged it, all right. Although he had wanted her physically, he resented her as well. Resented her for using his feelings for her to get what she wanted.

She couldn't blame him, really. She could remember several instances in the past when he had bullied her into doing something she didn't particularly want to do. She had resented his interference.

Now he felt the same way toward her.

Jennifer lay awake that night for hours, staring at the ceiling, thinking of everything that had happened. She had been on an emotional roller coaster these past few days. She tried to decide her best course of action, but nothing seemed suitable.

She was married to the man of her dreams, to her very secret lover, and he felt that she had trapped him into the relationship. In the small hours of the morning, Jennifer took a long, hard look at what she had done and was forced to agree with him.

The question was, what could she do about it now?

When Jennifer walked into the office Monday morning nothing had changed. Everyone greeted her as they always did, her desk was stacked with mail, as it always was, and the phone was ringing. Nothing new.

Only she was different. She wasn't the same woman who had walked out Friday morning, mystified as to why her employer had told her to leave with him.

If he wanted to punish her for what she had done, he could have found nothing more fitting than to give her a glimpse of what life would be like living with him, then to close the door.

She looked into his office. His out box was overflowing. He must have put in several hours of work before she arrived last Friday. Going into his office was difficult. It was so much a part of him and reflected his personality—organized, neat—and like her, waiting for his return.

By noon Jennifer knew she would have to talk to someone or go crazy. She called her mother and suggested dinner that night. Her mother was delighted.

"Mom, I have something to tell you that I know you're going to find hard to believe," Jennifer said that evening, over coffee.

They had enjoyed a leisurely meal at one of her favorite restaurants near where her mother lived.

Her mother smiled. "Nothing you could say would ever surprise me, Jennie. I have never known anyone with an imagination such as yours. I can remember so many of your stories—" She laughed. "But go ahead, dear." She patted Jennifer's hand. "Tell me."

Great. With a leadoff like that, Jennifer knew her mother would think she had made everything up.

"Mom. Some of this I have known for a long time. Some of it I've slowly found out over the past few months. Please bear with me, because I'd like to take it in sequence."

Jennifer paused, gathered her thoughts. "Do you remember the accident that caused Daddy's death, when two boys..." She began the story. She took her time, telling her the little bit that she could remember from that time. Then she told her all that Tony had shared.

Finally she told her mother how Chad had been able to mentally communicate with her.

Her mother's eyes had grown larger with the telling. But she had not interrupted Jennifer. Not once.

Jennifer continued the story through her growing-up years, and how she and Chad had finally lost touch with each other. Or so she thought.

"A couple of months ago I accidentally found out who Chad was."

Her mother looked confused. "I thought you said you knew. He was the young boy who—"

"No, I mean who he is now."

A tiny crease appeared between her mother's brows. "And who is that, my dear?"

"My boss, C. W. Cameron."

Her mother stared at her in astonishment. "I don't believe it. That cold, callous, arrogant man—"

Jennifer grinned at the description her mother had gained from the many stories Jennifer had told her. "That's right, Mom. The same man."

"But you describe Chad as so warm and loving, so very caring."

"He is."

"How could one man be so different?"

"I've given considerable thought to that over the past few months. I believe that the Chad I knew felt free to express himself. There were no conditions placed on him, no expectations of a certain behavior, no need to prove anything to anyone. In the fullest sense of the word, he allowed his inner self, his very essence, to unfurl and grow without hindrance."

Jennifer leaned back in her chair and sipped on her coffee. "I don't know the whole story, but from what I have learned through the office grapevine, Chad's father was a ruthless sort of a man, very demanding, who insisted on perfection from everyone around him, and considered that he gave nothing but the best, as well." She set her cup down and idly toyed with the handle. "I've tried to picture what Chad's young life was like. I have no idea who else was in his family, but obviously his father expected him to follow in his footsteps. So Chad did. He bottled all of his softer emotions away so that nobody ever saw them."

"Except you," her mother murmured.

They sat there quietly together, thinking about the young Chad Cameron and the conflicts he must have had to master.

"The only real coincidence in the story is that I went to work for Chad's company. That isn't as much of a coincidence as you might think, since the secretarial school I attended was only a few blocks away and the agency was always looking for stenographers. I understand the Camerons, both father and son, were difficult to work for, and they had a high turnover of personnel."

"I thought you said that changed, after you came to work."

"It did, and I'm beginning to understand why. Somehow I became a buffer between Chad and the rest of the staff. I was the one who caught most of the flak, and I could take it. At least most of the time. As he became accustomed to working with me, he calmed down."

"It probably didn't hurt that you were his childhood friend."

Jennifer grinned. "Good point. I hadn't really thought about that. But maybe he knew me so well he didn't need to intimidate or browbeat me into doing what needed to be done."

"As I recall, he did enough of that anyway."

"I know. I often look back and wonder why I stayed with him. He used to make me so angry!"

"I never could understand that, myself. You used to call me in tears. Whenever I suggested you quit, you said you didn't want to admit he could get the best of you."

They looked at each other. "I still don't, Mom, which brings us to the rest of the story, as they say."

"You mean, there's more? You know, this beats some of the wildest stories you used to tell as a child. I don't think even you have imagination enough to have dreamed up all of this."

"Just wait, Mom. You haven't heard everything. You see, last Friday, my boss, Mr. C. W. Cameron, and I flew to Las Vegas and were married."

Jennifer's mother looked as though a bucket of ice water had just been tossed in her face. She sat there staring at her daughter, her mouth slightly open.

Jennifer nodded. "I know, Mom. Unbelievable."

"But you never hinted, never by a word, that anything was going on between you."

"There wasn't, at least not in the way you mean. You see once I found out that Chad and C.W. were one and the same, I began to spot the similarities. He tried his best to keep the two personalities separate. But I started treating him differently in the office. I talked to him the same way we mentally communicated—easy, casually, and with a great deal of warmth."

"What did the people in the office think about your change?"

"Oh, they didn't see it. People avoid him as much as possible in the office, so no one would stick her head in my office whenever he was in town. It's almost comical, really, the lengths people will go to to avoid him."

"Well, what do they think now? Were they surprised to hear you're married to him?"

"Nobody knows."

"Aahh. That makes sense. He wants to keep it a secret."

"I have no idea what Chad wants, Mom. That's why I'm here telling you all of this. You see, he brought me back from Las Vegas after the most beautiful weekend, dropped me off at my car, told me he would be out of town all this week and he'd see me later.''

Jennifer's mother choked slightly on her water. Coughing, she waved away her daughter's help and eventually exclaimed, ''The man has to be the most insensitive, irritating, boorish oaf I've ever heard of.''

''That's one explanation. There might be others.''

''Name one.''

''I was a little underhanded in my attempts to get him to spend more time with me.''

''In what way?''

''Let's just say that I used our unique manner of communication to help him visualize some of the delightful ways we could spend our evenings, and nights, together.''

''Jennifer Chisholm! You didn't!''

''I'm afraid so, Mom. I can't say that I'm particularly pleased with my tactics, but they did provide some results. Not exactly what I had in mind, though.''

''Are you saying you were hoping for an affair with him?''

The way her mother said that caused Jennifer to bite her lip to keep from smiling. Her mother's words were spoken in a tone that indicated how hard she was trying to make an affair seem like an everyday occurrence. But Jennifer knew for a fact that her mother had shown no interest in a man since she'd lost her husband.

''I'm not sure what I was hoping for, to be honest. I hadn't given any long-range thought to what effect I was having on him and how he would handle it.''

Her mother sat back and studied her for a moment in silence. Then she smiled. ''So you're married, are you?''

She nodded. ''It looks that way, doesn't it?''

''What do you intend to do about it?''

''Fight for my marriage. What else?''

''Do you have any idea how?''

"No. I'm open to suggestions."

Jennifer's mother gathered up her purse and stood up. "Well, let's go home and see what we can do. At least you can't say you don't know the man. Surely with all that knowledge, you can figure out what to do to convince him the two of you belong together."

Jennifer followed her mother from the restaurant, a sense of expectancy invading her being. Somehow, someway, she had to convince C. W. Cameron that he had made the best decision in his life when he married her.

Chapter Eleven

"Chad?"

"?"

"Are you awake?"

"Just barely. What is it?"

Jennifer lay on her side in bed, Sam sprawled out beside her. She had been in bed for almost an hour, since eleven, and was unable to sleep.

"Nothing, really. I was just thinking of you, wondering if you were all right."

"Are you?"

She felt his concern. So he had been thinking of her. Three days had gone by since she had seen him. And three nights. Jennifer had discovered how quickly a person can become used to new experiences. She missed Chad in bed with her, holding her, loving her. She missed his presence.

"I miss you," she responded.

"I've got the same problem," he admitted.

"I had no idea being together could be so wonderful."

He didn't say anything for a moment. Then he said, *"I was afraid we might have overdone it a little. We were quite active for it to be your first exposure."*

"Let's just say that I haven't been in the mood to go to the club and work out since we got home." After a few moments of silence, she said, "Do you know yet when you'll be back?"

"No."

She tried for whimsical humor. "You can't stay gone forever, you know. Sooner or later you have to come home."

"I know."

"But you aren't looking forward to it," she offered gently.

"It isn't that. I just feel so—confused, somehow. I can't seem to get my life into any understandable order. All these years I've been in control of my life. Now...now I don't know what to think, what to do, how to evaluate what's happening."

"That's because feelings and emotions aren't that definable. We can't push them into little compartments and expect them to stay there. That's part of being human."

"If all this confusion is part of being human, I think I'll pass."

"And go back to being a robot?"

"Is that what I am?"

"I think that's what you've tried to be. Thank God, it didn't work."

They were quiet for several moments. At least he was communicating with her again, Jennifer was pleased to note. She was afraid their marriage had caused him to push that part of their relationship out of his life.

"Sunshine?"

She smiled at the familiar nickname. "Yes?"

"What are you wearing?"

She glanced down and grinned. "My flannel pajamas with the feet in them."

"?"

"Well, nobody's ever seen me in them but Sam."

"Have you ever thought about an electric blanket?"

"I have one. In fact, I generally keep it set close to broil."

"You didn't get cold while we were in Vegas."

"How could I, with almost two hundred pounds of brawn draped around me."

"One hundred eighty."

"Oh. Well, what's a few pounds here and there?"

"Sunshine?"

"Yes?"

"I know I wasn't fair to you last weekend."

"In what way?"

"I didn't give you a choice."

"Sure you did. Remember, you stopped me in the hallway and asked if—"

"You know what I mean. I never really asked if you wanted to marry me."

"I have never wanted to marry anyone else."

"But I know what you think of C. W. Cameron."

"If I'd had any idea all these years that my boss could read my mind," she teased, "would I have been embarrassed. I called you some pretty rotten names."

"After giving them some thought, most of the time I agreed with you."

"What about the times you didn't agree with me?"

"I waited to see if you were going to simmer down. No one would believe the temper you've got, just to see you and work around you. You keep it very well hidden."

"You've got the same abilities, you know."

"I'm afraid not. My temper seems to be legendary."

"I don't mean that. You have the ability to hide your

softer side, the Chad side that I love so much, from the outside world.''

"There isn't much call for him in the business world, I'm afraid."

"Perhaps not. But you don't have to think about business all the time. There are times for tenderness and love, for caring and comforting.''

"Not in my life."

"Of course in your life. You've done it for years. With me.''

"Oh, that."

"Yes, that.''

"But you're different."

"No. *You* are different when you're with me. But you don't seem to want to show it except in these conversations—and last weekend.''

"You mean I wasn't C. W. Cameron last weekend?"

"You were all that you could be, Chad. All your marvelous attributes and your loving disposition revealed themselves. If you gave yourself a chance, you could be that way more often.''

"If we spent all of our time together like that, the office would fall apart."

"I don't mean in bed. I mean relaxed, and friendly. We could joke and talk in the office the same way we did over dinner, or in the shower.''

"Now that might prove very interesting. I wonder what the staff would think?"

"You know what I mean. Don't be afraid to let your emotions show, Chad. There's nothing to be afraid of.''

He was quiet for several minutes. Then he said, *"I'm not sure I could ever do that, Sunshine."*

"It doesn't matter to me, Chad, because I already know they're there. But it might make a difference for you.''

After a while, he said, *"Good night, Sunshine."*

''Good night, Chad.''

She felt his love wrap around her and she smiled as she drifted off to sleep.

By ten o'clock Friday morning the office was in an uproar. Phones were ringing, people were having trouble with office equipment, and Jennifer was ready to storm out screaming.

Part of her problem was that she hadn't heard any more from Chad. She hesitated to be the one who always contacted him, so she had waited, but there had been nothing. That had never bothered her in the past, but things were different now. Or at least she hoped so.

Was he getting used to the idea that he now had a wife to return to?

The office intercom buzzed and when Jennifer answered the receptionist asked, ''Is there by any chance a full moon?''

Jennifer laughed. ''I'm not sure. Why?''

''Oh, everything's so crazy around here. Some of the questions I've been getting. I think some people think this office is run like Mike Hammer's.''

Jennifer grinned. ''We should be so lucky.''

''Well, actually, Mr. Cameron isn't bad, if he'd just unbend a little.'' There was a buzz in the background. ''Got another call. See ya.''

Jennifer shook her head, smiling. She wondered if Chad would like being compared with Mike Hammer? If only people knew how tedious investigative work was. Except for a few unusual incidents like the time when Chad got abandoned in a hunting cabin in southern Utah, it could be rather boring. She was smiling when she answered the phone.

''Mr. Cameron's office. May I help you?''

''Ms. Chisholm?'' She recognized his voice immediately. So. No matter what he might communicate to her privately, he was still going to be formal around the office.

Maybe it *was* a full moon, because she replied, "No, I'm sorry. Ms. Chisholm is no longer employed by this firm." She paused a beat and said in her most honeyed tones, "This is Mrs. Cameron, Mrs. Charles Winston Cameron. May I help you?"

The long distance wires hummed while she waited for a reply. "Jennifer?" he finally asked.

"Yes?" She kept her voice pleasant and very businesslike.

"Are you going by that name now?"

"I have a piece of paper, duly recorded, stating that to be my correct and legal name."

"I know. I just didn't realize you'd be using it around the office."

"I was forced to do so, sir, in order to stop all those nasty, vicious rumors going around about you."

"What rumors?"

"Those slurs on your manhood, sir. There has been talk about the possibility you weren't interested in women."

"What?" he yelped.

"Don't worry, sir," she said in a soothing voice. "I have certainly put paid to any such nonsensical remarks. I explained, in great and explicit detail, that after two and a half days of being locked up in a bedroom with you, there was no doubt in my mind as to your manhood." She paused for a couple of seconds and added, "Now, then, sir. How may I help you this morning?"

Jennifer was fascinated to discover that sometimes C. W. Cameron had trouble getting words out. He stumbled once or twice, cleared his throat and managed to say something that sounded like, "You're kidding, of course."

"You mean you don't want me to defend your reputation, sir?"

"You didn't really tell everyone about last weekend, did you?"

"It's nothing to be ashamed of, sir. You should be very proud of yourself. How many thirty-seven-year-old men could—"

"Jennifer!"

"Yes, sir?"

"Would you please stop calling me 'sir.'"

"Yes—What do you want me to call you?"

"What have you called me in the past?"

"Mr. Cameron. However, I refuse to call the man I sleep with by his last name. It smacks of class discrimination during the Edwardian era." She glanced over at his stack of calls. "Was there some particular reason you called? I can read you your messages or summarize the mail, whatever you wish."

Jennifer had the distinct impression that Chad was silently counting to himself. Yes, that was exactly what she picked up on him. So far he had passed twenty and was still climbing. Perhaps that was how he kept that ironclad control of his. He must be a mathematical wizard by now.

"Yes. I'd like to know what mail I have and any urgent messages."

For the next several minutes their conversation was filled with business. He gave her instructions for the other investigators, including the information that he would not be home for another week.

"I thought you said you'd be home in a few days."

"I had planned to. However, I ran into some problems that have caused me to change my plans."

"I see." As a secretary, it made very little difference to her whether he was there or not. She could take instructions in person or by phone. As a wife, it made a considerable amount of difference. Particularly since she was a new wife. A brand-new wife. With no husband in evidence.

Jennifer couldn't help but wonder if his delay had more to do with their new marital relationship than business problems, but she refused to ask. As she had pointed out to him before, he had to come home sometime.

Suddenly C. W. Cameron said something so astounding, she almost dropped the phone. He asked her a personal question. "What are your plans for the weekend?"

In all the years she'd worked for him, he'd never asked such a question. She had finally decided that as far as her employer was concerned she went up in a puff of smoke every Friday afternoon at five, only to reappear bright and early each Monday morning.

Maybe there was hope for them yet.

She didn't want to tell him that she had kept the weekend free just in case he were in town. Thinking quickly, she said, "Oh, I'll probably spend the weekend with Mother. She's always trying to get me to come visit."

"How is your mother?"

She stared at the phone as though he'd slipped into a foreign language. "Mom's fine. I had dinner with her Monday night."

"Oh."

She waited for him to say something else. She sure didn't know how to conduct this particular conversation.

"Did you tell her about us?"

"Yes."

"What did she say?"

"She wondered if she was going to have an invisible son-in-law and if her grandchildren would also carry the curse of invisibility."

"I'm looking forward to meeting her."

"She's looking forward to meeting you, too."

·

There was another pause. "I, uh, need to get to work. I'll talk with you next week."

"Fine. Is there anything else?"

She waited. Finally, in a low voice, he said, "I miss you, Sunshine."

Jennifer had difficulty concentrating on her work for the rest of the day.

"Definitely a good sign," her mother commented that evening. Jennifer and Sam had traveled out to Oceanside. Jennifer and her mother sat in front of the small fireplace, watching the flames while Sam checked out the place. A cat can't be too careful about the places he inhabits. Periodically he would leap up in Jennifer's lap and touch his nose to hers. Satisfied that she was behaving, he would jump down and continue his reconnaissance.

"I thought so," Jennifer agreed. "I don't think Chad consciously chose such a dramatic split in his personality. Little by little, through various circumstances and experiences, he worked out a pattern of survival."

"You know what I really find sad?" her mother asked.

"What's that, Mom?" Jennifer was enjoying some hot apple cider and she took a sip from the cup she held.

"What do you suppose would have happened to the Chad you know if he hadn't discovered how to communicate with you as a little girl? You took him out of himself, gave him someone else to think about, worry about, be concerned over. You've often mentioned how much company he was for you during those years. But what about him?"

Jennifer gave a light shiver. "I hate to think. The C. W. Cameron that we all know and hate would have been all that's left."

"Then he owes you as much gratitude as you owe him."

"Mom, gratitude doesn't come into this. Not when you love each other. Love is so much a sharing, a chance to be who you are, and accepted for who you are. I will never be able to understand how we managed to get together because neither of us has ever known anyone else with whom we could mentally communicate. The odds of our ever meeting were astronomical. And look at the age difference. He's twelve years older than I am. We could never have dated each other while either of us was growing up."

"And by the time you were grown," her mother continued, "and you went to work for him, he would have been too set in his ways to ever open up."

"He may still be, for all I know."

"Yet you're married to him."

"I know. And I'm not sorry. I'm willing to accept him as he is. It's the same as if your loved one was injured and became less than completely whole. He's the same person that you always loved."

"Yes. When your father realized that he was paralyzed, that he would never be able to walk again, he seemed to give up fighting for his life. I tried to make him understand that the important thing to me was that he would still be here with me."

"That's the way I feel about Chad. If we have to keep our lives together totally separated, the formal boss-employee relationship at work, and whatever he's willing to give me away from the office, I'll accept that. Because I know that he will be giving everything he's capable of giving. I can't ask for more than that."

By the time Jennifer arrived home on Sunday evening she felt pleasantly tired and truly relaxed. The visit had gone well. Sam had slain a few invisible dragons, which left him in a very benign mood, and she and her mother had grown closer than ever.

Jennifer felt blessed, even though she recognized that others might view her situation as bizarre, to say the least. She might go through life with a secret lover, while married to a cold, arrogant man in public. Sooner or later Chad had to realize that their marriage was workable because they wanted it to be. It might not be the usual arrangement that others shared, but why should it be? She and Chad were different. Hadn't she known that for years?

To be married to her invisible friend seemed to be enough of a bonus to Jennifer to accept whatever the future might bring.

A new serenity seemed to enfold Jennifer. She went to work the next week with an easy acceptance of her role in life. She kept the office running smoothly while Chad was away. Hopefully when he was back, she could find a way to keep his home life running just as smoothly.

The first thing she noticed when she walked in the door Wednesday morning was that the receptionist gave her a strange look. A very strange look.

Jennifer glanced down to see if she'd accidentally worn mismatched shoes to the office. She'd almost done that once. No. Her navy kid pumps gleamed back at her. As she walked toward her office she surreptitiously checked to see if her slip was showing. How could it? With the longer length in skirts, there was a good six-inch gap between her slip and the hem of her suit.

Shrugging, she walked into her office and stopped.

Her mail was stacked neatly on her desk, where it was always left by the receptionist. Right behind her nameplate. She did a double take.

Her nameplate read, "Jennifer C. Cameron."

Where had that come from? Glancing up she saw an ornate bouquet of red roses, which dwarfed the credenza behind her desk. After absently storing her purse she slid the card from the small white envelope attached to one of the roses and read, ''Thank you for the most wonderful honeymoon a man could ever wish for. All my love, Chad.''

Jennifer glanced around and saw that as many of the staff as could crowd into the area stood in front of the door to her office, watching her.

She turned around and gave them what she felt must be a very sickly smile. ''Good morning, everyone.''

''Good morning, Jennifer,'' came a chorused reply. They continued to stand there, waiting.

Now what was she supposed to do? Everyone's gaze seemed to move between the nameplate and the roses. No one said a word. She wondered if anyone was breathing, it was so quiet.

Chad, how could you do this to me!

She felt his love and amusement swirl around her, and she knew that he was paying her back for what she had said to him on the phone last week.

Where are you? she demanded.

There was no answer.

He could have had all of this done by someone else. In fact, he probably had. Although she felt sure he was wishing he was there to see her face.

''I, uh, you're probably wondering why—'' She waved her hand helplessly at her new name and the flowers.

All heads bobbed in unison. What had they been doing, for crying out loud? Rehearsing?

''Yes, well, I thought that—What I mean to say is, we had felt that perhaps—After all, he's been traveling and—'' She gave up. What was there to say, after all?

Folding her hands primly in front of her, Jennifer announced, ''Mr. Cameron and I were married in Las Vegas two weeks ago.''

Chapter Twelve

By the time Jennifer arrived home Friday evening all she wanted to do was to fall into bed, roll over and play dead.

She had not heard from her mysterious boss and so very secret lover. Which was just as well. She might have shot him. Actually, shooting was too quick and painless. Given enough time and energy, she was sure she could think of some really interesting and long-drawn-out ways to make him suffer.

Their newly announced marriage had created a minor riot at the office. "Too bad you couldn't be there to participate, my darling," she muttered to herself.

Of course everyone was shocked right down to their brightly painted toenails. And why not? There had never been a hint of romance between them. Not even a faint whiff. As a matter of fact, some of the women were embarrassed to remember going to her with complaints about him, only to recall that she had emphatically agreed with them.

And she married him anyway?

How could she explain? Jennifer saw him exactly as they saw him. He was just—most of the time—and fair—most of the time—but had never heard that justice and fairness could be tempered with mercy. More than once she had interceded on an employee's behalf.

But if she was happy, it was obvious they were happy for her. She had accepted their teasing and congratulatory comments with good grace, and tried to get some work done.

The next afternoon she had come back from lunch to discover a surprise shower, complete with cake and streamers, and gifts—all kinds of gifts, from gag to practical.

And poor dear Chad had missed out on all the excitement. Why was it she had a hunch he'd planned it that way?

What with all the added commotion in the office, Jennifer had gotten behind on her work. So she had stayed late tonight to catch up.

Chad hadn't called in during the week. Nor had he contacted her through their more intimate channel. Not that she could blame him. The man showed rare insight as to how she would react to what he had done.

She shook her head as she sank onto the side of the bed.

Well, she had survived, anyway. No doubt that by Monday something else would take precedence over the personal lives of the boss and his assistant. She hoped. In the meantime, Jennifer was going to fill the tub full of hot water and indulge in her favorite ritual of wine, music and relaxation.

By the time she got out, she was too relaxed and at peace with the world to be angry at anyone.

She wasn't really so very angry at Chad, anyway. She

missed him too much to be angry. They had been married two weeks today, and for most of that two weeks they had been separated.

Face it, kiddo, you're going to have a lifetime of that sort of existence, she reminded herself. She could handle that, if she knew a few of the particulars. Was he even going to live with her, or would they continue to keep separate residences?

Obviously, he was going to acknowledge her as his wife. There was no reason to wonder about that any longer.

Jennifer was looking under the cabinet for her small saucepan to heat some soup when the doorbell rang. She glanced down at herself in dismay. Since she wasn't expecting company she was padding around the house in her flannel pajamas. The ones with the feet in them.

She had no idea who could be there. Jennifer hadn't talked to Jerry in months. It couldn't be the paper boy collecting. He'd been by the week before.

She shrugged. When all else fails, answer the door and solve the mystery of the ringing doorbell, she told herself. Somehow that seemed to take all the fun out of the game.

"Just a minute," she called as it rang again. She ran for her bathrobe, the old fuzzy one that her mother had given her several years ago. The sash had pulled a hole in the side, which she fully intended to mend one of these days, and she had spilled hot chocolate down the front, which left a lurid stain, but it was comfortable. And who was she trying to impress, anyway?

Glancing through the security peephole suddenly reminded her of one person she might want to impress. Scrambling to take the chain off, she unlocked the door and opened it.

"I wasn't sure you were home," Chad said, standing in the hallway and looking at her rather uncertainly.

He looked so tired. There were lines in his face and dark circles under his eyes and she wanted to take him in her arms and hold him for at least a century or two for starters.

"Come in," she managed to say, stepping back and waving her arm.

He stepped in and looked around. Jennifer had decorated her apartment with various pieces of furniture that she had liked. Some of them she had refinished. Some still needed work. Bright prints and silk flower arrangements gave color to the room.

She had never looked at it from another person's viewpoint. Jennifer had filled her small home with items that meant something to her, so that old rubbed shoulders with new without much rhyme nor a great deal of reason.

It was home.

She had a sudden attack of stage fright. Jennifer had no idea what sort of home Chad had grown up in, or what his home looked like now. He was getting an idea of the type of place his wife lived in. He could very well turn around and run screaming into the night.

Only he didn't.

He's probably too tired, she thought to herself. "May I take your coat?" she offered politely. He slipped it off his shoulders with a sigh.

"Sit down. Anywhere. Can I get you something to drink?"

She was babbling. This was Chad, for heaven's sake. Her Chad. She'd known him forever. More important, he had known her for the same length of time.

Chad sank down on the sofa and said, "A drink sounds fine."

"Hot? Cold? Alcoholic? Non?"

"Anything."

"Hot coffee, hot chocolate, hot apple cider—"

He glanced up at her, a look of puzzlement on his face. "You're pushing hot these days?"

"That's because it's so cold these days."

"Cold?" He looked at her with surprise. "Fifty is not considered cold."

"It is to me," she responded emphatically.

"Coffee's fine."

She put on the coffee, then went back into the living room. "I just got out of the tub. I wasn't expecting anyone. If you'll excuse me, I'll go and—"

He grinned. "You look fine the way you are. The pigtails are a nice touch. I feel as though I kidnapped and married Buffy."

She'd forgotten that she'd tied her hair back. Hastily undoing the yarn, she finger-combed her hair. "Is that what you think? That you kidnapped me?"

Chad leaned his head back on the couch and closed his eyes. "Didn't I?" he asked wearily.

Cautiously Jennifer sat down beside him. She had never seen him look so tired. Defeated, almost.

"Chad?"

"Hmm?" He didn't open his eyes.

"You don't want to be married to me, do you?" She could feel the pain of the thought going through her like a laser.

Chad opened his eyes and saw her sitting by his side. He lifted his hand and rested it against her cheek. "I want to be married to you more than anything I've ever wanted in my life," he murmured. "I'm just not sure it's the best thing for you."

Jennifer could feel her pulse racing. "Why?"

"You deserve more. I'm so much older, so set in my ways, so used to being on my own."

She leaned closer, so that her mouth was only inches

from his. "None of that really matters, Chad, if you love me and want me."

He pulled her onto his lap and began to kiss her. Between each kiss he said, "I do love you...and I want you constantly. You brought sunshine into my life years ago...you are the greatest thing that ever happened to me." After a thorough, lingering kiss he added, "But I didn't give you a chance to say no."

"Why would I want to say no?" she asked, curling her arms around his neck and burying her head in his neck. "Those fantasies I was sharing with you should have given you some clue regarding my feelings about you."

She could feel him begin to relax beneath her. At least parts of him seemed to be relaxing. Then there were other parts....

Chad slid his hands into her hair and held her face still in front of him. "I missed you so much, Sunshine," he murmured.

"You did?" She was sure he could feel her heart racing.

"Very much."

"Why didn't you call?"

"I was afraid to, afraid to hear your voice. To be honest, I didn't need the distraction, if I was ever going to get finished and get back here to you." He kissed the tip of her nose. "We've got so many years to catch up on."

She nodded. "I know. There's so much I don't know about you, about your family, your friends...."

"You have been my closest friend. Always."

"But why couldn't I pick up on your thoughts the way you always have mine?"

"I wasn't sure you couldn't. I don't know. Maybe it takes practice. There were times when I purposely didn't want you to know what I was thinking. Particularly in the office. I felt as though I put up a mental shield between us, but I was never sure if it worked.''

"Oh, it worked all right. I never had a clue that C. W. Cameron was Chad.''

He hugged her to him, his hands sliding up and down her back. "Are you glad I'm home?''

"I certainly am.'' She leaned away from him slightly and announced, "I intend to kill you.''

He smiled and she noticed that he didn't look quite as tired as he did when he first arrived. "How interesting,'' he drawled. "Hasn't anyone ever pointed out that it makes it tougher when you announce your intentions to the proposed victim?''

"Why did you send that new nameplate and the flowers?''

His smile widened into a mischievous grin. "Didn't you like them?''

"They were beautiful. But you knew what a stir they'd cause.''

"But darling, I was only concerned about your reputation,'' he said, his expression solemn. "After you graphically depicted my sexual preferences in order to save my reputation, I didn't want anyone in the office to get the wrong idea about you. I wanted to be sure they knew that you were, indeed, a 'Sadie, Sadie, Married Lady.'''

"Ah, hah! You've seen *Funny Girl*.''

"A few dozen times, probably.''

"You mean you're a Streisand fan?''

"Isn't everyone?''

"Do you realize what this means?''

"What?''

"Chad! We've finally found something we have in common.''

He began to kiss her under her ear. "I think we've

already discovered a few others things we have in common, don't you?''

Of course he was right. They had shared memories of the past several years, even if he knew more about her than she did about him. The important thing was that he was now willing to share his life with her. He had come to her as soon as he reached town, even though he was obviously tired and in need of rest and—''Oh! Your coffee!'' Jennifer slid off his lap and hurried into the kitchen.

When she came back in carrying a tray she discovered that he had taken off his suit coat, his tie and his shoes, and had rolled up his shirt sleeves to the elbow.

He looked so good sitting there on her couch. She had messed up his hair a little, running her fingers through it, but it made him look more human, and less businesslike. The sizzling gleam in his eye also added to the more human and less business look.

She sat down beside him and handed him his coffee.

He accepted it with a smile that caused her heart to skip. He took a sip and asked, ''So how are things at the office?''

Obviously the office hadn't been on his mind for the past week or he would have called. Either that, or he trusted her enough to handle whatever problems might occur in his absence. In either event, she wasn't going to let him off lightly. ''Funny you should ask.''

''What's that supposed to mean?''

''Well, I'm not sure where to start,'' she said slowly, as though thinking. Tilting her head slightly she continued, ''Should I tell you first about discovering that the bookkeeper has been embezzling our trust funds, or that the receptionist ran off to Australia with your best investigator, or that the fire only destroyed the outer offices?''

She had to give him credit. He made a quick recovery. For a second she thought for sure he was going to spill the coffee down his shirt. Instead, he sat up abruptly and set the cup down.

"You're kidding me," he said, staring at her intently.

She shrugged. "Of course I'm kidding you. What else?"

He leaned toward her slightly. "You mean none of that is true?"

"Weelll, I did notice the receptionist giving Bill the eye the other day. But since he's got five kids already and is old enough to be her father, I kind of doubt he's going to take her up on anything."

He shook his head, and pulled her into his arms again. With deliberate thoroughness he claimed her mouth with his own, as though he couldn't get enough of her. Finally, he pulled away slightly, breathing unsteadily. "How was I ever so lucky to discover you?"

"You know," she said with a mock serious look on her face, "Mother and I were just discussing that very thing last week." She began to smile at the expression on his face. "We've decided you're very fortunate to have found me."

"You know," he said, "I believe you and your mother might have a point there."

Once again he began to kiss her—soft, nipping kisses that caused her toes to curl inside her pajamas. He played with her bottom lip, teasing her with his teeth, then licking away any hurt with his tongue. When she felt him groan, she knew that the teasing was getting to him as much as it was her.

And yet something still bothered her.

She pushed away from him. "Chad?"

"Hmm?"

"We can't just keep doing this."

"Doing what?"

"Falling into each other's arms when you're in town and never talking."

He nodded. "Good point. What do you want to talk about?"

"I need to know—" She stopped, and couldn't seem to go on.

After a few minutes, he prompted, "What?" "What is it you need to know? That I love you?" He nuzzled her neck. "I do. To distraction. That I missed you terribly? That, too." He kissed her once more.

What, indeed, did she need to know? Didn't she know everything that was necessary, after all? He loved her. She loved him. He had sought her out as soon as he got home, not waiting to rest. Obviously he wanted to be with her. Wasn't that enough?

"Nothing, really. I know all I need to know," she acknowledged with a smile, placing her arms around his neck.

He smiled, and she thought her heart would melt. He had the sweetest, most loving smile and he used it so rarely. Whenever he did, it had a very potent effect on her. Talk about a concealed weapon. This man could be downright dangerous to a woman's peace of mind.

Chad stood up, pulling her up beside him. "I have a great idea."

"What's that?"

"Why don't you show me around your apartment?"

She looked around the small area, perplexed. "But this is it. You can see the kitchen from here. The only other thing is the bath and bedro—" She grinned. "Oh. Okay. Why don't I show you the rest of my apartment?"

He nodded. "Good idea. I've never been here before."

"I know. I was surprised you knew where I lived."

"I didn't," he admitted sheepishly. "I had to look it up in your personnel file."

She laughed and took his hand. "All right. For the grand tour I would like to point out the master bedroom suite—Don't stumble over the chair there," she added, "and the adjoining bath." The room still carried the scent of her bath oil. Turning, she said, "Was there anything else?"

"I'm afraid it's too small."

She looked at him blankly.

"For two people," he added helpfully.

"I'm not surprised. I didn't rent it for two people. Sam doesn't take up all that much room."

He glanced around the room. "Ah, yes. Sam. I've been eager to meet him. Where is he?"

She shrugged. "I forgot to mention that he's very shy with people at first. So he's hiding somewhere. As soon as he knows he's safe with you, he'll come out."

"I see. Well, another time, perhaps."

She watched him, a little uncertain of his mood. She had never been around him in this relaxed, teasing mood. Except, of course, for their weekend honeymoon. Even then, he hadn't been this lighthearted. He'd been much more intense, almost desperate with her at times.

He looked down at the knot in the sash of her robe. Absently tugging at it, he said, "I didn't imagine your place would be large enough for two." The knot fell apart and the robe fell open. He slid it off her shoulders and let it drop on the chair by the bed. "My place isn't suitable, either. I've never cared about where I lived. I spend so little time there."

Chad found the small catch of her zipper underneath the collar of her pajamas. He tugged at it and watched with interest as it followed a path between her breasts, past her navel and down until it reached the top of her thighs.

Sliding his hands along her shoulders he eased the one-piece pajamas off her shoulders and arms and the garment fell in a heap around her ankles.

Jennifer stood before him quietly while he gazed at her beauty.

He touched the tip of her breast with one finger and watched it react to him. She could tell that he was not unaffected by his own actions. She had long since given up trying to control her uneven breathing. Her body quivered with every beat of her heart.

Chad leaned down and gently touched his lips first to one breast, then the other. He looked up at her, his eyes shining with love and tenderness and desire. "So I made an appointment with a realtor tomorrow, late tomorrow, to go look at houses. Or if you'd rather check out some condominiums, that's up to you." He pulled her unresisting body against him. "I've decided that I spend entirely too much time traveling. I have two other men who could help balance that load. And if they don't want to do it, I can always hire someone else who wants to travel."

So Chad had given a great deal of thought to their new situation. She should have known. He was a man who made his living solving problems. Their living arrangements had probably been a snap for him.

Jennifer began to unfasten his shirt buttons. His touch had already started its magical work on her. She wanted to feel him against her. When he stepped back and unfastened his belt, she quickly pulled the covers back from the bed.

They wouldn't need those heavy blankets. Jennifer had a hunch she was going to be warm enough without them.

"Oh, yes, there is something else," he said, reaching into his pants pocket. Once he stepped out of them and draped them over the bed, Chad held out his hand. Lying on his palm was a gold wedding band, intricately carved and studded with diamonds. Taking her left hand, he slipped the ring onto her third finger.

Raising her hand he kissed it, then looked at her with love-filled eyes. "Thank you for marrying me, Mrs. Cameron. I'm looking forward to many happy years together with you."

She smiled and hugged him around the waist. "I have a hunch that the pleasure is going to be all mine."

Epilogue

S*unshine?''*

"Hmm?"

"You've got to help me."

"Wha's wrong?" Jennifer mumbled, still more than half asleep.

"I can't move."

She shifted lazily in bed without opening her eyes. "Why not?''

"I'm being held captive by a wild jungle animal."

"Of course you are," she agreed sleepily, and buried her head deeper into her pillow.

"Don't you care?''

"I always care about you, love."

"Aren't you going to do anything about it?''

"Tell him to move," she mumbled.

"I tried that.''

"Wha' happened?''

"He licked my ear.''

She smiled into her pillow. "Tha's a good sign. Means ṇe likes you.''

"What would he do if he didn't like me?"

"He would never have let you near my bed. He's a trained attack cat." She finally opened her eyes and had to bite her lip—hard—to keep from laughing.

Chad was on his stomach, his head buried in his pillow. Sam had obviously taken the wide expanse of bare back as an invitation to stretch out, which he had done. Now Sam lay sprawled on top of Chad, occasionally reaching out enough to lick Chad's exposed ear.

While Jennifer watched, Sam waved his bushy tail regally in the air.

"It's no longer your bed, Sunshine. It is now our bed. Do you think you could explain that to him? I have just as much right to be here as he does." Since Chad was facing the other way he didn't know that Jennifer was now awake and enjoying the sight of him taking up a good-size portion of her bed.

"He knows that. See how willing he is to share with you?" she pointed out with a grin.

Jennifer stretched and almost fell off the bed. Maybe they should consider purchasing a king-size one for their new home.

"No way." Those words were the first ones he had spoken that morning. The sound so startled Sam that he leaped off the bed and ran into the other room.

Jennifer moved closer to Chad's side and began to rub the wide expanse that Sam had just vacated. "What do you mean, no way?"

"No king-size bed. I like being close enough to find you without hunting all over the bed."

"I see. You may not be able to find me one of these days after you've nudged me over the edge. I'll have to end up sleeping on the couch."

He turned his head and saw her watching him, her

smile gentle. "Do I really crowd you so much?" he asked, concerned.

"Well, let's face it. Neither one of us is used to sharing a bed." She paused for a moment with a look of inquiry on her face. "At least *I'm* not."

"You know damned well I'm not. I've lived practically my entire life as a monk, just because of you." He grinned. "I was always afraid of what you might be able to pick up and I didn't want to shock you, particularly when you were so much younger."

"I find that a little hard to believe, you know. Especially after that weekend in Vegas, not to mention the demonstration of your expertise these past several hours." They had gotten very little sleep the night before. Jennifer was a little surprised that she felt so marvelous this morning. She shook her head in mock concern at his relaxed position. "It's no wonder you're exhausted."

Chad turned over so that he was facing her. He slipped his hand along the nape of her neck and gently tugged. She fell against him with a breathless chuckle.

"You are a very apt student, you know," he admitted a few minutes later.

She raised her head slightly, enjoying the relaxed and contented look on his face.

"Do you really think so, Mr. Cameron? I appreciate those kind words, I really do. Does this mean I can expect my usual end-of-the-year bonus?"

Chad grabbed her and rolled over so that she was pinned to the bed. She started laughing at the look on his face. "I'm sorry, I'm sorry. It was just a joke, you know, a little fun and—"

"So you want a bonus, do you?"

His nonverbal response involved the total attention of them both for an extended period of time. Sam, peering through the doorway, was disgusted by the lack of attention he was receiving from his roommate. He stalked into the kitchen and waited by his empty food dish, feeling totally ignored.

Sam wondered if he could convince them that he deserved a friend of his own. Eyeing the door to the bedroom speculatively, he thought he might give it a try.

* * * * *

Take 2 bestselling love stories FREE

Plus get a FREE surprise gift!

Looking For More Romance?

Visit Romance.net

Check in daily for these and other exciting features:

Hot off the press

View all current titles, and purchase them on-line.

What do the stars have in store for you?

Horoscope

Hot deals

Exclusive offers available only at Romance.net

Plus, don't miss our interactive quizzes, contests and bonus gifts.

PWEB

MEN at WORK

All work and no play?
Not these men!

October 1998
SOUND OF SUMMER by Annette Broadrick

Secret agent Adam Conroy's seductive gaze could hypnotize a woman's heart. But it was Selena Stanford's body that needed saving— when she stumbled into the middle of an espionage ring and forced Adam out of hiding....

MEN IN UNIFORM

November 1998
GLASS HOUSES by Anne Stuart

Billionaire Michael Dubrovnik never lost a negotiation—until Laura de Kelsey Winston changed the boardroom rules. He might acquire her business...but a kiss would cost him his heart....

MILLIONAIRE'S CLUB

December 1998
FIT TO BE TIED by Joan Johnston

Matthew Benson had a way with words and women—but he refused to be tied down. Could Jennifer Smith get him to retract his scathing review of her art by trying another tactic: tying him *up*?

MAGNIFICENT MEN

Available at your favorite retail outlet!

MEN AT WORK™

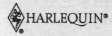

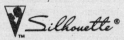